This Is No Time to Quit Drinking

Teacher Burnout and the Irish Powers

Stephen O'Connor

gatekeeper press

Published by Gatekeeper Press
2167 Strington Rd, Suite 109
Columbus, OH 43123-2989
www.GatekeeperPress.com

Cover illustration copyright © 2020 by The Briman (@briman_draws)
Cover design by Higgins and Ross Photography and Design
Interior book design and layout by Misty Horten
Author photograph by Molly A. O'Connor

First Printing, 2020
ISBN 9781642378139
Gatekeeper Press

For the late John Kent, descendent of the Irish rebel Éamonn Ceannt, and a dedicated and inspiring teacher.

"*Can it really be, Madame, that you are still to be seen in this age of railways and telegraphs?*"

"*What do you yourself think about it?*" she cried, in a silvery voice, straightening up her royal little figure in a very haughty fashion.

"*I don't really know,*" I answered, rubbing my eyes.

"*To know is nothing at all; to imagine is everything. Nothing exists except that which is imagined. I am imaginary. That is what it is to exist, I should think! I am dreamed of, and I appear. Everything is only dream; and as nobody ever dreams about you, Sylvestre Bonnard, it is YOU who do not exist.*"

—Anatole France, *The Crime of Sylvestre Bonnard*

"*The Celt, and his cromlechs, and his pillar-stones, these will not change much—indeed, it is doubtful if anybody at all changes at any time. There are, of course, children of light who have set their faces against all this, although even a newspaperman, if you entice him into a cemetery at midnight, will believe in phantoms, for everyone is a visionary, if you scratch him deep enough. But the Celt, unlike any other, is a visionary without scratching.*"

—W.B. Yeats

We are the gods
Who came along with you and joined your cause, when Troy
Went down in flames; we are the gods who crossed
The deepsea swell in ships at your command. . .

—Virgil, *The Aeneid*

Prelude

Bartley Kickham Hannigan was neither young nor old. He had reached the age at which he wore his years lightly or heavily, depending upon his mood and upon his current relation to the world around him. On this day, for example, the April sun did not cheer him; the cry of gulls was premonitory rather than stirring, and the distant thump of waves dull and monotonous. It was almost as if he could feel the declivity beneath his feet—the long slide toward middle age, lost opportunity, and irrelevance. His cigarette was stale, and he stubbed it into an ashtray outside the public restroom, a sand-filled planter out of which bloomed a bouquet of crooked butts.

Bartley was not only gloomy, he was excessively bored, since, on this brilliant morning of a so-called "romantic weekend getaway," his wife had predictably abandoned him for the glittering glass and marble of the "Galleria by the Sea," there to spend several hours perusing overpriced and meretricious merchandise for which she had no use. It was early for a seat at a bar, and cool for the beach; consequently, seeking he knew not what, he wandered absently, finally pausing before an A-frame sidewalk sign: "The cards tell all! Madame Veruschka Petrovna is a true-born Russian Romany card-reader. Your fate awaits. Twenty dollars."

Up to this point in his life, whether at carnivals, bazaars, or beachside boulevards alive with the diversions of summer, Bartley Hannigan had never paid attention to signs that announced, "Madame Fortuna: She Knows!" or "Fortune Teller! Clairvoyant Powers!" He had never sought the counsel of the world's innumerable palmists, crystal ball gazers, psychics, or spiritualists which one so often finds tucked into hole-in-the-wall closet-sized spaces between noisy arcades and pizza pie store fronts.

He stood pensively for a moment before this gypsy's sign, finally concluding that twenty dollars was too much for a lark. He was about to walk on when a voice from inside called, "You have questions. I will answer your questions."

I do have questions. Oh, what the hell. Bartley spread a gap in the oblig-atory bead curtain, inhaling the sandalwood incense. Madame Petrovna didn't look the part, which was disappointing. She did, at least, wear the requisite hanging earrings, gold hoops that nearly touched her shoulders. But Bartley was a traditionalist at heart; the head of a gypsy fortune teller should be wrapped in a scarf and encircled with a chain headband from which gold coins were pendent. Her shoulders should be wrapped in a saffron shawl, something like Esmeralda, the fortune-telling robot-gypsy in the glass case at the Hampton Casino when he was a kid, that lying gypsy who, after he had inserted his coin in a slot, issued a small card on which he had eagerly read: "True Love Awaits You." A bogus prophecy if ever there was one, but what can you expect for ten cents from a robotized psychic mannequin? The Romany Russian was at least real, even if somehow not thoroughly gypsy.

In fact, Madame Petrovna resembled some fashion fugitive from the 1960's, with a great pile of blonde hair piled up like a spool of cotton candy, a style that used to be known as a "beehive." She sat serenely shuffling a deck of Tarot cards. Her dress was what Bartley thought of as "psychedelic" in style. One side was patterned with colorful interlocking wheels, or maybe they were flowers, growing on smoky-swirling rainbow-colored stalks. The other side was solid in color, a dark blue, adorned with stars and other celestial bod-ies. Thick black lines of mascara and lengthy false eyelashes highlighted the veiled eyes which were cast toward the deck as she shuffled. Quite suddenly, she raised those eyes and fixed Bartley with a blue stare, somewhat startling since he had also imagined that gypsies must be dark-eyed.

With something of a theatrical flourish, she indicated a seat at the other side of the card table upon which a slim white candle burned. Madame Petrovna passed the deck through the candle's flame, then blew it out and moved the candle aside. She watched him for a moment in silence, and then asked, "Twenty dollars?"

"Up front, eh? You are a wise woman."

"Sometimes they don't like what they hear, and they run off."

She took his money and got up to put it somewhere behind a nearby counter. Bartley paid little attention to this operation, other than to note that Madame had apparently not skipped any of the Chicken Kiev. Her figure, unlike her style, was not reminiscent of undernourished 60's fashion queens. But Bartley was preoccupied with asking himself, "What is my question?"

When she had resumed her seat, she handed him her business card and said, "Tell your friends. Now what is your question?"

He pocketed the card and asked, "Where am I going? Am I on the wrong path? That's two questions, I know."

"No," she said. "It is the same question."

"I mean, personally . . . professionally."

"It is one life—it is one question."

She handed him the deck and asked him to breathe over it, and to shuffle the cards, and try to pass his energy into them. He did as he was told while the long-lashed woman studied him. He tried his best to play his part with a modicum of seriousness, though he didn't really know how to pass his energy into a deck of Tarot cards. How his wife, Adele, would laugh if she knew what he was up to. Yes, she would laugh, not with him, but at him, and so she would never know. He handed the cards back to the true-born Russian Romany.

She turned a card, laying it before them on the table. "The significator." A mounted knight. "The Knight of Pentacles," she said. "You value the old things. You are a man who keeps his word. One doesn't need the cards to see that you are unhappy. Maybe you will keep a promise that is old and worn out."

"A promise is a promise," he said, in his own defense.

She nodded as if he had confirmed her suspicion. "You lack imagination to see that sometimes a promise is a rusted chain attached to the corpse of yesterday."

"Hmm. An eloquent gypsy. Well, maybe so, but I believe you must try to keep your promises. Your vows. It's the way I was. . . ."

She began to turn over cards slowly, in a vertical line below the knight. "The Seven of Cups. Difficult decisions. You do not know which road to take, and so you take none, not realizing that that, too, is a decision. Eight of Cups. Again, stagnation, inaction."

At the next card, Bartley drew back a bit, eyebrows raised warily. A devil with great curving ram horns sat on a throne of sorts above a man and woman in chains. "The Devil," he said. "Nice."

"The Devil tells us that you have lost control of your life. You are a prisoner of forces you see as negative. At work, in the home, or both. You can free yourself, but you are chained to the world as it is, not knowing you can break the chains."

"Back to lacking imagination," Bartley said.

Madame Petrovna turned two cards in quick succession. "The Moon. You see the dog and the wolf, the civilized, the rational, as opposed to the wild, the instinctive, both under the sway of the mysterious. They bay at the moon together. Here, the Five of Swords. This is not the card you want to see for a relationship. It shows imbalance. One partner loves the other, but the love is not requited. Together with the moon, it means madness, harassment, maybe a woman who wants what you cannot give her and hates you for it."

"So, this is the life I'm to expect? Jesus, you were right to get the money up front, Madame Petrovna."

She nodded. "Of the fool's journey we call life, and where it will lead you, it is difficult to speak in absolutes."

"Why?"

"Because the end of the journey changes if the path is departed from. But I can tell where this path, the one you are on, leads." She turned a card, and Bartley studied it. Lightning struck a great tower of stone. Two figures plummeted earthward from the flaming citadel. "Yes, I am glad I have your twenty dollars," she said.

"That bad?"

She murmured to herself, "*Kak ty skazhesh' ispitania i nevsgody.* That is what I would tell a seeker in my country. *Ispitania i nevsgody.* The best translation in English, I think, is 'shit-storm.' Yes, the shit-storm is coming."

"Great. Thanks."

"A man forewarned is worth two."

"Shit-storm. Yup, that's sounds about right," Bartley said. "A lot of negative forces are gathering around me already. One shares my bed. Another is my boss at work. I'm an English teacher in a high school, which I used to enjoy, actually, but. . . ." He shook his head. "Don't get me going. Oh, and since my mother died, the old man is more batshit crazy than ever. He can be quite a negative force! Category five! So, bring on a few more. Why not?" Bartley raised his eyes and addressed the ceiling, or something beyond it. "Go ahead, Life! Just take another big shit on me!"

"Ah!" she said as she turned the next card. "The Star—hope."

"Thank you! That must have something to do with my son, Manus. If he's all right, I'll survive. Maybe someone heard my prayer."

"Did you make a prayer?"

"Mentally . . ."

"I thought you asked someone to take a shit on you."

"Just tell me about the hope part, will you?"

She flipped another card, to the left of the vertical line. It looked to Bartley like the Pope on his ecclesiastical throne. "Ah, the Hierophant. This is a mentor, a person of wisdom who understands the spirit world. A guide, like Virgil was to Dante." The next card in the horizontal line pictured an overflowing chalice surmounted by a dove. "A great and passionate love," she said.

"No, you don't understand, Madame P. My wife—I mean I've tried— that's what I'm doing up here at the beach, supposedly, but you see she's into some weird shit. . . ."

"A *new* love."

"Who, me?"

"I'm reading for you, no? The last two cards in the spread." She laid them down, forming a cross pattern on the table before him. "The Magician. This is a being who channels a high power. Be careful with that being. You will need the Hierophant, your adviser, to help you in dealing with this force."

"What kind of being? A man or woman?"

"I sense the power, but not the form. And finally, ah, the Ace of Swords! This portends the reaching of a higher plane." She raised her palms and shrugged. "Or, it could be death and the plane beyond. With such *ispitania i nevsgody,* is difficult to say."

"Oh, great." Bartley eyed the beaded curtain somewhat longingly but did not move.

"If it is not death, it is enlightenment. Seeing what is real and what is not. Understanding."

"Understanding what?"

Her gold earrings quivered as she turned her gaze on him sharply. "The true nature of things. The spirit world, Bartley."

"How did you know my name?"

"You said your name when you came in. You are a teacher."

"Yes, but, I don't think I did."

"I am sure you did. Your journey will be a trying one. Keep the balance. Trust your instincts. That is all."

He rose to make his exit but paused. "No other advice?"

"The love part. Don't make a mess of it, Bartley. You say, oh if my son is all right I will survive. This is all you want? Live your life! And stop smoking!"

He heard the rustling click of the beads as he exited, a sound which seemed to break a spell as he passed into what now seemed another world, the real world, the world that you could 'knock your sconce against.' It was a relief, somehow. The sunlight diffused the mysterious shadows cast by the cards and their portents, and now he chuckled to remember her serious airs over her cups and pentacles and devils, but the term "shit-storm" came back to him, ringing like the toll of an ominous bell within. *It's all a crock,* he reminded himself, rather sternly. However, he decided that it was not too early for a drink after all and set off for a little bar near the bay called the Windjammer, which served a peerless Bloody Mary.

One

Thirteen Months Later

Solicitous, head tilted in awkward sympathy so that she reminded him of a broken doll, Mrs. Julia Doyle touched his arm and cooed, "I'm so sorry, Bartley." She gazed wistfully in the direction of the open coffin in which his father was laid out.

"That's all right," he said. "I mean . . . thank you."

Not just her pupils, but her entire eyeballs dilated abruptly from time to time, as if there were extraordinary things going on around her. Her tilted head shook, and she bit her lower lip. Then she said, "So sudden!" She gripped his forearm—suddenly.

"Yes, it was a shock."

"It must have been such a shock. Such a sudden end."

Bartley nodded. He had already conceded that it had been a shock. He repeated, stupidly, "Yes, it was . . . a real shock. Quite a shock."

"If there's anything I can do. . . ."

"Thank you, Mrs. Doyle."

"Anything at all."

He tried to imagine anything helpful that she could possibly do. Bake him a cake? Make him a vodka martini? Pay the undertaker?

"Thank you."

"It would be no bother."

What would be no bother? He grimaced as his wife, Adele, who was posted to his left, stepped on his toe, her way of telling him to get rid of Mrs. Doyle and move the line along. But he was at a loss as to how to move a woman along who was planted in front of him in stolid sympathetic solidarity over the death of his father, Harry Hannigan, known, or formerly known, throughout Greater Lowell as "Happy Hannigan."

"For, well, it must be forty years, anyway, we bought our Christmas tree from your father every year," she continued. As a buttress to this assertion, Mrs. Doyle's head bobbled. "Oh," she continued, "he'll be missed. Believe me."

He tried to believe her, though he couldn't imagine who would miss the old blowhard, other than his cronies at the American Legion bar, and people who were accustomed to his gruff salesmanship of the trees or found it perversely endearing. But then he thought that, very probably, he would miss him, too. "Yes, he will be missed." He extricated his shoe from under his wife's foot as Mrs. Doyle leaned forward and whispered confidentially, "He looks wonderful. They did a marvelous job. He looks very much like himself."

"Yes, he does." *Who the hell else should he look like?*

"Dan wanted to come, of course, only he's suffering something awful with the shingles."

"Well . . ."

The line was beginning to stall, clogging the little room. Clusters of Happy's former acquaintances cast furtive glances at the names on the flower sprays, the photos of Happy in happier times, and the unhappy sight of his corpse laid out with a rosary he had never held in life entwined in his dead fingers. Bartley noticed that Gibby O'Malley, an old Navy buddy of his father's, appeared to have prepped for the wake with a bottle of fortified wine.

"Yes, I know. I know," Mrs. Doyle said. Bartley wondered what she knew. "There's no use complaining. Anyway, he didn't suffer."

No, he made everyone else suffer. "Thank you for coming to pay your respects."

"I wouldn't miss it," she said, as though his father's wake were a Broadway premiere. *Move on!* He screamed at her mentally, pulling his foot sideways to dodge his wife's attempt to re-crush his toes. Mrs. Doyle nodded and gathered wind in her lungs for what he hoped was her parting salvo. At that moment, Adele pushed the next in line against Mrs. Doyle's shoulder and said, "Bartley, this is Joe Keenan and his wife Margaret. Joe knew Harry from the Lafayette Club."

Another of his haunts.

He gave the slighted Mrs. Doyle a rapid final nod and smile and turned his attention to Joe and Margaret.

"Happy was a helluva guy. Helluva guy," the old geezer said. "Used to play cards with him down at the club. Pretty handy with a pool cue, too." He winked knowingly. "*Pre-tty* handy. Knew a lot about history, you know, military history, all kinds of stuff. Traveled all over in the Navy. Very classy guy. Knew all about fine wine, too, he had a wine cellar an' everything. Oh yeah, knew about cigars, everything! A true conna-sewer."

"Thank you for com—"

There was a loud crash near the casket, that turned all the heads in the line. Bartley saw Farmer Lambeau, another old pal of his father's, trying to haul Gibby O'Malley off the floor. Bartley went to assist him. Gibby was explaining that had intended to kneel and say an *Ave* for his friend but had quite missed the kneeler. "Damned trick knee," the drunkard muttered. And then, louder, "I'd like to say a prayer for ol' Happy. Can we all say a prayer for Happy?"

Smiling, Adele approached and, leaning toward his ear, gave Bartley the whispered command, "Get him out of here."

"Yes, sir." Since marriage counseling was proving futile, Adele had given up all pretense of respect for her partner as well as any attempt at working cooperatively with him.

Bartley and Farmer Lambeau each took one of Gibby's arms and guided the forlorn former comrade toward the rear exit. "I'm gonna miss ol' Happy," he mumbled. He was getting lugubrious, and Bartley feared he was going to start to weep on his shoulder. "He was never . . . he was never . . . you know. . . ."

"No, he never was. Now, if you could just. . . ."

"Lemme take you down to the Copper Kettle for a nightcap, Gibby," Farmer Lambeau said, "and I'll drive you home after." He winked at Bartley, who had extracted his wallet and was trying to press a twenty on Farmer for their drinks, but the rugged old French Canadian woodsman with the

Rocky Marciano face waved it off, saying, "I got it, kid." Gibby coughed and patted Bartley on the shoulder and said, "Buck up, Bar-Barley. He's in a bettah place!"

"Any place is better than this one."

Gibby's mouth twisted and his eyes rose toward his brows as he contemplated this remark; then he shrugged, and the two men set off. Bartley heard Farmer saying, "For Chrissake, don't lean on me so much, Gibby. I don't get the new knee till next week."

Bartley took advantage of the sanctioned escape from the wake-line to step outside, pulling from his suit jacket pocket the slim case in which he placed five cigarettes per day, down from seven. In this matter, anyway, he had decided to take the gypsy's advice. He opened the case and stroked the last two sadly. She was right. Coffin nails. Doctor Rivera had also told him to quit, of course. He lit one defiantly. They'd have us all eating carrots and drinking just one glass of red wine a day and getting on a treadmill every morning and living forever. As if everyday life wasn't enough of a treadmill. He exhaled noisily and shook his head in resignation as he recalled the 'possible death' in his cards. Death is always lurking in the cards somewhere. You don't need no gypsy to tell you that.

He closed his eyes and exhaled, tasting the tobacco in his throat and lungs, and wondering why God made bad things so good. Traps, everywhere! You go to the beach to enjoy the sun and you get a melanoma. Hike into the woods to appreciate the majesty of mountain and stream and you get a tick bite that knocks you on your ass. Try to maintain your equilibrium with a diet of well-shaken cocktails and your liver rots. Have a bit of a fling with a large-breasted and amiable young woman and you get a dose of the clap; or worse, another little humanoid that looks even more confused than you are, followed by years of diapers and temper tantrums and teenage angst and a woman stepping on your toes and ordering you to escort drunks out of rear exits. Relax with a bit of the aromatic smoke of golden flakes of tobacco and—

He felt his cell phone vibrate and started from his dejected reverie. "Hello?"

"Bartley!" An urgent sibilation.

"Louise. . . ." She was a fellow member of the D&E Book Club, a loose confederacy of local readers who enjoyed discussing books, and particularly liked to **D**rink and **E**at at their meetings, which were held on a rotating basis in the homes of members. Louise was also a published poet, though he had never had a look into one of her chapbooks. He cast a nervous glance toward the window of the parlor, as if his wife could tell that he was talking to another woman, and as if she cared.

"I haven't had a chance to speak to you," she said.

"Well, you know . . . my father's death and all that."

"Sorry."

"Yes, and Adele is in high dudgeon, as usual."

"I'm here if you need to talk. . . ."

"Very kind. Thanks."

Louise was not so different physically from Adele, Bartley thought. They were both attractive women of forty or so, and yet it was nearly incomprehensible to Bartley that they were really the same species of female *homo sapiens*. Adele was imperious, and not at all poetic. She preferred to be in charge, and she was quite good at it. She was a Senior Vice President for Operations at Dynamic Cloud Solutions. All that Bartley knew of her work was that it had to do with such things as data, "the cloud," and "enterprise network optimization." He understood none of that, and Adele certainly considered him too much of a simpleton to attempt to explain it to him. She had come to regard Bartley as one might regard a bothersome child who couldn't quite help being a nuisance, but with whom one needed to exercise discipline. For years, she had permitted sexual contact about once a month, during which she often requested that he "hurry up." She had things to do. Then a few years back, she began reading *Fifty Shades of Grey*, and a lot of other bondage fantasies. She decided that she wanted her husband to tie her up and beat her. Bartley had absolutely no interest in tying her up and beating her; consequently, their sex life had gradually "petered out" altogether.

Louise, on the other hand, did not strike him as a masochist, and moreover, she seemed to think that Bartley was not a simpleton, but a highly intelligent man. And on this matter, he believed that she was a far more astute judge than his wife. After all, she was a writer for a Boston-based magazine that covered books, culture, and the arts as well publishing political exposés, topical articles, and a section of personal ads that seemed to require a familiarity with an esoteric encyclopedia of acronyms. Yeah, Louise struck him as a pretty hip woman who was at least as smart as Adele. In a different way, of course. Hadn't the Romany woman mentioned a passionate new love? He chuckled at his momentary credulity. *All a crock!* Still, he wondered why, after more than a year, the gypsy's prophecies had been coming back to him so often lately.

"For better or worse." He had made the promise years ago, and he was determined not to be the one to break it. Stagnation and inaction? No. He believed that the words he had spoken on the altar of St. Patrick's Church constituted what Yeats would have called a "deep-sworn vow." A mistaken vow? Yes. Nevertheless, let her be the one to break it.

Still, he couldn't help comparing his life with Adele to what his life might be with Louise. Far from imperious, she was amiable and seemingly, even pliable; a quality which Bartley thought boded well for the bedroom. And though he had not yet begun an affair with Louise, she was his confidante, and he had hinted that, if and when his marriage finally unraveled, a likely eventuality, things might be different. It had crossed his mind that now that his father had 'bought the farm,' he and his brother would have old Happy's farm to sell, one hundred thirty-six acres of prime real estate just outside the city, a lot that developers would be eager to bid on. Strange, though, the premonition of which his father had spoken. He had seen the shadow of Death in the shape of. . . .

"There's something I have to tell you about all this, Louise, when I see you."

"All what?"

"The whole thing, my father's death. Something very odd."

"Odd?"

"I'll explain it later. Here's my brother. Gotta go."

Bartley's older brother descended the stairs and lumbered up to him. Harry Junior, whom Bartley referred to privately, in conversations with himself, as "Unhappy Hannigan," bulky, balding, bespectacled, stoop-shouldered and long-faced. "Adele says you should get back in there."

"When did you arrive?" Bartley asked.

"My plane got in four hours ago. I just stopped to shower at the hotel and came here." Harry Junior, an engineer, was working on various projects in the Gulf of Mexico which would keep him in Houston for the better part of the next decade.

"So, how are you, Harry?"

"Fine."

"That's good. Kids?"

"Good. Manus?"

"Good."

"Wife?"

Bartley shrugged. "Eh. Yours?"

"Okay." He paused and added, as though he'd just had an epiphany, "I can't believe the old man is actually gone."

Bartley nodded and took a drag of his cigarette.

His older brother frowned. "Those are bad for you."

"Living is bad for you."

Harry Junior waved a wisp of tobacco smoke away as if it were mustard gas and leaned back against the white clapboards of the O'Brian Funeral Home. The sky over the rooftops of Fletcher Street was violet, streaked with sooty clouds as the day died, a vision that seemed to prompt Harry Junior to uncommon contemplation. "Did you ever think, Bartley, how we just run all over the place, from our childhood on, going to school, chasing women and jobs, trying to make a living, yakking with people, and reading books and watching movies, drinking and raising children and all this *shit* we do, and nobody has any idea what it's all about, this weird trip, and then we all just end up stretched out here at O'Brian's with a bunch of people gawking at our corpse. What's it all *for?*"

Bartley dropped his cigarette on the sidewalk and crushed it under a wing-tipped shoe. "Hey," he said, "if you can't take a joke—*fuck ya.*"

Two

On a Saturday afternoon in April, close upon the fifth anniversary of his mother's death, Bartley Hannigan received a call from his father, the aforementioned Happy. The terse and doleful voice of the sober *paterfamilias* reached him like some desperate message from an outpost of the empire about to be overrun by bloodthirsty barbarians. "I need to talk to you."

"I was just . . ."

"*Urgently.*"

As he drove over the Rourke Bridge and along the river, Bartley thought about his father, and attempted, in a sort of Sherlock Holmesian fashion, to analyze his character. "It seems," he said, to an imaginary Dr. Watson in the passenger seat, "that somewhere along the circuitous road of life, my father, Harry "Happy" Hannigan, read, or was told, or concocted independently, the notion that solitary drinking is the most salient attribute of the alcoholic. Consequently, to ease his fears, he has established a rule, an unconditional precept to which he adheres with religious zeal: no drinking while at home alone."

Watson, scribbling field notes in a reporter's notebook, nodded and mumbled, "I see," as he took in these perceptive observations. Bartley continued, "There followed, ipso facto, two further consequences: 1) he is rarely at home, and 2) he is miserable when he is. The moniker of "Happy" has thus been clapped onto his out-of-the-house personality; while down home on the farm, "Ebenezer" might be a more suitable alias."

Concluding that he would never fully understand the dichotomies of his father's character, Bartley gave up the detective pose, and Watson's image faded. Soon after, he pulled into a gap in a ragged, unkempt barrier of hedges as his Honda Civic scrunched across a gravel driveway. Since his mother was no longer around to tell her husband to trim those hedges, or to scrape and paint peeling clapboards, and mow the lawn, the family home had begun to resemble what it was, the domicile of an increasingly eccentric and disaffected misanthrope. The farmhouse, which dated back to Civil War days, was slowly being enveloped in crawling, nondescript greenery that stole up the chimney and across the rotting sills to tear at the screens and finger the clouded windows.

Beyond his father's expansive property lay the 1,500 acres of the state forest. The low rolling hills of his father's land had been planted with Christmas trees, row on row like regiments in battle formation. Happy spent a good part of the year planting, tending, and trimming them. The day after Thanksgiving the onslaught would begin, and between then and Christmas his father and the local farm boys who worked for him would put three thousand trees in living rooms throughout the Merrimack Valley.

Upon entering the kitchen with a Dunkin' Donuts coffee in each hand, Bartley spied his father sitting at the kitchen table amid piles of old magazines and newspapers, one of which he was squinting at, since he liked to pretend he didn't need reading glasses. A black rotary dial telephone sat on top of a pile of *Muzzleloader* magazines published during the Eisenhower administration. Fruit flies hovered above a bowl of black bananas. Bartley set one coffee in front of his father, who picked it up with a grudging nod of thanks.

Bartley noticed a look of worry, an atypical anxiety, on his father's face. "Are you okay, Dad?"

"Dead man walking," he declared.

"What?"

"I'm gonna die!"

Bartley was surprised that this announcement, though alarming, produced no vibration of real concern in him. His father certainly did not appear to be dying. On the contrary, he appeared quite hale, a picture of robust health. Puttering about his trees and taking his daily walk to the

American Legion bar a mile down the road appeared to be sufficient exercise to keep him in the pink. His drinking had never stretched his belt a notch, made his nose bloom, his cheeks pallid, nor his blue eyes cloudy. His graying temples and square chin gave him a distinguished look, and he prided himself on what one drunkard at the legion called his "military bearing."

"Have you been to the doctor?"

"I don't need a goddamned doctor."

Bartley nodded and pursed his lips thoughtfully, wondering how to proceed. He peeled the lid from his coffee, cleared his throat and ventured, "It's just that, if you haven't been to the doctor, how do you know you're dying?"

Hannigan *pere* rolled his eyes at the enormous stupidity of Hannigan *fils.* "I didn't say I was dying. I said I'm gonna die! Soon!"

"Hmmm, so how do you feel?"

"I feel fine."

"You feel fine."

"Christ, is there an echo in here?"

"Okay so you feel fine, and the last I heard, Doctor Bleckman said—"

"That's bullshit."

"What's bullshit?"

"Whatever he said is bullshit. And it doesn't matter."

Lips pursed in thought, Bartley paused, wanting to appear as if giving his father's reply the consideration it deserved. Speaking with the old man, particularly when he was sober, was an exercise that required stamina and tact. He sipped his coffee, stroked his unshaven jaw thoughtfully and said, "So, this idea that you're dying—sorry! That you're gonna die soon, is just based on a feeling?"

"I told you, I feel fine. Are you listening?"

"I'm doing my best, Dad. All right, so, exactly why do you think you're dying—gonna die? Can you give me a clue?"

"I can give you more than a clue, wise guy, I can explain the whole thing."

"All right then."

"It's very simple."

"Okay."

"First, I'm gonna make a piece of toast." He rose and began to clear some plates, yellowed newspapers, a stiff paint brush, and a pearl-handled revolver from the counter. He dropped the plates in the sink and the rest of the junk into a wooden crate that bore the name of a tool factory in Union, Maine. From inside the oven, he took out a silver toaster that looked almost as old as the *Muzzleloader* magazines. The toaster reminded Bartley of a 1960 Winnebago.

"You want a piece of toast?"

"I'm all set, Dad."

"What, are you on a diet?"

"I had breakfast."

"Oh, he had breakfast. Excuse me." Hannigan Senior pulled a stick of butter and a loaf of Wonder Bread out of the refrigerator, slid a couple of pieces into the toaster, and jammed the lever down on the side. As he waited for his toast, he whistled 'Winchester Cathedral' with a sudden access to the Happy side of his character. He buttered the toast when it was done and slathered on a bit of Rolly's Farm Strawberry Jam.

He settled himself back at the table. "You know I was born in Ireland," he said, shoving a half slice of toast into his mouth and chewing around his words. He washed bite number one down with coffee.

"Of course. You came here when you were . . . eight?"

His father nodded. "And of course, I've been back. While in the Navy, and several times later, for funerals and such. Our branch of the Hannigans is from County Tyrone."

"Yes."

"As you know, your mother was a Cooley Kickham from Antrim, nearby, but that doesn't matter here. The point is. . . ." But before he could get to the point, another piece of toast disappeared into his mouth, and he sat staring gravely at his son while he chewed. Bartley shifted in his seat and drank more coffee, wondering what County Tyrone could possibly have to do with his father's impending death.

Hannigan Senior finally swallowed and ran his tongue over his teeth before continuing. "The point is, that in the sixteenth century, among the Hannigans, or back then the ÓhAnnagáins, there was a Hugh Hannigan, who followed a deer into some kind of sacred grove, an old Druidic place—Altadevon Glen it's called, where St. Patrick drove a devil off a cliff. It's a sacred place, a powerful place, Bartley. Hugh Hannigan followed the deer into the grove and put an arrow into it." He paused to let the significance of such an act sink into what he considered to be the rather dense cranium of his son.

"And what—does that portend some bad *ju ju*?"

"Does that portend bad *ju ju*? Does Howdy Doody have a wooden ass? Of course, he knew better—anyone would, anyone but you, I suppose." The older man shrugged. "But—he was hungry and a bit too bold for his own good."

"And this relates to your demise, how?"

"After that, soon after, but I don't know if it was that night or a week later, the story goes, Hugh was sleeping by the River Foyle, on an errand for the Ó Domhnaill. He awoke to the sound of a woman crying, *keening*, they would say. He rose and followed the sound and found her there in the moonlight."

"Found who?"

His father took a deep breath, his jaw set like a man resolved to face the firing squad without a blindfold. He nodded in the certainty of his knowledge. "The Washer at the Ford. My mother would have called her the *bean sidh* in the old tongue, the banshee, or woman of the *Sidhe*. Some might say the *Mór-Ríoghain*, the phantom queen."

"Fairy tales!" Bartley interjected.

His father ignored him. "She stood in the shallows of the river, her body, and her head, too, draped in white linen as she tried to wash the crimson stain of blood from her breast. Hugh was of stout heart and he called to her. He approached her like a good honest man to ask if there was anything he could do to assist her, you see? He tried to take her arm to help her out of the water, but before he could touch her, a piercing scream rose from beneath that shroud of white."

Harry Hannigan gazed upward and extended an arm, fingers spread as if to touch the vision he could see before him, "A sleek side, a thrashing of water, a clatter of hooves across the rocks of the riverbank—she was gone, in the form of a wounded deer, leaving a thin trail of blood."

Bartley shook his head and chuckled. "Yes, I'll remember that story when I'm around the campfire with the boys of Troop 22. So, once again, this relates how?"

"You'll be laughin' out of the other side of your mouth when your old man is cold and dead! Now listen to me. Not long after that, Hugh, leading a few chosen men, was carrying a message from Aodh Mór Ó Néill to the Ó Domhnaill at his keep in Ballyshannon. They were preparing to attack the English army on the Blackwater River, you see. They stopped at Binevenagh to gather pigeon eggs on the cliffs."

"He was a hungry fellow."

"The supermarket was closed! Everyone was hungry in those days. It's called survival. They gathered eggs, and that night they camped in the Ballycarton woods. They built a roaring blaze to keep the darkness away, but in the deepest night, they saw movement among the fitful shadows cast by the fire. Hugh raised a flaming brand and saw a wild boar glaring back at him. He jumped up, and hefting a spear, went after it. The men followed, but their torches went out, and they became lost in the forest and could not see Hugh's brand nor the light of their fire. They stumbled about in the darkness for a while, calling for their captain."

"And?"

"Well, finally they did see a light. Not a flame, but a white glow like moonlight. They drew near and saw a veiled woman, all in white, moving away from them. She moved not with steps but seemed to glide over the land. They followed her until she arrived at the top of the cliffs where they had gathered the eggs. They called to her, and she turned once, and raised her veil. It was a frightening sight. The men said she was pale, even her lips, and that surely, she had 'neither blood nor bone.' She moved off the clifftop, then, into air, but she never fell. She just *condensed* into a white vapor that drifted away and vanished with the light it held, leaving them in darkness."

"What about Hugh?"

"They found him in the morning, his spear, and his back broken on the rocks below that cliff."

"Who told you this story, anyway?"

"It's all written down in the Annals!"

"What Annals?"

"*The Annals of the Noble Families of Tyrone*, translated and edited by Fearghus Cosgrach, M.A., M.R.I.A.!" He raised a finger and both eyebrows: "And!" he cried. "And! There is such a thing as a generational curse, see. It's carried in the blood and can only end in blood. And you'd better be concerned, because you're Irish too, boy!"

"Let me remind you that I was born in Massachusetts."

"Christ was born in a stable, but he wasn't a jackass! It's Irish blood is in your veins, every drop! You don't get off the banshee hook just because someone took a boat ride!"

"Ok, fine. I'm screwed, too. But is there even any evidence that other Hannigans have been visited by this banshee, or phantom queen, or whatever she is?"

"Who knows? Lost in the mists of time! But she's back!"

"All right, slow down. So, you've seen her?"

His father's voice was low now, and for the first time that Bartley could remember, fearful. "I haven't seen her, yet. But I have heard her."

"How do you know it's her?"

"Who the hell else would it be?"

"What does it sound like?"

"A wail."

"Of pain?"

"A wail of pain and sometimes a screech of wrath. Sometimes just a forlorn cry."

"Of sadness?

"Sadness, yes. Have you heard the old Irish women keening over the dead?"

"Not really."

His father shivered. "God help us, Bartley, you've never heard anything like it."

"It's probably a barn owl, or a fisher cat."

"I know what they sound like, you ignoramus! It's Hugh Hannigan's banshee! The Washer at the Ford or some other vengeful spirit! If you heard the cry—it's part woman, part child, part human, part animal, and, I'm very much afraid, part demon. It's an awful thing to hear in the night."

Elbows on the table, chin resting on his fists, Bartley considered this for a moment, and in the most delicate tone he could produce, said, "Listen, Dad, do you think that maybe this might have something to do with . . . I mean, maybe, you might want to leave off the drinking for a while?"

"Pfff. This is *no time* to quit drinking."

"Do you hear what you're telling me? You believe you're haunted by a banshee!"

"And then there's the wee man in the cellar."

"You mean like a leprechaun?"

"I suppose."

"Wait! This is your idea of a joke, right?" Bartley's eyes narrowed, his head tilted skeptically. "Is this whole thing a joke?"

"Would that it were," Happy replied, unhappily. "Would that it were."

"All right, then what's this wee man doing in the cellar?"

The older man shrugged. "You know I never drink at home when I'm on my own. That's the first sign of an alcoholic! But I have developed a modest wine cellar, and on those occasions when I have the boys from the Legion over to play cards, I like to show off the vintages, bring up a few bottles, get some cigars from the humidor. Impresses the hell out of the guys. They may not be geniuses, and there's more fingers than teeth among the lot of 'em, but they do appreciate class."

Bartley looked around the littered kitchen, piles of dishes in the sink, peeling wallpaper, and black bananas. "Yeah, you got a classy place here all right. So, don't tell me—the wee man, the, ah, leprechaun is drinking your wine."

"That's *exactly* what he's doing. I hear him popping corks and singing old Irish songs down there, off-key, drunk as a lord. But anyway, I'm not so concerned about him. He's just a nuisance. It's *the other one* I'm worried about."

"Maybe the leprechaun could help you to get rid of the banshee," Bartley offered.

"At least that's a thought, Son. You're finally using your noodle. But leprechauns are, oh, you know, very *will o' the wisp* creatures, hard to catch, hard to even see. I'll tell you this Bartley. If you ever do catch him, don't take your eyes off him. He'll say 'Look over there! What's that?' And you look away, and he's gone! That's what I've heard, anyway."

"Dad, I think maybe you need to talk to someone about all this."

"I'm talking to *you*, numb-nuts!"

"I mean a *professional*."

"Oh, so that's the way it is, eh? Just because these things are outside of your little school teacher experience and your little tax-paying citizen world, they can't exist, right? What vanity! Ever been in the Altadevon wood at night, sonny boy? Visited the fog-enshrouded ruins of the Hellfire Club on the ridge of the Glenasmole Valley? Seen the Ardnamagh Fairy Rath bathed in an unnatural blue light when all around is black night? I have, and I'll tell you, you have *no idea*. And until you've been to places like that, don't tell me I need a *professional!*"

"Look, I'm not saying you're crazy, but sometimes—it can happen—you don't know if you're asleep or awake."

Harry Hannigan stood. He rolled up his shirt sleeves as if he were preparing for fisticuffs. "Come with me," he said.

Bartley followed him as he went to the cellar door, pushed back the sliding lock, and switched a light on—it was dim down there even in the daytime. He paused on the steep, narrow stairs, looking up over his shoulder at Bartley. "Now I swear on your mother's grave, I haven't been down here today, but yesterday I picked up two empty bottles of St. Julien. And last night around midnight, I heard the little bastard singing 'The Jug of Punch.' And I was *awake!*"

The "wine cellar," was in a small pinewood storage room in one corner of the rock-walled basement. Harry Hannigan tugged on the door handle, and with a creak of rusty hinges, the door opened. "Ha-ha!" cried the elder. "What do you say about *that?*"

Three empty bottles and an equal number of corks law strewn on the cement floor. Bartley's father picked up one of the dead soldiers and shook it in front of his son's face. "The son of a bitch drank my Chateau Haut Brion!"

Bartley recalled a certain Russian gypsy and wondered if this episode presaged the gathering winds of the shit-storm she had foretold. He pulled a dusty bottle out of one of the racks and to his father's inquiring gaze, said, as he remounted the stairs, "Don't worry, you're not gonna drink *alone.*"

Three

That evening, Bartley tried to explain his father's "situation" to his wife while she sat at her well-polished glass and chrome desk in what had been a video game room-cum-man-cave for their son, Manus, before he'd moved out. The video monitor and beanbag chairs had been moved out too, replaced by the desk and a credenza on which sat a fax machine, printer, and scanner. Manus's posters of *The Walking Dead* and *Fight Club* had been replaced with two large abstract works by some Boston artist, one of which looked to Bartley like oranges and empty Chinese food boxes floating in the Merrimack River, while the other resembled a jumble of nuts and bolts. The former was called "Dream States," and the latter, "Misapprehension." There could be no misapprehension about the function of the room, though. This was command central, a cyber HQ from which Adele sent out directives to her corporate minions and fortified her castle in the Cloud.

Bartley's story was interrupted by several interjections of "Wait a minute!" and sighs of disgust; whether at his narrative or at the utter incompetence of those with whom she was connected, he was not sure. He paused a few times in his narration while she tapped away, then continued until she had absorbed enough of what had unfolded at his father's place to stop, look at him, and say, "Your father has finally lost his mind."

"Maybe," he said.

"Maybe?" she laughed, and Bartley wondered how he would describe that laugh to Linda, their marriage counselor. A snicker? A disdainful giggle? Maybe a sneering chuckle.

"I suppose," he replied, attempting to maintain that equilibrium which he felt indicated a certain maturity, "that would be the *easiest* explanation."

"Bartley, darling. In twenty-two years, I really have heard you talk *quite a bit* of twaddle, but this—"

"Please, Adele. Linda said that we should try to speak respectfully, to just say what we're feeling without blaming the other."

"All right, let me rephrase that. When I hear you talk seriously about leprechaun infestations and banshee whatevers, it makes *me* feel . . . like I'm married to a fucking lunatic." She smiled and folded her arms, as though in eager anticipation of how being called a fucking lunatic made *him* feel.

With all the patience he could muster, he countered, "I don't know if that was exactly the tone that Linda was advising us to adopt in our interactions, but let me say that I respect. . . ." He raised a finger as if he were explaining a first principle to a novice. "I respect your feelings, *and* I believe it is possible—no, *probable*—that you are correct. However, when I hear you say that I am a fucking lunatic, I feel that maybe you, I mean, *I* feel that *I* am not being granted a completely open-minded audience."

"Audience? What am I, the goddamn Pope?"

"Yes, very good. Let's quibble about the connotations of words. That will be really helpful."

And there was the sneering chuckle again. "All right. How can I be *helpful*? Shall I go buy a net to capture the leprechaun? Keep an eye out for rainbows?"

Bartley exhaled and closed his eyes, a combination of nonverbal acts which was meant to signify that he was being patient and long-suffering. After an interlude of several seconds, he slowly opened his eyes and said, "This is called sharing, Adele. It's what married people do. I'm sharing a concern about my father, who, by the way, has never been given to hallucinations or irrational fears."

"Oh yes, he's a well-grounded individual."

Bartley ignored her ironic interjection and continued. "*And* I'm just wondering if there could be, *could be*, something improbable, something out of the ordinary, involved. That's all. I can understand you being skeptical, perhaps even dismissive, but I don't understand or appreciate your getting angry and judgmental."

She articulated each word: "Out-of-your-mind!"

His determined equilibrium was beginning to tip and wobble. "Maybe *you* were out of your mind to take me for better or for worse."

"And this is definitely *worse*. No, forget the comparative—let's go right to the superlative; this is *the worst*. I have an MBA from Bentley and twenty-seven people who report directly to me. I advise clients in six different Fortune 500 companies, and I come home to listen to my husband tell me that I'm 'judgmental' if I tell him it is plain ludicrous to talk about a banshee howling in his father's overgrown potato patch or a fucking leprechaun in his cellar."

Toward the end of this rebuke, her cell began to play a little salsa number. As she picked it up, the annoyed face gave way to a happy face, and she said, "Gary! Thanks for getting back to me. Listen, I sent you the updated Enterprise standard report. Yeah, if you could review the new tabs on servers and the client tab. . . ."

She launched into that foreign techie language that made Bartley feel clueless and inferior, so he went upstairs to look up 'banshees' on the Internet, wondering if there was some other way he could have approached the subject that might have elicited a different reaction. But a word kept banging about the dome of his skull like a bumper car driven by a reckless drunk. The word was *incompatible*. He wondered how his good friend Louise would have responded. Surely, it would not have been like this.

He read for a while. There was certainly no shortage of wild tales about banshees and a host of other supernatural creatures that occupied the Irish night. He didn't believe the stories, yet when his cell phone chimed, Bartley jumped. He closed the computer, picked the phone off the nightstand and saw that it was his father. He pushed the little green phone icon, and heard, over some background hubbub, the ol' man talking, or declaiming, "Gaius Julius Caesar—greatest military commander in history! *Audentis Fortuna iuvat!* General Mikhail Kutuzov, number two. Wellington, I put at three, General Patton at four—"

His father was holding court at the Legion bar once again. "Dad? Dad!"

"Hold on, boys! Bartley! Listen, I know I can be a nasty son of a bitch."

That was the first time he could ever recall his father making anything approaching an apology for his boorish behavior. "Really, I hadn't noticed."

"You hadn't noticed! Ha ha! You're funny, Bartley! Haaaaahaha!" He gave vent to the uproarious laugh of the well-lubricated, socially engaging Happy Hannigan. "Listen, I have a solution to our dilemma."

"*Our* dilemma?"

"Okay your haunted dad's dilemma! Ha ha! Listen, my cousin Mickey in Tyrone gave me the name of a man—Cornelius O'Tuama. Mickey says he's a bit peculiar, a bit backward in some ways, but he's the real deal when it comes to handling banshees. Anyway, I was able to communicate with O'Tuama! He thinks it's a serious case, all right."

"Who the hell is Cornelius whatever?"

"O'Tuama. He's a Cork man. From Ballyvourney, 'the town set in the morning.' More importantly, he's the seventh son of a seventh son, see? He's had dealings with banshees, routed a Grogoch up in Antrim, banished a Gray Man from the Tuscar Rock, and even took on a Dullahan up in Moneyscalp, though the outcome of that is uncertain from what Mickey says. Still, he'll know what to do."

"I have no idea what you're talking about."

"Gotta go, Bartley. My turn to break. Talk to you soon. Not to worry. O'Tuama is on the case. I've sent him the money."

"What money?"

"Why, for his ticket! And there's his fee! Talk to you later, sonny!"

"Dad!" he wanted to tell him that all the storytellers agreed: banshees rarely appeared to the person who was going to die; they always appeared to individuals to presage the death of someone else. But he couldn't tell him, because he had hung up, and because that was the last conversation that Bartley Hannigan ever had with his father.

Bartley woke near dawn. His wife's side of the bed was undisturbed, so she must have slept in the guest room. She did that when she was annoyed with him, and she was annoyed with him not infrequently. He knew that she was up, though, because he could smell the coffee.

For a few moments, he lay in bed savoring the remnants of his dream. He had been swimming in a deep clear pool of an ocean inlet, diving from a jetty into the cool water with a young blonde who, as they rose dripping diamond shards from the sun-stippled depths, asked, "Will you move to California with me?" Without hesitation, feeling no encumbrances, no complications, nor a single qualm, he said, like Molly Bloom, "Yes, yes, I will, yes."

After he had showered and shaved and was exiting the bathroom, Bartley glanced into Command Central. Adele sat in front of her computer, cradling her coffee. Her dark hair was loose, and in the light that streamed through the front windows he recollected something of the woman with whom he'd been in love when they were very young. Before she had become a manager, serious and driven. Before she had power suits and an office with a window and a thousand "endorsements" on LinkedIn. He watched her sip her coffee, put it down, and begin to type intently.

He had fought for a long time against the idea that his marriage was an irretrievable failure. Yes, it was true that if she had not become pregnant with Manus, the relationship might have run its course, and Adele might have been one of the women he had "known before." He imagined often what it might be like to be married to the right woman. He felt that he, too, would be another person.

However, her pregnancy put things in a different perspective, and he had vowed to her and to himself that he would make it work, and he believed he could. Adele had some good qualities. She was bright and intuitive, and she had sometimes shown deep emotion. He was struck with the wild thought that though she was under a lot of pressure at work, she must still love him a bit after all they'd been through together.

Determined, even at this late date, to try to soften her steely exterior, he approached her as she sat answering an email and leaned over to kiss her neck. She shrugged away from him as if he'd tickled her, and as he stood and moved back, the sleeve of his housecoat somehow caught her coffee cup, which fell and shattered on the hardwood floor. The coffee darkened and spotted the edge of the pale blue Oriental carpet.

She let out a growl of frustration, nearly slamming the lid of the laptop. "You are so careless!"

Bartley wondered: how fragile was a marriage that could very possibly be ended with the sleeve of a housecoat. The situation was hopeless, so he decided, what the hell, might as well throw a bucket of gasoline on the fire. "I'm sorry, Adele. A leprechaun *made me* do it."

But the real *coup de grâce* occurred just as Bartley turned to get a rag and some rug cleaner. He heard his wife shout the imperative, "Clean it up!"

He stopped in his tracks. "I don't think I will. I like it."

It was late April, and the school day had begun well, up to period four. He loved period four. It was a class of freshmen, and there wasn't a pain in the ass in the lot. They weren't all exactly scholars, but they gave it a shot. *That's all you can ask*, Bartley thought. Because it was a vocational school, where the students spent a week in academic classes and a week in one of the various trade shops, many felt that English, math and biology were just distractions from Carpentry or Masonry. The Massachusetts Department of Elementary and Secondary Education made no distinction between this urban vocational school and an academy in the wealthy suburbs of Westford or Andover. The students were expected to pass the same state-mandated tests. Courses like "English on the Job," had been replaced with "British Literature." The attitude of many students was summed up well by one of Bartley's Juniors, who said, "Hey, Mr. Hannigan, I don't need to know about no sonnets. I'm gonna be a plumber! All I gotta know is shit flows down and payday's Friday."

"You'll be a stain on the trade," Bartley assured him.

"Whatever that means," was his dismal reply.

With students like that, Bartley really appreciated the kids in period four. He could joke with them, and they didn't get carried away. And there were a few who were genuinely curious. Walter Zayas had approached him after class and asked if he had any other O. Henry stories. "Of course! I'll bring you a whole book-full tomorrow!" Wonderful young man. Then there was Justin, the Puerto Rican student who competed for grades with Wassla, the Brazilian girl. They tried to out-study each other. Imagine that. When he explained and illustrated the finely-crafted rhyme scheme of 'Stopping by Woods on a Snowy Evening,' he had their full attention. T.J. Doherty even nodded appreciatively and said, "Cool." And sometimes, when they were writing, he would put on, softly, something like Bach's *Well-Tempered Clavier*, and a few of them admitted *that they liked it*. Period four renewed his faith in education, and he tried to carry this faith, as vital as the lamp of knowledge, into other less motivated classes.

After lunch, the day devolved. There had been the scene with Alexandra, in period seven. She began sobbing hysterically because Bartley, *Mistah Hanna-gin*, told her she had to put her phone away. "You don't know what's going on in my life!" she shouted. He admitted that he did not but suggested that the middle of class was probably not the time to get into it. There was Frankie, in period ten, who came in twenty minutes late with no better excuse than, "I got lost." In his senior year, Frankie had suddenly been rendered incapable of recognizing any locale in the school. Bartley kept him after class and drew him a map from his previous class to his own class, hoping the insult to his intelligence would restore his memory.

The majority were decent kids, but, in this year's classes, outside of period four, he saw far too many of the sleepers, the whiners, the rude, the boorish, the chatterboxes, the gigglers, the sullen—all the types that he had been ready to blast out of the water in the fall, but who, by April, had utterly worn him down. As his friend and colleague Eric Harris had said, at this time of year, when the home stretch was in sight, it was all about self-preservation. His chief desire was to hunker down and await the resurrection of summer. But a teacher must keep teaching. That's the job.

And so, when the harried Harris whispered to him cryptically in the fluorescent-lit corridor, "We're like the *Andromeda Strain* in Level Four. We don't even know what's up there!" Bartley felt that, somehow, he knew what the beleaguered educator meant, even though he had never read the book or seen the film. He glanced upward at the bubble-eye of a camera, one of scores that turned the entire structure into an inward-gazing Argus. The old French Canadian custodian had confided in him, "Those cameras are not there to watch *the students!*" On an ironic, or professionally self-destructive impulse, he blew several kisses toward the camera and earnestly mouthed, "I LOVE YOU!"

Last period, there was a Special Ed "annual review" parent-teacher meeting for which the parent showed up twenty minutes late. When it was Bartley's turn to speak, he informed the woman that while he liked her son, the young man never did *any* homework, though he wasn't given much. She informed the gathering that he was not able to do any work on his own—he didn't 'get it,' and that his teachers should have him do all his work in class, where they were there to help him. The Special Ed liaison was nodding and taking notes, and Bartley wondered if it was even worth arguing the point. If the mother shared and reinforced her son's attitude, the student was not likely to accomplish much at home. "Learned helplessness" was how teachers, among themselves, referred to this attitude, which, it seemed, had begun to permeate the school like the noxious odors that sometimes rose through the vents from the auto body shop to nauseate entire sections of the school.

This was painful enough, but far worse for Bartley, when he returned to his room, was finding a dispiriting email reminder that there was a departmental meeting after school. He hated the meetings, and he hated his boss, Mr. Bede—not because he was a fat slob; not because he was unqualified; not because he was rude and condescending, though he was all of these. Bartley hated his boss because he was *utterly full of shit.*

Bede called the meeting to order promptly at 2:10, while stragglers were still looking for seats. Realizing that there were none vacant, they cast about, wondering what to do. Bede paused to enjoy their discomfiture and waved a churlish hand toward an adjoining room from which, they were supposed to deduce, they should bring chairs. While they scurried off, the unvenerable Bede launched into his pompous discourse.

"Strategic! Measurable! Attainable! Results-oriented!" he thundered.

Full of shit. Full of shit. Full of shit. Full of shit. Bartley countered mentally.

"And! *And!* And this is what I want to emphasize—*time bound!* SMART goals are TIME BOUND!"

Everything is time-bound, you asshole.

"So, when your PLC establishes SMART goals to improve the level of student achievement—we are working interdependently. . . ." Here he spread the fingers of both hands and inter-spliced them, as if his slow-witted English department needed visuals to understand English words, ". . . working *inter-dependently* to attain the intended essential learning." He moved his pudgy intertwined fingers back and forth as if he were demonstrating some hideous sexual act. "So, make sure that you establish a *timeline* for your goals. Remember that your goals should relate to your DDM's. This does not mean that you will not develop common formative assessments to help determine each student's mastery of essential learning standards. You will use the data you collect there to identify strategies and create instruments to assess the dispositions that students will acquire."

Bartley looked around at the sullen members of the department as the stragglers returned carrying chairs; he had seen brighter "dispositions" among the attendees at a wake. Bill Bergeron looked like his teeth hurt, Harris like he was sitting in the waiting room at the proctologist's. Some of the women, who made up most of the department, examined their split ends while others chewed gum joylessly. Only Bob Daley smiled contentedly. This was his last year, so he really didn't give a shit. In fact, he had told Bartley that he had Bluetooth in his hearing aid; he was probably listening not to Mr. Bede, but to Mr. Marley.

While Bede droned on, Bartley wandered along misty thought-paths where he searched out various characters in his life, characters whose intentions he would like to try to get to the bottom of somehow: his wife, his father, a banshee, and this seventh son of a seventh son. From time to time, a Bedian phrase would penetrate the mist: "Aligned with state and district standards," "bi-annual evaluation of adherence to team norms and protocols." Bartley would wince and retreat further into the fog. He glanced at his watch—only 2:28. Another half hour of this horse shit.

He recalled Harris's words after the last departmental meeting: "Was I kidnapped and taken aboard an alien space vessel? I feel as if I've been mind-probed—violated! It's like the Kennedy assassination. Nothing is the same afterward."

But as he pondered this Harrisonian commentary in grim empathetic recognition, there was a tap on the door and Fatima, the secretary, came in on discreet heels. She whispered something to Bede, who instantly turned his beady eyes on Bartley and nodded. Fatima looked at him too, eyebrows arched above her glasses, and signaled tactfully for him to follow her. A reprieve! But then, what could it be? Adele? He imagined her leaving the house angry and getting into an accident. That would be on his conscience!

Once out of the room, he asked, "What's up, Fatima?"

"Your wife says to call her. It's an e–eh, well, it's something important."

He headed toward his room to get the phone from his desk. In his fantasy, Adele would tell him that she'd had an epiphany. "What an insensitive bitch I've been!" She would tell him that she realized that the most important thing in her life was not the company, but her husband. She would beg his forgiveness, and—but along with the realization that none of this would happen came a cold flash of fear. Could there be something wrong with Manus? He broke into a run.

Adele was in the middle of a conversation with someone else when she answered the phone. "—then whose fault it is that the BDR's are not making their quota—excuse me, Jack. I have to get this—can you come back in ten minutes? Thank you. Bartley?"

"Is something wrong, Adele?"

"All right, listen. I'm at the office." This meant her work office; not her home office. "I checked the home messages—there was a call from Ray

Plouffe." She spelled out the name. "He's a policeman. I called him, and—it's about your father. He was in an accident, and I don't think he made it, Bartley. I mean, Bartley, he *didn't* make it. I'm very sorry."

She had no further details to relate. She gave him Officer Plouffe's number. She asked if he wanted her to accompany him, which was decent, but he could tell from her manner that she was eager to get back to who was to blame for the drooping BDR's.

She had never cared much for his father, anyway. Hell, *he* had never cared much for his father. He loved him, but he didn't really like him. Except in these last few days, when Harry Hannigan had suddenly and inexplicably called upon him as a sort of trusted friend.

Officer Plouffe was old school, and he did not want to discuss the matter over the phone. By 3:15, Bartley was in a conference room at Lowell General Hospital with a pathologist and a cop who looked familiar, probably from Dunkin' Donuts. The crooked nose suggested old battles, but the thin graying hair and comfortable paunch indicated that those days were done.

They accompanied Bartley down a brightly lit corridor, where he identified his father's body through a glass partition. He half expected him to sit up and say, "What the hell are you starin' at, numb-nuts? I told you I'd be dead soon!"

But this soon, Dad?

"So," Bartley said, when they had repaired to an interview room, "no one else was involved? I mean, I don't get it. Did he fall asleep at the wheel?"

"You see," Officer Plouffe explained, "at the scene we were able to identify some deer tracks on the edge of River Road, both on the river side, and on the other side—there was also deer hair on a spur of a barbed wire fence close to the scene."

"A deer ran in front of the car?"

"That's our theory."

"But when the car hit the tree, the airbag deployed. Why didn't that save him?"

The pathologist, a bald man in green scrubs and still wearing blue pro-phylactic gloves, took over. "When he saw the deer, or for whatever reason, he jammed on the brakes pretty hard."

"There were thirty feet of skid marks before the tree stopped him," Plouffe interjected, glancing at a small notebook.

"What we believe happened—very unlucky, by the way—you see, your father had a book in the back of the wagon, a very big, heavy book. He slams his brakes. Car goes from forty-five or fifty to zero, at the tree, in a matter of seconds." The pathologist held an imaginary wheel and slammed his right foot illustratively. "Consequently, this book in the back takes flight. Now this big old book, a very big, whattaya call it, *folio* sort of edition of several hundred pages, hardbound, you need two hands to lift it. And, sadly—laws of physics, you see—it flies forward and strikes your father square on the back of the head. Cracked his cranium. Death was probably instantaneous."

"Oh, shit," Bartley said. "Was the book called . . . some Annals of something?"

Plouffe glanced at his notes. "*Annals of the Noble Families of Tyrone.*"

Bartley felt the weight of his father's words strike him with the force of a hard jab: "You'll be laughin' out of the other side of your mouth when your old man is cold and dead!"

FOUR

A dele Smollet-Hannigan was taking it from behind, and she was not telling her partner to hurry up. On the contrary, she was shouting the kind of obscenities that her husband Bartley would have found neither exciting nor endearing. Her sweating partner grunted and growled and occasionally walloped her pale bottom as if she were a bucking bareback bronco, and he a rodeo cowboy hellbent to hang on. A resounding smack elicited an ecstatic tremor from the Vice President for Operations, along with a squeaky cry which punctuated the suggestive refrain of Frank Sinatra's "Witchcraft." (Old Blue Eyes' voice welled forth from two Acoustic Zen speakers, which employed declassified military technology to create the highest quality sonic transmission).

The pair need not have worried that such a frenzied ruckus, or *rumpus*, would vex the neighbors. Donald Delaney, her paramour, was a fellow VP for Sales and Marketing at Dynamic Cloud Solutions. Both his home and his property were spacious, and the two were quite alone. His wife had moved out just before Thanksgiving, when her nagging suspicions were confirmed by the discovery of a series of evocative texts between Donald and what Oscar Wilde might have referred to simply as "a young person" of the female variety. She was taking the counsel of her sisters and trying to find a good divorce lawyer, but Donald had as yet received no legal notifications.

When they had finished, Adele popped out of bed and into the master bath, where she straddled the bidet. After a quick adjustment to the temperature and strength of the spray, a skill she had mastered rather quickly, she pushed a button. Stainless steel water jets emerged noiselessly from the sides of the bowl below her and began to spray as she hummed along with Sinatra.

Donald had been reluctant to bring up the topic before they had sex, lest he kill the mood, but now that the deed was done, he called out his belated condolences. "Awfully sorry about your father-in-law."

"Oh, don't be," she replied as she emerged from the bathroom.

"That's a little hard-hearted, isn't it? Even for you?"

She jumped back onto the bed and ran her fingers over the hirsute chest of her companion. "Let me tell you about this guy. When we were first married, he and my mother-in-law came over to visit us. Millie, our little Bichon Frisé, goes up to smell my father-in-law, as dogs do, and he bends over and starts *barking* at her!"

Donald chuckled. "Sounds like a quack, all right."

"*Barks!* Like a rabid pit bull! The dog was terrified! Poor Millie! At least when Sheila, Bartley's mother, was alive, she kept him in check. After she died, God. One day, we met him at the supermarket, and Bartley says, 'Dad, Adele just got a big promotion in her company.' You know how he answers? 'It doesn't matter,' he says, 'in a few years, she'll still be old and ugly and smell like talcum powder.' And then he laughs like we should all enjoy this witty observation. The more annoyed you'd get, the harder he would laugh. That was my father-in-law. What a prick."

"Was he rich?"

"In cash, I don't think so. But in land, yes. His father, Jeremiah O'Hannigan, inherited a big farm in Tyngsborough from some uncle or great uncle, a horse breeder who had come over here back in the 1920's or something. The land must be worth quite a bit now."

"So, if Bartley sells it, you'll be rich? Which will make you *even more* attractive!"

Sinatra had now launched into "Nothing But the Best."

"Oh, I don't think I'll get any more attractive that way, Donnie. I'm sure he left nothing to me, land nor money. I've been thinking, if I can get through the funeral and everything, now that our son is out on his own, Bartley can have his father's money—I don't care—marriage counseling be damned, I'm *out*. An empty nest with that screwy bird? No, thank you."

"Please, don't call me Donnie. I told you I hate 'Donnie.'"

"I'm sorry. Donald."

"Has Bartley always been screwy?"

"He was never your typical buckaroo, for sure—of course, what did I know? I was a kid. A pregnant kid. But he's gone off the deep end now. He was telling me about a leprechaun that visits his father at his farmhouse—"

"Oh, saints preserve us!" Donald cried in a stage-Irish voice and pulling up the sheet to gaze down forlornly at his spent dick, added, "Bejasus, I am gettin' smaller!" The two of them burst into laughter. Finally, Adele wiped her eyes and shook her head and said, "And when I tell him that he's gone completely bonkers, he accuses me of being close-minded!"

"Close-minded! Because you doubt the wee folk! That's rich!" The fit of hilarity took them once more.

"So pathetic," she concluded.

A few last chuckles shook Donald's chest, and then he stopped as if he had just heard a strange sound. He propped himself up on his elbow: "Then what about you and me? I mean, after my wife divorces me."

"Oh, I think we're fine the way we are, don't you? I mean marriage is— well the next thing you know I'd be checking your texts and we'd have to sign all kinds of legal forms with the bank and the state, just to screw! And this way, when we're tired of each other, we can go our separate ways without ever calling lawyers to sue each other about it."

"You have a point," Donald said.

"And your point seems to have been lost!"

"For the moment!" He leaned over and kissed her nipple. He was a top salesman, but he didn't try to sell the marriage proposal because the truth was the deal she'd described was one he liked well enough.

Harry Hannigan's flag-draped coffin was carried up the granite steps into the vestibule of St. Patrick's Church, escorted by his sons, Harry and Bartley, Manus, who had flown in that morning, and three cronies from the American Legion, Post 147. Gibby O'Malley had requested that he be granted the honor of carrying old Happy's human remains, but despite the fact that the sun had not transited the meridian, Gibby's feet had evidently already transited the threshold of Cappy's Copper Kettle and placed him squarely at the bar all morning. Bartley prayed to a series of his favorite saints that Gibby would not drop the coffin.

Still, he felt bad for his father's old pal when Gibby asked, humbly, just as the priest was composing himself to lead them down the aisle, "Could I . . . could I say jus' a few words of fah-farewell at the 'propriate time?"

"Gibby, listen, this is a very solemn occasion, and you seem *a bit* unsteady. . . ."

"I wou' *nevah* dishonah my frien', Bar-ley."

"What do you want to say, Gibby?"

"Jus' what an honor it was to know him. He woulda wanted it, Bar-ley."

Bartley thought that he was probably right. "You know what? All right. But be brief! You'll miss him—good friend—honor to know him. That's it!"

"Thank you—I won' lech-ya down."

"Keep it brief! Right after my brother speaks." Harry Junior had decently volunteered to deliver a eulogy, a relief to Bartley.

The organ music began its slow lugubrious roll. The altar boy who led the procession, holding aloft the processional cross, seemed to have been told a joke by one of the acolytes, because it was obvious that he was trying his best not to laugh out loud, a task made more difficult by the solemnity of the occasion. Bartley watched his shoulders shake as he walked with downcast gaze.

The priest came up and waved the aspergillum, sprinkling holy water over the coffin, a good dose, and began the prescribed ecclesiastical rites of the Catholic Church according to the Code of Canon Law. It was their farewell to the soul of Happy Hannigan, which would perhaps send it off in the right direction. Bartley recalled once dipping into James Joyce's *Finnegans Wake*, in which the writer refers to this kind of service as a "funferall."

Danny Fesconi, a well-respected tenor in American Legion circles, sang "Be Not Afraid," and Bartley reflected that most of the people here were those who had known his father from the Legion, various other bars and pool halls, or the Farmers' Market. There were also those who had bought a tree from him every year for the past thirty Christmases.

One could not have chosen a gloomier individual than Harry Junior, Unhappy Hannigan, to deliver the eulogy. He was short on the sort of cheerful or humorous memories of the departed that formed the usual fare on these occasions and wound up telling a rather pitiful story about how he had once told his father that a boy at the park was picking on him. His father called him a "Nancy boy," and brought him right down to the park where the bully was sitting on the monkey bars. "Now you go right over there and bust him one in the chops, Harry, and he'll never mess with you again." Needless to say, Harry Junior went over and got his ass kicked royally. After which, Happy signed him up, not for boxing lessons, but for Irish step dancing lessons, which he said would build up his stamina and perfect his footwork. But, of course, when word got out that Harry Junior was wearing a green skirt and dancing with the girls after school in the church hall, he got his ass kicked again and became the punching bag for a host of new bullies.

"So . . ." Unhappy said at last. The assemblage sat despondently wishing for an uplifting resolution to the story, preferably one in which the young Harry learned a valuable lesson from Harry Senior, or the bullies got what was coming to them through the agency of Harry Senior. Instead, the speaker wound up the tale with a lame and pointless, "—you know, that was that."

"Jesus Christ," Bartley mumbled while Adele, like the altar boy, bowed her head and suppressed a smile.

"But, of course, he meant well," Harry Junior added, as Bartley cleared his throat loudly and told him with his eyes to SIT DOWN.

Bartley, hands folded in front of his crotch like a modest penitent, approached the lectern as his brother took his leave. "An old friend of my father's, Gabriel O'Malley, they were in the Navy together, and have been . . . were friends ever since, has requested to say a few brief words of farewell to Harry Hannigan."

Bartley resumed his seat. Adele whispered, "Oh, God help us. Nice move, Bartley," as Gibby drew himself up to his full wobbly height and haltingly approached center stage. He pulled a piece of notepaper from inside his jacket, but then began to fish around his pockets for his glasses, and being apparently unable to find them, stared stupidly for a moment at the crowd gathered before him. The paper slipped from his fingers and Bartley held his breath as Gibby bent to pick it up, remembering the "trick knee," but when his trembling hand was half way to the floor, he wisely thought better of it and stood back up, steadying himself with the lectern. Then he stood, not in prayerful, but in panicked silence.

Bartley was about to go help Gibby back to his seat when he suddenly began. "I am not a ejucated person. But *that* man!" He pointed to the coffin. "That man in there *was* a ejucated person. I mean he coo read *Latin!* Now, what I nevah understand, is why a ejucated guy like ol' Happy wanted a spend time with a bum like me. Probally I embarrassed him a cuppla times. I hope I'm not embarrasin' him now, but for some reason, for *some reason*, Happy latched onta me an' he decided you know— thass the way he was. . . ." Gibby's fingers were raised in front of him as if he were trying to open an invisible safe. "He jus' decided you know, this bum is all right. Yeah, he ain't too bright, an' he drinks too much—way too much. But you know he is who he is, an' he's all right. An' I'm gonna tell you people sumthin' right here. If Happy Hannigan thought you were all right, lemme tell you the God's hones' truth, he didin' care if you were black, white, ejucated, ignorant, rich, poor—din' mattah! If you were all right in his book, he would stand beside you 'gainst any odds. An' he took a beatin' 'causa me once or twice back in the Navy days. But you know, he nevah said, 'Whydja open your big mouth, Gibby, an' get us in that jam?' Nevah said that! Now I know if he thought you was a phony, yeah, he could be a *prick*." A ripple of the low laughter of recognition passed through the crowd. "Sorry, Fathah, my 'pologies. So finally, all I can say, I known a lotta guys, I'm tellin' you, all kindsa guys. But Harry Hannigan wuz the bess.' He wuz *the bess.*'"

The men of Post 147, and every bar where Happy Hannigan was known, erupted into applause. Adele did not applaud. She felt that she had been indirectly labeled a phony and was further agitated at the sight of both her husband and her son wiping tears away with sodden tissues.

A week after the funeral, Adele informed Bartley that she would not be going to marriage counseling with him, and that, moreover, she was finished with counseling, *and* she was finished with him.

To Bartley, it was as if the vet had just told him that his seventeen-year-old hound dog, who was deaf and blind and crippled, had to be put out of his misery. He only wished that *he* had been the one to tell *her* that *he* was leaving. In an attempt at sardonic wit, he said, "You forgot to say, 'It's not *you*, it's *me*.'"

"Oh," she said, unabashed, "it's you. It's definitely *you*."

He should have known better than to leave her that opening, and he thought sadly, the truth was that she was smarter than he was. Or at least cleverer.

"I won't be unreasonable, but this house will be considered marital property—"

"Like your IRA," he said.

"Yes, and your pension. I'm not threatening you, Bartley. But you really don't need this big house to live in by yourself. I will tell my lawyer to be equitable."

"Oh, a lawyer, great. They're always equitable."

"The court will decide. Nothing onerous. With my income and no dependents, I won't get much. It's just that we own this house and property together, that's all. And I hope we can continue to be amicable."

"Continue?"

"Look, we'll talk later. I have to get going."

"Right, then," Bartley said, "thanks for your time. It's been great."

She shook her head and was walking away when Bartley called after her, "Who's gonna tell Manus?"

"You tell him. I'll tell him. I don't think it will be a shock. I'll be staying with a friend until I find a place. My lawyer will be in touch."

He could see she wanted to leave, but she hesitated. She seemed to soften momentarily when she added, "Not to worry, Bartley. You'll be fine. Your inheritance will be considered 'separate property.' I'm sure your father left me nothing—we didn't like each other. But my lawyer will need a copy of the will, anyway."

"You've really thought this through."

"You know me."

Yes, he did know her.

"We have to be honest, Bartley. It's been bad for a while. We've just gone different ways."

"Fair enough," he said.

She went upstairs, to pack a suitcase, he presumed. As the initial shock subsided, to Bartley's surprise, he felt quite good. Yes, some twenty-odd years of effort were down the drain, but it had been a futile effort and defeat had been foregone and overdue. And he really was in no mood to go to counseling, anyway. The truth was that Linda was full of shit, too, with her "emotional avoidance," and "when I hear you say that, I feel," and her little games with the "sender" and the "receiver."

Bartley positioned his tongue under his front teeth, scrunched up his face, and curled back his lips. He opened and closed his mouth a few times, savoring the imminent mockery of Linda, and then sputtered, "Aw wight, now, teow me sthumthin *sspe-shew* abowt each otha. Say ditis *sspe-shew* to me becauth. . . ."

He snickered evilly at his mimicry and considered whether it might be time to begin an affair with Louise, something he had avoided because of some crazy sense of obligation to his stupid stupid stupid vows, and because he had never quite recovered full testosterone risk-it-all power-libido strength after watching *Fatal Attraction*.

But, by God, he was done. Done with vows. Done with fears of a rabbit boiling on his stove. Done with Honey I'm home, and Honey are you home, and do you mind if I, and are you okay, and what's wrong, and I'm sorry if I—done with excuses and lame explanations for imagined slights, and yes, I'll trim the hedges this weekend, and okay, I did forget the Q-tips! Done with the pathetic looks from women at her horrid company parties, women with whitened teeth and fake boobs and Cosmopolitan cocktails saying *a high school teacher? Oh*. Done with standing there with a hand on the door knob wondering what kind of mood she was going to be in. Done with a woman who would not even *consider* the possibility of a banshee or a leprechaun when *who really knows?* Done! Done! Done!

And he said, not in a soft voice, because he was done with whispering his malcontent, "What is weally ssss-peshew to me about you is that *you're leaving!*"

He decided it was time for a cigarette and a drink, or two cigarettes and three drinks, or—whatever! On his way out, disciplined by years of habit, he nearly called up the stairs, "I'm going out!" Then he remembered that he was done with all that and, laughing loudly, set off.

In celebration of his freedom, he slipped the Jimi Hendrix *Rainbow Bridge* CD into the player. Oh yeah, "Hear My Train A-Comin.'" He cranked it up, and it spoke to the unexpected springtime in his overflowing soul.

Like the engineer high up in the cab of the Advance Midnight Special, with an elbow resting across the open side window, Bartley was rolling down the steel rails of life toward the next chapter, or a whole new book, which began at American Legion Post 147, where the veterans still smoked at the bar. "It's Hannigan junior!" one of his father's pallbearers called out as he crossed the threshold into the dim interior. "Put him in Happy's seat!" He was ushered to an empty seat at the bar and installed there with deference.

"Thank you, gentlemen," he said. There were three cigarettes left in his case, but someone handed him a stogie, and he fired it up.

"It's Cuban," the guy said.

"I didn't think veterans would smoke Castro cigars," Bartley said.

"We prefer to think of it as burning the enemy's crops," the old-timer responded.

"Whataya drinkin' Hannigan?" another man asked.

"Bartley."

"Whataya drinkin', Bartley?"

"Got Sam Adams?"

"Charlie, give the kid a Sam and a shot of Irish."

Bartley sat back in the tall chair puffing the cigar, listening to the Zen-like sounds of clicking pool balls, men's conversations, and the therapeutic banter of Joe Castiglione and Don Orsillo as Red Sox Nation readied for battle against the Baltimore Orioles, whom Castiglione referred to as "the Birds." That was great.

So, Adele had finally pulled the plug on this moribund relationship. She was packing now, but her love had packed up . . . when? Probably years ago. Just as well. And no, Manus would not be shocked. During his visit for the funeral there had been a lot of eye-rolling and head shaking as he observed his parents' interactions.

Bartley decided he would watch two innings here, have another cold Sam, then go downtown, stow his car in the Market Street Garage and hit the Old Court for a couple of Guinness. Maybe he'd finish the evening dancing in a circle and knocking down ouzo with the Greeks at the Athenian Corner and take an Uber home, because he would barely be fit to walk, let alone drive. He relished the thought. It was the first day of the rest of his life, and *he could hear his train a-comin'!*

Bartley's outstretched hand touched vertical bars, and his first thought, hazy yet alarming, was, "Christ, I'm in fuckin' jail!" He opened his eyes. An operation that was unexpectedly painful, because his left eye was sore, or the orbital bone around it was sore. There was a blacksmith in his head slamming a great hammer onto the anvil of his frontal lobe, and Quasimodo was ringing his cerebellum.

The birdsong that filtered through the hammering was tuneless and annoying, and probably not from Baltimore, but he did see enough to conclude that he was not in a cell but in a big brass-frame bed. He closed his eyes again.

Fragments of the evening passed like a strange slideshow on the back of his eyeballs. These images coagulated and began to form a vague and disquieting memory, which accelerated his heart rate. His eyes opened again, wide.

He sat up, and instantly crashed back down on the pillow, pinching shut his eyes and clutching his throbbing skull. The view he had seen in the five seconds that his eyes were open had convinced him that he did not know where he was, but the brick walls and tall windows suggested that it was some sort of apartment or condo downtown in a rehabbed mill building.

"Ooooahh," he murmured, gingerly touching the sensitive area around his left eye. In those brief seconds of vision, he had seen something else: a long, Indian headdress hung from a hook on the wall. Had he stayed with Chief Red Cloud?

He heard singing in an adjoining room, a woman's voice:

Una flecha en el aire,
cielito lindo, lanzó Cupido,
si la tiró jugando,
cielito lindo, a mí me ha herido.

A woman's voice, drawing nearer. Slowly, cautiously, with some effort, he rose to a sitting position.

A dark, well-put-together Hispanic woman strode into the room, combing wet hair, and wearing an oversized plain white T-shirt. "Oh, you are awake, Barley! How did you sleep?"

"Did I slip? Is that what happened to my eye?" Fogs churned about him and the bright colors of the Indian headdress on the wall were making him dizzy.

"No, how did you *sleep*—in the bed?"

"Oh, uhhh, I slip—I slept okay." He recalled vaguely some kind of interaction with this woman the previous night.

She bit her lower lip and looked him over skeptically. "Let me look at your eye." He rose unsteadily as she came close. She held his elbows and peered up into his left eye. Even in his condition, Bartley queasily noticed that her own eyes were a lovely chocolate brown and that she smelled good. Really good.

"Aye." She shook her right hand rapidly as if she had burned her finger. "It looks bad, but I think is okay. You need to put the ice on it. And thank you for sticking up for me, Barley. That guy was a real yerk."

He had no clear notion of what had happened, but he had evidently gotten into some kind of jam or *yam* with a *yerk*. "Yeah, he must have been."

He sat back down and put his head in his hands again. "Ooof."

"You can drink *a lot!*"

"Ugh, yeah," he said. "Could I have some water?"

"In the kitchen, you can have water or *jugo*—yooce, I mean *juice*, while I get ready."

He stood again and, and glancing down, noticed that the front of his white underwear was stained a rusty red. "Jesus! My dick is bleeding!" he cried. The thought flashed through his mind that maybe this sweet woman was really a maniacal Lorena Bobbit! Maybe she had cut it off, fulfilling a long-held wish of Adele's!

As he pulled out the waistband to check the property, the woman laughed and said, "Your deck is not bleeding! You are so funny, Barley! You spilled a glass of wine on yourself!"

"Phew. Okay. I'm sorry. What's your name?"

"Violeta, silly!"

"Violeta Seely? Oh, *silly!*"

"You are making fun of my accent?"

"No, sorry, and you're from . . . Mexico?"

"*Si, claro que si*. We met at the Big Moon!"

"I was at the Big Moon? Oh, yeah, I *was* at the Big Moon." It was a strip club up on the river in Tyngsborough.

Now the headdress made sense. And another image squeezed through the haze and popped open, unfolding before him: Violeta undulating across a parquet dance floor under a spotlight, wearing only that Indian headdress. "You're a good dancer," he said. But he could say no more. He needed water.

"You are a good dancer, too, Barley!"

Oh, shit. "I'd better get some water. By the way, my name is Bartley, not Barley."

"*Bart*-lee? Last night you said it was Barley!"

"I guess I was having trouble with my name last night." He steadied himself with an outstretched hand and headed for the bathroom. He peed while he drank his third glass, wondering what, if anything, he had done with this woman. When he came out, she was standing there in jeans and a tank top with a bottle of aspirin, and as Bartley's head cleared, he noticed again, even more clearly, that she really was *kinda cute*.

She poured three aspirin into his open hand. "You want toast?" she asked. Where had he heard that recently—his father. And once again, he declined.

"You want to take a shower?"

"That would be great."

In the mirror, he saw that there was no blood in the eye, which was a relief, though he had a pretty good shiner. He gave his dick a quick inspection to gauge whether or not he'd used it, or attempted to use it, the night before. In that regard, it appeared his train had not come, but it was difficult to be sure.

He heard a hair dryer start in the next room. He showered and got re-dressed in his cigar-and-booze smelling clothes with many a groan and muttered imprecation and wondered about the etiquette of the situation. Did he owe her money?

He stepped tentatively back into the bedroom, where she was leaning toward the mirror applying mascara. Her dark hair was in a long braid. He loved long braids.

"Ah, did we . . . I mean things are a little hazy. Did we—?"

"No, we did nothing,' Bartley! You were very sick. An' I just met you last night! And besides, you said you were married."

Bartley frowned.

"Like they say on Facebook, is complicated?"

"Very simple, actually. My wife moved out yesterday. You see this gypsy told me that sometimes a promise is a rusted chain attached to something, um, attached to the corpse of yesterday, and now I see she was very correct. Damned what is it, Knight of Pentacles or something. Anyway, the corpse is buried. Ooof. I feel like dog shit, pardon my . . . my. . . ." He waved a hand at whatever he was asking her to pardon.

She made a pouting face. "I'm sorry, Bartley. For that reason, you were drinking so much? You were sad?"

"Long overdue celebration, really. Say, ah, listen, do I owe you . . . you know. For your time or anything?"

"Bartley! *I'm not a hooker!*"

He had stepped in it there, apparently. "I'm sorry, Violeta. Like I said, I'm very fuzzy this morning. Not myself."

"You are funny, Bartley! I asked you last night, *how much can you drink?* You said, 'I don't know, but I guess I'm gonna find out!' *Dios mio*, you can really drink *a lot*."

"Ugh. So you say. Um, I'll be off, then."

"I'm glad we met. I had a lot of fun, Bartley. That little guy, oh my God, he was something else. Seven hundred years old! *¡Que loco!*"

Bartley froze. "What leetle guy?"

"Come on, Bartley! You don't remember? When we left the Big Moon and we went to your father's house? I told you I am very interested in wine—in growing grapes for wine, and we went to your father's house—you showed me all the *vino?*"

"My father's house?"

"An' then we end up drinking with that crazy little man? *Pero*, it was *you* did most of the drinking. But the little man, he can drink a lot, too, especially for such a *little* man."

Once again, confused images squeezed through a hole in the curtain of alcoholic amnesia and popped open in Bartley's head, like scenes from a troublesome dream, snatches of phrases, and yes, a little man! "Was he wearing—?"

"A small green coat, how do you say, *la chaqueta con cola de pato*— you know, like the tail of a duck on the coat? Like the *mascota* of the Boston Celtics."

"The leprechaun on the logo."

"Yes, he has a curly moustache, it's like the handlebars on a bicycle. He has one of those old hats, you know, like Napoléon. And big red nose. Oh, he made me laugh so hard. He teach—he *taught* me that song he likes, let me see, goes, like, um:

> *I'm a rambler, I'm a gambler, I'm a long way from home*
> *An' if you don' like me, then leave me alone.*
> *I eat when I am hungry, an' I drink when I am dry*
> *An' if moonshine don' kill me, I'll live till I die."*

"'Moonshine is liquor," she explained.

"Yes," he said, rubbing his forehead.

"You do not remember the little man, Bartley?"

"Kind of, I think. Like a dream."

"He was funny. It was very difficult to understand his accent, so he was speaking to me in Spanish."

"He speaks Spanish?"

"He speaks very well Spanish. He says he was living for one hundred years in the wine cellar of *El Escorial* in Spain. He's so *crazy!*"

"Violeta, did the little man tell you his name?"

"A funny name. I don't—wait—he wrote it for me." She rummaged in a leather bag on her dresser and pulled out a piece of paper, which she unfolded. "Oh yes. His name is . . . there."

She handed the paper to Bartley, and yes, it was written right there, in a curious hand, all swirls and loops: *Don Nippery Septo.* Odd name, he thought, but then he reminded himself that he really had no notion of what might be a normal name for a . . . *leprechaun.*

A light sweat broke out on Bartley's brow. Yesterday, he had awoken in a home in the Highlands, clinging to the wreckage of a marriage and, if nothing else, at least a sense of normalcy. Today, he had awoken with a Mexican stripper in a strange apartment downtown after having drunk himself into oblivion in the company of a mythical being.

He looked out the window to get his bearings and saw the gray granite belfry of St. Anne's Church rising above the red bricks of the old city hall, and below him, the cobbled stones of Middle Street. He said, "Listen, Violeta, can we get a coffee? I need a very big coffee."

"I don't drink coffee, but I will go with you. I got nothing to do—it's Sunday."

For a moment, he felt an apprehension that someone he knew would see him, or that he would have to answer questions about Violeta. But then he remembered that he was *done with all that.*

A short walk down Market Street, at Brew'd Awakening, he got a large coffee for himself and a hot chocolate for Violeta. He was soothed by the sweet voice of Billie Holiday singing "I'll Be Seeing You." The aspirin had begun to kick in and the hydration helped, but it was the coffee, which he sipped with a nearly pious gratefulness, that began to inch him out of the deep hangover hole. He ordered two bagels.

"Okay, Violeta, so first of all, you're from. . . ?"

"I just told you! México," she said. *Meh-hee-co.* Then she repeated it, smiling, and trying to use the English pronunciation. "May-see-co."

"Right, right. Mexico, eh?"

"Uh-huh," she said, with that delightful, and he now noticed, slightly crooked smile, so endearing. "I'm a rambler, I'm a gambler, I'm a long way from home," she added.

If she said anything else, he missed it. He was temporarily absorbed in a vacant and fond admiration of her dark hair, the curve of her neck and the silver that adorned her in bracelets and rings, contrasting so beautifully with her bronzed skin. But it was her own radiance, the sympathy and intelligence in those almond eyes that began to dispel the fog of his hangover and haltingly reignite his heretofore slack and nauseated libido. He even felt a stirring in his wine-stained underwear, and beyond that, a sudden and powerful affection for her and a desire to kiss those lips that were not cherry red, but natural, glossed perhaps, and certainly inviting.

"You're very sweet. Do you mind if I ask how old you are?"

"I have thirty-four years."

"Jeers? Oh, *years.*"

"Are you making fun of my accent again?"

"You're English is excellent; it really is. In my condition, I'm just not as sharp as usual, and I'm thrown a bit by the slight accent, which is beautiful. Anyway, you're in fantastic shape, Violeta. Obviously." He didn't add that it might be working with a pole that kept her so fit.

"How many years, I mean, how old are you, Bartley?"

"I have forty-two years. I got married early. I have a twenty-two-year-old son, Manus."

She nodded but said nothing. Bartley continued, "And, you came up here . . . to dance?"

"I came up here to make money. I know that dancer . . . stripper, is not the most, you know, the most respectable job, but when I am finished with all this, I mean, when I make my money, I will go back to México to buy some land near Parras Valley in Cohuila, have a farm, maybe grow some of—*las uvas*—grapes for the wine."

"Grapes. Interesting."

"Grenache, dolcetto, syrah. That little man knows *a lot* about wine, Bartley. . . ."

"He certainly knows how to drink it from what I've heard. By the way, about that little man—I don't remember. Did—what—is he—did he say—he was, like, a *leprechaun* or something?"

A server arrived, staring at Bartley's black eye for a few seconds more than was polite, and set their bagels on the table. Violeta took a bite of hers, frowning in thought while she chewed. Then she shook her head and waved an index finger back and forth quickly. "No, no. He said he is *not* a leprechaun. He does not like the leprechauns. He said he is, oh, something else, but I don't remember—another funny name. But he is from Ireland. I think he's like a magic person or something." She nodded as if to say, 'Yes, that's it,' and took another bite of her bagel, chewing placidly.

"Magical people? That doesn't surprise you?"

"No. I have a hot chocolate here, but I don't understand how it got hot. Some energy traveled over a wire? That's magic, no? And your phone and the cars going by outside and airplanes and people in space and we hear music around us with no musicians. If a person came back from the past this all would be magic. And probably there is other kinds of things that are like magic to us that we don't know about."

"Well, that's all science," he said. "Laws of physics and all that."

"Yes, but on the news they say that there are US Air Force pilots, people who are trained to observe, smart people, serious people, who are reporting that they are seeing some crazy objects flying around that do not obey the laws of science we understand. And no one can explain how they do it, because it should be impossible to fly like that! And no trail of jet or heat from them. There's a lot of magic everywhere! People are too—I don't know the word in English—*presumido*."

"*Presumido*. Hmmm. They presume too much?" Bartley's cell phone began to sound. "Excuse me, Violeta."

Manus's voice awakened in him a feeling, for the first time, that it was perhaps sad that things could not have worked out. "Dad, I was trying to call the house, and no one was there. I called Mom and . . . Jesus, you guys have split up?"

"I was going to call you today."

"You all right, Dad?"

"Oh sure. Just having coffee with a friend. I'm fine. We're both fine, I mean your mother and I. Long time coming, son. I needn't tell you, or maybe I do need to tell you that your mother and I can't seem to get along very well any more. It's just one of those things . . . but we both love you, and that's forever."

"I know, Dad. I just wanted to check on you. You know, granddad and then this—it's a lot. But don't worry about me. I'm good, really."

"You'll be all right, Manus. How is Jill?"

"Oh, she's great, Dad. She's really great."

"You two seem like a good match. She's such an easy-going girl—and, believe me, easy-going is the best thing a woman can be. Best thing anyone can be. You guys will be fantastic together, really."

"Thanks, Dad. Means a lot."

"Stay in touch, Manus."

He pressed the little button and laid the phone on the table. Violeta had picked up a *Boston Globe* from a vacant table and was looking it over, but he was sure she had listened to his call because she seemed thoughtful and a bit sad.

Now the coffee was mixing with the remnants of whatever combination of booze he'd drowned himself in the night before, and now he felt a stirring not in his crotch, but in his bowels. "Violeta, I'm going to have to get my car and go home—my stomach is. . . ."

She seemed to sense his predicament. The bathroom door at the one-room café was two feet from their table and offered little privacy for such an emergency.

"Go and use my bathroom."

"I wouldn't do that to you. Like you said, we just met."

She laughed. "It's okay, we are animals, after all."

"Can I call you?" he asked. "To discuss this further?"

"Yes. My number is in your pocket—I gave it to you last night."

He extracted a crumpled piece of paper, and said, "Oh, yes. You're right."

"Oh, and Bartley, you are in great shape, too."

"Very generous, I'm sure. One thing, Violeta, this guy that whacked me. . . ."

"Oh, the *yer*—the jerk."

"Yeah, how did the jerk look? I mean, did I get a shot in at all?"

"He looked bad. I think his nose, it was broken."

Bartley gave a boxer's shrug. "Well, that's something."

"Yes, that is something."

She looked away for a moment, and Bartley thought he noticed a repressed smile as another scene swam into view in his fuddled brain. He recalled a mighty attempt to raise himself off the endlessly rocking ground while, he thought, someone had yelled—what was it? "The bitch broke my nose!"

Could *she* have. . . ? *No!*

Bartley's stomach renewed its rumbling, with a more urgent twist. "I'll call you." He ran out the door, glancing back once to see Violeta looking after him, smiling, perhaps fondly.

When Bartley had gone and she was alone at the table, Violeta wondered what this man must think of her. A woman who threw off her clothes before drunken men for money. She only cared because she kind of liked him. There was something about him; he seemed sad and lonely yet kind and good-hearted. She wished she could tell him the truth, that even her old father would be proud, though frightened, to know that his daughter was working to bring down one of the drug-running gangs who were destroying the country they loved, men who lived by the gun and worshipped *Santa Muerte*, the patroness of violence and death, men who were kidnappers, murderers, and drug smugglers. They were trying to extend their web of corruption here into the Northeast, through *mafiosos* like her boss at the club, Joe Catania, a man with loyalties, perhaps, but no ethics; devotion to "associates" and to family, but none to community or country. As an agent of the *La Policia Federal De México,* working with the DEA, she would take him down. But she could not tell Bartley that. She could not tell anyone.

Five

The pilot of Aer Lingus Airbus A330-300, Flight 2237, spoke with a clear, well-modulated, west-of-Ireland accent: "Ladies and gentleman, we are beginning our descent to Logan International Airport. Local time is 1:19 p.m. It is 77 degrees and partly sunny in Boston. We hope you have enjoyed your flight and thank you for choosing Aer Lingus. *Go n-éirí an bothar leat!*"

In window seat 28A, Cornelius O'Tuama fingered the Celtic knot tie tack stuck neatly into his University College Cork tie, black with red and gray stripes. (He had not actually attended UCC, but he had found the tie under a chair in a pub in Macroom and had taken a fancy to it). He closed his eyes, pulled his flat herringbone cap tighter over his shaggy mane, and whispered a brief prayer, too low for the passenger in seat 28B to hear, "Lord, keep your servant in the palm of your hand, and don't close your fist too tight."

The passenger in 28B was leaning as far away from Cornelius as possible, because the man from Ballyvourney, though rich in other qualities, was negligent in the area of personal hygiene. He had always hated the idea of immersing himself in water or scrubbing at his skin with a washcloth. Consequently, hovering about him was a miasma of sweaty staleness with a hint of dirty socks and a soupçon of pig farm, a mélange which most humans found disagreeable.

The plane descended toward the blanket of clouds and shuddered as it passed through them; vapors flew by his window like panicked ghosts. There was the sea, the white wakes of boats streaking across the blue, and then land—America! Wisps of clouds obscured his view again, and then he saw more islands, causeways, flooded plains, and then the vast green mainland dotted with homes and buildings and cut with long gray roads, as everything grew larger below them.

The wing to his left tilted upwards and the earth disappeared for a moment as the airliner banked into its turn. When the world below reappeared, he saw shipyards, cargo containers, sporting grounds, more houses, and a great oil tank brushed with long strokes of brightly colored paint. There was a bay with moored boats, and then the plane was over an expanse of naked water again, descending more rapidly. Cornelius thought they were about to put down in the sea, but as he held his breath, the edge of a runway appeared below them and soon after he felt the thump of wheels striking tarmac.

"Thank Jesus," he said. He had never been on a plane before in his life.

Cornelius picked up his meager luggage and his stout blackthorn and followed the line toward an exit. With his feet upon *terra firma*, Cornelius, like Antaeus of old, felt his confidence returning, his power growing. He was a mighty warrior of the realms of light, the seventh son of a seventh son of the House of the Red Lion, Guardian of the verdant lands of the *Ua Briain*, vanquisher of the Gray Man of the Tuscar Rock, strongest branch of the hazel, heart of the oak, scion of the tribes of Thomond, Ormond, and Desmond, most—

"Passport, please."

Shaken from his reverie, Cornelius O'Tuama stared blankly for a moment at the official before him. Here was a woman whose ancestors had no doubt crossed the trackless plains of Africa, noble hunters of the tiger, great conjurers of the spirits of—

"Hello? Do you speak English, sir?"

"Indeed, I do, yes. Where I come from, we call the language *Béarla*, you see, sometimes 'foul *Béarla*,' but yes, I do speak it. Indeed. Fluently, yes."

"Passport." She extended an open hand.

Cornelius was about to shake her hand, when by the expression on her face, he was given to understand that she would prefer to see his passport first. He reached inside his tweed suit coat and extracted the document.

The sudden movement that Cornelius had made set the aura that surrounded him trembling a bit, and a wave of fetid air particles traveled toward the official, whose face suddenly took on the aspect of someone who has bitten into a lemon.

She read his name.

"That's right. And what would be your name?"

"Would you put your . . ." She peered over the counter. "Where is your luggage, sir?"

"Luggage? Yes, now, this is it." He hefted a knapsack onto her counter.

"How long will you be in the United States?"

"So, you see there's a man is having a problem wid' a banshee. I think it's pretty serious."

"Mr. O'Tuama, I did not ask you the purpose of your visit. First, I'm asking you how long you will be in the United States."

The Irishman could see that he may have inadvertently taken the wrong tack with this official. She was probably very busy, after all, and had little time for banter. He decided to try to be more direct. "Based on my experience, I should think a month or so."

"What is the purpose of your visit?"

"The purpose, yes, well. A man from Massachusetts, he called his cousin, Mick, in Tyrone you see, who directed him to meself, as there's a banshee about the place—"

"Excuse me. What is a 'banshee,' sir?"

"Ah, now, there is some debate about that among scholars, but those that knows best, and I count meself among that number, believe that they are beings, well, of another plane, or a separate weave, you know, in this sort of elaborate tapestry that we call reality."

Cornelius remarked that the Irish people in line behind him were smiling broadly, and a few were laughing into their hands, shoulders bobbing. Cornelius bristled and turned a piercing eye in the direction from which he thought he'd overheard the term, "bog-trotter." The official was not laughing. She opened his bag and said, "You're coming to the US for up to a month, and this is what you brought? Two shirts, two pairs of underwear, a book, and a crucifix?"

"It has often been said," he replied, in his sing-song Corkonian, "and 'tis true, you know, like, you could be *too* prepared."

"What's this?" she asked, pulling a small glass bottle from a side pocket of the knapsack.

"Oh, yes, that is water from St. Patrick's Well. I expect that it may be efficacious."

"Against the banshee?"

"Right, so. That's it, exactly."

She unscrewed the cap and smelled the water. She frowned as she thumbed through the book. It was *Cré na Cille*, by Máirtín Ó Cadhain. "A very interesting book, there," Cornelius offered. "I believe it's been translated if you're interested. In English it's *The Dirt*, or, rather, *The Clay of the Churchyard*. It's about some dead people. . . ."

"Thank you, sir. I don't need to know what the book is about right now."

Lifting the small pile of clothes warily, she pulled another artifact out of the bottom of the sack, "Why are you bringing . . . a stick?"

"That's a hazel wand, actually. You're no doubt familiar with the Yeats thing about 'Wandering Aengus.' Now you might call this blackthorn a stick, or a *shtick*, you know." The woman appeared somewhat alarmed as he raised it to show it off, saying, "Sure you must have heard 'The Rocky Road to Dublin'? *Cut a stout blackthorn, to banish ghosts and gobbalins.* Great song, that. A blackthorn is a true friend on the strange road."

The customs agent looked at the Irishman as if she was trying to solve an algebraic equation in her head. Finally, she said, "Sir, I'm going to ask you to go sit on that bench right over there for a moment."

"Ye don't like 'The Rocky Road to Dublin'?"

"Please take a seat on the bench, sir, until you are called."

Cornelius complied, taking a seat with a couple of rather spectral figures, women who watched him out of narrow slits in black head-to-toe covering. In response to his inquiries, they explained that they were wearing "burkas." Ah, yes, he had seen something about that on the television.

"I can't say that I understand the purpose, exactly, being as it's not a popular look, say, in Balleyvourney. But I will aver that the two of you, if you'll pardon me saying so, have lovely eyes."

The veiled heads nodded.

"And I hope that was not too forward or impolite."

The veiled heads shook a negative, which the Irishman felt gave him license to continue in a forthright manner. "The 'borka' does draw the focus to the eyes, which is, after all, the most expressive feature of the female, don't you think?"

"Yes," they said, and out of modesty, he guessed, they drew a little farther away from him on the bench and began to speak their language. Like the Italians, they seemed to use their hands when they spoke, because one of them was vigorously waving a hand in front of her face. It was difficult to gauge their feelings exactly, because their eyes, though expressive, were not *that* expressive.

Cornelius watched the people, a human river pouring into the terminal from the sky and flowing toward baggage claim or departing planes. Through a plate glass window, he could see the great craft lowering out of the blue expanse onto the long runways.

"Ah, but we live in an amazing world, don't we?" he asked the two women. Silent nodding. "They put you in a steel tube with a crowd of people and lift you up eight miles over the Atlantic at some tremendous speed, and they put you down in Boston."

A blond pony-tailed woman in a short-sleeved blue uniform approached and directed Cornelius to a separate room. She might have been attractive enough, he thought, if it were not for the big gun that hung at her side, which was rather off-putting. She opened a door and closed it behind him. Two male customs agents inside offered him a seat and began to question him. Cornelius decided that Americans were rather dense and suspicious people. One fellow asked him what was inside his "cane." That struck him as a peculiarly daft sort of question. "'Tis a *blackthorn*, not a 'cane.' I suspect that inside there is more of the wood of the blackthorn, *prunus spinosa*."

"But people hollow out canes, and maybe *blackthorns* too," the man said. "They fill them with other things. Is this one filled with something else?"

Now the patience of the O'Tuamas was legendary in Ballyvourney, and all the way to Macroom, and Cornelius was blessed with more than his share. But by God, his patience was wearing thin, and when the fellow took a step closer, coughed, took a step backward, and choked out, "What's *inside* the blackthorn, Pat?" Cornelius could no longer stand it.

"Why don't ye chew through it and find out, Yank?"

That fellow was for sending him back to Éire on the next flight. But there was another fellow nearby, a P. Mahoney, according to his name tag, who appeared to have smiled slightly. He said his grandmother from Kerry had told him all about the banshees, and he concluded, "Let's not get overheated, here. The man is right. This banshee sounds like a serious case and he had better tend to it." He stamped the passport he held open in his hand. "B2 Tourist visa all in order. Six months. Off you go, sir. Enjoy your stay."

Thank God he had found one sensible man in America, and making so bold as to shake his hand, he picked up his "luggage." Mahoney held the door and walked out with him.

"Mr. O'Tuama, a word with you, sir. This is rather delicate, but between an Irish American and an Irishman, if you want to get on in this country, let me give you a bit of advice. Gets pretty hot here in the summer, which will be upon us soon. You may want to *bathe* a little more regularly and *thoroughly* here, people are quite sensitive to odors."

"Well, like, out on the pig farm—"

"This is the city, Mr. O'Tuama. People aren't used to strong odors, and you really need to bathe. I think you'll get a better reception."

"The problem, you see, is that you wash the *protective oils* off your skin, and you'll be sick."

Mahoney smiled at the way he said the last word: *seek.*

"That's a risk you'd better take. Good luck with the banshee."

"Ah, I've dealt with her like many's the time before," he replied, and following the instructions Harry Hannigan had sent to him, he took the Blue Line to Government Center, and from there, the Green Line trolley to North Station, where he was gratified to find the northbound train to Lowell, Massachusetts.

Six

One might reasonably have thought that Bartley would feel a tinge of pain or loss at returning to a house that was, and would remain for the foreseeable future, quite empty. That was not the case. In fact, there is nothing so pleasant as finding one's house empty when one is struck with a bout of intestinal difficulties. When he had noisily evacuated himself to his heart's, and his stomach's content, he re-showered, tossed his smoky, wine-stained clothes down the chute, took two more aspirin, and clad in a clean terry cloth robe, and with an ice pack over his black eye, collapsed onto his bed where he lay under the hypnotic, slowly rotating blades of the ceiling fan. He farted a few last times and fell into the profound sleep of the innocent for three and a half hours, when incessant pings from his cell phone violated the tranquility of this blessed state.

It was a text from Louise. "How r you? Call me?"

It was after midday, and Bartley was feeling much better. He went downstairs, made more coffee, and boiled an egg. He put on the classical radio station softly to soothe his head. He ate the egg on toast and sat dumbly listening to Elgar's *Cello Concerto* for a while, as he felt his energy and focus returning, as well as a bit of shame at his boorish, repetitive questioning of Violeta. "Where are you from? Where did you say you were from?" God, how embarrassing.

Oh well, in all likelihood, he would not see her again. He punched in Louise's number.

"Bartley!"

"Hi, Louise."

"How are you? How are things with Adele?"

"She moved out."

"No! And, how are *you?*"

"I'm good."

"Do you want to get together for a drink?"

Bartley shivered and blessed himself. "Oh, no. I mean, I had more than enough yesterday. I think I'll be on the wagon for at least a week—give my liver a chance to recover."

"I understand. Hey, what were you going to tell me—something 'odd' about your father's death?"

Now, for some reason, Bartley didn't want to get into it. He was still digesting it all himself. He didn't think Louise could help him figure any of it out, and there was the danger that he would sound as if he should be committed, that, as Adele had put it, he was talking 'twaddle.' He left the table and started to pace around the house with the phone. "Oh," he said, dismissively, "it's just that he had a premonition. He told me he thought he was going to die. A dream he had."

"What kind of dream?"

"Ah, that he was crossing a road and a big bus came out of nowhere and hit him."

"That is odd."

"Probably just a coincidence."

"Yes. A strange one, though. Bartley, I'm doing a reading of my poetry at the Pollard Library in a few weeks, if you can make it."

"Sure. Let me know."

"I'll text you the date."

"Right. I'll put it on the calendar."

"You know, Bartley, it's better this way. That bitch never appreciated you."

That was a tone he had not heard from Louise before. She was trying to be sympathetic, no doubt, but it grated a bit. She was a bitch, of course, but she was still Manus's mother, and somehow, he didn't like people to presume that he wanted to hear her insulted. Maybe that was what *presumido* meant.

"Are you lonely?" she continued, "Do you want me to come over?"

Glancing down, Bartley saw an envelope from Hannafin and Kane, the legal office that was handling his father's affairs. He had left the previous day before the mail arrived. Adele must have taken it out of the mailbox and left it on the table in the hallway.

"Bartley?"

"I'm sorry. Louise, I'm feeling kind of sick and hungover today. I'll be in touch, or I'll see you at the reading."

"Okay, then." Did she sound a little offended? He hoped not. "Take care, Bartley," she said.

"Thanks, Louise. I will." Bartley wondered what had happened since yesterday, when he had conceived the notion that he should begin an affair with her. He no longer even wanted to confide in her. And yet she hadn't done anything to annoy him. She was very nice, and the thought of her naked was not unappealing. He thought it was his mood and that he would feel differently the next day. Or maybe it was just that after escaping from a vexing relationship of such long duration, he wanted to enjoy his liberty for a while. He had to be damned sure before he involved himself in any new relationship. For, as someone had said, the term "soul mate" was very close to "cellmate."

And then, of course, there *was* that inexplicable good vibe, despite the monster hangover, that he'd begun to feel with Violeta. He took out the piece of paper on which her name and number were written and studied her handwriting. Feminine! Endearing! *But come on, Bartley! She's a stripper! You can't start dating a stripper!*

He told himself to toss the number in the waste basket, but when he stood in front of it, he was unable to let go of the paper. After all, she'd had a conversation with his father's leprechaun, or whatever he was. She was the only person in the world who would know for certain that he was not crazy! Moreover, she was a hell of a nice person. He opened his wallet and slid the slip of paper behind his driver's license.

He poured another coffee and sat down at the table with a document of several pages from the law firm. He read it over twice, slowly, because it was full of terms such as *testator* and *testamentary trust* and *equitable title* and *pour-over provisions*. Finally, he let it fall out of his hands and said to the ceiling, or maybe to heaven, *"What the fuck, Dad?"*

Jack Carnadine was a developer who was widely believed to have Mafia ties. And here was his name in his father's will. He had sold thirty-six acres to Carnadine and had been in receipt of the sum of $450,000, and yet his cash reserves totaled only twenty-five thousand, with another estimated fifty-two thousand in stocks. If he read correctly, nearly half a million dollars had disappeared. What was even stranger, he had left nothing to Harry Junior, five thousand to Cornelius O'Tuama, the banshee-hunter, and five thousand to Gibby O'Malley. And the rest to Bartley (not Bartley and Adele), along with the entire property, the farmhouse, and all its contents, (including, the will noted, books such as *An Introduction to Growing Christmas Trees, Starting a Christmas Tree Business, Understanding Agriculture,* and, of course, *Annals of the Noble Families of Tyrone*) as well as "any other possessions not heretofore mentioned in the will."

The proviso to this latter bequest was that the home and property would be held in trust for Bartley Hannigan, who would be *unable to develop, sell, or substantially alter the remaining one hundred acres of farmland for fifteen years.* Thanks a lot, Dad. I'm now heir to a Christmas tree and produce business that I don't know how to manage, a ramshackle farmhouse with an unwelcome tenant, several dumpsters full of shit, and a trans-generational family curse!

Along with the will was a map of the property on which the proposed subdivision was shown, replete with new roads. Six houses per acre—two hundred and sixteen houses, most of which were in the wooded area on which no Christmas trees were planted. His swimming hole, too, would be subsumed.

If only his father had left him some of the ready cash from the sale of the thirty-six acres, and his brother the encumbered farmhouse. He could have left the school and never sat through another departmental meeting. The seventy-five thousand, or so, his father had left him would, he hoped, cover the work that needed to be done on the dilapidated farmhouse just to keep it standing.

Coincidentally, there was also a letter from Adele's attorney. She certainly hadn't wasted any time. It must have been mailed before she had definitively left him! He tossed it in a drawer, unopened. There would be no one at the law offices of Hannafin and Kane today to discuss the mystery of the missing money, even if they knew anything.

Later that afternoon, Bartley decided to drive out to his father's house and try to gauge just how bad this real estate albatross now hung about his neck really was. His first reaction upon studying the farmhouse with the eye of a new owner was a gigantic sigh, followed by a mighty swing at something invisible, and the utterance of a string of several words, most of which began with m, f, c, b, and s.

Then he heard a sound, a wavering, dolorous strain. Someone was singing! Quietly, he moved in the direction from which the song emanated. The singer was in his father's garden! Bartley's back pressed flat against the side of a tool shed, he listened.

> *When my heart was as light as the wild winds that blow*
> *Down the Mardyke through each elm tree*
> *Where we sported and play'd 'neath each green leafy shade*
> *On the banks of my own lovely Lee.*

It had to be that little Septo Nippy whatever character with his bicorn hat and his bulbous nose!

The singing stopped, and he heard, "Ah, what kind of a respectable farmer would let a patch go to seed like this?"

He edged around the shed, heart pounding. He saw an article of clothing, not a green coat with tails, but a tweed jacket slung over the picket fence of the garden. Beside it, the gnarly length of a blackthorn stick rested in the sun, but there was no sign of the creature.

> *And then in the springtime of laughter and song*
> *Can I ever forget the sweet hours?*

He glimpsed him through the green leafy shade—a tweed cap bobbing as he crouched, apparently plucking weeds between the rows of cukes and summer squash his father had already planted. And what had his father told him—catch him and don't take your eyes off him! He charged.

With the friends of my youth as we rambled along
'Mongst your green mossy banks . . . aaAAAARGH!

Bartley tackled the figure and the two of them crashed into a tent-shaped cucumber trellis, rolling through various plastic-covered frames. It struck Bartley that the prey he had captured was rather large for a leprechaun, and a damned sight stronger. He quickly found himself on his back and realized that in any case he'd rather surrender than continue to breathe the foul exhalations which had enveloped him in a choking cloud since he had joined the scrum with the melodious intruder.

At the first opportunity, Bartley worked himself free and stood. The other man jumped up, too, and faced him in a wrestler's stance. "Who are you?" Bartley demanded.

Cornelius spat in his hands and rubbed them together. His cap having been lost in the fray, he looked, with his long, wildly tussled hair, his stained linen shirt and rustic farmer's suspenders, like a figure out of Grimm's tales. "I am the broom from the top of *Cnoic na Síofra*," he said, "and you come at me again, I'll sweep the floor with you, boy, as it looks like someone has done recently."

Bartley fingered the tender area around his eye, which was hurting again thanks to this scuffle. "Oh, God. Are you that Cornelius something? The banshee hunter?"

"I am Cornelius O'Tuama of Ballyvourney," the figure retorted haughtily. "And I don't *hunt* banshees. I may have to face them down if they are angry spirits, but that is rare." He brushed the dirt from his pants. "And why didn't you ask me to begin with, or is it the custom in America to greet an honest man by sneakin' up on him and throwing him to the ground, ye gouger?"

"Sorry, I thought—"

"Are you Harry Hannigan, then?"

"No, I'm his son, Bartley."

"Then is the man himself about?"

"He's dead."

"Ah!" he said. "Then she'll have to be dealt with, all right." He picked up his cap, and pushing the long hair back behind his ears, replaced it snugly on his head. Bartley thought that he must be about forty. A few gray strands mingled with his shaggy auburn locks. The mutton shop sideburns would have been in style during the psychedelic era, or the Civil War.

Bartley patted his pockets; he had left his cigarette case in the car, and he wished to put some smoke between him and the banshee-hunter. "I'll tell you the story later. The house is a mess, but I'll show you in. Let me get you a towel, so you can take a shower after your trip."

Cornelius picked up his suit jacket. "I'll just wash my hands," he said. "Someone needs to tend to this garden."

Bartley's cell phone sounded, but he saw that it was Adele. He didn't want to talk to her, so he ignored it.

"We'll see about the garden, but I'll let you in. You can make yourself at home and take a shower."

"I'd rather not, thank you."

"You'll feel better."

"No, thank you."

"Go ahead."

"I'm fine, thanks."

"No wonder the banshees run," he muttered.

"What was that?"

"Nothing. Can I get you anything?"

"Tea and biscuits?"

"I'll go to the store."

"And a few bottles of plain?"

"Plain what?"

"The black stuff."

"Guinness?"

"That'll do."

On the front porch, Bartley picked up several days' newspapers, which he had apparently overlooked the previous evening, and unlocked the door. O'Tuama did not seem to find the house particularly disorganized, though empty wine bottles littered the kitchen table where Bartley had apparently sat with Violeta and "the leetle man." Beyond that, the clutter and debris in which his father had lived since the death of Bartley's mother were visible all around them.

Bartley cleared the table and collected the empty bottles for the recycle bin, the whiff of stale wine making him somewhat queasy for a few seconds. Cornelius laid his stick and coat across a chair and spread a week-old newspaper on the table before him.

Bartley was about to head out to the store when he paused at the door and said, "Oh yeah, my father left you five grand."

"Five grand *what?*"

"Five thousand dollars."

He shook his head without looking up from the paper. "He paid for my ticket, so lodging and six hundred is sufficient."

"You got five thousand."

Bartley returned with supplies, but he did not, could not, invite Cornelius back to his own house until he had gotten him to bathe. He stopped by the farmhouse each day for a week after school, to check on the workers who were cutting trees, stripping and re-shingling the roof, replacing windows, scraping and painting, pointing the foundation and chimney, rebuilding stairs, and fortifying sagging porches.

They hauled away old clothes, volumes of ancient encyclopedias, laceless, sole-worn shoes, pre-war Christmas decorations, bald tires, the stereo phonograph console on which his father had spun Clancy Brothers records when Bartley was a kid, a broken, or as Cornelius called it, "banjaxed" couch, ugly lamps with dust-laden lampshades, antiquated telephones and TVs, tennis rackets with sprung strings, threadbare rugs—the detritus, inherited and accumulated, of a lifetime, of several lifetimes. Cornelius assisted Bartley in stripping faded, flowery wallpaper and spackling and repainting walls. Until he could find a way to get the banshee-hunter to bathe, Bartley found it necessary to keep several yards between himself and his guest at all times.

Finally, Bartley was able to have a sit-down with Joe Hannafin, whose law offices had executed his father's will. However, the meeting proved unsatisfactory. In response to Bartley's questions about the missing money, Joe would say only, "Talk to your brother."

The subsequent call to his brother revealed an interesting transaction. His father had bought Harry Junior and his wife a four hundred-thousand-dollar home in Houston. "He said he'd buy me the home, and he was going to leave you the farm," Harry Junior explained.

"I thought homes down there were cheap," Bartley said.

"It's a pretty big lot, in a gated community backing up to Lake Houston. Four bedrooms, and—"

"That's great. Obviously, it was Dad's land and his money, and he can—he could—do what he wanted with it. He left me the farm, but I can't sell it! His final joke was to try to turn me into a farmer."

There was silence on the other end of the line while Harry Junior absorbed this information and tried to think of a response. Finally, he managed a mumbled, "Oh, mmm, sorry."

There was nothing for Bartley but to continue with his life, the principle fact of which was his so-called career at the high school. Each day, except for one very rainy day, he visited the farmhouse and found Cornelius tending the garden and singing.

By the end of the week, Bartley had conceived a plan. Friday afternoon was warm. His father's land included a large pond and a smaller sort of frog pond, which were called Top Pond and Bottom Pond respectively. He convinced Cornelius to take a hike up to Top Pond just after supper and brought along a couple of towels.

The path forked near the approach to Top Pond, and as Bartley headed to the right, the Irishman froze for an instant, head raised as if sniffing some scent in the light breeze. He was watching a pair of dark wings that swept among the trees. He began to run up the left path.

"This way!" Bartley yelled, but eventually he shook his head and followed Cornelius. He caught up with him as the Irishman, wide-eyed, was slowly approaching a circle of stone pillars on a wooded plateau overlooking the Merrimack River.

Cornelius placed a hand on one of the standing stones, which was about his height, and said, "Why did you not tell me about this?"

"Nothing to tell. It's what they call a 'Victorian folly.'"

"I don't believe it is."

"It is. My father had a lot of notions about it when he first moved in. He even got some people from Harvard, an archaeological team, interested in it, and they came up one summer when I was a youngster. Dug test pits—they found some arrow heads, Indian arrow heads and a polished stone axe head, but those things are not unusual around here."

"But sure, Indians didn't build stone circles—"

"No, but the team excavated around the pillars. They found that at the base of the stones there were pavers, the kind used on the cobblestone streets in Lowell. So, they said it was probably erected in the late 19th, early 20th century—a simulacrum, if you will."

"Look at the weathering of the stone. And if they were quarried at that time, where are the drill marks?"

"I suppose they *wanted* it to look like an old circle, so they chipped them away. The stones may be older, but they were placed here much later. Maybe Jeremiah O'Hannigan put them up to remind him of home."

"And wouldn't a folly be in a more accessible place? Near a garden or something?"

"Who knows? Maybe they liked to come up here and have a picnic, meditate among the old standing stones. Nice view, especially if you cleared the trees on the river side."

Bartley walked to the western edge and, peering through the trees, took in the panorama before him—he never tired of it. A few yards out, the land dropped off in a sharp declivity down to a shore where hardwoods and hemlocks gripped the stony soil with twisting roots.

When he turned back, Cornelius had his two hands upon one of the stone pillars, head bowed against it. His eyes had been closed, and he opened them. "Feel my hands, Bartley."

"What for?"

"Just feel my hands."

Bartley took the outstretched hands in his own. They were as hard as cured leather. He released them, and Cornelius said, "I know stone, Bartley. I've set stone in miles and miles of pasture walls in my day."

"You don't wear gloves?"

He shook his head. "You need to have the *feel* of the stone in your hands, so you know how it will balance, how it will hold and work with the others." He ran his hands along the stones. "Oh yes, and I've visited a fair number of dolmens and stone circles, henges, and monoliths, in Ireland, Scotland, England and Wales. And I'll tell you this—these stones have not been here for a hundred years. They've been here for a *thousand* years."

Bartley shrugged. "Harvard disagrees."

"And how did I know to come up this way?"

It struck Bartley then that the stone circle was not visible from the fork. He paused.

"How *did* you know?"

A crow passed overhead and let out three sharp squawking cries. "I knew rightly," Cornelius said, watching the bird settle on a pine bough. "For as Madame Blavatsky once said, 'If coming events are said to cast their shadows before, past events cannot fail to leave their impress behind them.'"

"God help us, when did my life become a Lewis Carroll novel?" Bartley asked no one in particular. But if he remained skeptical about Cornelius's theory, he was at the same time troubled by the fact that the circle was within the thirty-six acres marked off to be developed by Jack Carnadine. "Let's go for a swim," he said.

They left the circle and headed to the pond, and Bartley turned the discussion toward 'the situation,' assuming that there was a situation. Cornelius had been staying at his father's house, *his* house now, without supernatural adventures. "Have you had any sign of this leprechaun at all?"

"First of all," Cornelius said curtly, "this Don Nippery Septo fellow is not technically a leprechaun."

"What is he, just a tiny, housebreaking, alcoholic thief?"

"He's what's known as a *clurichaun*. There can be little doubt. A sort of cousin to the leprechaun."

"And what do they do?"

"Precisely what he was doing at your father's house. Drinking him dry. Think of them as little Irish Bacchuses."

He was sort of wishing that Cornelius would laugh and slap him on the back and say, "Of course *it's all just old stories anyway!*" But he didn't. In fact, he looked quite serious. And, in any case, Violeta had verified *something*.

"Look at this!" Bartley cried when they arrived at the pond. "The 'green mossy banks,' just like that song you sing about your own lovely Lee." He threw the towels over a low branch and stripped down to his jockey shorts. He took a deep breath, plunged into the cool pond, and came up sputtering and shouting as enthusiastically as his shrunken privates would allow. Cornelius O'Tuama sat on a rock and watched him.

"Come on in, Cornelius! It's . . . as you would say, it's *grand!* Invigorating!" On his back, he moved across the water, legs churning. "Ah, refreshing!" he shouted at the sky, "What are you waiting for?" Since his ears were underwater, Bartley heard only a muffled reply.

He rolled over and began a slow breast stroke toward shore. "What did you say? Don't you want to take a dip?"

Cornelius stirred uneasily, kicking a stone toward the water. "Sure, you know yourself."

"I know *what* myself? What does that mean?"

The Irishman pulled his suit jacket tighter about him and said, "I think you're trying to drown me."

"You'll feel better, O'Tuama!"

"I can't swim."

"I'll teach you to swim."

"I'll teach you to stay dry."

"Very funny! Come on!"

But Cornelius, as the sun set, had become engrossed in another phenomenon. He appeared more surprised at the tiny flickering lights that flashed in the air about them than he would have been had the Washer at the Ford suddenly appeared in the water before him draped in white. His head moved from right to left and up and down as he studied the movements of the tiny creatures flitting about the water's edge flashing sparks of light.

Bartley, having given up on Operation Pond Bath, stepped out of the water and grabbed his towel. He saw that Cornelius was awestruck, his face creased with lines of close observation and intense thought. "What are they?" he asked, pointing vaguely into the air.

"They call 'em fireflies, but they're more like beetles than flies. That's how they attract a mate." The time seemed right for a subtle hint. "We can't light up our ass, so *we* attract a mate by bathing, and using deodorant, a comb and a little cologne."

"How *do* they do it?"

"It's called bioluminescence, but how it really works, I don't know." Recalling Violeta's philosophy, he concluded, "It's magic."

"Fireflies, eh? I've never seen them in Ireland! Amazing!"

Bartley stepped into his tennis shoes and lit a cigarette, and as they walked back to the farmhouse in the dying light, he began to work out Plan B, because he could not deal with any clurichauns or banshees at all until he dealt with the B.O. of C.O. And Plan B was a masterpiece.

At school the next day, during his prep period, Bartley saw that he had an email from Adele, in response to the copy of his father's will that Hannafin and Kane had faxed her office.

It appears that your housing problems are sorted out. How nice of your father to tie up his property so that it will do you no good. I suppose that was his idea of a joke. Funny. You're getting rather difficult to communicate with. Don't ignore my lawyer's communications. Or mine."

He scrunched up his face and said in an obnoxious squeal, "Don't ignore my," (here he paused to snort three times like a pig), "my lawyer's communicashuns!" He pressed "Delete" with a flourish.

The phone by his desk rang. It was Fatima, Bede's secretary. "Did you forget your evaluation meeting?" she asked.

He had forgotten. "Of course not! Just got held up with a parent phone call! I'm on my way." He grabbed his spurious "evaluation binder" and ran down the green-tiled corridor.

Mr. Bede was on the phone, but he motioned Bartley to have a seat before his desk. Like a reprobate school boy in the principal's office, he sat, hands folded over his binder. His seat seemed lower than Bede's. The pudgy fingers of the big man's free hand impatiently rapped a pencil on his desk as he spoke. "I believe that *authentic* lesson plans should include power standards, mastery objectives slash essential questions, key content, assessment of objectives, teaching and learning experiences, and list of resources aligned with state frameworks."

The King of All Bullshit—exercising his dominion. Bartley stifled a groan as Bede's mouth continued to exude streams of bullshit. Finally, the pompous administrator muttered that he had a meeting, and without a word of farewell, terminated the call.

"So! *Mis-ter* Hannigan. Now, in this folder, I have your team goals and self-assessment, but what were your professional goals for this year?"

"My professional goals . . ." Christ, he had written them back in September, when, swamped with paperwork, Individualized Education Plans to read, and classes to organize, he had no doubt tried to crank out some of his own *ad hoc* bullshit that sounded plausible.

Bede smiled indulgently at this not uncommon lapse and said, "Wait a minute." He tugged on a drawer in his desk and rummaged among some files. He pulled out a folder and read, "Okay, so your goals were to raise ACCESS scores for at least ten percent of your students by one level.

Okay, we're still waiting for the results, but do you expect you achieved that goal?"

Bartley tried to look thoughtful for a moment and then nodded. Obviously, he had pulled the ten percent figure out of his ass. High enough to seem ambitious and low enough to *perhaps* be achievable. But a vision of the vacant stares of some of the students he'd had this year at Slug Central caused considerable misgivings. Bede would call them "struggling students." Bartley would call them, in private conversation with Harris, "lazy sacks of shit." In fact, some proclaimed their laziness via T-shirts with such mottoes as, "I Don't Do Mornings," and "You're Talking But All I Hear is Blah Blah Blah."

"You have your evaluation binder?"

"Here you go." He handed the sacred portfolio across the desk where it was received in Bede's beefy hands.

He flipped through the pages. "Hmmm. Hmmmmm. I see you didn't write the standards you were teaching on the cover sheets for the various indicators. You need to get those on there. Let's see—now you don't have any artifacts to provide evidence for the Indicator Five under Section Three, 'Maintains a Safe Classroom Environment.'"

"I can get a notarized statement that no one has died in my room."

Bede was not amused. "Let's get serious, Hannigan. Maybe take a photo of some anti-bullying posters, classroom rules on respect, oh, the fire escape plan, exit sign . . . those would be acceptable artifacts."

DING! Bartley had never been so happy to hear the summons: the B-flat of the bell tone. "I have a class!"

"Just work on those things I mentioned, and I'll talk to you again before the school year ends." Bede heaved his bulk into a standing position. "By the way, Bartley, sorry about your father."

"Thanks," Bartley murmured. He saw by Bede's sonorous intake of breath and sudden upward gaze that he was about to wax philosophical, or to offer some particular consolation derived through personal experience. He bolted.

Seven

Nothing of preternatural or numinous note had transpired at the farmhouse. A Brazilian "Do Any Job" guy had hauled away a third dumpster full of junk. The carpenters and roofers were done, and a landscaper was grinding the stumps of the last felled trees; but a plumber, two electricians, and a mason were still traipsing in and out. They were all very busy.

Cornelius continued to work in the garden and stink up the house. Bartley would have preferred him to leave, at first, but he found, in spite of his odor, that there was a lot that he liked about him. He was certainly amusing, quite helpful, and knowledgeable, particularly about the garden, and of course all sorts of inexplicable phenomena. And now that he had some evidence that the "clurichaun" existed, he had a feeling he might want to consult the Irishman.

But something did have to be done about the mephitis that occupied the atmosphere around Cornelius. Bartley decided that the time had come to implement Plan B. Its genius was its *simplicity*. Eric Harris, his fellow inmate at "the institute," as they referred to the high school, owed Bartley a favor. He had taken care of Sparky, Eric's beloved Black Lab, for a week over Christmas vacation while he visited his brother in Colorado. His friend was grateful, but had sincere reservations about the return favor that Bartley was now calling in. "Jeez, Hannigan, I've never stripped a male before, and damned few females, for that matter."

"He'll be drunk as a skunk. I got a bottle of Irish Distillers' Redbreast, 12-year-old cask strength, 117.2 proof whiskey. And three four-packs of his beloved Murphy's Stout from Cork. When he's plastered, we just get his clothes off and stick him in the shower. How hard can it be to get a drunk in a shower?"

"This is your 'ingenious' plan?"

"Can you think of a better one?"

"No, but stripping a dude! That's like—I don't know—I might get homosexual panic."

"Harris, I'm trying to clean the house and it smells like a swamp with a dead moose in it, and I've got other things to worry about."

"Like what?"

"I told you about the leprechaun that's not a leprechaun, and. . . ."

Harris raised both hands in surrender. "OK, never mind."

"Well, you asked. And it so happens this creature. . . ."

His hands were waving in front of him now. "Dep-se-yep, yaah!" Bartley understood that these sputtered syllables were meant to signify that Harris could not think quickly enough of the correct words that would immediately terminate this line of conversation. Finally, he pulled himself together enough to manage, "I don't need to hear anything about your . . . nightmares!"

Bartley's shoulders sagged. "Right, I'm crazy."

"Whatever. I like to stick to reality. And, *I'm* just saying, to get back to the issue at hand, undressing men, drunk or not. . . ."

"The guy will thank us. I have fresh new clothes for him, too, and sneakers in three sizes—he can wear whichever ones fit. We are doing a good thing for the guy. It's just sticking a drunk in a shower!"

"Let's leave his underwear on!"

"Hell no, we're going all the way. He can't put on new clothes over dirty underwear. Besides, I intend to burn his old clothes."

"Oh, God."

"Come on, get tough, Harris! Do I need to enumerate the things I've done for you? What about Sparky? And who got you a key to the gym so you could swim before school? Who—"

"All right all right all right."

"Friday afternoon—it's important that we get him drinking on an empty stomach."

Cornelius O'Tuama was getting quite relaxed with Bartley and his new pal, Harris. The workers had been sent home early to enjoy the weekend, and the three sat on the porch by the newly-restored trellis. The low sun cast dappled light through the latticework.

"Banshee!" Harris objected. "Come on! Have you ever *seen* a banshee?"

Cornelius began to speak about the banshee he had met on Allen's Bridge. "One fella described the banshee's eyes this way: 'as cold as a moon reflected in the water of a bog.' And so they were. Ice blue. Her skin and hair as white as snow. But—" He paused and held out his glass. "*Is túisce deoch ná scéal.* A drink precedes a story."

Bartley refilled the Cork man's tumbler with the golden whiskey. Cornelius thanked him and added a splash of water from the beaker, "to open it up."

"I stood on the bridge just starin' at her, and she let out a keen that would make your blood curdle. It frightened me, lads. I staggered backward, for I was new to the game, but I raised the Brigid's cross, and the iron triskelle broach I had in the vest pocket, and I recited the old prayer that begins:

A Naoimh-Mícheál Árdaingeal
cosain sinn i n-am an chatha,
bí mar dhídean againn in aghaidh urchóirde
agus chealgaireachta an diabhail."

Harris looked blankly at Bartley, who shrugged.

"And at that, the eyes went back in her head. She turned away and rolled over the stone balustrade into the River Dalua, with never a splash, and nor did she rise, but a wisp of smoke, or of swirling fog, rolled away from the spot and floated along the dark water and into the night."

"Jesus," Harris said.

"And Sean McCarthy, patriarch of the McCarthy clan in nearby Kanturk—didn't he die that night, and they say for as long as anyone can remember or history records, that same woman appears, or can be heard, preceding a death in that family."

Bartley responded with tales of "the hatchet man," of the Dracut State Forest. Cornelius paused in his appreciation of the whiskey and said, "Augumtoocooke."

"What?"

"My research. That's what the Indians called your *Dracut:* Augumtoocooke, the wilderness north of the river."

"Interesting. Anyway . . ." Bartley recounted all the other wild stories he could think of, continually refilling Cornelius's glass, while he and Harris nursed their drinks. "Pour him another pint of Murphy's there, Harris, to wash it down."

At one point, when Cornelius had stumbled off to what he referred to as "the jacks," Harris leaned over and said, "I don't like this."

"It's not a murder! It's a shower!"

"Can't we just convince him?"

"I've tried that."

"I thought he was Irish. Why is he speaking Polish?"

"He was speaking Gaelic. They call it Irish."

"I thought the Irish spoke English, with an accent."

"Most of them do, today, but they have their own language. Cornelius grew up speaking Irish. There are remote areas all around the country, the *Gaeltacht,* where the people still use it as a daily language. West Cork, where Cornelius is from, is a *Gaeltacht* area. And most people learn it in school."

"So, it's a real language?"

"What do you think?"

"I guess I thought it was just like, gibberish."

"Okay, so before their *saviors,* the Anglo-Saxons, arrived, you think Ireland was full of people all hanging around speaking *gibberish* to each other? It's a *language,* you mow-ron! Jesus, are you drunk, too?" Bartley realized that he was beginning to sound like his father. Maybe it was the influence of his house. Or, maybe Harris was just being a mow-ron.

Cornelius came back, humming a tune, which was a good sign, and trying to say *Augumtoocooke,* and making a hash of it. "Agumatoo—tugooma-took . . . agatookoke . . . ." Finally, he gave it up and said, "Jesus, Bartley, I'm fockin campeetlee twisted! *Langers!* Washin' the floor!"

By seven o'clock, step one had been achieved, the Irishman was thoroughly anesthetized, mumbling incoherently and seemingly ready to pass out. Zero hour had arrived. "Listen, Cornelius! It's hot out, and you smell bad, and I'm tired of arguing with you! You're gonna take a shower!"

He muttered something about "pah-tective oils" and "bad luck on a Friday." There was a feeble struggle, and the two men nearly gagged as they lugged him upstairs, stripped off the filthy clothes, and stuck him under the running shower. Bartley squirted shampoo on Cornelius's head and rubbed it in roughly, while Cornelius sputtered. Bartley stuffed a facecloth into his hands.

"Wash!" They pulled the shower curtain closed and stood there for a minute in case he should fall through it. But soon they heard a melody:

When my har wass as light as the wil' winat blow
Down the Mardyke through cheechemree. . . .
Da daa da da da da da
Da da da da my own lovely Leeeeee.

"I told you you'd love it, you silly bastard!" Bartley yelled. "Protective oils! There's a towel and some brand new clothes here—even got you some sneakers!"

"Da da da da my own lovely Leeeee."

Bartley grimaced as he picked up the noxious clothing and explained to Harris, "We're gonna burn this crap; otherwise, he'll fish it out of the barrel."

"The suit jacket too?"

"Everything but the tie. He loves that tie—I'll wash it. The fire pit is ready to be lit."

"You've given Plan B a lot of thought, Bartley."

"Oh, yes."

They went out to the pit and Bartley lit a match. The fire began—a low flicker as the birch bark he'd set in the base kindled and the smaller sticks began to flare. "Just like McGregor taught us in Troop 22 of the Boy Scouts," he said with satisfaction. Soon the fire blazed, and with a stick he began to lay the clothes on the fire. "I'm going to bury the sandals. He looks like the Wandering Jew in those things! And look, the strap's broken on this one, and he repaired it with a plastic six-pack holder!"

Just then they heard tires crunching the gravel of the driveway. "Who the hell is that?" Harris asked. A car door closed, and as the two men stood by the fire pit, Bartley holding a rancid pair of underwear on a stick, Adele came around, pausing for a moment to take in the scene. Bartley imagined that scene as she saw it and let the foul skivvies drop into the fire.

"Hi, Adele," he said.

Harris waved and inclined his head politely, "Hi, Adele."

"Hello boys. A little campfire fun? Are you going to sing Kumbaya?"

The "boys" chuckled as if they recognized good-natured fun when they heard it.

"Bartley, you seem to be avoiding me. I don't know if you received the letter from my lawyer, so I brought out a copy personally to put in your hands. Just so there's no—"

At that point, the screen door flew open. Like a tree gone suddenly and shockingly leafless, the denuded Cornelius O'Tuama, his Gaelic *wahoo* gloriously pendent in the evening air, emerged from the house and cried, "Ye get me dthrunk, shtrip me nay-kid, and force me to do summin' I tol' ye I *didn't want* to do! Though I'll admit, verr mush t-to my s-surprise, "I *did* enjoy it so I did!"

The generally calm and collected Adele was aghast. Her jaw worked two or three times soundlessly. The lawyer's letter fell from her hand just as a fortuitous breeze rose and carried it into the billowing flames. Adele looked from the fast-withering letter back to the naked man and said, "I'm calling the police."

Eight

It had taken some very rapid explaining, some earnest reassuring, and some desperate promises to convince Adele that no crime had been committed. One promise was that Bartley would begin to cooperate with Adele and her lawyer. So, within a week their home was up for sale, and Bartley started to prepare to move permanently into the farmhouse, which was beginning to shape up. And he had to admit that Cornelius was doing a hell of a job in the garden.

They had taken out a second mortgage on the house to pay for Manus's tuition at B.U., and they had agreed to pay off that loan for him when the house was sold. Adele had never been good at living within her means, and after they paid off the rest of the first mortgage and all of the second, and she took half of the remainder, there would not be much. But at least Manus would start life with no debts, and that was something that he and Adele could agree was good.

Louise had texted Bartley that she was giving a poetry reading at the Pollard Library at an odd time, 6:00 on a Thursday night. He thought that the least he could do would be to go and show support. She had been a good friend, and though he hadn't attended a D&E Book Club meeting in a while, it had been therapeutic during a difficult time for him. Bartley, feeling as though he might have treated her a little shabbily recently, asked Louise if she'd like to get something to eat before her reading. He hoped it would not be awkward, since he wasn't quite sure what he really wanted from her, if anything, beyond friendship.

They sat in the Athenian Corner, quite near each other in a snug upholstered seat beside a small bay window. On the whitewashed brick walls were photos of Santorini, the Acropolis, and other scenes of Hellenic beauty. The waiter came and lit a candle on their table though it was not yet dark; bouzouki music sounded softly from recessed speakers. Louise ordered white wine, and Bartley a Hendrick's gin and tonic.

He told her about his father's place. She got very excited and said, "I've gotten my Christmas tree there every year since I moved down here!" He thought it was nice to hear her enthuse about the farm.

He liked her style—jeans and a white shirt, sleeves rolled up, collar unbuttoned to reveal just a bit of cleavage and a stylized octopus pendent on a silver chain. They spoke of generalities for a while, the book club, his job at the school, her job at the magazine.

When their drinks arrived, she got to the point. "You know, Bartley, I thought, as the English say, that you were 'fond' of me."

"I am fond of you, Louise. That's why I asked you to dinner. I'd like to get to know you better." She looked good, and he gulped the G&T gratefully and tried to relax. He decided to be honest. Not *totally* honest—he didn't even like to do that with himself. "It's just that, I've been in a relationship, a marriage, for a long time, and I need to take it slowly."

"That's entirely understandable," she said. *Such a pleasant woman*, he thought. "You know," she continued, "I'm surprised she let you go so easily. If I were married, and my husband wanted a divorce, it would be *really messy*."

What? This was the first discordant note of the evening. He was going to say that his wife had wanted the divorce, but he thought she knew that. Anyway, he didn't want to get into it. But why throw what seemed to be a veiled threat into the middle of a first date? She was sitting very close to him, and under the tablecloth, she petted his thigh reassuringly, rather close to his crotch, which redirected his attention away from what he told himself must have been an idle remark. After all, a woman is supposed to want to hang on to her husband.

He gulped the remainder of his drink and ordered another. She *really was* a wonderful friend. Lovely eyes. A woman like that might also understand that a man had certain needs, and that in a *friendly* sort of way, she might assist him with them. Would that be wrong? Didn't necessarily imply commitment; then again, would commitment to a woman such as this be so bad? Nothing like Adele, who took every opportunity to prove that her estrogen trumped his testosterone. Louise was different. And for a moment, as she told him about a poetry workshop she had attended at Naropa University, he lost track of her words and became slightly lost in her eyes, the fragrance of her hair and the femininity of her voice. A kind, sensitive woman—a poet in fact—and as he thought of all this, and inhaled her fragrance, he began to feel like Joe Namath on the sidelines with the attractive female commentator. He wanted to kiss her, but the waiter had brought their tray, and then she was chewing spinach pie.

They ate dinner in a sort of easy companionship. After drinking their demitasses of Greek Coffee, he paid the tab and they walked over to the library. "I hope you like the reading," she said.

"Oh, I'm sure you'll be wonderful," he replied. "Just be yourself." Throughout dinner, the old feeling of intimacy he had sometimes experienced talking with her after book club meetings had begun to blossom again in his gin-warmed interior. He wanted, even more than before, to kiss her.

"The poetry has to come from an honest place," she said, "and some people are troubled by that. They'd prefer me to put on an act."

He slipped an arm around her waist and said, "I can think of an act I'd like to perform with you."

She laughed in receptive complicity and returned his squeeze. Bartley thought that things were going well. There were only about fifteen people when they arrived, and Bartley took a seat in the second row. People continued to arrive, though, and by 6:05, she had managed to attract a decent crowd of about thirty people.

The librarian, a serious, bearded fellow of the requisite literary bent, closed the door to the room and introduced her. "Louise Andino is a native of Nashua, New Hampshire. Her poetry has appeared in *The Musgrave Quarterly*, *Funky Zombie*, *The New Reality*, *Mutton for the Masses*, *The Tie Rod Review*, and elsewhere. Gail Lambeer, of *Depressing Vistas Magazine*, writes, 'Andino's voice is a wail of pity for the human condition. Her poetry forces us to confront the shame of our own existence.' Ladies and gentlemen, Louise Andino."

She stepped up to the lectern and cleared her throat. Bartley noticed that she must have rather large ears, because they sort of peeked through her long hair. So cute! She *really was* cute.

Blue jays are bullshit! She cried without warning. Bartley was startled. He had always liked blue jays, actually. She continued, as if she were suddenly angry.

> *All the pretty birds are bullshit,*
> *The flowers all stink like shit!*
> *Nature is bullshit, and who wants to see another fucking sunset?*
> *Fuck you, with your calendar pictures of butterflies!*
> *Fuck you with a big unlubricated dildo!*
> *Fuck your blue lagoons where the dolphins play!*
> *Fuck your cute puppies in a fucking basket!*
> *I'd like to throw them all in the fucking incinerator*
> *And hear them whimper as they burn!*
> *Now that would be beautiful!*

The crowd clapped appreciatively. *Okay,* Bartley thought, *hyperbole for comic effect? I guess?* Admittedly, he didn't "get" a lot of modern poetry. If he read poetry at all, it tended to be older stuff. He loved Emily Dickinson, Robert Frost, and—but Louise had begun again.

> *Red is the rose that in yonder garden grows*

Ah, she was quoting the old Irish song. He liked the sound of this.

> *Green its loathsome creeping tendrils*

Not the song—losing the tone of the song! Bartley thought.

> *Like a hungry cancer they wrap the trellis round*
> *Gripping in barbarian fingers the enemy's dripping heart*
> *Fabulous! Great war hero! You Dane! You Hun! You Saxon King!*
> *Alexander and his horse his horse and Alexander*
> *   You King of Kings from Bethlehem*

The war began in your liver and spread from land to unholy land
     Terrible evolution! Skanky lawnmower of royal gardens!
Your insides were ugly and now the world is ugly too.
Red is the rose! Red is the blood!
My curse on the rose! And the thorny stem!
A silent Inquisition! Interrogation without questions!
Each day a torture without tools but the ticking clock
The light in the tunnel the pheromone in the air the lapse in judgment
And there you are smiling and dopey until the skanky lawnmower roars
Atop your green and the ocean is dumped on your flame
Your wretched rose-red flame! I could scream! I could scream!
Paltry rose! Withering petal! Beauty so dirt beauty so dirty!
AAAAAAAAAAAAAAAARRRRRRRRRRRRGGGGGGHHEEEEEAH!

The sudden scream stunned Bartley. Allen Ginsberg never let out a howl like that! In addition, Louise had glanced his way, and he wasn't sure whether she expected him to smile appreciatively at the performance or take on a look of consternation induced by the contemplation of such heavy and inscrutable plaints. He supposed they were heavy and inscrutable because after all, the other members of the audience appeared to register some kind of comprehension or appreciation. They were applauding. But then again, so was he. And he had no fucking idea what he had just heard.

Louise looked his way again. He felt bad, but how to react? He didn't know. Had he been thinking, as little as thirty minutes ago, that he'd like to get her in bed? He didn't want to perform any sex acts with her anymore! What if she let out a Yoko Ono screech like that during orgasm? Holy crap, that would be like having sex with Regan MacNeil! And she might write a poem about it! What happened to the warm and relaxed woman he'd just dined with at the Athenian Corner? "Interrogation with no answers? Torture without tools?" Jesus Christ, listening to this shit was like a waterboarding with no water.

Oh, crap! She was beginning again. "This is a poem I wrote about the taste of semen," she said.

Now *Bartley* wanted to scream! He shifted in his seat and tried holding his breath. No torture but the ticking clock, all right! The taste of . . . God help us! Now he didn't even want to kiss her! Christ, he'd rather hear a poem about peristalsis! And just an hour ago he'd had such pleasant fantasies. Dean Martin had sung it, and *so* aptly, "Ain't that a kick in the head?"

He sat for another forty-five grueling minutes listening to Louise intone about "her soul being sucked into the cracks in the sidewalk," "the snake that sits polishing lug nuts," and the fact that "stones are stones." And once, (embarrassing even to recall), she had the temerity to admonish a member of the audience for yawning!

Then, after the reading, he'd had to tell her that he found it *interesting*, but of course that wasn't enough; she wanted him to say that it had been—what, fun? Stimulating? Inspiring? Thought-provoking? He was afraid he'd left her all unsatisfied on that score. And, he, of course, was unsatisfied as well.

When Bartley returned home, he found Cornelius at the kitchen table reading *Annals of the Noble Families of Tyrone,* which the police had returned to him the day before. A bit creepy, that. But he supposed having Cornelius "on the case" was a good thing.

There were other books on the table beside him, *Life Along the Merrimac: Collected Histories of the Native Americans Who Live Along Its Banks,* edited by John Pendergast, *An Atlas of Colonial Middlesex County,* and *Vital Records of Early Massachusetts Settlements.* Bartley refilled Cornelius's glass and joined him in a generous tumbler of Bushmill's; the cask-strength Redbreast was a memory.

"Where'd you get those other books?"

"Took a walk to the Tyngsborough Historical Society."

"They let you take them out?"

"They're not supposed to, but the woman said she trusted me to bring them back. Eva Angelina—lovely name. Her grandmother was a Murphy from Youghal Harbour."

He took a deep breath and said, "You smell mighty good, Cornelius. She wouldn't have let you in before, let alone trusted you with that material. You just have to shave those mutton-chop sideburns—they went out of style many moons ago."

The Irishman nodded absently and continued to pore over the super-sized pages of the antiquated tome. Bartley thought, the trick will be to *keep* him smelling good. He couldn't get him drunk and wrestle him into the shower every few days. He would have to formulate another plan. Finally, he picked up the *Globe*, and the two of them sat at the table like two old pals. For although neither spoke, they were glad of each other's company.

Bartley could have poured another whiskey, but it was a work night. He left Cornelius to his reading and went upstairs. He lay awake for a while, wondering what Manus was really thinking about his parents' divorce, and what, if he could go back, he would have done differently. What *could* he have done? There were also a few stray thoughts of Louise, and how things might have gone if her allure had not so quickly turned to revulsion. And he found that now, when his imagination put a woman beside him in the bed, she resembled no one so much as the Violeta he had spurned.

Like a character in a gothic novel, *he fell into a troubled sleep* in the bedroom he'd once shared with Harry Jr. in the old farmhouse. The digital clock said 3:12 a.m. when he awoke, or was awakened, by the sound of a woman sobbing. He froze for an instant, then sat up quickly, listening hard. Nothing. Had he been dreaming? He rose, went to the window, lifted a slat of the blinds and peeked out. Before him lay what might be a painted scene: "A View from the Childhood Bedroom in Half-Moonlight." But just then a motion detector activated the double lights over the back steps, and in their brilliance, he saw a deer move quietly across the yard and into the dark woods.

He let the slat slip out of his fingers and went back to bed, talking himself out of the unease he felt with reminders that dreams sometimes seem real and that there had always been deer in the woods. Still, he opened the drawer in the night table slightly—the drawer in which he had thrown his father's pistol and a box of bullets. Cornelius said he did not sense evil about the place, but, well, one never knew.

Bartley hadn't slept well, and he was tired in the morning. At his marital home, the one that was now for sale, he might have checked the news online, but he had no internet connection at the farm as yet.

He retrieved the paper from the porch, looked over the headlines, and drank three coffees in fifteen minutes. A quick shower, a comb through the hair, shirt and tie. He gazed into the mirror and said, "Now go and pretend you really care about standardized education, state testing and data collection and analysis." As Harris was fond of saying, "Fakin' it is makin' it."

The coffee caught up with Bartley by the end of first period. When the bell rang for change of class, he walked briskly to the men's room. On the way back, he spotted a couple making out in a recessed doorway. "Save it for the drive-in!" he said.

"What?" the young man asked, befuddled by the reference.

Bartley realized that they had no idea what a "drive-in" was. Why would they? "Just get to class," he said.

He rounded the corner of the corridor. There was Bede standing outside his classroom door, as welcome to Bartley's sight as a red dawn to a sailor. What he wanted to say was, "Fuck!" Instead, he called out, as affably as possible, "Good morning, Mr. Bede." The fat fucking fuck assumed his most tutorial, supervisorial air. He opened the door, raised an index finger and said to the class, "I'll be speaking to Mr. Hannigan here for a moment. Keep it down."

Turning to face his prodigal "team member," Bede said, "Bartley! You should always be in the class to greet the students and get them going on a 'bell ringer.' What if a fight broke out while you were not present? You'd be responsible."

"Sorry. I had to run to the men's room."

"If you need to use the men's room during scheduled class time, call Fatima and we'll send an aide to cover for you as soon as we can."

"Right. I thought I could make it. I mean I'm only a minute late."

"But you're *responsible*," Bede reminded him once more.

From inside the class, they heard laughter and a girl's voice: "Shut the fuck up, Angel!"

"If there's nothing else, I'd better get back in there," Bartley said.

"There is one other thing," he said. He took a step closer and Bartley took a step back. He didn't like to be too close to the belly, which had assumed frightening proportions, as if Bede were with child, probably with one of those creatures from the movie *Alien.* "I had some extra money in the budget, which I need to spend before the end of the fiscal year, so I've asked a consultant to come in and work with you and a couple of other people."

"A consultant? This year?"

"I need to spend the money, or we'll lose it."

"Why me?" He was aware, too late, that he sounded like Job, or Nancy Kerrigan.

"She can go over the template for the Teacher Action Plan with you, for one thing. Your self-assessments were a little vague, didn't really measure effectively whether you've met your goals. She has a very thorough knowledge of state mandates. Speaking of, the state is requiring us to create Model Performance Indicators for content areas. Esme can help you with writing effective MPIs. And while she's here, she can observe your classes and give you some input. Shouldn't be painful."

"Esme?"

"Esme Gath, highly regarded educational consultant with the 'Access for All Collaborative.'"

"She's going to observe me during the last two weeks of school? Is that fair?"

"Oh, just do whatever you normally do. Remember, Esme's here to *help* you."

Louder this time, the voice inside the room shouted, "Shut the fuck up!"

Bede's jaw seemed to tighten, and his head bobbed as if this overheard bit of classroom anarchy represented Exhibit A in the case for Bartley needing the advice of a consultant, and why he should never allow his alleged need to urinate to make him late for class.

"This is why you need to be there to greet them," he said, slowly, like a Scout troop master explaining the importance of dry matches to a tenderfoot.

"I would be in there, if you weren't keeping me out here."

"Go then, and remember, Bartley, the skilled teacher always gives them a 'bell ringer assignment' to occupy them as soon as they get in the room."

"Right, I'll put it in my Teacher Action Plan."

"Good idea."

As Bede receded down the hallway, Bartley threw open the door to the room, glared at the class, told them to be quiet, separated Angel and Josefina, and told them all to open their books to page 214, "The Road Not Taken." Turning his back on them as he erased the dopey faces they had drawn on the Smartboard, he closed his eyes and whispered to himself, "*Esme Gath!* This can't be good. And *what the fuck* is a Model Performance Indicator?"

Longingly, he thought back to the simple days when he had started teaching. There was reading, writing, discussing ideas. There was spontaneity, creativity, and individuality. The days before DDMs and formative and summative assessments and growth tables and impact ratings and norms and roles and the endless stream of *drivel* that distracted everyone from teaching. And now, Esme and her MPIs! Hopeless! Why couldn't he have become something simple and straightforward, like a banshee hunter?

He recalled that character his father had told him about in Irish mythology who charged into the sea, slashing at the waves with his sword. A druid had cast an enchantment over him which made him see the rollers as charging ranks of enemy warriors.

Bartley was under no such druidic illusion. He *knew* that none of it was real; the 'experts' had taken over the schools with all their so-called "best practices" and their "presentation and response accommodations." They were always "having conversations around" issues and "unpacking rubrics" and "engaging in collaborative inquiry." Meanwhile, half the kids couldn't read a goddamned analog clock or find Australia on a map.

And Esme would be his own personal emissary from the ivory tower of educational bullshit—there could be no doubt. Suddenly he was longing for fresh air, maybe a drop of Bushmills, and the sight of something wild and natural, a deer moving toward a darkened wood, or through it on some inviting road he had not taken.

Intermezzo

Setting: Bartley Hannigan's Property, circa 1000 AD

Batuckweh understood why the strange warriors had built it. It was a place to call their power. The circle of the sun and the stone of the earth. They built their fort in a circle, too, in a high place near the sky, and the river flashed its silver back below. All the power was here. That was why he had to kill them. For three summers, he had let them be, but now they were growing strong. They would grow stronger still and their number increase, and maybe more would arrive, and their gods might be strong, too, and one day in the days that come, they would challenge the Penakuk for the land by the falls where the salmon come to give themselves to be eaten. So, they and their allies from the Sokoki and Weshacum surrounded the strange warriors and let them starve, and their gods were not strong enough to save them.

After eight nights, they heard the men in the high place singing their death song. None of the Penakuk could ever describe it after, but sometimes they heard it in the wind when they hunted near the high ground.

When the sun was rising from the place where the river runs, Batuckweh attacked. The men with hair the color of the sun or the color of flame and hair on their faces fought hard, but there was death in their eyes for they were weak with hunger and thirst and only wanted to die swinging their great knives so that their ancestors would welcome them. That was good.

Their chief led them out, a giant of a man, shouting in a language that sounded like water roaring over a shallow rocky place, churning gravel. He fought like Kunnaway, the bear. He killed Otenka's son, and Witighese too, but an arrow from Batuckweh's bow pierced the pale flesh beneath his ear, and the heart went out of his warriors when they saw the heavy blade drop to the ground and the giant fall, choking on blood. After that, the strangers only fought to die fighting, and they were outnumbered and overrun. And Batuckweh let them die like warriors in a rain of arrows.

When the battle cries had ceased, and the blood of the strange warriors flowed over the earth, Tecoun brought the women, there were twelve of them, and five small children, wide-eyed, crying. But the women did not cry. They were a hard people, proud, and they buried their fear deep in their hearts. They would be adopted by the tribe, and their blood would mix with the blood of the Penakuk, and their gods would be happy.

He gave a signal to Tecoun, and the women and children were taken away. He walked through their camp, looking at the bodies in their bright-colored clothing and wondering how they had made it. He looked around at the stones they had raised to stand in a circle on the earth. They had some strong knowledge, and if there had been more of them, they might have driven the Penakuk away from the rich fishing grounds.

Tecoun came to him then, holding in his hands a flat stone into which was cut three turning circles which held within them many more circles. "Is this one of their gods, Batuckweh?"

And Batuckweh understood this, too. "Yes. It is the Spirit Mother. She knows the things that began, the things that are now, and the days that will come. She knows the earth and the moon and the sun, all turning, and the river, flowing to the big water forever. Everything turns in a circle, and the bird builds his nest in a circle."

"Shall I break it, Batuckweh?"

"Do not break it. You will release the spirit to do us harm. We will keep her in the stone. We do not want their tribe to return and prosper and grow strong here. Bury it in the earth in this place, outside the circle of the stones, where no sun will reach it, where it will be held in darkness forever while the days move on."

They took the long knives and the colored garments and other things from the dead. Some things they understood, and some they did not understand or know how they were made. And they dropped the bodies down the steep banks to the running water to be carried away from their grounds. Soon it would be as if the strangers had never come up the river to die.

Batuckweh called out and raised his war club, and the men followed him back to the falls, carrying the bodies of Otenka's son and Witighese and the others. He wondered as he walked if one day greater war parties of these men would arrive and if it would be they who would run far to the north and disappear, leaving no tall stones. When their villages were burned, and the paths they used grown over, and their tools scattered, there would be nothing. Sokoki, Mahican, Nipmuc, Pocumtuc, Susquehannok, Wampanoag. All might one day pass like these men, and the strangers would move over the river in their canoes and drive the salmon into the seines of wild hemp, and their smoke would rise as they dried the salmon on the river bank.

And as he drew near the village, Batuckweh watched the wide river fall from its high path and crash onto the rocks below and run to that place where the people of the dawn look over the endless, bitter water. The strange warriors were gone, but that night, when the moon made the river a silver snake, the people of the tribe by the falls heard a cry from the hill where the strangers had died. It was like the howling of wind, like the scream of a woman, like the cry of the crow.

Nine

"Es-me?"

"That's her name."

"But there's only two weeks left!" Harris said.

"No shit."

"The kids are off the walls."

"Crazy. Hey, you know what a one of 'em asked me today? Why America wanted to kill the tourists. He said he heard someone on TV say that America had to kill all the tourists."

"What tourists?"

"Terrorists!" Bartley's chest swelled and deflated in a dismal sigh. "What's it like out, do you know?" There were no windows in the classrooms—a design flaw, to say the least.

"I hear it's beautiful out."

"Okay, I'm going for a swim at the pond. You wanna go?"

"Forgive me, Bartley. Believe me, I take no pleasure in reminding you of this, but there's a departmental meeting in five minutes."

"No, no, no, no!"

While Bede rambled about the tangled undergrowth of educational newspeak and droned on interminably in the stuffy, fluorescent-lit room, Bartley thought, a little angrily, about his father. If he had just left him the farm, unencumbered, he could have sold it all and disembarked from this ship of fools. But having worked his way up the longevity scale, he couldn't find another job that would pay what this one paid—and then there was the pension system. Traps, everywhere!

With the word *trap*, came thoughts of Adele. He tried to recall the time when he had really loved her. They were in her parents' home in Connecticut, young. Her hair was long back then. And she was eating a cracker or something, looking out the window of the kitchen, and she turned and looked at him and smiled this great smile, like she approved of him. Was that what he wanted? Approval? She *did* approve of him then. And he felt it for her there in the kitchen—love. Yes, he had loved her.

But she was so different in those days. He supposed he was, too. Some couples grow together, and some grow apart. That's just the way it is. He sent a silent prayer upward past the fluorescent lights. God, please let Manus and Jill grow together.

"Soooo, when you get together with your PLC, and review your norms and protocols—"

Harris passed him a note. As if he had read his mind regarding the ship of fools, it read: "Where is there a Mr. Roberts who will throw the captain's palm tree off the ship?"

Where indeed? Having Harris around helped him, somehow, to cope. Maybe it was just good to know that there was a friend beside him on the bench rowing the galley to the beat of the same crazy drum.

When, *finally*, he could leave the building, he nearly ran to his car. The days were getting longer, and there was still plenty of sun. He ran into the house—no sign of Cornelius—put on his bathing suit and sneakers and sprinted up the trail, a towel over his shoulder.

He was carrying a book, his cigarette case and lighter. No phone, no electronics, nothing to disturb the silence but the occasional bird call and Mozart's *Requiem* in his head.

But when he was on his back, churning slowly across the pond and squinting at the clouds sailing the troposphere, he became aware of a different music. At least, he thought he did; his ears were underwater, but he was sure he'd heard a voice:

I'm a rambler, I'm a gambler, I'm a long way from home

He righted himself, and treading water, listened.

. . . if you don't like me then leave me alone

Rolling his body toward the direction from which the sound seemed to be coming, he noticed puffs of smoke rising from behind a thicket along the embankment, not far from where he'd left his towel and book.

Stealthily, he swam a breast stroke toward the shore while over the water a thin, hoarse voice carried the old song:

Oh, moonshine, dear moonshine, oh, how I love thee
You killed me poor father, but damn ye try me
Now bless all moonshiners and bless all moonshine
For their breath smells as sweet as the dew on the vine

Bartley rose dripping from the pond, grabbed his towel, and crept along the bank to peek over a tangle of wild morning glory vines that encompassed the tumbled trunk of a dead, bleached tree. Though he was already sure what he'd find there, it was a jolt to his senses, a traumatic injury to his reason, to find in clear daylight before him, the bicorn hat adorned with a "panache," or sweeping black feather. From under this arcane headgear, puffs of smoke floated up between refrains of the song.

Without taking his eyes off the hat, which was trimmed with gold braid, Bartley stepped around the flowing undergrowth and was face to face with a little man smoking a clay pipe. He saw now that the black feather was held by a green rosette, in the center of which was silver medal engraved with a harp.

"Ah, Bartley Hannigan, there you are, as large as life." The figure puffed again at the pipe, humming his song.

Bulbous nose, green coat, and, what had Violeta said, "a moustache like the handle bars of a bi-ceecle."

"Don Nippery Septo, I presume?"

"Presume away. Ah, Bartley, as they say in the West, '*Is beo duine gan a chairde ach ní beo duine gan a phíopa*.' 'One may live without one's friends, but not without one's pipe.' Very true, that."

"You're the . . . lep . . . I mean, the, what, the—*clurichaun*."

The black feather waggled as he nodded. "Accurate. Yes. Not that it matters to the popular mind."

"You haven't been in the wine cellar lately."

"Respect, Bartley, respect. I shouldn't like to steal drink from a man so recently dead, God rest his soul, be it ever so tasty. The wine, that is. Albert Boxler Riesling Grand Cru Sommerberg, Vendange Tardive, 2005—a vintage I won't soon forget. But no, I have me principles, so I do. Except when you invite me, as ye did before, you bein' the rightful heir an' all."

"Of course." Bartley knew that Cornelius had set a few things on the wine cellar door—a pine cone and a horseshoe, and he forgot what other ridiculous articles. Or at least he had thought them ridiculous, but he wondered now whether it had been those talismans rather than Septo's principles which had kept him away from the Grand Cru whatever it was.

"God's teeth, but you were pissed as a fiddler. I see yer shiner has healed well. Bejasus." His eyes took on a dreamy look as he peered through a cloud of smoke. "*Violeta Martinez.*" He said her name in a most refined Spanish, or at least it sounded so to Bartley. "Oh, but she's a rare bird. Reminds me of the lovely Concepción Castellví, a woman I knew in Castille back in the days of the Felon King. We cracked a few bottles the day he abdicated, I can tell you."

"What the hell are you talking—"

"Have ye called her at all? What are ye waitin' for? I could see she liked you. I can't imagine why, knackered as you were." He shook his head. "No, that's a mystery, that is."

"First, regarding the woman in question: *mind your own business!*"

"I hope you're not put off because she makes a few extra quid as an exotic dancer? And she is exotic, bejasus. But if you can't see she's a lovely soul as well, why then you're as blind as one of those craychers at the bottom of the sea where they've no light, nor any use for light."

"I do not have to explain myself to a person who . . . who I'm not sure even exists."

"Hah! 'Tis a rum sailor you are, to take that tack. Do you not have the evidence of your senses, as Marley said to oul' Scrooge? He was a right bastard now, wasn't he? I mean until the spirits set 'im straight. Do *you* know that seventy percent of the people in Iceland believe absolutely in gnomes? Ah, but *nowadays*, 'round this place, no one believes in anything, except—" His bushy eyebrows lowered as he seemed to hunt about mentally for what it was that people believed in. "*Cyberspace!*" he proclaimed, finally. "That's your Otherworld!"

"All right," Bartley said, "let's say that you do exist."

"Yes, let's do. And let's say that *you* exist, too, since I am not in the habit of discoursin' wid nonentities, though I must say, at times . . . *your damned close!*" He clamped down on the pipe stem again, his mouth invisible under the great moustache, while wreaths of smoke clouded the dusty old hat and rust-colored hair.

"Very funny, well, let's say *I* exist because I'm not usually *invisible!*"

"Gaps and folds in the curtain—it's not that we're *invisible* really—it's just that you don't notice us."

"That makes no sense. Listen, Septo. Why would a gnome or a leprechaun or a clurichaun or anything of the kind appear to *me?*"

"Oh, there he goes. *Why me?* Listen while I tell ye, Bartley boyo, sure I wouldn't be wastin' me time in confabulation with such as yerself were it not for—*her!*" He nodded gravely and thrust the bit of the pipe in the direction of the stone circle. "Only thank heaven you have Cornelius O'Tuama about. He'll sort things out, if they can be sorted."

"Why don't you appear to him then, and . . . and confer on it."

He smiled. "Why don't *you* call Violeta?"

Exasperated, Bartley cried, "Where the hell do you *come from?*"

"Not from bloody *cyberspace!*" the little man chortled.

"Another planet, then?" Bartley asked.

"Do I look like a bleedin' alien? Haha! No, no. Ireland, in the main. We're small enough, and willing enough, and clever enough, to find the doors between places that occupy nearly the same space and move about. Not across the stormy main, mind you! Oh no! Had to slip aboard the *Happy Return*, a foul barky, for that crossing. 'Twas in October of 1882."

"You came in 1882? No one lives that long, my friend."

"No humans, you mean. We're a different race. Not a drop of Adam's blood, don't you know. Sad, that. Quite. Closes the big door. All a question of *time*, and I confess I don't even know what the word means. No one does. Not a bit of it. Not even the fellah in the wheelchair. I suppose we are *out of time* at this point. Nearly. Hmmm. Tricky thing, time—very! When you've a proper perspective, it seems to me everything is happening at the same time somewhere."

"At the same time? What? I'm pretty sure that yesterday was yesterday, and tomorrow is, or, will be, tomorrow."

"'Tis what time seems to you, Bartley bucko. But then it also *seems* that the world is flat, doesn't it now?" His bushy brows descended over his blue eyes. He blew a pensive cloud and said, "Sure, what seems to be almost never is." He cleared his throat and continued, "Listen to me now while I tell ye." He winked one eye shut and tapped his temple with an index finger. "O'Tuama! Clever fellow. Strong will. Great perception. Subtle, very. Of course, he smells like a piece of French cheese. Rancid stuff. Don't know why he hates the wather so. Comes from dacent people."

He rapped the bowl of his pipe against a rock and blew through the stem to clear it. "You must take his advice all the same. He *has* the power. God knows *I wouldn't face her,* bejasus."

"Like I said, why don't you talk to Cornelius? He gets this stuff—why are you talking to me?"

"Don't like to get too close to a seventh son of a seventh son. An individual like that—humph! He might beat you at your own game and that would be humiliatin'. No, prefer *the Bartley intermediary.* For a fellah never cut himself on a dull blade!"

"Thanks a lot!"

Septo looked as if he was about to take his leave. "Wait a minute," Bartley said, "Face whom? Give me a little more than this. I've been waiting—"

"What in the name of the seven stars is *that?*" Septo cried, pointing up into the branches of the trees. Bartley turned to look, and seeing nothing, turned back. The little man was gone, leaving only a lump of charred tobacco and a wisp of smoke dissipating in air.

Bartley was wishing, then, that somehow, he would find himself awakening from a nap, stretched on his towel by the pond's edge. He recalled what he'd said to his father: "Sometimes you don't know if you're asleep or awake." What a stupid thing to say. He was awake, and he was either insane, or he'd just had a conversation with a mythical being. A creature who was giving him love advice! "In Ireland, anything can happen, and it usually does." Bartley had read that in a book by Mervyn Wall. But this was not Ireland. How could they suddenly be overrun with banshees and clurichauns?

He went back to his spot by the pond and smoked a cigarette in the lowering sun. He watched the water striders skating over the surface of the pond, just like Jesus in the Gospel, and remembered Cornelius's fireflies. *Anything can happen.*

When Bartley got back to the house, he found Cornelius sitting on an overturned bucket with an upended bicycle before him, and a lot of tools he had no doubt pulled from the shed. "Can you credit it, Bartley, that someone actually tossed this bicycle away? I found it sticking out of a dumpster!"

"What were you doing. . . ? Never mind."

"'Tis a perfectly decent bicycle." Bartley smiled as he appreciated the Irish twist on the words: ". . . a pour-fectly daycent boy-sickle."

"Great. Listen, I just met the—"

A canary yellow Volkswagen Jetta pulled into the driveway. "Oh, Christ. It's Louise." She had texted him several times over the last week—all caps—ANSWER MY TEXT! But he just didn't know what to say. So, he hadn't answered her, hoping that some way to extricate himself would occur to him or that she would take a hint.

"Bartley! Where have you been?"

She was looking fine in white jeans and a loose V-neck top, but all he could remember was that horrid unpoetic howl. Still, he felt a bit overmatched as he stood there dripping wet in a baggy bathing suit, a *Star Wars* beach towel over his shoulder. "I've been super busy, working, fixing up the place."

She was watching the long-haired Irishman oiling the bicycle chain. "That's Cornelius," Bartley said. "He's visiting from Ireland. Cornelius, Louise."

She cast a cold glance in his direction. "Nice to meet you."

He stood, wiping his hands on a rag, and tipped his cap. "Good afternoon, Louise."

She looked from Bartley to Cornelius and then scanned the whole farm, house and garden. "Can we talk, Bartley?" The question brought Joan Rivers to mind, except that Joan Rivers had always followed that question with something funny, and Bartley was pretty sure that whatever Louise would follow up with would not be funny at all. In his experience, that question never introduced what would be a pleasant discussion for the male when it was posed by a female.

"Sure," he said in as innocent a voice as he could muster, "go ahead."

Her eyebrows rose, and she cocked her head so that only one of her ears popped through her long hair. "I mean in private." Her tone of voice suggested that he should already have guessed that she wanted to talk to him in private and that he was stupid for not having realized this.

"Oh yeah—let's, ah, do you mind if I throw a shirt on?"

She nodded, and he jogged into the house and returned a minute later with combed hair, wearing plaid shorts and a wrinkled Lowell Spinners T-shirt, the last cigarette of the day drooping from his mouth. The bicycle was right-side up now, and Cornelius was extolling its virtues to Louise, who was not even pretending to be interested.

He walked over and said, "Can I get you a drink or anything?"

"No, thank you. Let's walk."

He followed her like an obedient dog up the broad shallow hill planted with Christmas trees, which were now beginning to cast shadows twice their lengths. "Bartley," she said. "One thing you should know about me is that I believe in honesty. I'm very honest."

"Yes, of course."

"Are you honest, Bartley?"

"Oh, most of the time, I think, you know. . . ."

"Then be honest with me. Why haven't you responded to my texts or my calls?"

"I've just been really busy with. . . ." This was torture. Why did everyone want to torture him? He looked at the octopus hanging on the chain about her neck and felt as if he were trying to extricate himself from its writhing tentacles.

"Honesty, Bartley! Ever since you went to my poetry reading, you've gone dark on me. You didn't like it, did you? Admit it!"

"Well, I, no, yes, I did. But you know, I mean, what do I know about poetry?"

"You're an English teacher, for God's sake!"

"Yes, but in college I read the Romantic poets, and Shakespeare, and Yeats. Alexander Pope and Chaucer and . . . I didn't really read a lot of *modern* poetry, so it's just that I know very little about it, but it seemed, you know, very interesting."

"You didn't like it! You hated it! Can't you be honest, or is that just too difficult for a hypocritical toad like Bartley Hannigan?"

Hypocritical toad? Now she was throwing down the gauntlet, and, since his irritation was beginning to banish his scruples, he decided to pick it up. What the hell was he doing in this situation anyway? He was *done* with all this! All those years of trying to please Adele and avoid arguments and grovel—*done!* "You're right, Louise. But I'm not a hypocrite. My reaction was based on the simple desire not to offend, which may seem cowardly to you but was really just good manners. However, since you want *total honesty*, here it is. No, I didn't like your poetry. I thought it sucked and I hated it. 'Alexander and his horse his horse and Alexander' and 'stones are stones' and 'I want to throw the puppies in the incinerator'—give me a fuckin' break. And now you come up here berating me like I broke some vow? We had a date—it didn't work out. What do you want me to say? I'm sorry."

Her face flushed, and her eyes were suddenly—weaponized. "You know *nothing* about poetry!"

"I already said that!"

"Ignorant philistine! That's what you are! I don't care that you slighted me. What sickens me is that I thought you were a kindred spirit. Then you slighted my *art!*"

"Maybe I can't appreciate your art because it's too *sublime.*"

"I thought you were an intelligent man! You're just plain *stupid!*"

"Fine, I'm stupid."

"And, you're a prick!"

"Well, you wouldn't *let* me be nice. What did you want me to do? Cry?"

"I *despise* you, Bartley Hannigan. You have *no soul* at all."

"Who the hell made you the judge of who has a soul? Oh, I forgot—you're a *poet!* Unfortunately, you're not a very nice person. You know, whatever art you produce, and no matter who you are, everyone doesn't *have to* like it!"

He turned and walked down the hill, sucking the last of his cigarette. He heard her shout after him, "No soul!" and he muttered to himself, because, even in the mood he was in, it was too cruel to shout, "Go write a stupid fucking poem about it!"

He went down and into the house, where Cornelius was once again ensconced in a chair with one of his old books and poured himself a Jameson. He heard her car door slam and the sound of gravel flying as she gunned it out of the yard.

The *Boston Globe* was lying on the countertop, and Bartley noticed an article, "Hawking Says Black Holes Are Door to Other Dimensions." Hmmm. *The fellah in the wheelchair.* What a coincidence. He looked it over quickly:

If you're Stephen Hawking, the most efficient way of visiting another dimension is to bravely throw yourself into the gaping maw of a black hole. During a speech at Harvard University last night, the British physicist claimed black holes have a "back door" and "aren't the eternal prisons they were once thought. Things can get out of a black hole, both from the outside and possibly through another universe," he said.

"I'd like to send her to another universe," Bartley muttered.

Cornelius looked up from his book. "Workin' the charm on the lasses again, eh Hannigan?" he asked. And then, snorting and shaking his head disapprovingly, he added, "What, did you use the poor woman for your dirty pleasure and now yer tossin' her aside, ye brute?"

Bartley poured another glass, handed it to the Irishman, and sat in a chair by the coffee table, which was scarred with burns from his father's cigars and rings from his coffee cups. "I never even had sex with the woman! A few conversations and a dinner and she acts like I'm breaking an engagement the day before the wedding!"

"Ah, she's mad, then."

Bartley swigged the whiskey and blew a big sigh of relief as he leaned back in the chair. "Speaking of madness—I was visited up at the Top Pond by that Don Nippery Dippery, and I guess he is, kind of real."

Cornelius leaned forward. "Tell us."

"He said that you would get to the bottom of things. He knows your name. And he said to stay clean—washed, not to disgrace your people."

"Sure, I'm clean—I took a shower."

"That was two weeks ago, now."

"And in two more weeks I'll take another. Once a month, you can't ask fairer than that!"

Bartley decided to put aside the hygiene question for the time being. "We'll discuss that later. Are you getting to the bottom of things?"

"I believe I'm onto the game or will twig it soon."

"Twig it?"

"Suss it out, like."

"Oh, by the way, he mentioned a lot of stuff about time and space, sounded like science fiction bullshit. But he said that his kind 'don't have a drop of Adam's blood' and how that was sad. What's all that about?"

"I can't say, definitively, you know, what it's all about. But I have heard stories. In my grandfather's time, in the parish of Ballysadare in the County Sligo, a priest was walking home in the small hours of the night from the deathbed of an old woman. His road led through Sliabh Gamh, where he heard music. And looking into a sort of glen in the hills, he saw a fire and a lot of wee folk dancing 'round it, you see. There were a couple of fiddlers playing the jig called 'The Gold Ring.' Now, of course, the priest was amazed, and he stood by watching, but they'd seen him, and the music stopped. He hurried on his way, but soon they were all around him. One of them, the head man, I suppose, spoke to him in the old tongue, and he asked, 'Father, can we ask a question of you?' And your man the priest, says, 'You may ask me anything, and I'll do my best to answer you honestly.' So, the leprechaun asks, 'Father, can we get to heaven?' Now the priest answers, 'It's not for me to say which of you may pass through the gates of heaven, but I can tell you this: if you've one drop of Adam's blood, you've as much chance as any man to enter the Kingdom of Heaven.' And at that, don't you know, a great lamentation arose among them, and they faded into the darkness until the whole glen was quiet but for a rising wind in the bell heather, and the priest wondered whether the whole encounter had not been some kind of dream, but likely 'twas no dream, Bartley. Septo would seem to affirm its veracity."

Bartley was thinking back to the conversation he'd had with his father in this house; it seemed long ago now. He'd been so ready to assume that old Happy was delusional, and now here he was listening to this seventh son of a seventh son explain the nature of some other order of beings as if he were explaining the rules of cricket. Bartley had always felt he had a firm grasp on reality, yet when these very unreal events had begun to occur around him, somehow, it didn't seem as much of a shock as he might have thought. As if, at a subconscious level, he had suspected all along that things might not be so neat and intelligible as they seemed. *What seems to be almost never is.* Hadn't science shown that time itself, which we imagine evenly divided into days and years and measured with clocks and calendars, turns out, as Septo said, to be a "tricky thing," relative and shifting, not linear at all.

Bartley sipped his whiskey and leaned back in his chair. "Where do they come from, then? I mean what's *your* theory?"

"My mother told me that they were the angels who sat on the fence, would not take a side in the war between God and Lucifer, and they were thrown from heaven. I don't believe that story."

"Sounds pretty far-fetched, but then far-fetched doesn't mean much anymore."

"There is another theory that they are the *Tuatha Dé Danann*, the tribe of the goddess Danu. The ancient text, the *Lebor Gabála Érenn,* known in English as *The Book of Invasions,* says that they arrived in Ireland in a dark cloud. They were a magical people, and their champion was the god Lugh. Three of them were the goddesses Ériu, Banba, and Fodla. The name of Éire derives from Ériu, but the other two are also synonymous with Ireland in poetry."

"Kind of a pre-Christian trinity?"

Cornelius nodded. "And there was another trinity of war goddesses born of the same mother; they were called Badb, Macha, and the Mórrígan. But eventually, according to the texts, the *Tuatha Dé Danann* were defeated by the Milesians, with the help of the poet-magician Amergin. And the *Tuatha Dé Danann* agreed to a division of the land of Ireland, but Amergin tricked them, and they were given the land beneath Ireland, and so they became the *aes sidhe,* the people of the *sidhe,* or the fairy mounds. These are the earthen mounds you find all over Ireland. And as they shrank from memory, and as fewer people believed in them, they grew smaller; hence, the wee people."

"Not a drop of Adam's blood. Arrived in a cloud. I'd dismiss the whole business were it not for having seen this little fellow. Does mythology have some basis in reality? Can mythology be history?"

"What becomes history is what's easy to explain. Then there are the stories we tell to explain the things that can't be explained, or that we don't know how to explain. How do we account for all of the strange things that occur around those fairy mounds, or fairy forts, or raths, or *sidhe,* or whatever you want to call them, and around stone circles as well? Listen to me Bartley. In 2008, the developer Sean Quinn was the richest man in Ireland. Worth six billion US dollars, he was. In 2011, he moved a 'fairy fort,' an ancient circular earthen enclosure, to the other side of the village of Ballyconnell. He was financially ruined within the year—filed for bankruptcy. Oh, there are stories enough like that to fill a library, explain them how you will."

Ten

The next morning, Bartley was off to the teenage wasteland and Cornelius was speeding away on his bicycle, the University College Cork tie flying over his shoulder.

Before beginning his lesson on inferences, he decided to do one of Bede's "Bell ringers," a quick assignment to "get them going." He had typed a sentence on the digital blackboard—the "Smartboard."

It read:

Ugh, she said, look at those maggots! Their disgusting!

"All right, boys and girls. Let's begin by correcting this sentence. First, what is missing?" They stared at the board with pursed lips and furrowed brows. "Come on, now, what's missing? If the sentence says, 'she said,' then I need to put in—*what?*"

Danilo, a chubby Portuguese kid, threw a hand in the air, convulsed with the answer. Before Bartley could call on him, he blurted, "Parentheses!"

"Not parentheses, *but—*"

"Those *thingies!*" Swansel cried.

"And, what do you call the thingies?"

"Commas!" someone said.

"Not commas. . . ."

"Parentheses!"

"Not parentheses."

"Commas!"

"Not commas!"

"Those thingies!"

"All right! That's enough with the commas and the thingies!" Bartley said. "After about five minutes, he got Eliezer to go up and put in the quotation marks and explained (for the tenth time this year) that they were called quotation marks, and why 'she said,' was not included within the quotation marks. The explanation was punctated with various commands. 'Put your phone away, Jennifer.' 'Brandon! Wake up!'"

At this point the door opened and Bede came in like an unwelcome draft with a pale, frizzy-haired woman—the consultant whose coming was foretold. She looked like she was wearing a tent and was carrying an enormous Barnes and Noble bag, from which a laptop and a pair of knitting needles protruded. Bartley thought, "Oh shit," but he nodded toward them and mouthed, "Good morning."

Mr. Bede whispered, as if he understood what discretion was, "Mr. Hannigan, this is Esme Gath. She's just going to take a seat. You can carry on." Then he said softly to Esme, "We'll talk later," and flashed the phony smile.

Bartley briefly shook the bony hand that Esme held out as she passed. She lugged her bag to the back of the room, sat down, pulled out the laptop and started typing away like he was on trial and she was the stenographer.

He pointed with the yardstick to the Smartboard, where the corrections to the sentence had begun: *"Ugh," she said, "look at those maggots! Their disgusting!"*

"Any other mistakes you see there, besides the quotation marks?" Silence reigned. He knew that the consultant would say that it was important to give the students "wait time," and so he waited for an answer until the silence became grueling.

"There's *one* other mistake. Something we went over last week."

Miguel, a sweet kid, had been sitting there quietly; English was not easy for him, and he lacked the confidence to throw his hand up. But now he was sure he had the answer that was stumping the rest of the class, and his hand rose tentatively. "Um, Mr. Hannigan? I think I see the mistake."

"Great, Miguel. What is it?"

"The 'm' in 'maggots' should be an 'f.' It should be 'Look at those ff—'"

"No, no! Thank you, Miguel! That's not it." The poor kid was as sincere as he was clueless; he wasn't mean; he just didn't *get* things. Bartley was relieved that the rest of the class had not burst into laughter—they hadn't quite seen where he was going with his 'correction,' or they were lost in their own hypotheses as to where the mistake lay.

He noticed that Maria Luisa had understood—she was smiling to herself, but she was too classy to call attention to the error, and too kind to humiliate Miguel. Maturity was such a rare treasure in this building, as was compassion.

Bartley thought it best to point out the actual error and initiate a quick review of the oft repeated yet somehow ne'er recalled distinction between *there, their,* and *they're*. Esme was tapping away at her laptop, hardly looking up. Hopefully, she hadn't noticed Miguel's proposed correction either.

He launched into the lesson on inferences, beginning with a simple explanation, and then projecting on the Smartboard a series of Norman Rockwell paintings. The first one showed a boy in his pajamas standing facing the viewer, wide-eyed and open-mouthed in shocked disbelief. Behind him, a Santa Claus suit was pulled halfway out of an opened drawer in a dresser.

"Now, let's make an inference." Bartley pointed the yardstick at the picture on the Smartboard. "What is the boy feeling and why? Can you make an inference based on what you see?"

"He los' sumthin'."

"Did he lose something or find something? What did he find?"

"Red pajamas?"

"What do you see?"

"Um, is that a Santa suit?"

"Yes. So, what is your *inference* about why the boy looks shocked? Whose dresser do you think it is?"

He coaxed and cajoled, suggested and hinted, and was eventually able to haul an answer out of them. And so, bit by bit, he slogged through the pieces of art, trying to get the students to look, and to think, ever uncomfortably aware of Esme tap tap-tapping away, like the wireless operator on the *Titanic*.

Just before the bell rang, he asked them to write in their notebooks what they understood by the word 'inference.'

"What?"

"Write what you think *inference* means. The word, *inference*. We've been talking about making *inferences*. Remember?"

"What is it, Mista?"

"That's what I'm asking *you*. Remember? I explained it, and then we've been going over examples. . . ." He cast a glance at the minute hand of the clock, which seemed almost to be in retrograde. ". . . for the last forty minutes." God help us.

Doing his best to maintain that cheerful pedagogical exterior, he walked around while they wrote, and peered at what they were writing. If they were writing nothing, he tried to prod them along with reminders and suggestions.

Finally, the bell rang, and he began the same drill with the next class. Esme's tapping seemed to become louder to Bartley, like the heartbeat of the dead man buried under the floorboards in Poe's "The Tell-Tale Heart." Finally, three quarters of the way through that class, she packed up her laptop and trundled away with her giant bag, and Bartley felt a surge of positive energy as the door closed behind her.

"*Debrief?*" Bartley asked. "Esme wants to *debrief*? What are we, Seal Team Six? And during my prep period?"

"How can she assist you if she doesn't debrief, or, call it something else, discuss things with you?"

"Email? I mean, Mr. Bede, contractually I have a prep period. And I don't want to spend it with Esme."

Bede's eyes narrowed, and he nodded slightly, body language that said, "So, you wanna fight, eh?" He picked up his pen and made a note to himself. "All right, then, I'll get you coverage during your last period, so you can debrief then."

"What did she say? Did she think the class was subpar?"

"Oh, this is all confidential, Bartley. She doesn't talk to me. This is between you and her. It's to *help* you."

Confidential, my ass, but Bartley was out of dodges. There was nothing for it but to meet with Esme, which he would do that afternoon at a table in the back of what was known officially as "the Media Center," and perhaps, more accurately, to the students as "the lie-berry."

She'd asked him to bring his lesson plan, which meant he had to spend his prep writing a goddamn lesson plan. His plans were in his head. He decided to make it as tedious as possible for her to read. You want a lesson plan? I'll give you a damned lesson plan! As Zorba would have said, "The whole catastrophe!"

He began to type, trying to think like a functionary of the Department of Elementary and Secondary Education in Malden, Massachusetts.

Materials required: Smartboard, pointer, notebooks, pencils

WIDA Standard: The Language of English Language Instruction

ELA Standards: (Here he opened the book of *Common Core Standards* and typed out a foot-long string of numbered standards).

Objective: Inferencing having been identified by MCAS and DDM data as a weak point for our students, the lesson will attempt to scaffold instruction in the standard. (Here he wrote another paragraph of thick *educationalese* buzzwords and Department of Ed-approved bullshit).

That took up the first page. On the second, the bullshit grew deeper:

Assessment Criteria, Evidence, Resources, followed by Stages of Lesson—Introductory 'bell ringer' reviewing previously taught concepts. Stage One: Interactive Tasks, Activities, Challenges. Stage Two: Developing Concepts, Elaboration. Stage Three: Conclusion—Review of Key Terms, Ticket to Leave.

The hour of doom arrived, and a sullen Bartley trod the long corridor that lead to the Media Center. The consultant was chatting with a librarian. When she saw Bartley, she smiled and the two of them walked toward a table at the back of the room. She took a chair, her bag took a chair, and Bartley took a chair.

Esme stuck an elastic band in her mouth while she gathered in her bony hands the rampant hair behind her head. Then she took the band and did that thing women do, inserting the hair and flipping the band until all but a few rebellious strands were held firmly at the back of her head.

She requested his lesson plan, which she perused as if it were a court document in a murder trial. "You should include some strategies for *differentiated instruction*."

Differentiation! Shit! How had he forgotten that buzzword?

"Well, Bartley," she said in what was supposed to be a chummy voice, "how do you think the class went?"

"How do I think it went? Not bad. Pretty typical for that class and for this time of year."

She got that look of concern, then, like a doctor might have if you told him there was blood in your stool. She was opening the laptop again with officious state-sponsored eagerness. Looking at her screen, she said, "Your objectives were on the board, but I noticed you didn't *interact* with your objectives. You have to interact continually with the standards and objectives that are posted for the lesson."

He nodded. "Uh huh." *Let me out of here!*

"The artwork you showed. Why did you choose that? I'm just curious." She looked like she was curious all right. In the same way that Tomás de Torquemada was "curious" about the views of Jews and heretics. If the inquisition was a stretch, he at least felt like a witness before the Senate Select Committee investigating Lesson Plans.

"It struck me that Norman Rockwell captures a lot of those moments in which something is revealed. Often, they kind of tell a story if you read into the visual. The sweet little Black girl in the white dress being accompanied to school by the burly US Marshals, the racist graffiti visible on the wall behind her. The students are doing the Civil Rights Movement in history class, so hopefully they can put together what's happening. Very basic inferences, but not so easy for them. I thought we'd begin with those, and then go on to look at written pieces that require inferences."

Her curiosity lapsed into skepticism. "Hmmm. Wouldn't you say it would be advisable to use more culturally diverse artwork?"

"I'm not against that. It's just that I had this kind of epiphany that the Rockwell paintings suggest a lot. There are relatively simple inferences to be made. That was the point of the lesson. And since the students do live in America, it's probably not a bad thing to become familiar with a well-known American artist."

The expression on Esme's face now shifted further, from skepticism to distaste, as if she had suddenly noticed an odor, like Bartley had dog shit on his shoe. Apparently, she suspected that she was dealing with some kind of jingoistic *patriot*. "The data shows that students learn better, that they can relate to material better, when it's presented from a culturally appropriate background. A sort of space in which the teacher invites inclusion and validates the 'other.'"

He knew that it was pointless to argue. "Oh, well, if that's what the data shows, then, you know, I'll have to toss out the Rockwells. Don't want anyone to feel invalid."

She did not require very finely tuned radar to sense the sarcasm in his tone, so she dropped the bomb. "To be honest, Mr. Hannigan, I was surprised that you allowed that young man to make a homophobic slur without using it as a teaching moment and referring him to a counselor."

Oh Christ, Miguel! "Esme, if I thought the kid was being mean, I would have certainly said something. But you have to know Miguel—he wouldn't want to insult anyone. He's a very nice young man. He's just confused, really, about, well, almost everything. I don't know if you noticed—he talks to himself a lot. He's very low-functioning. He asked me the other day where the sun goes when it goes down."

She was typing again, and he began to lose his train of thought. "He may be low-functioning," she said, "but I'm sure he and the other students could profit from a conversation around issues of homophobia. And frankly, an observer might wonder whether your reluctance to engage the student on this issue is really symptomatic of a larger issue."

"A *larger* issue. Oh, so *I'm* homophobic?" *Listening* to bullshit was bad enough, but now he was being *accused* of bullshit. He felt the blood pulsing in his temples.

"I'm not saying you're homophobic. I'm just saying when these issues come up in a class they have to be addressed. And an unwillingness to do so. . . ."

In that instant, and quite out of the blue, he had a vision of Mr. Roberts hurling the captain's palm tree off the bridge of the ship, into the wild and wasteful sea. "I'm gay," he declared.

"What?"

"I'm gay. I've always been gay. My wife just left me because she found out. Now, I'm in love with an Irishman who lives with me. So, I don't see how I could be homophobic. In fact, the accusation of being anti-gay is the sort of micro-aggression that is triggering. . . ." He didn't really know what the hell it could be triggering. Feelings of invalidation? He didn't even understand clearly what constituted a "micro-aggression," but he had noticed that very often the only defense against bullshit is denser bullshit. And sadly, in this case, outright lies.

His declaration seemed to be working. Esme looked as if he had tossed a bucket of cold water in her face. "Okay, I see. Sorry, I . . . I'm sure you're right; this Miguel meant no harm. Anyway, let's, let's move on."

It was strange, but her attitude toward him shifted abruptly after that. Soon she was smiling carelessly, as if intent on demonstrating that his revelation had in no way lowered his standing in her estimation one iota. On the contrary, his standing had risen. It was as if he'd given her the secret code—the password into the *sanctum sanctorum* of the tribe. A white male, yes, but he was not the oppressor—he was the oppressed!

At the end of the school day, Bartley, hobbled by the reality of his day-to-day existence, flung open the exit door and inhaled the warm air gratefully, like a deep diver breaking the surface. Was there ever a man, he wondered, whose work life was so painfully real and mundane, and whose home life was so fantastical and weird? In the parking lot, he noticed that a knot of teachers had formed around his car. They nudged each other as they saw him approaching. Some shook their heads—others smiled stupidly or exchanged knowing glances.

They parted as he approached. What the hell! Letters, in orange spray paint across his white Ford Tempo read: NO SOUL. He circled the car and read across the other side: LYING FUCK.

Louise!

Bartley saw a math teacher, Mr. Silk, raising his phone to take a picture. "Put that away, Silky! Jesus Christ, I don't want this all over the damned Twittersphere!"

"Oh, Okay, sorry, Bartley. But you need to take a photo as evidence, you know."

Ms. Montoya, the Spanish teacher, clenched her fist and said, "Some goddamn people." He wasn't sure if she was referring to the vandal or to himself, the soulless lying fuck.

"Jesus, Bartley," Silky said, "reminds me of that movie *Fatal Attraction*. You seen that movie?"

"Yes!" He wanted to shout: *But I didn't even have sex with her!* That fact, however, would certainly make him appear even more ridiculous than he already did. He scanned the lot looking for cameras on the light poles, but there were no cameras here, just up in the administrators' lot. Wordlessly, feeling a bit like Hester Prynne, he jumped into his shame-mobile and watched the gawking mob grow smaller in his rearview mirror.

He had considered stopping at a bar in Lowell for a tall beer—there was a Flower Power IPA at Cobblestones that was particularly good—but he was reluctant to take his fluorescent orange message to the masses. He drove home and found some black spray paint in the cellar. The car was a '94 he'd bought used in 2004; it now had 210,000 miles on it, so he decided not to bother with insurance agents and deductibles and auto body repair guys. He spray-painted black patches over the orange words.

He was wondering how he had not seen, or how Louise had hidden the fact, that she was out of her mind. The best woman he'd met in a long time, he concluded, was Violeta. She was not crazy or mean. And she was the only one who could assure him that *he* wasn't crazy.

But she was a *stripper!* How would that work out? What if he started to fall for her? He imagined the relationship: "How was work, Honey?"

"Oh, just another day of shaking my ass for drunks!"

He cringed at the thought. No, that wouldn't work out at all! He didn't feel he was a prude, but . . . oh screw it! *You think too much, Bartley! You're dying to call her, so call her.*

Besides, he needed her help for the next plan; he had gotten Cornelius clean once, but the trick would be to *keep* him clean.

He pulled her number out of his wallet and looked at it somewhat apprehensively for a moment before he dialed. His name must have come up on her phone—he could never get used to that technological advance. She answered as if she'd been expecting his call. "Hello, Bartley. How are you?"

"Oh, I'm fine."

"Your eye is okay, right?"

"Fine," he said. "I miss you." He didn't know why he said it, and in a way, he wished he hadn't, but hearing her voice made him realize it.

"Eh?" She spoke the interrogative syllable as a challenge. "That is your fault. You never called me!"

"I know. It's just that, I figure you probably meet so many guys at the club."

"Too many!" she said, words which made Bartley's heart sink momentarily. "But mostly they are *pinches cabrones*. You know, jerks."

"Right." His heart rose again.

Her tone brightened. "Have you seen the little man?"

"Oh, yes. He's quite impressed with you. I'd like to talk about that, and a few other things. Are you free tonight?"

"No, I have to get ready soon. I have to work until I have Sunday and Monday off."

"Okay listen. I need you to help me." He explained the problem, his proposed solution, and reminded her of the most essential part of the plan—when she came into the bar, she should pretend she did not know him.

"You are crazy, Bartley, but I will do it for you."

Once again, Bartley felt an overwhelming affection for her, as he had in the coffee shop, and he understood why love had always been portrayed as coming suddenly, an arrow from the bow of a playful god. "Barley, I mean Bartley, I have not had the time to tell you I am sorry you lost your father. It must make you sad, no? Tell me about him."

He was touched by her interest in the old man. "Happy Hannigan? What can I say? Larger than life. Often cantankerous . . . I mean, bad-tempered. All right, here's a story for you that kind of illustrates my father's character, or what it was like having him as a father." He took the phone out on the porch and sat down. "When I was in third grade, I woke up one morning for school. It happened to be March 18th, the day after St. Patrick's Day, and it was snowing to beat the band—snowing hard—a lot of the schools around here were canceled, but not St. Stan's down the road, where my brother and I went. Harry Junior pulled the sore throat routine that morning, and my mother wouldn't believe we were both sick. She was single-handedly doing the chores—she made me oatmeal and went out to milk the cow and feed Old Joe, our horse. My father was in bed with a hangover from the high holiday, St. Patrick's Day, a time when he felt it was the obligation of every Irishman to get particularly drunk, and I set off to school, but with the drifts and the wind and the snow blowing in my face—"

"Oh, poor Bartley."

"I made it to school, *I thought*, just in time. But, Sister Mary Michael, the principal, from her office by the main door, spots me coming up the stairs, and out she flies like a black cloud with her robe, her habit, swishing. 'You're late, Mr. Hannigan,' she says. I pull the glove back from my Timex and say, 'Sister, it's eight o'clock.'"

"Oh, I know what time it is, Mr. Hannigan. Oh yes, I've been able to read a clock for quite some time now. I'm really very good at it. You are supposed to be *in your seat* at eight o'clock!"

"*¡Que bruja!*" Violeta interjected. "What a witch!"

"But it's snowing, Sister," I remind her. "Pretty hard."

"'Really?' she says. She turns on the sarcasm. The nuns were masters of sarcasm. 'Oh, it's snowing! Yes, that *does* happen in New England from time to time in March, doesn't it? I guess we should plan accordingly, shouldn't we? Do you have a note to explain your tardiness?'"

"No, Sister."

"Listen to me, Mr. Hannigan, you march yourself right back home and have your mother or father call me and give me a reason, other than the obvious fact that it's snowing, to explain why you are tardy."

"Go back home?"

"What a marvel!" she says, "The boy understands English. You heard me, Mr. Hannigan!"

"So, I set off back through the snow, and when I got home, I could see my mother, you know, barely, through the snow, in her big coat, carrying a bucket into the chicken coop, so I have to wake up my father, which takes a while. Finally, I get him to sit up with his wild hair and red eyes, and I tell him the story."

"He was mad at you?"

"Didn't seem to be. 'All right,' he says, and he has me look up the number and dial it for him, and I'm kind of pacing around the room saying, 'What are you going to tell her, Dad? Tell her the alarm didn't go off—tell her. . . .' But he raises a hand to tell me to be quiet. 'Hello?' he says, 'Is this Sister Michael Mary, or Mary Michael, or whatever the hell it is?'"

Bartley heard Violeta laughing.

"I was ready to die right there," he continued, "but *then* he says to her, 'Listen, Sister! What the fuck is wrong with you? Are you some kind of fucking mental case?' And I'm there waving my arms and saying, 'No, Dad! Dad! No!' But he says, 'I'm sending the boy back to school, and if he comes back here again, I'll be bringing him back personally, and you can believe me when I tell you, *you do not want me* in that building this morning because I'm *really* hungover and there will be *hell to pay!*' Then he hangs up, and says, 'You're all set, kid, go back to school,' and he lies back down."

"What happened, Bartley?"

"I trudged back to school, and the snow was getting wetter and heavier, and the slush was seeping into my old shoes, but I walked really slowly, and then I walked around the building three times, terrified to go in, but finally I was getting so cold and wet, I had to go in. It was almost 9:00, but to my amazement, no one said a word, not Sister Mary Michael, and not Sister Benedict, my teacher. And no one ever said a word. So, for better or worse, that was my father."

They talked about their families for a while. Her mother had died when she was very young, and she had taken over a lot of responsibility, cooking for her father and her older brother, and cleaning, and doing some farm work too, which she grew to love. They spoke of the work and the people and the places that had shaped them, and by the time he hung up, nearly an hour later, he was half in love with her. But then he reminded himself, he had felt quite sanguine about Louise not long ago. And, that Violeta was a stripper.

A little while later, Bartley heard Cornelius clattering across the gravel on his rattletrap dumpster bicycle. He walked out on to the porch, noticing some books and what looked like a bottle in a bag tied with twine to the rear fender rack of the bicycle.

Cornelius was staring at Bartley's vandalized vehicle. "That's a grand upgrade to the machine," he said, nodding toward the fresh rectangle of black paint.

"There was an attack of the psycho poet."

Cornelius handed the bag to Bartley, who slid a bottle out of it and read, "West Cork Whiskey." He nodded approvingly and said, "Let's crack it."

They went in and Cornelius poured a couple of glasses of the golden liquid, raised his glass and said, "*Sláinte mhaith!*" Which sounded to Bartley like "Slawncha wah," and meant nothing to him, but suggested convivial good health.

They sipped the whiskey appreciatively. "Smooth, light and malty," Bartley concluded. And then he asked, "What's your opinion so far, Cornelius?"

"Sure, I would concur with that assessment."

"Not the whiskey—I mean, in general. Mystically, if you will. What's going on?"

He set his whiskey down. "Listen to me now while I tell ye."

"I'm all ears."

One might say that Cornelius took on a pensive look, but his look was always somewhat pensive. "My examination of the situation, Bartley, has led me to a cuppla conclusions. Hypotheses which are becoming firmer each day. Number one, your father's death had nothing to do with Hugh Hannigan's banshee."

"Was there a banshee who turned herself into a deer?"

"Who knows what there was or what there is. The old books do speak of shape shifters—the *Cailleach Bhéara*, Fliodhas, the Mórrígan, could all appear as deer. A Celtic god, probably Cernunnos, appears with antlers on the Gundestrup Caldron."

"But there's no 'generational curse' in your opinion?"

"There never was. There is a line in 'The Book of Lamentations,' that says, 'Our fathers sinned and are no more, but we bear their iniquities,' but that Jeremiah was a gloomy fellah anyway. It may be true in that if an ancestor pisses away the family fortune, for example, or allows the usurper to take his freedom, or marries his sister, there are repercussions throughout time. But the idea that later generations are punished for an individual's sin just doesn't seem to fit with my understanding of, oh, I dunno, Celtic karma. It's daft to think your father would be punished because hundreds of years earlier your man Hugh Hannigan was too hungry to show proper respect in a sacred grove. Sure, we must all have some awful chancers and gits back in the family tree."

"Gits?"

"You know—whores' gits! Disreputable gougers!"

"I see. Yes, I'm sure we all must have ancestors like that," Bartley admitted. "Then what happened to my father?"

"Probably, as they told you, 'twas just physics, Bartley. There are deer about, and that book of annals is heavy and hard! A strange coincidence,

I'll grant you that, but life is full of strange coincidences. Why, Edwin Booth—the brother of John Wilkes Booth, saved the life of Lincoln's son, Robert, and don't you know it was just a year or two before John Wilkes shot the president?"

"I never heard that."

"Ah, look it up, sure."

"So, what *is* going on here?"

"It's the stone circle is at the center of it all. I felt it as soon as I went up there—"

"But I told you, when they excavated it, there were pavers at the base of the stones! It's a fairly recent construction."

"Ah, I'm certain 'tis otherwise." Cornelius got up and pulled a book from a pile on the counter. He laid on the table a great, leather-bound tome with gold tooling around the edges. He opened it, showing the marbled end paper. A musty smell rose as he turned the old pages. "Now here is an early map, something not so formal as an ordnance survey, but a piece of work done by an amateur cartographer in this area in 1788."

He showed Bartley the map. Some names were recognizable; others, he had never heard. There was a Tyngsborough Parish, but it was still part of Dunstable at that time. He studied the heavy black line that ran like a fish hook from the White Mountains to the sea. Along its length were the words "Merimake River." Spelling was as mutable as were the names. The town of "Dracut" appeared as "Draucutt," and the present-day city of Lowell was nothing but a cluster of farms over which was written East Chelmsford.

Cornelius turned a few more pages. "All right, now look at this: the area north of Wickasee Island, now Vesper Country Club, just south of us. The home of Chief Wannalancit of the Pennacook Indians, until he left in 1696, I believe it was. Now, you say that the stone circle was erected one hundred years ago because of the pavers at the base. But, if you look at this map plate from over a hundred years earlier. All right, here's the river. Your father's land is here. What's the name you see right there?" He placed a finger on the spot.

Bartley pushed his drink aside and leaned over the book to examine the small, stylized script. "Dru-id Hill. Druid Hill!"

"Right enough. Early settlers found some reason to name the place Druid Hill. Drombeg Stone Circle in Cork, which goes back to 1100 BC, by the way, is known, coincidentally, as 'the Druid's Altar.' Now, this was all Pennacook land, you see, though none are left now. How do you think the Indians would have felt if some band of Irish, or let's say Celts, arrived and followed the river to this point, where they tried to settle? There were fish, and a good stone quarry nearby that was used well into the last century, good hunting. And if the Pennacook killed them, would they leave their sacred place standing?"

Bartley nodded slowly. "They might knock it down."

"Yes, but the tilted or toppled stones were still recognizable as being somehow Celtic or 'Druidic' to later European settlers. And at some point, someone, Jeremiah O'Hannigan, for example, might also recognize what they were, and may have had the stones hauled upright again, and set pavers at the base so that they would stay up." He pulled from the back of the book a drawing he had done of the stone circle. "What you have on Druid Hill is a classic axial stone circle—found only in the southwestern corner of Ireland."

Bartley laid a finger on the one flat stone. "Why was this one never set upright?"

"This is the recumbent stone, the one that is always lying flat like an altar. And there are always an odd number of stones in the circle, from five to . . . I believe nineteen. There are seven here. Finally, if we draw a line from these two portal stones, the highest two, over the center of the recumbent stone, the line will always point south-southwest, as it does here."

"Why?"

"No one knows why at all. There's an archaeological controversy about it. And out here," he continued, pointing to the stone outside the group, "is the taller stone, sometimes called 'the piper.' It's as if the others are dancing in a circle and the piper is playing the tune."

"And the Harvard archaeologists didn't know all this?"

"I'm sure they did, but even Harvard professors have their biases. I think they came here with the idea that it *must be* a 'Victorian folly.' They were only looking for something to confirm their theory, and with the pavers, they found it. We humans don't like to change long-held beliefs. But you know it's proven and accepted now that there was a Viking settlement in Newfoundland, over a thousand years ago, and that they explored coastal North America as well. They just found evidence of another Viking settlement recently in New Brunswick. Why not Celts?"

"So, if it wasn't the Hannigan banshee my father heard, what was it?"

He tossed back the last of his whiskey and squinted at Bartley. "I believe that what he heard, or whom he heard, was the Mórrígan."

"*The Mórrígan?* Do I even want to know?"

"I'd say she was there, present, like, the day we went up together. That crow that seemed to be watching us is indicative, you know. The *Badb Catha,* 'the battle crow,' according to numerous ancient sources—it's one of the forms the Mórrígan takes."

"And, assuming just for a minute you're right . . . is she good? Bad?"

He shrugged. "In the old stories, her nature would be to pursue, to hunt, to avenge. Only there's no one left to take vengeance on. The old enemy they faced here has vanished, another sad story—been killed or emigrated to Canada. But she's still here—alone."

"Strange, to say the least. You know, I'm not sure if I was dreaming the other night, but I thought I heard a woman crying, or as my father said, *keening.*"

"I heard her as well. And when I fell back to sleep, I dreamed of the circle, and the *Badb Catha,* and two lines kept running through that dream. *Bhí an míádh ag siúl, ag rith, leo.* 'They were dogged by misfortune.' *Bhí sí á crá féin i ndiaidh a clainne.* 'She tormented herself over the loss of her children.' There are stone circles all over the British Isles. But I sense that this one is different. Something *cataclysmic,* in its way, happened there. Near that circle, Bartley, two civilizations clashed—two sets of gods and their tribes, and then those tribes were erased from all but the memory of the land. She was brought here, far from the seat of her power, and her strength failed, and when she lost her children there was nothing and no one for her on this side of the vast sea. None to venerate her. None to sacrifice to her. None to believe in her or her power, and, I think, she was stranded here. After all, Bartley, where does a dying god go?"

Eleven

"A gentleman is one who never hurts anyone's feelings unintentionally."

—Oscar Wilde

"Tomorrow is the last day of school, Mr. Bede," Bartley said. "What does Amy Proctor want with me?" Amy Proctor was the Director of Human Resources at the school. Whatever she wanted, it couldn't be good. *Mr. Hannigan, we'd like to give you a gold star for all your effort!*

"I'm just informing you that she needs to see you," Bede said, rifling casually through some papers on his desk in what Bartley felt was an attempt to conceal his private (and malicious) agenda.

"Well then, your job is done. Tell her I'm on my way."

He got up, and, muttering expletives, strode out of the office and down the hall, descended a flight of stairs and passed along another corridor to the Human Resources office. He knocked on Amy Proctor's door and walked in. She was just getting off the phone, probably with Bede. Was her smile forced? Definitely.

"Have a seat. Mr. Hannigan, please."

He almost felt sorry for her as she sat fidgeting with her pencil. She was young, good-looking, with dark hair, turquoise earrings. A few years ago, she was probably watching tennis matches at Smith College, going to dances over at Amherst, Saturday morning yoga classes, and cocktails at the Tunnel Bar. And now here she was caught up in the real world, like the rest of us, in the storm of pointless bullshit and petty politics, so far from the theoretical discussions, the dramatic readings, the sincere friendships—everything that she had no doubt loved about college life. Gone, alas, are those days, too soon.

"You can call me Bartley—we've known each other for a couple of years."

"Of course."

"I mean I hope you don't mind if I call you Amy."

"That's fine, Bartley."

"So, what, as they say, seems to be the problem?"

"Ah, yes, um, I don't know if I would call it a *problem*, it's just an issue we're trying to *clarify?*" She was speaking in 'up-talk,' so that the statement sounded like a question, a habit that had always troubled Bartley, since it seemed to suggest a lack of confidence.

"What do you need to clarify, Amy?"

"I has to do with the consultant—Ms. Gath?"

"Oh yes, charming woman."

"Um, yes, well, in your interactions with her, did you indicate to her that you were gay?"

"Yes, I did."

"You did."

"That's what I said, yes. Is that all?"

"What we're trying to clarify. . . ."

"You don't seem to know how to proceed. What is it exactly?"

"So, you told her you were gay."

"You typically like people to tell you the same thing twice?"

"No, sorry. Okay. But here's the thing." She poked at some invisible balloon in the air with the point of her pen. "You're *not* gay . . . are you?"

"Why? Does it matter?"

Words formed on her lips, but Ms. Proctor would not utter them until she had made some rapid diplomatic calculations. Then her mouth closed on the unspoken words and when it opened again, she said, "Well, no."

"All right, then. Thanks for your time, Amy. Hope I've *clarified* the situation."

He rose, and as he was about to leave, paused with the doorknob in his hand, turned back, and said, "By the way, I was given to understand, by Mr. Bede, that my conversations with Ms. Gath were . . ." he whispered the word, "*confidential*. So, I must say I don't much care for your *demarche*." He raised his eyebrows and sniffed indignantly before closing the door. Back in the corridor, he smiled as he imagined the captain's palm tree hurtling once more through the air.

His smile might have been broader if he could have seen the woman behind the door he had just closed. She sat quite still for a moment or two, gazing into the now unoccupied space before her desk. Her brow furrowed, and her right thumbnail slid between her teeth. Then she opened her laptop and went to dictionary.com to look up the word 'demarche.'

Harris always said that when he left a departmental meeting, or any meeting with a school official, he felt like Sparky, his Labrador Retriever, climbing out of some murky pond. He said that sometimes he actually shuddered involuntarily. It was as if he wanted to shake off the accumulated bullshit, in the same way the dog would shake the water in sheets out of his dense coat. Bartley understood the physical response entirely, and as he drove away from the school that afternoon, he did shiver suddenly in Harrisonian solidarity, or maybe due to a similar unconscious need.

The mechanism he had developed to survive was to compartmentalize his life. Once he left the building, he tried to enter fully into his other life, a world which did not include Bede, or DDM's, or PIMs, or MPI's or artifacts or Department of Ed-approved consultants. Outside of work, there would always be papers to correct and lessons to prepare, but that was the part of the job that was *real;* he didn't object to that, and certainly not to actually *teaching*.

Once again, he realized that leaving the building was the high point of his existence. What had the little man said? That he was "damned close" to being a "nonentity." It hadn't always been this way. If they would just let him teach! But they don't want the students to read something and then say how it makes them feel or why they like it or dislike it. Talk about it. No, they want them to write a five-paragraph analyzation of the theme proving something or other with evidence and quotations in MLA format! No wonder they hate reading! It's always followed by a punishment! "And it's a vocational school for God's sake!" he said aloud. He was sure it would be better to try to give them some positive experiences with reading, help them to see the beauty of a well-written sentence, to visualize a scene.

His gloomy mood began to lift, though. The June air was intoxicating. One more day in this place and then he would have the long summer to recuperate! He could, for a while at least, forget all the drivel. Forget the resigned weariness of Harris as he sat filling out Individualized Education Plans. Forget the hopeless face of the young teacher who told him that they had mixed non-English speakers with her regular students and told her to teach them all *The Odyssey*. When she asked Bede how she could teach Homer to students who would not know how to say, "Could I have a ham sandwich and a cup of coffee to go?" she was told—Bartley's hackles rose at the ignorant presumption—"you need to *differentiate* the content lesson plans." It infuriated Bartley to think of this dedicated young teacher asking for advice—for help—and getting meaningless and impracticable jargon.

Oh well, summer first. He pulled out of the school parking lot and saw the narrow pine woodland beyond which the river flowed. A few hundred yards upriver, it flowed around Wicasee Island, where, a mere few centuries ago, Chief Wannalancit had his lodge and raised his arms to hail the morning sun.

When workers built the foundation for the school, they had found an Indian graveyard. The dead were buried sitting up, with bows and arrows and war clubs, facing the East. Descendants of the tribe came down from Canada back in 1977 and reburied the remains in the state forest in accordance with the ceremonies of the tribe. The Indians returned to Canada, leaving the dead in their new graves in the whispering shade of oaks. All things must pass—even, he thought with satisfaction, the Department of Ed!

Bartley uncorked a bottle of Vouvray Moelleux from his father's cellar and threw some steak tips on the grill, while Cornelius leaned back in an Adirondack chair on the porch, absorbed in some texts he had ordered through the Royal Irish Academy. These works had titles like *Codices*

Hibernenses Eximii I: Lebor na hUidre, Aon Amharc ar Éirinn: Gaelic Families and Their Manuscripts, and *Gein Branduib maic Echach ocus Aedáin maic Gabráin.* There were also two volumes of a scholarly journal called *Ériu.*

At one point, Cornelius looked up and, as if awakening from a dream, leaned forward and asked, "Would you be wanting me to make a salad?"

"I'm all set—just get to the bottom of—all that!"

Cornelius rubbed his eyes, stretched and sat back. "That's the problem, you know, it's bottomless. The more you know, the more you realize what you don't know."

"Keep digging. After dinner let's go downtown for a pint or two of Guinness stout. We can certainly get to the bottom of *that*." Cornelius didn't protest, which was good, because the trip downtown with the lure of stout was all part of Plan C, code-named in Bartley's mind "Operation Maintain Cleanliness."

And so, it came to pass, that less than two hours later, Bartley Hannigan and Cornelius O'Tuama were perched at the bar of the Old Court in Lowell, each with a tall black pint of Guinness in front of him. It was still early; the college crowd had not yet arrived and were not likely to appear in force on a Monday night anyway, so there was plenty of room at the bar and at the tables along the wall. There was a muted soccer game on the TV, and softly, over the bar's speakers, a traditional Irish band was blazing away on tin whistles, pipes, and fiddles.

The tranquility of the scene was ruffled by the entrance of a woman—ruffled in the way that a delicious summer breeze ruffles the placid waters of a forest lake. She was a Latina with long dark hair and almond eyes. Bartley saw Cornelius take in her shapely figure with a sheepish glance and heard him murmur something in Irish. Though he didn't speak the language, he was pretty sure it might be translated accurately as, "Goddamn!"

The woman took a seat a few bar stools away from them.

"Hi," Bartley said. And as his head was turned away from Cornelius, he gave her a conspiratorial wink.

"Hello."

"I hope you won't be offended if I say you look lovely this evening."

"No, I am not offended. *Gracias*."

Cornelius cast an innocent sidelong glance at the newcomer, lifted his Guinness and took a long drink.

"What are you drinking?" Bartley asked.

"Let me see. I am going to have a Cosmo."

The bartender had been pretending to be busy straightening the beer bottles in the cooler, while, like Cornelius, he awaited with interest the outcome of this conversation. He was giving Bartley a minute to work the charm he had never known him to have. "Jimmy," Bartley now called, "make this young lady—what's your name?"

"Violeta."

"Beautiful name—charming name—would you please make Violeta a Cosmo, and don't stint on the vodka."

Jimmy was about to protest that he never stinted on the vodka, but decided, like a pal, that he should try to make Bartley look good. With an obsequious nod, he replied, "Coming right up, Mr. Hannigan."

Bartley addressed himself once again to the dark beauty to his right. "I'm Bartley Hannigan of the Hannigan Tree Farm, and a teacher at a local institute of learning. This gentleman on my left is my excellent friend Cornelius O'Tuama of Ballyvourney." He raised his glass in convivial cheer. "Would you care to join us, Violeta?"

She nodded obligingly. "Yes, I will join you," she said. She slid off her stool and took the one beside Bartley. Suddenly, she paused and with nose in the air said, "Mmmm. Bartley is your name?"

"That's right."

"Aye, *Dios mio*, I love your smell."

"Really?"

"You have just little light cologne. What it is called?"

"You know, I couldn't tell you. My son gave it to me for Christmas—it's in a blue bottle about this big." He made a "C" in the air with his index finger and thumb.

"I *love* it. And then, like beneath that I can smell some good, clean soap . . . like. . . ."

"That I know. It's Irish Spring," he said.

"I like it!"

Jimmy set down the Cosmo and Bartley told him to put it on his tab. Violeta sipped it and said, "Mmm, that is good. Thank you, Jimmy! Now, Bartley, if you don' mind, let me see your fingernails."

"My fingernails? Okay." He held his hands out as if he was about to begin a piano piece. She took them in hers and said, "Now. See? You have what they call the whole package! Nice clean, cut fingernails, you smell so good—smell is the most important thing for the woman! Your clothes are so fresh, too."

Bartley felt almost cruel, because he had sensed Cornelius drawing farther away from him and Violeta, and he had seen his hands slip under his arms. And he felt even worse when the Irishman spoke. "You know, Violeta," he said, "in addition to bein' a clean fella, a very clean fella that smells like a daisy, or, I mean, smells very good—also, Bartley here is also a fine man. A good fella, you know."

"Oh, thank you for telling me that, Cornelius. I love your accent! You look like a very big, strong man, too. Handsome, but you are more like the farmer, down-in-the-earth, type, right? Yes, I can see that— my father is a farmer in *Mexico*. That is very attractive also, only men like that got to try even harder. It's hard when a strong man works hard. A teacher—at an *institute*—he's not going to get his soft hands dirty anyway."

"I'm not sure I like the implication," Bartley began to protest, but she leaned in front of him and whispered to Cornelius, "I will tell you something. With your looks and strong body, if you clean up like this guy here? You will knock the ladies down!"

"Knock them down?" Cornelius never took his eyes off her as he swallowed some stout.

"You know! They will fall for you! They will fall down!"

The Irishman was mesmerized. He had a fleeting vision of a long row of women falling like dominoes before his clean, spruced-up, and sweet-smelling figure. "F-fall down?"

"Hard!"

"Wait just a minute, Violeta" Bartley interjected, "now my friend Cornelius here doesn't like water much, or soap, and I've tried to change that, but you know, I've decided to accept him the way he is. Maybe we should not try to change him. He has a very interesting theory that it's healthier *not* to bathe regularly, and that we all worry too much about odors. Hey, maybe he's right! Protective natural oils, you see? And if you're *too clean*, you have no *antibodies*. Maybe he'll live longer than all of us and be happier. I'm not going to try to change him anymore!"

"Hmmm, maybe you are right," Violeta said. "Maybe, Cornelius, you are like a philosopher, so that you don't care about women and like you are thinking about deep, things, *cosas profundas,* and you have no time to think about the females!"

"Well . . ." Cornelius ventured, in philosophical tones.

"Yes, that's it," Bartley said. "Very deep things. You are quite perceptive, Violeta. And not just of smells."

"Thank you, Bartley."

"Tell us about your farm in Mexico."

"My father, he grows coffee and sugarcane in Cazones, Veracruz. The coffee is like part of a cooperative that exports to America, but the sugarcane is for the domestic market. Also, he grows the pineapples, mangoes, cacao, and vanilla. It's beautiful."

"And did you not want to stay there?" Cornelius asked.

"Very much. But it does not produce big income, an' I want to save some money for land, maybe in Parras Valley in Cohuila, where I would like to try to have a wine-yar'."

"Vineyard." Bartley interjected. "It's pronounced *vin-yerd.*"

"Oh, *bin-yar.*"

"*Va*-vin-yerd."

"*Va*-vin-yerd."

"Perfect," Bartley said, imagining the little man sitting on a barrel of wine cheerfully waving an overflowing goblet in the cellar of Violeta's Mexican farm, singing away in his crooked Napoleonic headgear.

"But getting back to Cornelius," she said, and at those words the man from Ballvourney's head lifted and turned to her, hauled out of God only knows what fanciful dream or arcane Gaelic bypath. "I would like to take you shopping for some clothes. Oh yes, I can do it this week. And I can take you to the Portuguese lady that cuts my hair. She's very good."

"Oh, I can see that," Cornelius began.

"Just leave him the way he is! He's happy!" Bartley insisted. "Cornelius, tell her to stop!"

"Well now, you know, Hannigan, like, as my brother Dermot has often said, and 'tis true, 'A change is as good as a rest.'"

"But what about the protective oils? Remember? You'll be sick!"

In all his days, Cornelius had never seen the kind of magic that Bartley's *smell* had achieved with this creature. Soap—shampoo—clean fingernails—light cologne—he had never suspected that these things had such power to charm. And for the first time, he imagined himself not with a stolid woman of the rugged farmlands or the black shadowy mountains, trudging along the *boreen* in a shapeless coat and Wellington boots, lugging a bucket in each hand, but with a—what was the word the Americans used—a *babe! Who cares* if she could not make boxty or a pot of colcannon? "You know, Bartley," he concluded, "I think I'm going to risk it."

And thus, was the reborn Cornelius conceived in innocence and dedicated to the proposition that women prefer soap and scissors to natural oils and boggy animal health.

They ordered some sandwiches and Bartley basked in the glow of Violeta's feminine allure, and a mission accomplished—a Cornelius devoted to cleanliness. Not to mention that tomorrow was the last day of school!

At the height of his elation, he thought of his son for some reason, and was struck with the sudden desire to speak with him. He excused himself and went to the lobby.

"Dad, this is spooky. I *just* told Jill that I was going to call you."

"Strange. Just wondering how you were doing."

"We're getting married, Dad."

Bartley was stunned into silence, dismayed somehow to hear those words from one he still thought of as so very young.

"Dad?"

"Sorry, Manus. You took me by surprise. Congratulations!"

"Jill is here. Let me put you on speaker, Dad."

"Hi, Jill," Bartley said.

"Hi, Mr. Hannigan," she said, rather shyly, as always.

"Call me Bartley! We're going to be family. That's great. You two are wonderful together." There was so much he wanted to say, but he didn't know how, or where to begin. *Be patient! Talk things over—you have to be able to talk about everything—money, sex, relatives, goals, all honestly and without fear. Be patient. Take love easy. What did the old song say? She bade me take life easy, as the leaves fall from the tree. . . .*

Ah, but who was he to give advice? And at Manus's age, would he have listened? Did he listen when his father told him, "You'll make a hash of it, marryin' that *Smollet* one!" No, but without Adele, there would be no Manus, and so he contented himself with the mistake to have the miracle.

"When is the wedding?"

"October. It's just a wedding party, Dad. I mean, we'll be married at city hall, and then there'll be a party after at the Mt. Pleasant Golf Club. We don't want to blow, or have our parents blow, thirty grand on a wedding."

Bartley was still in shock. "You mean October of next year?"

"No, October of this year. Dad? There's only one thing. And I hope it's not too awkward. Mom said she'd like to bring some guy named Donald to the party. He's a salesman at her company."

"Not a problem. We're all adults."

"Do you think you want to bring anyone, Dad?"

"Yes, maybe."

"I mean, are you seeing anyone?"

Sure son, I'm crazy about this Mexican stripper. "Well, not seriously, you know, but maybe just for company. I'll let you know. Hey, congratulations again! This is exciting. Sudden, but exciting. We'll have to talk about your plans, see if there's any way your mother and I can help, all that."

"All right. Are you okay, Dad?"

"Oh, absolutely. I'm just having a beer with a couple of friends downtown."

"Okay, that's great—I'll let you go. We'll send you an invitation this week with the details."

"My love to both of you!"

They signed off, a duet of goodbyes and well wishes, but Jill still called him Mr. Hannigan, for which he couldn't blame her.

He stopped in the men's room, and saw that someone had written on the wall above the urinal:

Things I hate:

1. Vandalism

2. Lists

3. Irony

Bartley pulled a pen out of his pants pocket and scrawled—

4. *Donald*

Childish, yes. He shrugged. So be it. He wondered if she had been screwing old Donald while they were still married and in counseling. *Oh, who cares.* His father had it right long ago—one big hash.

Soon after Bartley returned, Cornelius began to chat with a grizzled English chap they called Step-and-a-Half, or Steppy, because of his limping gait—the result of a compound fracture sustained in a rugby match in his youth in Liverpool. Bartley leaned closer to Violeta and said, "I love your smell, too." She smiled, and Bartley saw something—was there a little timidity behind the smile? But how could an exotic dancer be timid? Only if she cared about him.

"My son, Manus, is getting married."

"Oh, that is great. Are you happy?"

"Yes, I suppose—I just hope everything works out for him. But I was wondering, if you're around, if you'd like to go to the wedding—in the fall?"

"Soon! Yes, I would like to go if you don't disappear on me again before that."

"I've had to admit to myself that that was a mistake. It's just. . . ."

"My job."

He nodded, somewhat apologetically. "Yeah, your job. It's none of my business, but honestly, that's why I've hesitated to call. It's not what a man hopes for in a woman he really likes."

"Bartley, I don' like to do that job. I put aside my pride because I have to do it."

"For your farm?"

"I do want a farm. This face you see, in a while will be wrinkled, this hair will be white. You know the woman's beauty fades. But the land is beautiful forever, just like the good heart like yours is good forever. And I have other reasons that I can't explain now. You have to trust me. I do it, just for a while longer."

He nodded. "I understand. It's just—you understand. It's difficult for a man."

"Oh, yes. Of course." She took his hand and squeezed it softly, "You know *why* I take, why I took care of you the night you came in, and then I went with you and we see the little man?"

"In fact, I've been trying to figure out how a woman like you would have ended up with a drunken disgusting lout."

"You don' remember the guy, the jerk, he said a bad comment to me, and you told him, 'Hey, show some respect, asshole!' I laughed at that. And the guy, he said, 'Shut the fuck up, who is talking to you?' And he said, 'I'll tell her whatever I want! She is just a stripper.' And then, Bartley, I heard *you* say, 'Just because she is a stripper, that does not mean she does not have a *soul*.'"

Bartley saw her eyes fill, and he leaned closer and put his arm around her. In his memory, the entire incident was little more than the shadow of a dream—some noise and confused chatter overheard in another room. And yet her words brought to mind what Septo had said: *If you can't see she has a lovely soul, why then you're as blind as one of those craychers at the bottom of the sea where they've no light, nor any use for light.*

"Yes," he said, "Drunk as I was, I could see that."

Violeta turned her head upward and they kissed, a romantic gesture which raised the bartender's eyebrows considerably as he passed with a flowing pint. Then she drew back. "And then the guy, he said something stupid again an' you tried to fight with him, but you were very drunk, oh, but you broke his nose, and then the bouncer came and Mr. Catania, he's the owner of the club, I tell them I know you and it was not your fault and then we put you in a seat until I drive, I *drove* you to your father's house, because you say it's not far and you don't want to go to your house in Lowell because—well, anyway, you don't want to go there." She paused and asked, "How did you get out to the Big Moon, anyway?"

Bartley squinted as he peered through the mists of alcoholically-fogged memory. "I was drinking with some guy I used to know at the Old Worthen. And he said, 'Let's go to the Big Moon.' So, I went with him, and then I lost him, I guess."

Violeta nodded as if all that was perfectly understandable. "I was just going to get you onto the couch there, but we heard the little man singing in the cellar. . . ."

"Ah, the little man."

"And then, later when I was leaving, you got in the car with me, and you know the rest."

"Weren't you kind of *shocked* about the little man?"

"No, in Mexico, we have *duendes*, little people with long hair who like to run around naked. They live in the . . . the *selva*, but you don't see them unless they are drunk, and they forget to hide. Maybe that's why we see Don. . . ."

"Nippery Septo."

"Yes. My grandfather met one *duende* who was drunk. My grandfather was leading his *burro* along at night, and the *duende* asked him for a ride. My grandfather was scary, I mean scared, and he said okay. The *duende* rode for a while—then he disappeared."

"Did you tell anyone about Don Septo?"

She wagged an index finger. "In Mexico, the people, they might believe me about that, because also they have the *alux*, which appear like little Mayan people, yes. But here, I don't say anything because you tell that stuff to Americans and the conversation is going down the hill very fast. They will say, 'The Mexican is *loca*.'"

"'Down the heel?' Oh, *downhill*." Her accent still tripped him up from time to time. "I know you're not crazy. *And* if it were not for you, I would think that *I* was crazy."

He was getting to the bottom of his Guinness, and decided it was time to call it a night. As a teacher, he had to be very careful about the .08 alcohol limit, which he had always considered a dangerously low threshold. He didn't want to leave Violeta, though. Not at all. "Listen," he said, "it's the last day of school tomorrow before vacation, so I have to leave the house early, but would you like to come out and see what we've been doing at the farmhouse, and maybe spend the night? I mean, since I smell so good and everything?"

"If I spend the night, you're not going to disappear to me again? Hmmm?"

"I can't do it. Like Sinatra said, 'I've got you under my skin.'"

"Okay, then come fly with me."

He almost spit out the last mouthful of Guinness.

"I know Sinatra, too," she said. "Of course."

What a woman, he thought. "You want to follow me?"

"I remember where was the house. I was not drunk!"

When the three of them were leaving, Steppy, the Liverpudlian, nodded toward the departing figure of Cornelius and whispered to Bartley, "Nice fella, but I wouldn't bring him to the Adelphi."

"Are you referring to his odor?"

He grimaced and nodded. "It'd frighten a police horse."

"After tonight, he may be cured, Steppy."

"Jasus!" Cornelius said when they were in Bartley's car, "You say she's comin' home to see your wood etchings? I didn't even know you made wood etchings!"

Bartley cracked his window. "Actually, she's coming home because I think we are going to do that thing that male and female *homo sapiens* do sometimes when they get together. Don't worry—I'll turn up the radio! But—shit—I have to stop at the Pawtucket Pharmacy for some protection."

"From Violeta?"

"From babies!"

Cornelius shook his head. "Male and female *homo sapiens*. By God, Bartley, never again in this life will I underestimate the power of soap."

While the moon, with sad steps, mounted the sky above the farmhouse and, on a ridge above the river, bathed the circle of stones in its light, Bartley, in sleep, relived what had been. The supple warmth of her, the fragrance of her, the bare smoothness of her, her breath on his neck, her hands caressing him, her mouth on his, softly, then harder; her dark hair brushing his chest, her breasts, paler than her body, gleaming in the dimness of the room and swaying gently as she moved, like a censer on a golden chain, a tender offering; her body enclosing him, enfolding him, wholly at one with him, moving in a rhythm as old as the race—she whispered words he could not understand, and yet did understand, more fully than any that had ever been spoken to him.

The next morning, a little after dawn, Bartley awakened, gladdened to see the dark hair and olive skin of the woman who slept beside him. He raised himself on his elbow to watch her sleep. As if she felt his gaze, she opened her eyes, blinked, and smiled. He leaned to kiss her just as she rose to kiss him, and their foreheads collided.

"Ow!"

"¡Ay!"

The two of them rubbed their heads, but they were soon laughing, not only because the pain had faded, but also because they could hear Cornelius in the shower. Bartley jumped up and opened the bedroom door, so they could listen to the Irishman singing one of the plaintive airs of his nation:

> *"Damsel of the queenly brow"*
> *I spake, "my life, my love,*
> *What name, I pray thee, bearest thou*
> *Here or in heaven above?"*
> *"Banba and Éire am I called*
> *And Heber's kingdom, now enthralled*
> *I mourn my heroes, fetter-galled*
> *While all alone I rove."*
>
> *Together then in that sweet place*
> *In saddest mood we spoke*
> *Lamenting much the valiant race*
> *Who wear the exile's yoke*

Most of the lyrics that followed here were rendered incomprehensible, suddenly inter-spliced as they were with a lot of blubbering and sputtering, regaining comprehensibility with the final lines—

> *And see naught but the willow withe*
> *Or gloomy grove of oak.*

"I would not have believed it," Bartley said to Violeta. As Cornelius exited and padded down the hallway in his towel, Bartley yelled after him, "You Irish and your gloomy groves!"

They took turns using the bathroom; Violeta came out complaining that she'd had to brush her teeth with her finger. Bartley said that he would make them coffee and a quick breakfast—but in response to a certain look in Violeta's eye, a certain arch in her left eyebrow, and in her back, (clad though she was in one of his own tee shirts)—he cranked up the radio, just in time to hear Teddy Panos's daily radio salutation. "*Gooooooood morning Merrimack Valley! And welcome to the dawn of a new day!*" They jumped back into bed and welcomed the new day.

The silver case now held only one cigarette. As he drove to school, he cracked the window and fired up the first of the day, and what he decided would be the last of his life, while listening idly to Red Sox chatter on the sports channel. As he pulled into the school parking lot, his cell phone rang. It was Sheila Vondersaar, the unofficial chief of the D&E Book Club. Bartley considered her a friend, so he was somewhat taken aback when she opened with, "Bartley—what the hell is wrong with you?"

"Good morning, Sheila."

"You know, I never took you for such a *prick!*"

"So, you've been talking to Louise—"

"You took her out, went with her to her reading, and then told her, if I'm quoting correctly, 'Your poetry sucks and I hate it.'"

"Was that wrong?"

"Not funny!"

Bartley got out of the car, grabbed his briefcase, and took a few drags of his first and last cigarette as he walked across the parking lot. He decided that his need for nicotine had already left him; the coffin nail tasted stale. He let it fall to the asphalt and crushed it under his shoe, saying, "Listen, I *tried* to be nice. I *tried* to be diplomatic and circumspect—she was having none of it. She called me a cowardly hypocrite. She *demanded* the truth, so I gave it to her. Then she spray-painted my car with a lot of . . . aspersions! She's psycho."

"Oh, I don't think she'd do that. Are you sure it was her?"

"Sheila, vandals write, 'You suck.' Only psycho poets write, 'No soul.'"

"That's not her version. All I can say is you are none too popular at the book club."

"Oh well, that's too bad. You know, aside from Louise, I've been a little preoccupied with death and divorce and other stuff."

"Sorry. The club sent flowers."

"Thank you. They were beautiful. What are you guys reading, anyway?"

"We're reading *Massacre on the Merrimack*—it's about Hannah Dustin and how she was kidnapped by the Indians in 1687, but then she murdered ten of them with their own tomahawks one night and escaped. It's a fascinating book, but I honestly don't think you're welcome."

"You don't imagine that *anything* would induce me to return to the book club to chat with Louise about a woman murdering a bunch of men with a tomahawk!"

"She wrote a poem about her."

"Oh, Christ. I'll bet she did."

"Louise says you left your wife to move in with an Irish guy? Did you come out of the closet or something, Bartley? I mean, I don't care! You know me. I was just wondering."

"*I'm not gay!*" he said, a little too loudly, just as Mr. Silk, carrying a bag lunch even on this half day, walked past him, nodding discreetly, and smiling faintly. "My father invited him over from Ireland, and he arrived after my father's death."

"A relative?"

"No, not a relative."

"A friend of your father's?"

"Ah, yes. Cornelius O'Tuama. Just come to experience America. I'm in love with a woman, actually."

"Louise?"

"*What?* Have you been listening?"

"It's just that the whole thing does suggest *a kind of* passion. And I know relationships have their ups and downs."

"Sheila, I don't have a *relationship* with her. I never did! I liked her. We had dinner. We may have flirted a little bit. That's it. Then I changed my mind about her. Can I change my mind?" He gazed up at the looming high school. "I have to go into the building."

"All right, all right, goodbye."

"Just tell the others that there is another side to the story."

"I'd rather not get involved."

"Like the angels who sat on the fence. . . ."

"What angels?"

"Never mind. I have to get in there, Sheila."

"I said goodbye, then you started talking about angels."

"All right. Sorry. Goodbye. But she's psycho!"

"So you say. Goodbye."

"And her poetry really *does suck*."

"Goodbye!"

"Goodbye."

Of course, the students had no intention of doing anything on the last day, that is, the half of them who showed up. Grades had already been submitted, and they knew it, so there really wasn't much point in trying to pretend. Bartley thought he should try to pass on some parting wisdom to them, something they might take away if they had learned nothing else. "You know," he began, when he had got their attention, "I know you guys think that some—a lot—of what we read this year was boring, but it's all part of expanding your mind, and helping you grow as a human being. The more things you're interested in and passionate about, the more alive you are, you see? Education is just learning to appreciate things. And the more you appreciate, the more interesting life becomes. Go to museums. Learn about where you came from. Read books. Learn to paint or write or play a musical instrument. Talk to people who don't see the world the way you do. You'll be surprised! You'll find out things in the world are not the way you thought they were, believe me. Life is more than a video game. Watch a sunrise. Witness the glory of Nature. Get out in the woods and the mountains!

You may even sense something like God out there, or maybe a goddess! Get passionate about life! Can anyone tell me something that you're really passionate about? One thing that you think is amazing or fascinating or that you'd like to learn about or that you can't wait to do or experience?"

He looked expectantly at the group of passive faces. "Anyone?"

Tentatively, a hand rose. "Yes, Jaylein?"

"Can I go to the bathroom?"

Bartley's shoulder's slumped and he shook his head sadly.

"I thought you were done talking," Jaylein said.

"Yes. I am." He went to his desk and wrote her a pass, muttering to himself, "Where is Doctor Kevorkian when you need him?"

Harris, who had a "prep period," came in during what was the last class of the school year. A few students played hangman on the blackboard, while others chatted about their summer plans or played checkers at a board Bartley had found in the closet.

Harris sat down beside Bartley at his desk. "We survived another one," he said. "You going to Boomer's for a twenty-two-ounce IPA when we get outa here?"

Bartley smiled and nodded. "Oh yeah." Then he said, "I think I'm in love, Harris. No, *I am* in love."

"How do you know?"

Most people would have asked, "With whom?" Bartley reflected, but Harris wanted to know how he knew. He thought about it for a minute, and then said, "When I was a kid, I had this dog, good old Prince. He was a Springer Spaniel I got at the pound—his master had died, so I got him when he was already three years old. Anyway, I loved that dog right away, and pretty soon, he loved me. Once, I thought he was in the yard, but he got out somehow—I got on the bus, and I was halfway downtown when someone said, 'Look at the crazy dog chasing the bus!' And there was Prince, ears back, tongue hanging. He would have chased that bus until he dropped because he knew I was on it. I became so attached to that dog—it was like we understood each other. I had to leave every morning to walk to the school bus stop, and I would sneak out the front door, 'cause he was in the fenced-in back yard. But no matter how quietly I went out, he sensed it, and he would go to the part of the fence where he could see me walking away. He didn't bark or cry, but he would just stand there, with his ears raised, watching, and I used to feel broken-hearted that I had to leave him, and he didn't know why or for how long. I always wanted to run back and hug him and reassure him, but I thought that would just make it worse."

Harris was listening intently, though Bartley thought he must wonder what any of this had to do with his being in love. "Anyway, when I left . . . this woman this morning, I felt a kind of pain at leaving her, like I used to feel when I had to leave Prince. I know it sounds strange. It was like it hurt to leave her. I wanted to run back and hold her and kiss her and tell her that I wouldn't—that I *couldn't* leave her."

Harris nodded, and made a sort of duck face for a few seconds. "Wow," he said finally, "an affection that can be compared to a boy's love for his dog? All I can say is, you really got it bad. God knows I love my Sparky. Best friend a man ever had." There was no note of sarcasm in the comment. And Harris never did ask who she was.

A few minutes later, the students were standing by the door, watching the clock. The bell rang for summer vacation, and they shouted, "Have a good summah, Mista Hannigan!" and exited into the general chaos of cheering and howling in the corridors.

The teachers had to complete the end of year "checklist" before signing out with their supervisors. It was at his sign-out that Bede informed Bartley that he had been seen smoking a cigarette in the parking lot, and reminded him that smoking by anyone, anywhere on school grounds, was illegal under chapter something or other of some law and would not be tolerated. "By the way," he added, with condescending solicitude, "if you'd like to quit, we do offer a program through the Employee Assistance Program."

"Not necessary," Bartley responded. "I don't smoke."

"You don't smoke?"

He shook his head. "Nope."

"And yet, as I said, you were smoking this morning on school grounds."

"I quit."

"You quit this morning, after you were seen smoking?"

"Bingo."

"I don't know how to say this, exactly, Bartley, but it seems to me that . . . sometimes, for you, that truth is . . . how shall I say it?" He tented his fingers and puckered up his face, as though he were a real wordsmith searching for sublime expression. "That, very often, the truth is whatever is convenient for you at the time."

"Is that so? I'm sorry to spoil your Holmesian deductions, but if you want to test your hypothesis, you might take a stroll down to the waste bin in the Teachers' Resource Center, the one near the copy machine. An examination of the contents therein will uncover a silver-plated cigarette case—probably worth a few bucks—evidence of a final, resolute act performed on the final school day of this school year, by a man who has committed himself to a smokeless life." Bartley smiled.

Bede frowned, and said, "Fine." He quickly regained the upper hand, however, by informing Bartley that his evaluation binder was missing a "Pre-Assessment Analysis." *Analysis Paralysis*, as Harris would say. In this case, it was Bede's way of keeping Bartley for another hour in the building fiddling with bullshit paperwork while his friends drank end-of-the-year beers at Boomer's.

"Is this *really* necessary?" he ventured. "I didn't see it on the checklist."

"It wasn't on the checklist because it was due *last November*."

Bartley did his best to quell a surge of bitterness as the words *analysis paralysis* bounced vexingly around his cranium. "I was busy *teaching*."

"And how can we evaluate your teaching *performance* if you are noncompliant with teacher evaluation protocols?"

"So, you decided to solve this little paperwork problem on the last day of school."

The bastard suppressed a smile. "I can't sign you out until the paperwork is complete."

The two of them sat there staring at each other for a full ten seconds in silence, Bartley looking as if he had just caught wind of a foul odor, and Bede as if his dignity had been impugned by an unworthy personage. It was obvious to Bede that Hannigan wanted to lean over his desk and shout, "Shove your protocols up your fat ass!" And it was obvious to Hannigan that Bede didn't want to say anything, but that he was *thinking*, "Go ahead, you fake homosexual! Make my day. Let me add 'insubordinate' to 'noncompliant,' on your personnel file, and push you into a corner from which you will only escape by leaving my department, and preferably the school."

He spoke the following words as if he might choke on them. "Neglected to hand my analysis of the pre-assessment, eh? Well, to quote Marc Antony, 'if it were so, it was a grievous fault indeed,' and I will see to it immediately. I will review the pre-assessments, which are in my cabinet, and analyze those outdated and useless results and fill out the little forms so that you can put a check mark somewhere and stuff them in a folder, and stuff the folder in a file drawer, never to see the light of day again." He scratched an eye with his middle finger, rose, and headed back up the staircase and through the deserted corridors to the room he had hoped not to revisit until the last week of August.

Twelve

"There are more things in heaven and earth,
Horatio, than are dreamt of in your philosophy."

—Shakespeare

By the time he made his escape from the institute, Bartley was hardly in a convivial mood. For fear that he would be a downer to his celebrating colleagues, he skipped the celebration at Boomer's and drove back to the farm.

Cornelius was sitting on the porch. At least he thought it was Cornelius; the transformation was stunning. The raggle-taggle gypsy had gone GQ. The mutton chop sideburns had disappeared, revealing a clean, well-shaven jawline. The herringbone cap was gone, too, and the shaggy mop of locks had been lopped and trimmed with a professional flair that left the Irishman looking— Bartley searched for the word—handsome? *Dapper?* Anyway, much improved.

And that was just the start of it. He had been clothes shopping, too, and Violeta (Bartley knew that Cornelius could not have done this on his own), had decked him out in a sort of urban cowboy look, complete with jeans, a pale blue denim shirt with mother-of-pearl buttons, and Frye boots.

"Holy crap," Bartley said, "you're gonna get more women than Robert Redford!"

Cornelius blushed and said, "'Twas only a bath, a bazzer and a rake of clothing."

"A what a what? What's a 'bazzer'?"

"A bazzer—a haircut."

"It's a stylish bazzer. And now that we can discuss such things *reasonably,* what kind of woman are you interested in, Cornelius?"

"I dunno, Bartley. Sure, I suppose I'd take any woman who'll have me. I believe I mentioned the lovely woman works over at the Special Collections

room of the Dunstable Library." He said her name wistfully and with rever-
ence: "Eva Angelina." His countenance took on a far-off look, as if the mere
mention of the name had raised him to some higher plane of contemplation.

"Pull yourself together, O'Tuama!"

"Right, well, Eva let me borrow a little mp3 player loaded with the songs
of the Beatles. It's great stuff altogether."

"Yeah, I've heard of the Beatles."

Bartley's cell sounded. He rolled his eyes as he looked at the screen. "Hi,
Adele." He got up and went into the kitchen.

"How are you?" she asked, but before he could answer, she continued.
"The agent says we have an offer on the house."

"Is it a good one?"

"About ten grand below asking price."

"That's fine."

"I think they'll split the difference."

"Okay. Who are they?" Bartley pulled the bottle of West Cork Whiskey
out of the cupboard and poured himself a generous tumbler.

"Young married couple. One daughter, two years old, but the woman is
pregnant. He's a fire fighter. She's a nurse."

"I hope they're happy there." *Happier than we were.* "Just accept the offer."

"You're not exactly a bazaar Arab when it comes to negotiations, Bartley."

"A couple of thousand isn't going to change my life."

"After we pay the rest of the mortgage and college loans there may not
be much more."

He swallowed some whiskey. "You make plenty. I make enough for me.
I don't spend much."

"Exciting news about Manus, isn't it?"

"Yeah, it's great," he said, saying a secret prayer that it would be great.

"I'll let you know about the signing, then. And, of course, I'll see you
at the wedding."

He knew her well enough to sense some tension, some unspoken question in her voice. "Are you bringing anyone?" she asked.

"Yes, I will be bringing someone, I think."

"The Irishman?"

He held the phone away from him and made a face at it, as if she could see him through the phone. "Why would I bring *a man* to my son's wedding? I mean, if I'm not gay, why would I do that?" He sipped the whiskey.

"*Have you* switched sides, Bartley?"

He laughed as he was swallowing, and sprayed the whiskey across the kitchen floor, doubling over in a bout of wild hilarity. The humor faded somewhat as he wondered if the rumor he had instigated in a moment of pique had percolated through the school and into the community, but then he reminded himself that he was done with caring about what other people thought and laughed some more.

"That's just like you," she fumed. "I try to have an honest discussion with you—ask you a simple question, which by the way, I think I have a right to ask—and you have to trivialize my feelings."

Bartley pulled himself together long enough to say, "Honey, I don't have to *trivialize* your feelings. They're *already* trivial."

"Oh yes, let's get right to the insults. The bottom line is you left your wife and moved in with a man."

"You skipped the part about you telling me you were divorcing me. Look, whatever. Think what you want, rewrite the story however you like. I don't care!"

"I just find it odd that as soon as you left, or I left, or whatever, you moved in with a man!"

"So, find it odd! You're not my wife! Listen to me. I *don't care* what you think!"

He heard her familiar puff of frustration. "Just don't embarrass me at the wedding party, Bartley."

"Goodbye," he said. But then he added, "And why would it embarrass you, anyway? Weren't you always the one talking about honesty? If your husband *was* gay, why would his honest expression of that fact *embarrass* you?"

"Oh, please. Don't get sanctimonious with me."

"Say hi to *Donald*," he said, but she'd already hung up, so, holding the phone at arm's length as if it were Adele herself facing him, he shouted, once more "I don't care!"

Cornelius passed by on his way upstairs and said, "Givin' out to the telephone are ye, Bartley? I shouldn't think you'd be in such bad humor and you starting summer vacation."

"You're absolutely right."

He finished his whiskey, flicked on the classical radio station, kicked off his sneakers and stretched out on the couch. He thought about Adele and all the years he'd wasted with a woman who made him feel small. How fucked up was their marriage that after so much time together, she wasn't even sure who he was? Did she think he might be gay because he wasn't into her S&M fantasies? Whatever!

Ah, but it was over, thank God, and it was *summer*. The accumulated stress of the years of a sucky marriage and the grind of a school year ebbed from his psyche in the golden light of that word. All the self-evaluations and goals and five-year professional development plans and common assessment sheets and DDM's and MPI's and PIM's and everything that distracted teachers from teaching—in short, all the *bullshit*—would wither and fade in the high burning sun of summer. Evaporate! The murky web of catch-phrases and buzzwords produced by people who needed a topic for their doctoral dissertations in Education but who had little or no real experience in the trenches of an American school, all would grow lighter and float away like the beautiful balloon in the song, while the corn in the field ripened. On the radio, a string quartet played Bach's "Sheep May Safely Graze." *Sheep may safely graze where a good shepherd watches.*

What serene harmony. The orderly strains, the finely-orchestrated variations washed over him as he slipped the bonds of consciousness. His body loosened the cords that connected muscle to brain and blurred and blunted the surrounding stimuli and his response, as he sank deep into the cushions of the couch. Soon, shifting images fluttered before his closed eyes and people visited like spirits, uttering words whose nonsensical nature troubled the sleeper not in the least. A parade of characters, often people he knew only vaguely, wandered through, and he found himself in a stream of various locations—a busy city, a small town, and a football field of his high school days on which the players all peered into a deep ditch—a grave, in fact, a neat rectangle cut into the turf in the end zone. *Touch down.* The goal of all our lives.

When he awoke it was dark, and someone—Cornelius, of course—had thrown a sheet over him. God, he had slept into the night, and so delicious was his relaxation that, after a stumbling visit to the bathroom, he went back to the couch and fell once again into dreams of which he would later remember nothing, until deep into the night. Then he seemed to walk, in a downpour, the street where he had lived with his family. There he met Manus, who told him, "I'm sorry, Dad."

"You have nothing to be sorry for!" Bartley said.

Finally, he was on a boat, rocking and bucking as it shot the rapids of a river. The helmsman was calling his name, loudly, when he realized that no, it was not—he was not—"*Wake up*, Bartley!"

Cornelius stopped shaking him when he opened his eyes, very wide, regaining his bearings. "Jesus," he asked, "wha—what's up?"

"Come on, we've got to start out while it's still dark."

Bartley could smell coffee. "Still dark. Where?"

"To the circle. It's June 21st."

He ran his hands through his hair. "Meaning?"

"And you the son of a farmer!"

"The summer solstice?"

"Ah, and who is it says you're not the full shilling, Bartley boy?"

"I've never heard *anyone* say that," he said as he sat up and stretched.

Toast sprang from his father's old toaster, and after they had slathered the golden bread with rhubarb jam and washed it down with coffee, the Irishman took his blackthorn from behind the door and they set out on the long path to Druid Hill. A waning crescent moon floated behind them in the south, while the sky was lightening to their right in the east. And though the sun had not yet risen, the dawn choristers of robins, goldfinches, sparrows, starlings, and nuthatches already charmed the air with a riot of song. Bartley recalled the words of Thoreau: "Only that day dawns to which we are awake," and rarely had he felt so awake.

When they arrived, Cornelius had them take up their positions at the western end of the circle, facing the two portal stones. The trills and melodies that emanated from the bird-rich trees seemed to reach a crescendo as the last vestiges of night fled before the brightness unfurling in the east. A thin ribbon of purplish cloud sat on the horizon, or what they could see of it through the trees; they watched it lighten into gray and finally pink as the sun peeked over the rim of the earth.

"'Dawn spread out her fingertips of rose' as oul' Homer put it," Cornelius said.

Then the sun rose and stood like the god that it was between the two portal stones, its rays illuminating the recumbent stone at the opposite side of the circle. The rising sun, or something, hushed the birdsong.

Cornelius handed the knobby blackthorn to Bartley. He stepped to the center of the circle, arms raised to the sun, and began to intone in the old tongue:

Sith co nem.
Nem co doman.
Doman fo ním,

nert hi cach, án forlann,
lan do mil, mid co saith.
Sam hi ngam, gai for sciath,
sciath for durnd.

Bartley stood still as the words filled the grove. Although they were strange to his ear, he sensed a power in them.

Dunad lonngarg; longait-tromfoíd
fod di uí, ross forbiur
benna abu, airbe imetha.

Mess for crannaib, craob do scis
scis do áss, saith do mac
mac for muin, muinel tairb
tarb di arccoin, odhb do crann,
crann do ten.

Tene a nn-ail. Ail a n-uír
uích a mbuaib, boinn a mbru.

Bartley sidled along the exterior of the circle, seeing Cornelius' face in the rosy rays, his eyes closed, arms still spread, the morning resounding with his strange incantation. The Irishman's hair stirred, and Bartley felt a breeze that seemed to sweep upward from the river and move the now silent boughs of pine, birch, and oak. Cornelius continued, his voice growing louder.

Brú lafefaid
ossglas iaer errach,
foghamar forasit etha.

Iall do tir,
tir co trachd lafeabrae.
Bidruad rossaib, síraib rithmár,
'Nach scel laut?'

Bartley heard a flutter of wings and then a sound behind him, like someone running hard through the woods. His back against a stone, all his senses alert, he watched and listened. There was nothing, only the trees, their trunks bathed in the glow of the dawn of the year's longest day. Certain that he had heard something, he peered as deeply as he could into the woods, moving now to his left as he searched for some sign.

When it came, it came suddenly. Air rushed past him—he heard a fhwacking *pop* like a parachute opening. Bartley whirled about and saw that Cornelius had been knocked to the ground and seemed to be struggling to pull something from his pocket. Over him stood a creature the likes of which Bartley had never imagined, let alone seen.

In her bare feet, she was taller than either of them. Her wild hair was black, and she wore a headdress or perhaps a crown spiked with the feathers of a raven. On one bare, muscled arm, he saw a tattoo of a triskelion, and about her neck, a string of wolves' fangs. A mantle of what looked like the fur of a gray timber wolf was cinctured at the waist with a great belt from which hung, beside her powerful legs, a sword in a silver scabbard engraved with a complex lattice work of Celtic interlacing, the work of a master metalsmith. The grip of the sword was green, and the pommel formed the antlered head of a stag.

He could feel his heart beating in his mouth, fear tinged with awe. "Cornelius!" he cried.

She turned her gaze on Bartley; it was a cold gaze indeed, for her eyes were yellow, and he felt as if some strange bird were examining him. But he was beneath her notice, and again she faced Cornelius, who was back on his feet, holding a St. Brigid's Cross before him, speaking rapidly, at first in Latin, and then once again in Irish.

He seemed to be asking her a question. Bartley watched closely, gripping the blackthorn and hoping that her hand would not touch the hilt of that great sword. And then she spoke, in a voice that defied nature, defied imagination.

It was three voices, sometimes sounding individually and sometimes in unison. The voices were those of a child, a mature woman, and an old woman, but the language was Irish.

More than anything up to this point, that voice, or those voices, frightened Bartley. His knees were actually shaking, and Cornelius, sensing his terror, moved closer to him and whispered urgently, "For God's sake man, *fill yer boots!*"

Just as urgently, Bartley shot back, "I'm about to fill *my underwear!*" He supposed the Irishman was telling him to buck up, which he made an effort to do, taking some deep breaths.

The creature was still speaking to Cornelius, more softly now. He lowered the cross and bowed before her, at which point she took a step toward him, reached out and touched his head, fondly, it seemed, the way the master would touch the head of an old hound, and Bartley was surprised to see what looked like tears glistening in those cold eyes.

The sun began to rise above the portal stones; dawn, as the poet wrote, was going down to day. She said something else that sounded like a plea, and her image grew translucent in the brightening air—then, a sudden swirling darkness enwrapped the wild woman. She stepped back and looked skyward before she was lost in its purling vortex. The inky cloud erupted in a piercing *caaaw* and a beating of wings. The men ducked as a shadow swept close overhead. And Bartley thought, *the goddess is gone!* For such she must have been.

"Jesus Christ, Cornelius! Did you know that was going to happen?" Cornelius was deep in thought, or trying to collect his thoughts, or something. "Cornelius!"

Finally, he looked at Bartley squarely. He pulled his cap more snugly over his head and said, "Listen, *me buachaill*, nobody ever knows what's going to happen, and that is particularly true when you're dealing with the otherworld, a glimpse of which you've just taken in. I took a chance based on experience and a hunch. I was shocked, yes, but not surprised."

"Jesus, Mary and Joseph. But who or what is she?"

"Have I not told you about the *Badb Catha,* 'the battle crow?'" Cornelius began to amble down the path while Bartley followed, casting apprehensive glances over his shoulder.

"I remember something about it. Then, you're saying, she was—"

"The Mórrígan, yes."

"Unless—maybe—we convinced ourselves somehow that we saw something that was illusory in nature, like a whaddayacallit. . . ." His hands moved in circles before him, as he tried to coax the words out of his brain. "Some kind of a shared delusion."

"Then let's compare notes." And Cornelius described the creature that he had seen, in detail.

"All right. My theory is shot to hell. I'm still adjusting to my new reality, or unreality. The little man was tough enough. But at least he was smaller than me, and he didn't have a fucking sword! Come on! What's she doing here? How did she get here? What does she want?"

"There's a problem, Bartley. I was speaking modern Irish to her, and she was answering me in Old Irish; I understood about half of it, maybe a bit more as she continued to speak. I've studied it on paper, you see, but I've never heard it spoken—no one has."

"What did you gather from what you *did* understand?"

Cornelius stopped short as they emerged from the wild woods and sat on an outcropping of rock from which they could see, on the descending slope, the orderly rows of Christmas trees. The thought struck Bartley that he would have to figure out what to do with all these trees—his father had had a routine in caring for them and getting them ready for sale. Cornelius answered, "One thing I understood was something like, 'You see me not as I am, but as I was.' Do you remember that I once told you that the 'wee people' were thought to have been descendants of the *Tuatha de Danaan*, and that they grew smaller as people ceased to believe in them?"

Bartley sat down beside him. "Yes, yes, I remember that . . . *story.*"

"I was reading a book about James Joyce by a Belgian fellow, a Dr. Lernout—and in the introduction, he discusses a passage from 'The Book of Matthew.' The evangelist recounts therein, you see, that Jesus remarked, on a visit to his hometown of Nazareth, 'A prophet is not without honor, save in his own country, and in his own house.' And Matthew concludes, 'He did not many mighty works there because of their unbelief.' St. Mark goes farther, and says, 'He *could not* do mighty works there.' Belief—or faith, if you like—maybe it really has power, Bartley. Gods grow strong in our faith or by our faith. Jesus *could not* perform miracles in Nazareth, because the people did not *believe* that he could. Their disbelief weakened him."

Bartley said nothing. It was as if some instinct or intuition grasped the idea, but reason would not allow him to accept its implications.

"She came here with them, Bartley. The stone circle was built to focus the power. There was enormous faith in her all over the Celtic world, including the band that came here to find a new land for the tribe. They crossed the ocean with her, and on her strength, and then they died. In this place."

"And so, you're saying, without their faith, she grew weak here, as Christ was weak in Nazareth?"

"Just so."

"If she was so powerful at that time, why did they lose?"

"Did you study the *Aeneid* in school? You remember that Carthage fell, even though Juno, the Queen of Heaven, loved Carthage above all lands?

Here were her arms, and her chariot; the goddess
Nursed the hope that should the Fates permit,
This race would rule all others, but anxiously she heard
that of the Trojan blood there was a breed
then rising, which upon the destined day
should utterly o'erwhelm her Tyrian towers,
a people of broad reach and conquest proud
should compass Libya's doom; such was the web
the Fatal Sisters spun."

"How much stuff do you have memorized, Cornelius?"

"Mnemosyne, Memory, was the mother of all the Muses, Bartley. People today believe in a new goddess, named Google. She sees everything, and she knows everything, and she understands nothing. I still believe in Mnemosyne."

"So, what you're saying is that Fate is more powerful than the gods."

"That would seem to be the consensus of all the ancients. Poseidon wanted to kill Odysseus while he was alone on the sea, but the Fates were against it. Even Juno couldn't save Carthage, nor could Apollo save Hektor from Achilles after Zeus weighed their fates in the balance—and the Mórrígan couldn't save those who called her here if it was their fate to die. As Horace wrote:

Ah! how oft shall he
Lament that faith can fail, that gods can change

Anyway, I think all these gods were, how can I say it, the sort of embodiment of the spirit of the tribe. Inspirational, I think, more than powerful in battle. Like, you know, in *The Iliad*, the gods take a hand in the fight in small ways, Apollo gives Patroclus a bit of a push in his fight with Hektor—that sort of unearthly help or hindrance we sometimes feel—but the gods don't win the battle for you—the belief gives you the strength to win it. And in that way, maybe *Kitchi Manitou* was helping the Indians while our Mórrígan helped the Celts, but fate, and numbers, still matter more than prayers."

"Gitchee who?"

"*Kitchi Manitou.* The god of the Algonquians," he said, "the Great Spirit," and in answer to Bartley's uncomprehending look, added, "Have you not read the history of your land, Bartley?"

"I guess not. And where is that god now?"

"Probably with the remnants of the tribe, far to the north."

"You talk about all this stuff as if it were *real.*"

"Millions of people, over thousands of years, have imagined it, and believed in it. So, in a way, it's more real than we poor creatures of a day."

"I know if I were to start to tell Harris, or people in general what just happened, they'd throw a net over me. Outside of you, and of course Violeta, the only person I tried to discuss it with was Adele, and she moved out shortly after. Not that that was a bad thing, but I learned my lesson."

Cornelius frowned. "This American insistence on a merely observable reality is all very queer, because where I'm from, folk tell stories about the fairies and the *daoine sídhe,* the supernatural beings, all the time."

"That's what Violeta said about where she's from."

"There are ancient stones in Mexico, too—bloody pyramids!"

"Honestly, Cornelius, when people tell these stories in Ireland, do others believe them?"

"In the cities, probably not. They might think you backward or superstitious. But in the country, well most people have caught a glimpse of something on the boreen of a dark night, and the nights are very dark away from the city lights. In the country pubs, the conversation often turns to strange figures seen under the stars near ancient sites."

"Anyway, this isn't Ireland."

"That hill, and the circle up there, is a portal to Ireland, or to an Irish otherworld. I can't explain how it is, or why it is, but that's *what* it is."

"This is crazy."

"Or maybe it's quite in the order of things—who knows? Definitive conclusions about the nature of this universe, boyo, are premature and arrogant." Bartley appeared to struggle to accept this observation, and so Cornelius added simply, "You know yourself. You saw her."

"I did," Bartley had to admit. "Let's go have a whiskey. Two whiskies. As my father once said, 'This is no time to quit drinking.'"

Thirteen

In smoky North End back rooms where men wearing large rings and dark suits sipped demitasses of espresso, Joe Catania was known as "*Il Maestro,*" or "The Teacher." This was due to his fondness for such expressions as 'I'll teach that Hatchet Burke a lesson he'll never forget,' and 'Lou DaSilva is gonna need an education.' To say that he was a guy who held a grudge was an understatement. Sometimes, especially when the rain gorged the gutters of his stately colonial home in Groton and splattered on the flat roof outside his bedroom window, he lay awake plotting ways to get even with double-crossers, snitches, and punks. This was not an unusual pastime among the members of the Dodge Square Gang; what was unusual was that some of the individuals on whom he planned a glorious revenge happened to be guys who had disrespected him in the schoolyard when he was twelve.

In his office in the back of the Big Moon, the Teacher was giving himself the evil eye in a full-length mirror, while threatening his image in the assumed characters of a menagerie of Hollywood tough guys. "Are you talkin' to me?" he asked his reflection. Two vertical creases formed between his lowered brows; his head tilted slightly and the dark eyes went blank in the pudgy, clean-shaven face. He lowered his voice a half-tone and repeated the question, adding a sharper edge to the word 'me.' "Are you talkin' to *me?*" He nodded, and as his mouth turned slightly upward in what he considered his "dangerous smile." He laughed softly, satisfied with the implied violence in his expression. "Go ahead," he said, "make my day . . . *punk!*"

He turned to view his profile and sucked in his paunch. Then he patted his slick, dark hair, stretched his neck like Rodney Dangerfield, as if his collar was too tight, though he was wearing not a dress shirt, but a Ralph Lauren polo shirt. He gave his shoulders a Cagney-esque shrug and sauntered over to a humidor that sat on an oak credenza. Raising the lid, he selected a 5 Vegas Classic, which he slid between his nostrils and upturned lip, inhaling appreciatively.

He leaned back in his ergonomic reclining leather chair with built-in lumbar support and deposited on top of his desk his three-hundred dollar Firenze Verona ox hide loafers with the elegant horse-bit buckle. He stared pensively at the ceiling for a moment, then shouted, "Franky!"

There was a stir in the adjoining room, followed by a crash, and Joe Catania exhaled noisily. The door opened and in popped a thin, angular face with wisps of hair sensing the air above a nearly-bald head. "Yes, boss?" the head asked.

"Frank, try to have a little fuckin' *dignity*." The Teacher raised a professorial finger. "Like the Bard said, 'Assume a virtue, ah, even if thou hast it not.'"

Frank the Plank's lips puckered and the head shook narrowly. "I don' know dis 'Bart,' but he talks kinda funny."

"Jesus, Frankie, 'the Bard' is Shakespeare! You know—from back in the 1800's! Din' cha go ta school? Is Vie-letta in yet?"

"Yeah, she's here. I seen her talkin' to—"

"Send her in."

The head withdrew, and Joe Catania unfolded the *Boston Herald*. He rubbed his smooth cheeks with the back of his fingers while he perused the box scores and waited. He felt lucky that he had found the Mexican girl. He smiled remembering what she had said. "Some people know how to keep a secret, Mr. Catania, and some do not. I know how to keep a secret, and I keep it deep. Like my father used to say, 'You live longer that way, *m'hija*.'" He had reason to believe her. He'd had other girls at the club try to get information out of her that he had told her was personal, and she had always been as quiet as the grave, which is where she could end up if she flapped her jaws. That would be a shame—good-lookin' girl.

Violeta was talking with Cesar, a Peruvian busboy and dishwasher. He was telling her that the menu, which consisted mainly of rice pilaf and fried chicken, should be expanded, but she reminded him that people—men—didn't come to the club for the food. She was feeling sorry that, when the operation went down, Cesar would be out of a job, and he had no papers.

The squirrely Frank ambled up and, jerking a thumb over his shoulder, said, "The boss wants ta see ya, Violeta."

"Tell him she's busy! She's talking to me," Cesar said, and Frank and Violeta both chuckled at that.

Inwardly, Violeta composed herself. She assumed the personality of the hapless illegal immigrant, grateful for a break. "Showtime," she said to herself.

Catania took his feet off the desk and sat up as Violeta came in. She stood meekly in front of his desk like a school girl in the principal's office. *Her* smile was not dangerous; it was tentative, ingratiating. She nodded, bowing slightly, as if she were in the presence of Juan Jurado Íñiguez, the Archbishop of Guadalajara, "Good morning, Mister Catania."

"Ah, bwenis dee-ass, Vie-letta. Pull that chair ova' here. Have a seat."

She complied, and he continued, "How's everything goin'? You still like the club?"

She said she did.

"No one givin' you any shit, right?"

She said that everyone was very nice.

"Good, good. You got a problem, you jus' let Mr. Catania know—it'll be taken care of. I like my girls happy, you know?"

She nodded and thanked him.

"OK, listen. I got another opportunity for you 'cause you're a good girl an' you talk Spanish. You can do me anotha favor. You're a rare typa girl. You don' get drunk, or fight with nobody, do drugs—I got no problems with you since you came here. In fact, I respect you very much."

"Oh, that is good to hear, Mr. Catania."

"Yes. Very much." He nodded. "So I got somethin' for you." He opened a drawer, took out a box, and slid it across the desk. "Just a little somethin'—don't tell the other girls—they get jealous."

"That is very kind of you, Mister Catania."

"Open it."

"*¡Madre mía!*" she said as she pulled up the lid, trying her best to be expressive. "But it's too much. I cannot take it."

"Take it," he said.

"Oh, but . . ."

"Take it."

"You are very generous," she said.

"That's a Jacques Cartier—that ain't no Walmart watch."

"I can see that. It's very nice," she said, thinking that his lack of class was evident in his need to point out how expensive his gift had been.

"I'm glad you like it. It makes me happy, you know?"

"It's beautiful," she said, infusing her voice with an awe of which she felt no trace.

He waved a dismissive hand. "Eh—fahget about it—it's nothin'. You're a good girl, Vie-letta. I consider you a friend who I can trust."

"Oh, yes. Of course."

As she drew a wayward strand of hair from her eyes, she glanced quickly and involuntarily at the power cord that was just visible at the foot of the curtains, into which a lamp, a Bose radio, and an exercise treadmill were plugged. It had been given to her by Ricardo Perez of the Criminal Investigation Division, and a Detective Chief Constable of the DEA named Sandoval. "Direct from Operational Technology Division," they said. The sight of the cord made her nervous for an instant. It looked like the power cord she had removed, but was actually a "room bugging electrical mains power transmitter" through which an agent was even now listening to their conversation. Perez thought it a perfect device for this situation; since it was plugged into its own power source, it would transmit 24/7. Violeta felt her heart beating faster for a moment, but she imposed a calm on herself and reasserted the trusting face.

"Oh, by the way," the Teacher continued, "you remember those guys that came in here that day back around February—the two Mexican guys—we had that business deal, an' I had you here 'cause they were talkin' a lotta Spanish to each other. You kinda kept me in the loop, which I 'preciate."

"Oh, yes—I remember." *How could she forget? Cachorro and Payaso. The shaved heads, the hard eyes, and the horrible tattoos of Santa Muerte, like the Virgin of Guadalupe in her starry robe, but with the skull face.*

"What did you say their names mean, in English?"

"Puppy and Clown."

He shook his head. "The tough guys I know got names like Hatchet and Cold Fingers and Hammer. What, are they trying to say that they're so bad that they can take funny names, weak names, and it don't matter?"

"I think, yes, that is what they are trying to say. They think it's more scary that way."

"Hmph. Strange. Now, you know this is—well, it ain't exactly legal. But you gotta do what you gotta do—like you crossin' the border in the trunk of a car, right?"

She understood the implied threat, that someone could call ICE at any time and have her deported, or so this man thought.

"I know you unnastan' the situation, so I took a chance on you, an' it worked out fine, 'cause I got a pretty good sense of people, Vie-letta. An' a'course I pay you well for your assistance."

"Oh yes, thank you."

"An' I mean, you know that if I don' take advantage of the opportunity, someone else will. It's supply and demand here in New England jus' like everywhere else. It's what people want, that's all."

"It's what *los gringos* want."

He laughed. "Yeah, it's what the gringos want, all right. Stupid muthafuckas that they are, pardon my Fran-say. And you never mentioned that deal to anyone, right?"

"Oh no, that's your business, Mr. Catania. I don't mention your business to nobody. That's personal, and could get *me* in trouble. I never want to mess up, you know, a business deal. I am not stupid."

"All right—just a reminder, an' it appears you understand the situation perfectly. I can see that, an' that's why I 'preciate your friendship so much." He paused and said, "Do you mind if I smoke a cigar? I know some women don't like it."

"Oh, I don't mind—my father smokes the cigars all the time."

"What does he smoke? What kind?"

Her father didn't smoke cigars. "*Te Amo. Puros.* All Mexican tobacco. He's a patriot."

Catania grinned. "A patriot, eh? That's rich."

He picked up a personalized silver-plated cigar cutter that looked to Violeta like a tiny guillotine and neatly snipped the end off the cigar. He leaned back and thumbed a flame from a matching lighter, engraved with the initials J.C. "Now, these guys will be coming back, with the, the stuff. I gotta pick it up—me an' a couple of my business colleagues. I would like you to come along in case I need you to translate something, an' just to keep your ears open—make sure we undertand everything that's going down."

"Yes, I can do that for you. When? Is it far?"

"Right down the river—not far, and I'll let you know when. It might be short notice, but don' worry. I'll pay you for your services, which I 'preciate, and again, as you say—this is my business, so it's personal. You don' mention it to boyfriends or BFF's—no one, or my colleagues get angry, and I'm afraid they have very bad tempers when people discuss their business. Like you said, it would be very bad for you. And for me."

"Not for anything do I talk about your business. Where I am from, you don't do that. Like my father used to say. . . ."

"You live longer that way."

"And I want to live a long time."

He smiled and nodded in a way that suggested that the interview was over. "That's why I like you," he said. "You know the shot." Violeta rose, but Catania leaned over the desk and whispered confidentially, "Leave that box here." A wink and a nod. "Just slip the watch in your pocket. The girls get jealous." He raised a finger to his lips. "*Mum's the word.*"

She had never heard the expression before, but she understood it well.

"Bartley! Bartley Hannigan!"

Peering out his bedroom window, Bartley saw a long black vintage Cadillac that looked like an antiquated batmobile. Next to the vanity plate, which said "FARMER," was a bumpersticker featuring a skull and crossbones and the words: DEATH TO TAXES. It was Farmer Lambeau, an old friend, or old former friend, of Happy Hannigan's.

"Bartley Hannigan!"

The window was open; he raised the blind and shouted to the caller, "Coming!"

He ran down the stairs and opened the door. The porch was vacant, but he saw Farmer limping up the hill away from the house. He wore baggy jeans, a short-sleeved plaid shirt and a porkpie hat with a wilting brim. Bartley trotted after him, awkwardly, in the flip-flops he sometimes wore around the house.

"Hey, Farmer—howsa goin'?"

The older man turned and extended a hand, a great calloused paw into which Bartley was almost ashamed to place his own soft teacher's hand. "Sorry I couldn't make the funeral. They had me scheduled for a new hip right after the wake. Still breakin' it in."

"That's your second one, right?"

"Second hip—got a new knee, too, and a pig's valve in my heart."

"Jesus, Farmer, you're like the Bionic Man."

He nodded and gazed skyward for a moment, serious and reflective. "The Bionic Man. Jesus, that sonuvabitch could run, couldn't he?"

"Yes. Yes, he sure could."

He withdrew from his bionic reverie and looked at Bartley. "So what are you doin' here, kid?" Farmer had called him "kid" since he was a kid.

"You mean about the trees?"

Farmer frowned, but didn't answer. *Of course he means about the trees.* "I haven't given it much thought, really," he said.

The older man's brow furrowed, his eyes narrowed, his lips pursed, and he shook his head discontentedly for a few seconds. Then he responded, slowly, as if he were addressing a child. "Don't you think it's time you *gave it* some thought? You have a working farm here. A hundred acres—roughly fifteen hundred trees per acre. That's one hundred and fifty thousand trees."

"That many . . ." Bartley said, scanning the serried rows.

"Your father would sell three thousand trees in the four weekends, not counting the weekdays, pay the help and pocket. . . ." His lips moved as he made a rapid mental calculation. "Over fifty grand."

"That much. . . ."

"If you never planted another tree, you could sell what you have for another ten years, but there are some things you gotta do, kid."

"Yeah, I was going to look into that. So, for example?"

"Every kind of tree has its own diseases—needle casting disease, fungus. The Scotch pines have a lot of issues. Spider mites, aphids, the pine spittle bugs. *And* different insecticides are good against different insects. Come on, let's take a walk."

He pointed to an outcropping of rock, a gray hump among the trees. "I was out here with your father one day. We saw a puma right up on those rocks. Some people would call him a catamount. He was watching us. You're so close to the state forest here, you can run into anything—coyotes, fisher cats, badgers, even black bears. You see a black bear, Bartley, you stare that son of a bitch in the eye while you back away. Don't run. Don't *ever* run. Unless he charges. Then you're screwed anyway."

"'A gentleman never runs,' as the Englishman said. Any wolves in the state forest?"

"Don't believe there are. But I was snowshoeing out near Gray's Landing on the Quabbin in western Mass. about twenty years ago. You feel like you're in Alaska. I saw two big gray wolves eatin' a deer on the ice, blood drippin' outa their jaws. I was damn glad I was upwind. I hid there, pretty still, for a long time until they were full and trotted off."

"Did you have a gun?"

"I had a 12 gauge shotgun."

"Which could kill a wolf, or anything else."

"Sure, but I was hunting pheasant, quail, rabbits. I was loaded with bird shot, which probably just would have pissed them off. Didn't expect to see any damn wolves!"

Bartley followed Farmer Lambeau as he strolled among the trees, feeling like a boy again, following his father, which made him kind of miss the old man. He watched the old farmer and woodsman while he paused here and there to wave a hand among branches and look a tree up and down like a hussar examining a war horse. "Not bad," he'd mutter, and continue.

But on East Hill he stopped short and said, "These trees here are all fucked up, kid. You got bugs sucking the juice out of the needles." Then, holding his hat down with one hand, he kicked a five foot tree, which immediately fell over, its root system exposed. *Pretty good kick for a guy with a new hip*, Bartley thought. Farmer reached into the clotted earth and came out with a fat white grub squirming in his fingers. "They're eating the roots," he said. He threw down the grub, pushed his hat back and said, "They become June bugs later on. Shit, kid, you gotta spray these trees, and mow around them. Your father used a Gravely mower with sickle bars. It's in the barn. Might want to change the oil and grease the gears."

"Really?" Bartley asked, uncomprehendingly, and unenthusastically.

"Damn right, *really!* What are you gonna do, let all this shit spread?"

"No . . . uh . . . well, yes, I think the mower is in the barn, and—"

"Luckily most of 'em are all right. Your father went in mainly for the New England historic Balsam Fir, and they grow good here. He got away from the Scotch Pines and the Fraiser Firs, for the most part. He's got a few oddball Cork Bark Fir trees. But you gotta nip this bug stuff in the bud. I'll tell you what to get."

"Okay, then."

"For cryin' out loud, you were raised here. I used to see you drivin' the tractor when you were a nipper."

"Sure, but I never stuck with it, and I never managed the farm."

"You'll do fine."

As they descended the long hill, they could see the house at the far end of an unplanted corn field; Bartley stopped short and said, "Oh, shit!" There was a yellow Volkswagen parked beside the greenhouse.

"Whatsa matter, kid?"

"This crazy woman—I had one date with her and she keeps haunting me because I didn't like her."

"Crazy woman?" Farmer asked. "I believe that's what they call *redundant*."

Bartley recalled that Farmer had had some problems with a highly volatile wife from whom he'd separated many years before. "No, they're not all crazy, but this one is *wicked crazy*—mad as a March hare. I just hope she's not spray painting my house." He set off, jogging and half-tripping in his flip-flops, while Farmer limp-trotted behind him.

As he approached the house, he saw the psycho poet coming down the back stairs. He froze. Adrenalin shot through his system. There was a gun in her right hand.

He was about to run, but she'd spotted him. A gentleman never runs!

"Bartley!"

He raised his hands. "I'm unarmed, Louise! I'm very sorry if I insulted you. Let's talk this over. Don't do something that you'll regret for the rest of your life! Anyway, I'm really not worth it. I'm a just a regular schmuck! I'm not Tom Cruise for God's sake!"

She looked at him quizzically as Farmer arrived on the scene. "Stay back," Bartley said, over his shoulder. "She's got a weapon."

Farmer passed him, mumbling, "What's she gonna do, staple you to death?"

Bartley lowered his hands, seeing now that she was actually carrying a staple gun. Louise, delighting in his terror and subsequent embarrassment, began to laugh, enjoying the joke.

Bartley scowled. "What do you want, Louise?"

"I just came by to share a little impromptu piece I wrote for you."

"Grrrreat. I can't wait to read it."

She raised her hands as she walked back to her car and said, "I'm unarmed! Don't shoot!" She aimed the stapler at him and said, "Bang bang!" Then she laughed.

Bartley made a face at her and said, "Stay off my property!" Then he added, for good measure, "You're no Emily Dickinson!"

"And you're no man!" she shouted back. "Otherwise, you would have told me you were *gay!*"

"I'm not gay!" he shouted. And then, turning to meet Farmer's curious gaze, he repeated, less fervently, "I'm not."

This, of course, in the odd karmic scheme of what his life had become, was the signal for Cornelius to sail in on his bicycle wearing a pink helmet and lustily roaring the Beatles classic 1965 hit, "You've Got to Hide Your Love Away."

"None of *my* business," Farmer said.

Bartley heard the land line phone ringing inside the house and trotted in, ripping from the door, as he passed, a poem that the mad poetess had stapled there. "Hello!" he shouted into the phone.

"I'm sorry—Mr. Hannigan?"

"Bartley Hannigan, yes. What is it?"

"This is Brendan Barry. Manus said you were living out there, so I found the number online."

Brendan was a friend of Manus's, going back to elementary school. They'd played soccer together, gone on camping trips, and sat in his son's room thumbing the controllers of Super Mario and Zelda video games through interminable hours of what Bartley heard when he passed his son's bedroom door as beeping, trilling, and detonations punctuated with exclamations and expletives.

"Sorry, Brendan—didn't mean to yell at you. A little problem here."

"Should I call back?"

"No, no. What's up?"

"We're planning a bachelor party for Manus in a couple of weeks."

"Oh, that's great."

"Yeah, he doesn't know about it. We're gonna grab a bite at the Whalebone Grille at 6:00, and then take him up to the Big Moon to see some strippers. Should be fun."

Bartley made a face at the ceiling and clenched his fist at God, who he figured must be laughing His ass off. He composed himself and asked, "When is it?"

"October 15th, a Friday night. Anyway, keep it open."

"Yes. Right. I'll go to the restaurant. I think I'll skip the strip club—that's a bit awkward." *Jesus Christ is it awkward.*

"Whatever you like, Mr. Hannigan. We have a room reserved at the restaurant."

"Good, good."

After he hung up, he fell into a chair and let his head sink into his hands. And here was the reason that going out with a stripper was a bad idea. The thought of his son watching his father's girlfriend—who knows, maybe his future stepmother—fling her clothes off piece by piece . . . it would gnaw at his soul like those little grubs gnawed at the roots of the Christmas trees.

He stood and walked to the window. Farmer and Cornelius were at the garden, in deep conversation. He looked at the poem he'd torn off the door and paced through the house, reading:

He's a tiger for the ladies hear his low and bitter growl
He's got a pocketful of lye to throw on bodies when he prowls.
He's got a shoe-box full of smiles with which he tries to win their hearts
And a dagger that he rips them with instead of Cupid's darts.

He's as smooth as flowing water and as hard as Spanish steel
He likes his girls submissive—just don't tell him what you feel
Trophies on his mantle bear the names he's tossed aside
He wishes he could skin them all and wear a lily hide.

And so on—a full page of this *crap* until the final couplet:

And having now abused all the women that he can,
He's about to drop them all and try it with a man!

What the fuck? He marched to the kitchen, opened a drawer in the counter, pulled out a red pen and wrote BULLSHIT across the page, and at the bottom: NO EMILY DICKINSON!

Farmer came in while he stood their fuming, and mistaking his red-faced rage and bachelor party befuddlement for sexual embarrassment, said, waving vaguely toward the garden, "Quite a knowledgeable guy—knows his stuff—and hey, what the hell, honestly kid, I don't care what you're into."

Bartley was quiet for a minute, just looking at honest old Farmer, as solid a man of the earth as Farmer Oak in Hardy's *Far from the Madding Crowd*, a book Bartley had loved in college. Finally, he spoke, slowly and more calmly, "Thank you, Farmer. I know you would be above such prejudices, and it does you credit. However, your consolation is misplaced, because I am *not gay*."

At this point, Cornelius threw the screen door open and entered stage left like a character in some dreadful farce, caught sight of his fine figure in the mirror over the mantle and said, "Jaysus, Bartley, my outlook has certainly changed since those days you had to get me dthrunk and forcibly strip me to give me a wash!"

Fourteen

Bartley Kickham Hannigan, Gentleman, spoke into the tiny microphone.

"Violeta, it's me."

A dull buzz sounded, and he pulled open the door. He mounted the broad wooden stairs that mill workers of the late nineteenth century had used on their way to the clanging belt-driven looms, and a minute later, Violeta opened the door. She was wearing an apron and holding a wooden spoon in one hand. She kissed him and hurried back to the kitchen leaving him in the brick-walled living room with its views of downtown. The air was redolent with a wonderful aroma of some kind of soup—chicken, herbs, and spices. He heard the notes of some sort of breathy flutes punctuated with the rhythmic chords of a stringed instrument. A woman's voice began to float above the music and intertwine with it. A sad song. Bartley thought that if he and Violeta stayed together, he would have to learn Spanish, or try. After all, he reflected, he had gotten good grades in Spanish in college, though after so many years all he could really recall was, *¿Dónde está el baño de caballeros?* Where is the men's room?

She returned without the apron and said dinner would be ready soon. It was an awkward way to begin the evening, but the weight on his mind had to be relieved. "Listen, sweetheart, you have to take the fifteenth of October off. It's a Friday night. My son will be there for his bachelor party."

"Aye," she said, biting her thumbnail and looking pained. "I will try."

"Violeta, please. Don't *try*—do it! Tell them you can't work that night!"

"Bartley, some things are going on that I may have to be there. I cannot explain, you have to trust me. If I can, I will take off the night."

"I don't get it. My son will be there, Violeta!"

"I will try. But Bartley, if I was an actress, would you go crazy because I am without clothes in a film?"

"I'm not going crazy. I'm just asking you to do this as a favor. Manus would never even go to the Big Moon unless his friends were bringing him."

"If I can. . . ."

A photo in a simple square black frame caught his attention. A little girl in a flowered bonnet on a horse. A man held the reins, his weathered, sun-bronzed face and sweeping moustache shadowed under the brim of a well-worn straw hat. "Is this you?" he asked.

"Yes, with my father, Don Ramon."

"What an angel. Your father looks like a solid man, a good man. Another farmer, like my dad."

"He is a good man."

"You come from good people, Violeta. Honestly, I don't want to judge you, but do you think they would want you to be working the Big Moon?"

"No . . . I don't know, but. . . ." The internal strife was written in her narrowed brows, her troubled eyes.

"What is it?" Bartley asked. "Tell me."

At this, she seemed to impose a calm over her features, a mask of insouciance. "It's nothing. I won't do it much longer."

"You're such a good person, beautiful, inside and out, and you know how I feel about you. But if you work my son's bachelor party, how am I going to be able to explain that to him? I mean, I know you, but he doesn't."

At this, she turned aside. There was a cactus in a clay pot by the window. Leaning against the window frame, she touched the needles that sprouted from its green skin. "But if I have to work, would it be so easy for you, to say it's over?"

"No, it would kill me. But—can I bring you to the wedding after that? I can't tell Manus, 'This is my girlfriend—remember her from your bachelor party?' I don't care if he *finds out*—I just don't want . . . I mean, the idea of my son and his friends ogling the father's girlfriend—it's just kind of awful."

She looked into her hand, and Bartley saw a tiny spot of blood there. "I understand," she said. "But you must understand that when I say it may not be possible, that I am saying the truth."

He nodded. "Okay. And you can't tell me *why* it may not be possible?"

"I'm sorry. Not right now. You have to trust me."

"I just don't understand." Bartley told himself that he should make a resolute exit. There was nothing more to say, and they both knew it. I love you? Very nice, but how could that rearrange such discordant circumstances? Someone, Bartley recalled, once said that the Irish were the Mexicans of Europe. Whether or not that was an apt analogy, he knew enough about Violeta and himself to suspect that both were stubborn, and that neither one would bend the will to accept what was unacceptable—not for love.

Perhaps not for love, but hunger was another thing, and in the space of the few seconds that Bartley hesitated to make a dramatic exit, Violeta sensed her opening. "You are not going to leave before you eat the *pozole* I make—*I made* for you?"

"Of course not," he said, "that would be boorish."

The question of the bachelor party, he decided, could be put off, maybe because the inner voice that told him he was being a sucker was not as strong or insistent as the voice that told him that, in fact, he did trust her. If he had to explain these things to Manus, why then, he would have to explain them to Manus.

In the kitchen, he told her the story of the encounter with Mórrígan, which did not leave her aghast. Her only comment was, "I wish that I was there. Poor . . . *criatura!*"

"It would have amazed you, greatly."

She nodded, wide-eyed and serious, and said, "Maybe she will come again."

"I'll make sure you're there." Bartley was getting very hungry. He asked her about the ingredients of *pozole*, and together they went into the kitchen, where a bottle of "Armonia de Tintos," a Mexican wine, was breathing beside two glasses, and where, from a Bluetooth player, Bartley now heard a plaintive voice crying, "*Aye, amor, amor.*"

As he watched Violeta standing over the stove in the cloud of soup steam, ladling the *pozole* into two bowls and grinding pepper over them, he felt a pang of what he knew was a deep love for her, a powerful love. Someone said that music is the space between notes, and maybe love is the space between words—between thoughts. He felt that wordless swelling emotion, and his next thought was a decision, for now, to put off demands and consequences, and simply enjoy the warmth of her company, and of her affection. He rose and poured two glasses.

After all, running his life according to the expectations of others? Wasn't that what he had sworn he was done with? *Done!* God, she looked beautiful. He pulled his phone out and tapped the camera app. He called her name, and when she turned, took her photo as she broke into one of her sunburst smiles. "Why you are laughing?" she asked.

"I don't know. I guess I'm just happy. You're wonderful."

Violeta laughed too, pleased with the compliment, and even more pleased with the change in mood. She carried the bowls to the table and Bartley set the wine glasses beside them. All resentment forgotten, they embraced warmly, and she whispered something in his ear in Spanish—Bartley did not understand, but the sound was so beautiful that he had to respond in kind—in the only way he knew how: *¿Dónde está el baño de caballeros?* She laughed and said, "*¡Qué romántico!*"

But the mood was not so merry in the courtyard below, where Louise Andino, psychotic daughter of the Muse, watched the windows of the one-bedroom apartment, and cursed when, a while later, the electric light in one went out, and was replaced with the pale flickering shimmer of a candle in another.

Farmer had instructed Bartley to spray around the roots of the trees on and near what he had christened "Grub Hill" before a rain, so that the insecticide would soak into the soil and kill the little tree-killers. And so he found himself traversing the hills under a cloudy sky carrying a spray hose attached to a large plastic container. He hated chemicals, and so he wore gloves, a mask, and his father's "moon suit." But he finished the job by noon and went through the bulkhead to the sink in the cellar, remembering what Farmer had told him, wash your gloves before you take them off. Put the coveralls in a plastic bag until you launder them, and wash goggles, hats, and boots in warm soapy water.

Bartley noticed that there was a horse shoe, a pine cone, and a cracked wine glass hanging by its stem on the door of the wine cellar. On a whim, he removed them, opened the door and announced, "Come and have some vino, you crazy, drunken little man—you're invited!"

He was about to head up the stairs when he heard a crash and saw that the little creature himself had seemingly fallen out of the ceiling and was dusting his hat and smoothing his moustache.

"Sudden, that! Very! Jasus, ye took me by surprise so you did with yer generous invitation! I see the nasty artifacts are stowed and the door is open. Let's crack a bottle, shall we? Too bad Violeta's not about. By heaven, I enjoy her company, and that's no lie. How is the strappin' lass?"

"She's fine."

"I'm glad to hear it, so I am."

"Where the hell did you get that Napoleon hat?"

The clurichaun held the hat at arm's length before him and declared with quiet pride: "A gift from a good old Irishman, Captain Thomas Foley, Knight Grand Cross of the Order of the Bath. Yes, He commanded HMS *Goliath*, seventy-four guns, at the Battle of the Nile. Led a squadron that outflanked the Frenchies, twenty-one of his crew killed, forty-one wounded. Grisly. Quite. But he helped the one-armed Admirel carry the day. More importantly, the man was a true oenophile."

"Eena-file?"

"A connoisseur—of wines. From the Greek *oinos*, 'wine.'"

The little man replaced the hat on his head and rubbed his hands together lustily as he began to browse among the rows of bottles. "*Côte de Nuits,* some of the best burgundies. HOH! *Regardez,* Bartley, eh? *AC Chassagne-Montrachet Premier Cru*—hoh hoh! Let's open it!" He produced a corkscrew from a vest pocket and went to work. Pop! Two goblets flashed into his left hand through some kind of prestidigitation. He uttered murmurs of delight as he poured a goblet and handed it to Bartley. "There y'are, boy. Put that under yer shirt."

They sat on empty crates, and the clurichaun grew reflective. "I wonder sometimes Bartley Hannigan, if I've wasted me life. What have I really accomplished in seven hundred years? There are still so many vintages I haven't tasted at all. And will I ever get the chance? That's what I want to know. Another few hundred years, and I'll be pretty much done for. Maybe four hundred if I can find a few more bottles like this. And there are so many more wine-growing regions than there used to be! How will I keep up at all?"

"I can't imagine," Bartley said, "but you've got a good glass of whatever it is in front of you right now—so just enjoy it." He swigged his own glass; he was no connoisseur, but even he knew that it was a superior vintage, light and tasty.

"Ah, I see. You're one of those fellows is what they call an *optimist,* damn yer eyes. Ye can't grumble or complain about anything, but they say, 'You know it could be worse! Look at the bright side of it!' We Irish know, or we damned well *should know* by now, there's no bright side to anything, boy! If things are good, bejasus, they're soon bound to get worse, and that's a fact!"

"Don't get yourself worked up, Don, or Don Nippery or Septo or whatever they call you—how the hell did you get that name, anyway?"

"*As ucht Dé!* I didn't name meself, did I?"

"Did you ever ask?"

He looked puzzled. "With all the pressing questions a gorsoon may have for his muther and fadther, I hardly think that flogging the origins of me moniker out of 'em woulda been the best use of the interrogative. Anyway, as Shakespeare said, what's in a name?"

"It's just odd. It doesn't sound Irish."

"And what the hell do you know about my people, or the human Irish, for that matter?" He drank, then smiled dismissively. "Ah, why would you know anything about it, I suppose. Anyway, thank you for invitin' me. I was coming to see you soon."

"You want to drink upstairs?"

"Ah, sure I like it right here where I can see all them bottles. Now if you tell me Violeta is upstairs. . . ."

"Why did you want to see me?"

"Right, so. You've seen the Ancient One." Bartley noticed the raised eyebrows under the brim of the great headpiece. "What a piece a' work, eh, the Mórrígan?"

He nodded. "She was impressive."

"Aye." He twirled one end of his curling mustache nervously. "She scares the livin' shite outa me to be perfectly honest. Seems you are witness to a great accident of history, Bartley. How many human men, do you think, ever see a goddess?"

"Not many?"

"Damned few. Especially these days. But listen, if the circle is destroyed—if that old magic enclosure is violated. . . ."

"She will never return?"

"The door will be closed. Quite. The last remnant of the old world. She will live for some time, trapped in this place where no one believes in her or prays to her or sacrifices to her—where no one even *knows* her. And she will grow thinner and less substantial and soon, cease to be." His face grew long and seemed to droop like a flower in the rain. "Gods shouldn't die, Bartley. Gods should never die."

"And back in Ireland. . . ."

"Her places will always be revered—the *Fulacht na Mó, Dá Chich na Morrigna*, her cave, *Uaigh na gCat*, at Rathcroghan in Roscommon, *Gort na Morrigna* in County Louth, *Gleannfreagham*, the Glen of the Ravens, in County Kerry—and her power will live there. She can live there—if only she can find her way back."

"But which place will she go back to?"

"That's why I wanted to see ye. There are two mounds close to *Brú na Bóinne* known together as *Mur na Morrigna*. Can ye remember that?"

"*Brew na Bon-yah. Moor na Mooreeg-na.* Let me write it down." He pulled a ballpoint pen from his pocket and scribbled the words down phonetically on the back of a sales slip from the supermarket.

"She's not your all-powerful biblical God, you know, rulin' the universe. Or his son goin' to weddins' and turnin' wather into wine. Miraculous all right, that. Very. Jasus. Transforming elements, you see? Difficult. Like to get the hang of that trick. No, no. You see, Bartley, 'tis not yer Christian heaven that's in it a'tall. 'Tis known as *orbis alius*, the 'Otherworld,' but it's Other *Worlds*, really. Right enough. Summon her when the door is open, yes, but then someone's got to light the way, call her across the void, show her the road back to Ireland, and there's only one, do ye see? Otherwise, she might wander forever through time, through space, through dreams and songs and in the fogs that roll over the boundless wat'ry main. You must . . ."

"Dad?"

He would have heard Manus descending the stairs, but he had apparently come down the open bulkhead, and now he stepped into the threshold of the wine cellar, the length and breadth of the man he had become nearly filling the doorway. His expression was one that his father recognized as "a look of concern." The young man scanned the room—his father scanned it with him, and the two men seemed equally surprised to find that Bartley was its sole occupant. "Who were you talking to, Dad?"

He patted his pocket. "I just put my phone away."

"I thought I heard someone else."

"I had it on speaker."

"Oh. Why are you sitting down here . . . drinking wine?"

"I was organizing the bottles, just seeing what's here—decided to try this one. I'm just taking a break. Let's go upstairs."

"Dad?"

"What is it, Manus?"

"Why do you have another wine glass, there—half full?"

"That? Oh, a friend was coming over—I poured a half glass for him—he doesn't drink much, just to let it breathe, you know." Bartley waved his free hand in the air to suggest wine breathing. "But, that was him on the phone. He can't make it."

Bartley was amazed at his own facility with lies. He had always been a lousy liar and was inclined to just tell the truth and face the consequences as a way of avoiding the ensnaring strands of the tangled web. But a rapid calculation of the situation had convinced him that to attempt the truth in this case was an utter and absolute impossibility. That would be asking for more trouble than he could contemplate right now. Manus would be on the phone to mental health professionals in a jiffy. Anyway, as far as he could recall, "Thou shalt not lie" was not even one of the commandments, never mind that it was a question of a harmless lie.

Bartley grabbed the bottle and closed the door after them as Manus headed up the stairs. He quickly re-hung the pine cone and the horseshoe on the door, making a sour and challenging face at the air above him.

In the kitchen, father and son took seats at the table, and Bartley recalled how he and his own father had sat at the same table on the day the old man told him that he had connected a nocturnal wailing to his own impending death. So, now Bartley had learned that belief, especially a determined belief, could have sustained, maybe even created, the gods of old. And yet, he still believed that reason, in general, was best, and was glad that his son would not have believed him. In short, he didn't know anything anymore.

"Care for a glass of French wine, Manus?"

"Bit early. Got coffee?"

God, he was sensible. "Sure." He corked the wine and set about making coffee while Manus regarded him somewhat skeptically.

"So, who is this Irish guy who lives here?"

"He's from Balleyvourney. Your grandfather was friendly with his family. He just wants to experience America, so he's got a base of operations. He'll be heading back before Thanksgiving." He poured water into the reservoir, slapped the lid shut and flicked the switch. "How's Jill?"

"Wonderful."

"Are you guys getting nervous?"

"Not really. We're looking forward to it. Jill is not one of those *prima donnas* who wants some fairy tale wedding where everything has to be perfect. Remember when you told me that 'easy-going' is the best thing a woman can be? She's easy-going. We're pals. We're getting married at Lowell City Hall, having a little party, and we're off to the Hotel Frontenac in Quebec."

"Believe me, Manus, everything you say bodes well, indeed. Quebec City is wonderful. And the bar at the Frontenac—it's the best. View of the St. Lawrence—professional bartenders—you'll love it."

The young man smiled. "Sounds good, Yeah, she thinks that show where the woman cries and agonizes and gushes over the perfect wedding dress is really stupid. She's just going to wear a regular dress, and I'll wear the suit I got for my job interview."

The late Happy Hannigan's antiquated coffee maker hissed and bubbled steamily like an enfeebled geezer gargling, as the water percolated through the coffee basket. "Of course," Manus, added, "no matter how low-key you try to keep it, it's still a big day. You know, you and Mom, splitting up after all those years, it doesn't really inspire confidence in marriage."

"I realize that." Bartley wasn't sure what to say, and he didn't want to blame it all on Adele. "Sorry, Manus. You know, I tried to hold it together, but. . . ."

"I know, Dad. Are you all right now?"

"Yeah. To tell the truth, I was getting tired of trying so hard. They say a relationship is work, and I understand that, but it can't be *just* work, all the time. And I probably drove your mother crazy, too." He shrugged and held his hands before him, palms upward. "Our personalities are just very different. And over time, small differences became big differences."

"I'm glad you're happy, anyway. I got a little worried when I found you drinking in the cellar. Divorce and losing Grandpa together—must have been rough."

"Not to worry, Manus."

"I met this guy—Donald, Mom's 'friend.' She says she's bringing him to the wedding. You know that, right?"

"Yeah, that's fine."

"Honestly, Dad, the guy strikes me as a total dick. One of these guys who seems to think, 'It's me against the world, and I'm winning.' Wants to talk about all the upgrades he gets at hotels, the great deals he gets on everything, how he reamed out some poor waiter to get a better table. I can't understand what the hell she sees in him, other than that he's the opposite of you." He paused, and with a pained expression, added, "That didn't sound right. I mean . . ."

Bartley smiled. "Doesn't bother me. Listen, I wouldn't worry about it, Manus. I doubt that she's serious with the guy. I mean, what do I know, but, I just doubt it."

Manus nodded and took a deep breath to signal a new topic of conversation. "So, you mentioned that you might bring someone to the wedding? Who is that?"

"She's very nice. A very nice person. We get along quite well, so far. She seems to like me for some reason."

"For a lot of reasons, I'm sure! What's her background? Is she Irish?"

"No, no, she's not Irish. She's Hispanic, in fact."

"Oh yeah? From where?"

"From Mexico, originally."

"Interesting. How'd you meet her?"

Bartley got up and pulled a couple of coffee mugs out of the cabinet and got a quart of milk from the refrigerator. Manus, like him, took whole milk in his coffee. Over his shoulder, he said, "She's interested in farming, actually. I met her at the Nashua Farmers' Exchange."

"No kidding?"

"Yeah. I mean, no. No kidding." Bartley poured the coffee and returned to the table with a mug in each hand, setting one in front of his son.

Manus chuckled. "I can't quite picture you hitting on a woman at the Farmers' Exchange, or anywhere, for that matter."

"It has been a while, but, you know, we just started talking . . . and, well, I am still quite attractive as you can see."

"Ha! And when can I meet her?"

"Soon, I think. Very soon." He tried not to think about that meeting at the Big Moon.

"I'm sure I'm gonna love her."

Bartley nodded, "Yeah, I'm sure you will."

He changed the subject quickly then, because he felt as if he might throw up. They talked for a while, and Manus, in parting, asked him for some advice on marriage. *Imagine that.* "Oh, I don't know," Bartley said. "Save your money. Be patient with each other. Assume good intentions—I'm clearly not one to give advice."

But Manus listened intently to those simple precepts, saying, "To tell the truth, Dad, I'm amazed you stayed with Mom as long as you did. Not many guys could have managed it. That's why I still think you're pretty good at figuring women out."

"Oh yeah, they call me 'the estrogen detective.' What have you figured out so far on your own?"

Manus smiled. "She wants me to tell her I love her—very often."

"Yes, keep that up."

After Manus had left, Bartley flopped back in the kitchen chair and pulled out his cell phone. He tapped it a few times, calling up the photo he had taken of Violeta, with her warm smile, standing in a column of soup-steam, ladle in hand. He felt his heart twist as he stared at the image. His emotions were in turmoil. Love and forbearance battled with a renewed desire to have it out with Violeta. Maybe love and conflict were intertwined; he recalled an interview he'd seen with a French singer who referred to love as "the tender war."

What to do? He wished he was "pretty good at figuring women out," or even at figuring himself out. The image on the phone screen dimmed and went dark. He tossed his coffee in the sink and pulled the cork out of the vino.

Fifteen

Bartley was trying to sort out his problems, which seemed slightly less overwhelming when he had got halfway down the bottle of— what did that little Nipper say it was? He picked up the bottle and inspected the label. *AC Chassagne-Montrachet.* "Thanks, Dad." He toasted the air.

He turned his attention back to his problems: there was Violeta, of course, and the bachelor party. He nodded gravely to himself. Front burner. There was Mr. Bede and the tidal wave of *bullshit* that had become his so-called career. Back burner, only because it was summer. There was the psycho poet with her 'slighted art.' Fuck her—back burner. There was this minor thing that some people now thought he was gay. Who cares? Back burner.

Finally, there was this phantasmagorical thing about saving a goddess. Back burner? He reminded himself that it was not really phantasmagorical. He *had* seen her, and heard her voice, or her *voices*. It was like one of those books, like *The Lord of the Rings*, when Frodo says, "Why me?" And Gandalf sagely assures him that he was chosen for some deep reason, some quality as yet unrealized in his character that made him the one who must be trusted with the mighty task of delivering the ring that rules them all to Mount Doom.

What if Frodo had decided it wasn't his problem? Middle Earth would have been fucked! Maybe that problem was on the front burner, in front of all the other burners. Maybe. Probably. He took another sip of the wine and nodded. Definitely. Unmistakably.

He decided it was time to tell Cornelius that Jack Carnadine was now the owner of the "magic enclosure," and might start developing that land at any time. He should find out *when*.

He took out his phone and typed in *Jack Carnadine Lowell.* There was the link—Carnadine Development LLC. He dialed the number. The idea that his father had sold all those acres he'd roamed as a boy had not seemed real until he told the secretary who he was and she responded immediately, as if she knew him, "Oh yes, Mr. Hannigan. He's on the other line. Can you hold?" He held, nervously.

Bartley had invited Violeta to dinner, along with Cornelius. Less than romantic, but he had to speak to both. She arrived with a bag out of which she pulled a tall, slender bottle of Milagro Silver Tequila, a bottle of Quantro, and some limes, announcing that she would make them some real Mexican margaritas. Bartley kissed her and uttered one of the simple phrases he'd been practicing, *"¡Cada día más linda, tú!"*

"Oooh," she purred, and kissed him again, smiling a little at his gringo accent.

Cornelius examined the tequila label. "Be careful with that stuff!" Bartley warned. "That's a Mexican that'll knock you on your Gaelic ass!"

He told them of a conversation he'd had with the mason who pointed the chimney. "I asked him if he wanted a beer one day after he finished. 'No thanks, Bartley,' he said, 'I ain't had a drink in twenty-three years.' So, I asked him why he quit. He said, 'Tequila was my drink. One night I drank too much of it. I threw a chair through the plate glass window of the Copper Kettle, smashed my car into a cruiser, punched Mickey O'Keefe and another cop in the face, and woke up in a cell on the floor, under the bunk, in a puddle of vomit. 'Yeah,' I said, 'That's it for me, kid. I'm done!' Ginger ale and lime—that's been my drink for twenty-three years."

Cornelius listened gravely to this cautionary tequila tale, and said, "We'll just have one."

"Maybe two," Bartley said. "Two, and then maybe we'll split one—any more, you start chasing cars."

"The dinner smells *delicioso*," Violeta said.

"Just your basic American chicken dinner with stuffing, potatoes, sweet potatoes, and vegetables."

The stove made the kitchen a bit warm, and Bartley turned on the new overhead fan and began to set out the plates while Violeta made the drinks. The screen door let in the cooler air of early evening, as well as the golden light of the declining sun that felt to Bartley like a divine presence, or at least a gift of Divine Nature.

The three friends ate in such companionable conviviality that Bartley wondered what the hell he had been doing for so many years, determined, for some reason, to hold together a marriage that was nothing more than the familiar order of things. Familiar and hopeless! Imagine having to be so careful of what you say to the person you live with! Bartley shivered at the memory. Done!

The dinner over, they took their drinks out to the porch. As the sun descended toward the lush tree line of summer, Bartley laid out for them what he knew. First of all, his father had sold some of the property to a developer named Jack Carnadine. And Carnadine had told him over the phone that he had a couple of other projects going, and when he was finished with them, he would begin development on the 'Stonehenge Condominiums.' "He says he came up with the name himself after scouting out the land."

Cornelius leaned forward. "Did he give you an estimate?"

"Middle of October."

"That's two weeks before Samhain!"

"And right in the middle of Manus's wedding preparations."

"Sow-en?" Violeta asked.

"You tell her," Bartley said and sat back with his Margarita.

Cornelius explained that, according to the ancient Celtic calendar, there were four major holidays, Samhain, Imbolc, Beltane, and Lughnasadh. "It was Samhain from which you got your modern-day Halloween. It was a liminal time for the Celts."

"What is this 'liminal time'?"

"From the Latin, *limis*, or threshold. The end of the harvest, the beginning of the winter. Halfway between the autumn equinox and the winter solstice. The *Dumha na nGiall*, a Neolithic passage tomb going back 3,000 years before Christ, is aligned with the sunrise of Samhain. It's the time when the doors between this world and the other world are open. It would be the only logical time to try to get the Mórrígan back to Ireland."

"How are we gonna do that?" Bartley wanted to know.

"We'll do a ritual here, and some associates in Ireland will perform another at a sacred site in Ireland. I'll take care of that side of things. So, if this Carnadine fella will call it 'Stonehenge,' does that mean he'll keep the stone circle?"

"Well, he says he does not want to knock it down—"

"Jesus, that's a relief!"

"But he wants to move it."

"Move it? Where?"

"They're putting in a road for the new complex about a mile and a half down Sherwood Ave. He wants the circle relocated to the entrance to give it that 'Stonehenge' flavor—shine lights on it at night. Anyway, there'll be a house foundation laid beside the spot where the circle is located now."

"Didja explain, Bartley?"

"Cornelius—how the hell am I going to *explain?* I have trouble explaining all this, any of this, to *myself.* I said that I had an expert from Ireland who believed it was a pre-Christian circle constructed by early Celtic visitors. He had found out about the excavation that turned up nothing and suggested that it was a Victorian folly, but he said that if there was any *real evidence* of pre-Christian origins, he might be willing to redesign the configuration of the development and leave it where it stands. 'Might enhance the value of the property,' he said, but I think he was just trying to humor me."

"That is not unreasonable, I suppose," Violeta ventured, "for a businessman."

They nodded, resignedly. "With any luck," Bartley said, "he may not get to it before November. Or he may even wait until the spring."

Cornelius appeared depressed. He finished his drink and picked up a book on a side table, saying he would clean the kitchen and go upstairs to read, and that he would "leave them to it" on the porch.

"I will help you clean," Violeta said, rising.

"We'll clean in the morning," Bartley said. "What are you reading now?" Cornelius held the up the cover and Bartley read, "*The Metrical Dindshenchas*, Author: Unknown."

"Ancient Irish place name lore. I'm trying to decide on the best point of re-entry for *her*."

"Let me see?"

He handed the book to Bartley, who opened the academic text and saw, but could not read:

Cathir Chrofhind, nírbo chamm,
a hainm ac Túaith Dé Danann,
co toracht Tea, nar chlé,
ben Erimóin co n-ard-gn

"Jesus, I thought Spanish was tough. And listen, I almost forgot, while you're doing your research, check this place." He pulled out his wallet and extracted a piece of paper, which he handed to Cornelius together with the book. "That's where the Nippery guy thinks she should reenter."

Cornelius glanced at the paper and tucked it into the *Dindshenchas*. "I'm lookin' into it," he said. "And I think you'll hear her tonight."

"Why do you say that?"

Cornelius pointed to the full moon a hand's breadth over the horizon. "It's what they call here 'the Buck Moon.' When the buck deer start to grow those fuzzy, hair-covered horns. They also call it the Thunder Moon because of the prevalence of thunderstorms."

"How does he know all this stuff?" Bartley asked no one in particular.

"For Jesus' sake, Bartley, I should think you would know by now that you must pay attention to the movements and evolutions of the sun, the moon and the planets. And you must attune yourself to. . . ." His eyes closed, and he traced circles in the air with the book in his hand while he searched for the words. ". . . to . . . to the mystical tension of the night."

"Hmm," Bartley said, sipping is drink. "I'll try."

Cornelius went in, and soon they heard the clinking of plates and running water as he cleaned up. Violeta went in to help him, but he would have none of it, so she made more drinks and she and Bartley sat on the porch.

"I've got to sign the papers on the house sale on Saturday," he said. "And I have the court date in a few weeks for the divorce."

"Does that make you stress out?" she asked.

"Nah, I have a lawyer friend who is looking things over. But it's a no-fault deal, and we're leaving it up to the judge to do an 'equitable distribution.'"

She asked him about his marriage, about why he had tried so hard for so long to hold it together. He tried to explain this sense he'd had that a vow was a vow, until it just didn't make any sense at all, and still he persevered until she thankfully shot the crippled dog that was their marriage. "I have to thank her for that," he said.

"I suppose I do, too," she said. "How was the . . . the things in the bedroom?" she asked.

"Not good," he said. "Not like us, now. This is just between you and me, of course. Adele, you see, she read this *Fifty Shades of Grey*, and I guess it spoke to, or awakened, some masochistic part of her nature. She wanted me to tie her up, and gag her and beat her, and I'm just—I just wasn't into that at all."

"Ah, *Cincuenta Sombras de Grey*, I read about half of that book. It was silly. I don't want to be beaten."

"And I don't want to beat anyone. I don't get it. And it was strange how a woman who was so dominant in every other aspect of her life wanted to be humiliated in bed all of a sudden. I mean we all have fantasies—it's just that mine never involved whips and gags and all those porno movie props. She said I lacked adventurousness, and I said—well, anyway, to answer your question is no, things were not good."

Violeta shook her dark head, her brow furrowed in thought. "No, I don't understand that." Then she seemed to relax and leaned closer to him and said, "What *do* your fantasies involve?"

"Oh, ordinary male fantasy stuff I suppose—you in nothing but high heels, and maybe. . . ." He buried his head in her hair and whispered in her ear.

She smiled. "A doctor? With an . . . *estetoscopio?*"

"Stethoscope! Yeah, you know. 'It's probably nothing Miss Martinez, but if you'd take off your shirt I'd like to listen to your heart. Hmm. I'd better check your reflexes, if you'd just raise your skirt.'"

"Oh, I think you are going to have to do a thorough exam. I know it's OK because you are a *doctor!*"

"Absolutely! We wouldn't want to miss something—*anything! * That would be unprofessional!"

The tequila made the doctor scenario more comic than erotic somehow, and they laughed while the landscape before them began to lose definition and the tapering pines on the hills seemed to gather more thickly, standing in the silvery gloaming under the swollen Buck Moon like a silent regiment awaiting the fateful order. They relished the tranquility of the view until another regiment began its attack. The humming flyers of the mosquito squadron arrived with nightfall, and the couple made their way up to Bartley's room.

They were awakened in the deepest part of the night, when, as the tequila induced life-is-a-carnival attitude no longer held sway over their minds, more pressing thoughts returned. She was silently praying for the end of the operation at the Big Moon, and he was thinking of the impending marriage of his son and the party at the strip club. Was either able to speak to the other of the concerns that lay deep in the heart? They were not, and were forced, therefore, to suffer the consequences of their silence. She was sworn to secrecy and he—reason told him to make demands on her, but love bade him trust her.

The moon was at the zenith of its arc when the stillness was splintered, and these thoughts scattered. They heard a wail of pain, a forlorn cry that rose from the wooded hills. Bartley opened his eyes, and on the pillow beside him, saw Violeta's eyes, tear-bright in the moonlight that filtered through the curtains and infused the bedroom.

He recalled his father's words: "God help us, Bartley, you've never heard anything like it." In the ensuing silence, Violeta reached out under the sheet and took his hand and whispered words that sounded like a prayer in Spanish.

The room darkened as storm clouds rolled across the heavens above the Merrimack Valley; all was still once again. Then the curtains stirred, and the air was rent with a low rumble followed by a booming crash of thunder. Bartley pulled the blanket at the foot of the bed up over them, and soon a dismal rain hammered the roof of the old farmhouse, and the windows flashed with the strobes of billions of joules of energy shooting veins of light that resembled skeletons dancing across the face of night.

Rushing currents of power—Bartley imagined them in cartoon form—particles shifting, colliding, charging, and discharging. Who could ever explain the world? He thought of the millions of bees, following some silent command, creatures of a month's span, working in unison to construct perfect rows of hexagonal honeycombs. The birds 'in chevron flight' and their miraculous migrations. Neither Aristotle nor Einstein could say how it all came about and followed certain laws or mathematical principles to put us here, with our big brains, yet not big enough to figure out what the hell we were doing on this mostly wet rock tethered by invisible cords to a star and riding it round and round like a crazy amusement park carousel, with nary a glimpse of Holden Caulfield's gold ring nor any other prize or purpose! A little man in the wine cellar or a lost goddess was a minor mystery compared with all this! Who could explain *anything*, really?

Sixteen

Summer's lease hath all too short a date indeed! Bartley thought as July passed, and Cornelius, in the fields he'd tended so well, gathered tomatoes, eggplant, sweet corn, lima beans, peppers, squash, and of course potatoes, or as he called them, "spuds." Sometimes Bartley helped him, but more often it was Violeta who would come over, don the gloves, and pick up the garden shears or the curved harvesting knife while the Corkman hefted the potato fork. Meanwhile, Bartley tried his hand at trimming the trees, which Cornelius declared to be "in fine fettle."

It was on such an August day that Bartley found them tending and plucking and brought cold Smithwick's ales for Cornelius and himself and an iced tea for Violeta. Quoting from his Shakespeare calendar, he cried, "You sunburned sickle men of August weary, come from the furrow and be merry!" They laid down the tools and the mesh produce bags and came up to sit in plastic lawn chairs in the shadow of the barn.

The conversation was pleasantly rustic, and Bartley felt relaxed while the other two spoke of blueberries and pears; he gave himself over to admiration of the woman he loved—the glow of her eyes and her slightly perspiring skin—until Cornelius mentioned that apple-picking time would soon be upon them. Violeta sensed his altered mood.

"What's wrong, *mi amor?*"

"Ah, it's just that apple-picking time is school time! I hate to see the apples ripening."

"It's necessary to do this job that you don't like? Why you don't quit?"

"After Adele's lawyer got through the separation agreement and the divorce, there wasn't a whole lot left from the home sale transaction."

"But the students, you don't like them?"

"There really are a lot of good kids. Most of them are good kids. It's just that they don't let you teach anymore. Every five minutes there's some new theory—paperwork to complete so it can gather dust. I have a very low threshold for tolerance of bullshit."

"No one likes bullshit," Cornelius concurred, swigging his Smithwick's.

"Bartley," Violeta said, "your wife left you, and you never cried over it or anything! You were happy! You tell me you are so happy to be 'done with all that.' But your wife made the decision! You would still be with her, I think, if she had not ended it. And now, you hate your job, but you keep doing it! Why don't you leave, Bartley?"

"I don't know. Some gypsy told me that my card was the Knight of Pentacles if I recall correctly. And that meant that I was afraid of change, or afraid to initiate change. And maybe she was right—and you're right. In retrospect, my marriage was like a purgatory for sins I didn't even commit. And now, I don't know, it's just that I've always been a teacher! I really don't know how to do anything else. I do like helping the kids. And I'll never be a farmer—I don't have it in me. Anyway, I'll deal with it, later."

"Later," Violeta echoed, dubiously.

"Look, right now we've got to keep our eye on the ball. I'm committed to getting this being off my property—Carnadine's property, and through the door to the Otherworld." Bartley nearly shivered, recalling the lost look in those strange eyes the color of yellow columbine, and reflecting that, thank God, he was with perhaps the only two people in Massachusetts for whom the appearance of such a creature was not particularly stunning or bizarre.

Cornelius pulled his chair back as the shadow of the barn shortened, and said, "Then I'll be goin' back home meself soon after." At these words, Violeta made a sad, pouting face at Bartley, for she had grown fond of the Irishman—they both had.

They finished their drinks, and Bartley suggested a swim at Top Pond. Cornelius begged off. "You've got me bathing right enough, but you'll never get me swimming. There must be frogs and leeches and water snakes and God knows what, old skeletons and queer creatures up in that dark water!"

"It's just a pond! And you're the guy who back in Ireland faced the Gray Man of the Tuscar Rock and the banshee on the bridge and that other creature that's like a Headless Horseman. . . ."

"A dullahan," Cornelius interjected.

"How could you do all that and be afraid of a pond?"

"Sure, you know yourself," he said, his catch-all answer when Bartley suspected he didn't know himself.

A half hour later, when Violeta was ready, she and Bartley set off to the Top Pond for a swim. Fearing that she might be bashful, he refrained for a moment from suggesting a skinny dip in broad daylight in this wood-enclosed oasis—but then he remembered that she was a stripper.

In a trice, they as were naked as babes, she, laughing at the sudden hat-rack that had appeared on his person. A naked man can hardly hide what he's thinking, and she led him to a secluded hollow, where she lay down their blanket, and herself.

It was those moments he was trying to recall one day after the apples had ripened and he took his seat in the lecture hall for opening day of school. The opening day was for teachers only. The superintendent took the stage. She was a short, stout, unduly cheerful woman, wearing oversized glasses and the gray, close-cropped haircut of a former nun (though she was none). She almost appeared to be wearing a silver helmet and needed only a breastplate, buckler, and sword to lead the hopeless charge. Yes, there was something of the military about her. She always wore, rather proudly, one of a variety of dragonfly brooches on the lapel of her power suit as if it were a military decoration awarded by the educational brass.

"Well!" she said, turning this way and that to take in the whole stupefied audience of the lecture hall, "I hope you're well-rested, and your batteries are recharged, and you're ready . . ." (here she switched the microphone to her left hand and raised a clenched fist), "to take on the challenges of a new school year." She shook her tiny fist at the imaginary challenges, and Bartley groaned.

"And now let's get down to business," she said. The smile disappeared, and the get-down-to-business face turned toward the big screen behind her on which appeared the first of an interminable series of bar graphs and pie charts, new state-gathered testing data on their students. A laser pointer appeared in her hand and flitted about the screen like a tiny firefly. When he heard the words, "preliminary embargoed accountability data," he lost consciousness of his surroundings altogether and sank into a dejected reverie of the lost summer, margaritas on the porch, Violeta's naked body in the stippled light of the greenwood by the pond, and the honest work of the farm.

He was jarred from the comfort of these memories. "And now!" the superintendent cried in bouncy tones, "Students arrive tomorrow! I'll let you get together by department in your professional learning communities! This morning's breakout sessions are based around the theme of 'Unpacking the Rubrics!'" Her job for the year was done, and now she would disappear into the office with the big-screen TV, like Oz behind his curtain, rarely to be seen again until she handed out diplomas at graduation. Bartley envied her escape as the teachers milled out of the hall in docile compliance, like cattle to the slaughterhouse. For him, there was only one thing worse than listening to the superintendent—that was listening to Bede.

Harris sidled up to him in the sullen exiting cortege and said, "Coming to a theater near you—'Unpacking the Rubrics.' What balderdash! Hong Kong fooey! Poppycock! Gibbily gock! It's like the brain falling into mental quicksand. Over and over again." He shook his head, and raising his eyes toward the concrete ceiling, concluded, "There goes another summer-mellowing of our souls."

Meanwhile, at DEA headquarters at 50 Sudbury Street in Boston, Violeta Martinez flashed her identification at the front desk. The ID that she showed did not identify her as Violeta Martinez but as someone else. The guard nodded, and she passed to an elevator where a barcode on the ID was scanned before the doors opened with a sibilant hiss. A few minutes later, she was seated in an office on the third floor, feeling uncomfortably like a patient waiting for the doctor to arrive.

It was, instead, Detective Chief Constable Ricardo Perez who arrived, somewhat out of breath. He explained that he was using the stairs rather than the elevators in an attempt to stay fit. *In an attempt to have a heart attack is more like it*, she thought as he flopped into the chair behind the desk, but she refrained from offering the suggestion that he try to lose thirty pounds before pounding the stairs.

They spoke in Spanish; it was a relief to Violeta to speak easily and fluently, never at a loss. "I want to pull out of this operation as quickly as I can," she said.

Perez nodded, still catching his breath, ran one hand through his thick, if graying, mane and pushed the bridge of his eyeglasses up with the other. Finally, he leaned forward, arms on the desk, and grimaced as he loosened his tie. "We can't do that. This operation is top priority, Sofia."

"Call me Violeta until it's over and I am out of it."

"All right. But this is the beginning, not the end."

"I don't think so. You have enough evidence against Catania, and you can arrest the two from the Airport Cartel too. Three buys I have made with them. Why do you say this is the beginning?"

"Sof—Violeta! We've learned a lot from the bugging device. Number one, they like you. Number two, they trust you. Number three, this Cachorro likes you a lot. You give him a smile and a wink, and he'll take you back to Torreón, where you would come into contact with Gustavo Mejias, the head of the cartel. Think about it, Violeta! We'd be working with a very limited and incorruptible number of *Policía Federal*. When are we going to get another chance to infiltrate the cartel? So, this isn't about a relatively small drug bust up here. It's about bringing down an international ring."

"Incorruptible my ass! Take the small drug bust, Perez, because I played the stripper, but I'm not going to be El Cachorro's whore so that you can get to Mejias." In English, she added, "No way, José."

"Just think about it. You could be one of the biggest—"

"Whores!"

"—undercover operatives in agency history."

"Not for you, not for the agency, and not even for Mexico. You understand? They asked me to help you get a gang in New England who made contact with this cartel, not to become Mata Hari. I did my job. Finalize it, Perez. I'm tired of shaking my ass for a lot of *pendejos*. I still can't believe I agreed to that!"

"And now you want to throw it all away because you're in love?"

Violeta stood. "Since you want to talk about our personal lives. . . ." She snatched from his desk the framed photo of his wife and two daughters. "Would you tell one of them to go fuck a killer twice a day so that you could make a headline—a big international bust?"

He was about to speak but leaned back in his swivel chair and half-turned, looking away out the window and shaking his head. She set the photo squarely in front of his chair.

"I didn't think so, *cabrón!* End it! Soon!"

"All right. The end of next month, or the next big shipment."

She threw open the door and exited without closing it, muttering, "*Pinche puñatero*," and a string of other Mexican curses.

Perez stared out the open door and listened to her receding footsteps. He had had a feeling she would react this way, and there was no sense arguing with her when she was in that mood. But then he hadn't yet played his ace. She may yet change her mind; yes, she would see things differently. She was working with the DEA now, and in *this* organization, every private should know his, or her, duty.

He gazed at the photo of his wife and, just for a second, thought that she was scowling at him.

Donald had grown tired of Adele. They were too much alike. He didn't like to be reminded of what a selfish bastard he was, and, somehow, he was constantly seeing his own reflection in her unblushing narcissism. He missed the innocuous naiveté of his wife, who liked to see the best in everyone, even in him, a tendency which allowed him to imagine that she might be right. Besides, Caroline had actually loved him! And he missed being with a woman who loved him, having sex with a woman who really loved him. He suspected that Adele didn't really love anyone.

A few tentative emails to Caroline lamenting his stupidity and expressing his repentance had not been met with a categorical rejection, and divorce proceedings appeared to be on hold. He was sure he still had the charm (and of course, the financial reserves) to win her back.

"Are you dumping me?" Adele asked as he began to question, in a vague, exploratory way, the future of their relationship.

Donald had always considered himself a master of diplomacy. He cleared his throat and shook his head gravely, *diplomatically*. His puckered visage indicated that he was weighing all the evidence mentally, like Sherlock Holmes without the pipe. "*Dumping?* Hell no, that's not how I would put it," he said.

"No? How *would* you put it, Donnie?"

He paused like a patient schoolmaster with an irksome child. "I think I've told you I don't care for that name, if you don't mind."

"Yes, you did tell me. But I just don't listen." She took a step closer and ran her fingers along the notched lapel of his Brioni suit, a lovely blue-gray material. "Mmmmm. Wool and silk blend—don't you just love the feel of *quality*, Donnie?"

He took her wrist in his thick fingers. "I said, don't call me 'Donnie,' Adele."

"What are you going to do, put me over you knee and give me a good lesson. . . ?"

Yes, he was tired of Adele. He was tired of spanking her and tying her up and gagging her and calling her a dirty whore. Humiliating her had become like a part-time job—fifty shades of tedium. He was beginning to feel like some old torturer in the Tower of London who was ready for retirement. Sex with Caroline was much less of a project.

He released her hand and straightened an already straight tie. "As I was saying, I just don't think this relationship is going anywhere, Adele."

She folded her arms and smiled, quite amused, a broad sort of smile bordering on laughter. "And where were we supposed to *go?*" she asked, looking around as if they had missed a bus.

Donald was abashed. First, because he had no answer, and second, because her total indifference to his declaration was apparent. A man doesn't want to hurt a woman's feelings, of course, nor cause a scene. But on the other hand, he would like to feel that by ending an affair, he would evoke some sensible tremor in the emotional life of the female in question.

He began to speak but found himself as flustered as a debutante. His diplomacy had floundered in a swamp of self-doubt. He stammered, quite undiplomatically, and she silenced him with a raised palm and a look of scorn.

"Listen. Here's the deal, *Donald*. As I told you months ago when you suggested marriage—God, imagine that—you are *free*. We have no lawyers nor contracts nor judges here. It was fun for a while, but it was just one of those things, and fortunately there is no shortage of men. However, you must accompany me to my son's wedding party and act as if you're happy to be there. Can you do that? That's not too taxing, is it? And then you can crawl back to your wife or to some other lucky woman."

She was giving him orders! By God, Donald Delaney did not take orders from women! Yet, instead of the unqualified *no* that was longing for release, he raised the qualifying question: "And *what if* I were to say no?"

"You have every right to do so. It might be slightly awkward for me, since I've already told Manus and the guests that my friend Donald would accompany me, but I would manage. I always manage. However, bitch that I *can be*, I might find it necessary to make you pay at some later point, to a far greater degree, since I have come to believe that the proper response to a shot across the bow should always be a full, hull-shattering broadside."

One part of Donald's mind, a small corner not yet subdued by her superior ability and intellectual capacity, hankered for total war with Adele. He saw himself on the deck of HMS Victory, absorbing her timber-shivering broadside, standing like a British admiral in the shifting smoke beneath his streaming banner. His gun ports open, and out of the darkness emerge the death-dealing maws of black cannons in bristling rows along each of the triple decks. "Fire on the roll!" he commands, and the world erupts beneath him. The bitch runs below as her decks are raked with grapeshot. His cheering crew toss the grappling hooks and board her battered flagship, sabers flashing. She strikes her colors and surrenders her sword. What a sweet victory he might achieve! A true spanking!

But the three sensible corners of his brain flash a picture into his visual cortex of his own ship afire and listing awkwardly, the mighty mast cracking and toppling sideways into the sea like a spent penis, while Caroline's ship flies toward the horizon under a full press of sail.

"Donald? *Hell-O-oh.*"

He tore himself from these reveries and chuckled graciously—generously. "Hey, let's stop this quarreling! We're friends after all! If you'd like me to go to Manus's wedding, of course I'd be happy to oblige." He held his arms open in a welcoming embrace, and she came to him.

"Oh," she said, taking hold of his crotch, "you're such a dear."

Catania told Violeta that she would have to be on "stand-by," at the club, because the exact date of what would be the big drop depended on things like the weather outlook offshore or whether there were any Coast Guard interdiction patrols about. But Perez had already told her that, and she prepared to let Bartley know that she would have to work the night of his son's stag party. She wondered how she could explain and how this might work out. Maybe later, when he knew the truth, he would forgive her. But for now, she had to focus on the operation, or she might not be alive to explain the truth.

She called her father in Mexico every week, and it was during a call in the third week of September that he gave her the news. Since NAFTA was passed, there had been a lot of pressure on small farmers. Cheap US corn exports to Mexico had quintupled, driving farmers off their homesteads and northward in search of jobs across the Rio Grande.

Her father, Ramon, was clever, and he had found ways to move to more profitable endeavors. With the help of a *Pro-Campo* cash transfer subsidy, he had managed to survive. Now, without warning, they had sent him a letter stating that he no longer qualified for the subsidy and that they were calling in taxes that had been in arrears from the bad years—taxes that he'd been told were written off when he got the subsidy. "It's finished here, Sofia," he said. "I will have to go to America to pick lettuce."

"This just happened—unexpectedly?" she asked.

"*Sí, m'hija.*"

An hour later, she was once again in Perez's office, and it was she who was out of breath, because she had run from the Parcel 7 Parking Garage. Again, they spoke in Spanish. "You think you can blackmail me, you son of a bitch?"

"Calm yourself, Violeta! There's no blackmail here."

"You arranged it all! And if I agree to go to Torreón to get evidence on Mejias, my father keeps his farm, right? This is not blackmail?"

"Wait just a minute. We helped your father to get the subsidy."

"Which he qualified for!"

"We helped, and as a favor to us, the Mexican government helped him because we explained that you were assisting them and us in the war against narco-traffickers. Now you want to take your ball and go home, so we reported that you're no longer as cooperative as you have been, which is true. If you decide to work with us on this bid to get Mejias, I'm sure we can get them to rescind their decision. It's very straightforward—*tal para cual*—'tit for tat' as the Americans say. It's how the world works. It's not *blackmail!*"

"I call it blackmail because that's what it is!"

"You help us, and we help you. Just think it over. We'll be watching out for you all the time."

"Oh, of course you will!"

"Your father—"

She didn't want to hear him talk about her father, so she got up and left, quietly this time. She cried as she drove along 128 South, exiting the highway in Burlington, where she sat for a while in her car in the

Starbuck's parking lot, thinking, and listening to Vicente Fernandez singing *Cielito Lindo.*

There was no way out; she called Perez. "I'll do it," she said. "*¡Qué cabrón eres!*"

She didn't hear his reply, which she was sure was some patronizing bullshit about what a great thing she was doing. She turned off her phone and cranked up the music. Her father always said that no one could sing *ranchera* like Vincente Fernandez.

Seventeen

The 15th of October was a bad day for Bartley Hannigan. First, he awakened to the faint but discernible rumbling of tractors, which he knew, before even opening his eyes, was the sound of the road going in for the Stonehenge Condominiums. Second, his son's stag party was set for that evening, and Violeta had gone dark on him. He supposed that she would be working.

For the last week, she had not responded to his calls or texts, and their last conversation had been ominous. Suddenly serious, grave even, she'd said that she would have to go back to Mexico soon to attend to a family problem, but had been vague about when, or even if, she'd be back. Cornelius said she had come by once after that when Bartley was not home, but she had left no message. He wondered if the whole affair had been a misunderstanding, a grand illusion, much like his marriage.

And finally, "to put the tin hat on it," as the Irish say, he was to meet with Bede to review his SMART goals for the upcoming "evaluation cycle." He could hear the fat bastard now, "Specific and strategic goals! Attainable and action-oriented! Based on data! Focused on outcome and not process!"

He felt nauseated as he sat up in bed and searched with his feet for his slippers. This low tide in the sea of his being was not helped by the fact that the night before he had walked in his father's footsteps down to the American Legion, where the old veterans set him on his father's barstool like the rightful heir on his throne. He had knocked back more than a few in an attempt to forget everything he was now remembering in the cold light of morning.

He saw that there was an email on his phone from Sheila Vondersaar of the D&E Book Club: "You were right. Louise is nuts. She told us you are having a *ménage a trois* with a stripper and an Irish farmhand. She wants to 'out' you. Strange. Be careful. She read a poem about a guy I think was you. It was *bizarre*."

Whatever. He showered and dressed and descended to the kitchen to drink two strong black coffees. Ten minutes of peace before the onslaught of the tsunami of bullshit.

The hole into which he felt he had sunk felt somehow deeper as he listened to Cornelius, who was chopping wood out by the back porch, singing one of his typically mournful Irish songs:

Then it's farewell darling I now must leave you,
No more to meet you on yon moorland dale.

Could it be? Was he no more to meet Violeta? What happened?

For I've travelled England, I have travelled Ireland,
I have travelled Scotland o'er and o'er,
May the heavens above now protect my darling,
Near the mountain streams where the moorcocks crow.

May the heavens above protect her, even if, for some reason he could not understand, he was no more to meet her. He could not protect himself, though, from an aching sadness as he remembered her dark eyes and crooked smile.

Fall was in the air as he stepped out the door, and Cornelius, leaning on the axe handle, said, "*Dia dhuit ar maidin! Aon scéal?*"

"You sound cheerful, whatever you're saying."

"Ah, it's a fine day. Much better than July around here, when the sun is splittin' the rocks."

Bartley nodded and descended the stairs in the same way that a convict might ascend the stairs to the gallows. "I'm off to work."

The Irishman frowned, "Oh, what can ail thee, knight-at-arms?"

He stopped, shook his head, and shrugged. He felt powerless and somewhat broken. "It seems Violeta is tired of me. Not surprising. I'm tired of myself."

Both hands on the top of the axe handle, now, he leaned toward his friend. "I wanted to speak to you about her. She is troubled, Bartley. There is a great weight on her mind. Something that has nothing a' tall to do with her feelings for yourself."

"Did she tell you that?"

"She did not."

"How do you know?"

"I know rightly, and you can chalk it down."

"Yes, but *how* do you know?"

He swung the axe up onto his shoulder and smiled. "I've six older brothers. Me dear father had six older brothers, don't you see?"

"Oh, right. Seventh son of . . . right."

"Maybe that's it, or maybe it's just obvious, Bartley. Like it was obvious the night you 'met' her that you already knew her."

"Oh."

"You're not *that* smooth, boy. But, you've been so kind, and I thought if it was that important to you that you created all these daft schemes . . . and I have been more welcome at the library—everywhere, suddenly, so 'twas for my own good, and now I'm quite accustomed to it. Anyway, I can tell you that it's not yourself is the problem, Bartley. But there *is* a problem. I'm afraid that she's in some kind of peril."

"Really? Hmmm. You could be right. You know, there are all these problems, let's say whatever Violeta's problem is, and that goddess up there on the hill, and the maniac poet, and my job—and well, I mean, Septo is, I guess you would have to say, some kind of magical creature. And so, I mean, can't he help?"

"In what way?"

"I don't know, but in *some* way—sorting things out, using his magical talents or whatever—just to help us in whatever way we need help? Because I feel like we need help."

"Yes, yes, I see. 'Tis true for you, Bartley." The Irishman swung the axe down casually, burying the head in the top of a log. He gazed up toward the hill where the stone circle had been erected long ago to honor a spirit that still ghosted about the wood. Cornelius squinted in a way that Bartley had come to recognize as his skeptical squint. "But you see, there are all kinds of forces out there which operate for good or ill. And they can't really be harnessed for our ends in any dramatic way, nor change the facts of who we are and what we do and our causes and effects and our what-have-you's. It's they who need our help, you see, and not so much the other way about."

"But this guy can appear and disappear. He's got some real power there."

"Ah, sure, but he could never really focus it on a great purpose."

"Why not?"

"He's a bit of a ball hopper."

"What?"

"Well, in the first place, he's interested *mainly* in drinking. D'ya know like?"

Bartley nodded resignedly. "That is true."

The squinting eyes now began to spread into his other features so that even his mouth squinted skeptically, and his shoulders rose in skeptical apology. "And so, you know, he'd *like* to help, I think, but he would be a fierce unreliable ally for any serious undertaking. That's why he wants *us* to do it."

"I get the picture. Well, I'm off to the institute."

"Right, so."

Bartley heard the thwack and crack of log-splitting behind him as he walked toward the car with his briefcase, and he envied Cornelius that honest and simple labor.

The day was grueling. It wasn't just the hangover, or that he had a contest of wills with Yahaira about texting during class. He usually treated that young woman with kid gloves; she was a volatile creature of whom Mr. Dillon in the Discipline Office had once said, "She would *beat the shit* out of most of the boys in this school." However, today he was in no mood for her insolence, and her reluctance to accept his request that she put her phone away resulted in an escalation of a mild admonition into a loud confrontation and her ejection from the room.

No, it wasn't that, nor that Jeremy fell asleep once again and began to drool on his desk, nor that the one millionth student in his wretched career found it necessary to inform him that he "*hated* to read," nor that

Raphael said he "didn't need to know" the word *antonym*. "Why can't I just say *opposite?* Nobody uses these words! 'Oh, it was very *tranquil.*' Nobody says that!"

He didn't have the energy to rebut even this facile argument. "You're right, Raphael. Knowledge is bad. Ignorance is good."

It wasn't any of the hundred minor debasements that it was the lot of the high school teacher to endure day in and day out, nor even when Yahaira's counselor called him during last period to ask about *his version* of the *incident*, since she had already heard some twisted tale from a perpetually resentful Yahaira. Certain counselors and 'advocates' were inclined to believe the student and not the teacher. All of that was just the job, like correcting papers over the weekend. Enduring adolescent irrationality and the wacky advocates and enablers of spoiled, unwilling, unresponsive, and uncooperative slugs—that was the job.

But this new ignominy—the insinuation of corporate culture into education, this obsession with data collection, and this robotic adherence to laid-out daily objectives and numerically-categorized standards—to gathering "artifacts" of compliance with fifty shades of "indicators," this mother lode of drivel that was heaped once more on his aching head by the overbearing Bede in a meeting which it was too painful, later, for Bartley even to recall—this was the final and ultimate degradation of the teacher.

And all the while, even as Bede thumbed through his "evaluation binder," complaining once again that the standards were not written on *each* cover sheet, Bartley's deeper thoughts were with the woman who had come into his life so suddenly and in such a strange fashion. And now, it seemed, would disappear with equal suddenness. In some dim, incense-laden corner of his mind, he could see Madame Veruschka Petrovna leaning over a deck of Tarot cards. How her words had ignited the cold candle of hope in his soul when she foretold, albeit amid the 'shit-storm,' the arrival of true love. Ah, well, what could you expect for twenty bucks from a seaside gypsy? Or from anyone.

"So, either tonight, tomorrow night, or at the latest Monday night, we'll need you. Just plan to be here—you work tonight, anyway, so we'll let you know. It will be a late pick-up. Now I know, Violeta, that you never did any work 'OTC.'" Catania was referring to work "outside the club," in other words, turning tricks. "You're a dancer, not a working girl. You're different. To tell you the truth. . . ." He raised his palms and patted the air as if he were playing patty-cake with an imaginary friend. This gesture was designed to indicate that he was surrendering to a desire to tell the truth. "To be *perfectly* honest with you, I feel protective of you, Violeta."

"You are very good, Mister Catania."

"Well." He nodded to admit that this was true. "Anyway, our new business partners—these countrymen of yours with the strange names—the character—Cachorro? I understand he's taken a shine to you. He's been callin' you here, tryna charm you I guess, with what little charm he has, an' askin' you to go back to Mexico with him?"

"Yes. You think I should do that? I don't really know him. Is he a good man?"

"No, Violeta, he is not a good man. He is a strange man, I think, and a bad man. Violent. He got money, yes. But it's a dangerous life, you know? I would advise you against going away with him."

She nodded, silent for a while, and said, "I think I would like to go to México with him." She could imagine Perez, probably later, when Sandoval played the edited tape for him, pumping the air with his fist.

"It's your decision, sweetheart. It might even be good for our business relationship. But I would advise you very strongly not to become involved with this guy."

"I know how to handle this kind of man."

"A killer? You know how to handle a killer, Violeta? I mean I got protection, from Dodge Square, from guys like Hatchet Harlow and Cold Fingers. They're bad guys, too. An' up here, you're with me. With us. I'm jus' sayin' you go down there, what protection you got? You're on your own, kid. I told you I would like to protect you—I can't protect you there.

It's your decision. I'm not your father, but what do you think your father would tell you?"

At this, Violeta, in one instant, forgot her training, her experience and her courage. She lost her cool. She rose and ran from the room, fearing she would burst into tears. Catania's words had struck the heart that she was sure she had hardened. She knew what her father would say, and she also knew that Catania, this dishonest gangster and strip club impresario, cared more about her than the bastards for whom she was risking her life. She got in her car and dialed Perez.

"I'm done," she said.

"Wait a minute!" he shouted into the phone.

"It's over! Take the evidence you have and do what you want with it. I will never see Catania or Cachorro or any of them again."

"But your father!"

"*Chinga tu madre, Perez!*"

Bartley had spent an hour after school with the well-meaning Hadeel, a gentle soul who had come to America as a refugee from Iraq. His heart went out to the young man, who, after only six years with the English language, was trying to plow through *Macbeth*, with its strange prophecies, supernatural creatures, inhuman or perhaps too-human ambition and bloody vengeance, all expressed in a rich and arcane language which Bartley had to explain nearly line by line. But the young Iraqi tried his best, and that was all anyone could ask of anyone.

When they had finished Act I, Hadeel leaned back and pulled a Hershey bar out of his backpack. "You want some?"

"No, thanks."

Hadeel looked at the wrapper as he chewed a piece of chocolate, and read, "*Hershey's Since 1894*." He looked up, aghast, and said, "Mister, this thing is *expired!*"

Bartley got a laugh out of that, but as he headed back to the farm, Macbeth's words reverberated in his cranium: "Make dust of our paper and with rainy eyes write sorrow on the bosom of the earth." God help us. He needed something, a cigarette and a drink? No, a walk in the woods, to clear his head and restore his serenity.

His serenity was knocked on its ass when he saw Violeta Martinez in his driveway leaning against her car. But if serenity fled, then Hope, "the thing with feathers," in the words of Emily Dickinson, was now perched, somewhat timidly, on a nearby branch.

"Violeta," he began.

"My name is not Violeta."

"*What?*"

"My name is Sofia Garcia Reyes," she said. "I am—I was, an agent of *La Policia Federal De México*, working for the D.E.A. on one *línea de investigación.* . . ."

She gazed upward as if reading from a PowerPoint presentation above his head, or something memorized in her own. ". . .working one line of the investigation into a Mexican drug cartel to obtain, analyze and study their routes of supply and distribution and to collect evidence to persecute, to *prosecute* them. That is why I am—why I was working at the Big Moon."

Bartley had gone pale. This struck him as far stranger than a little man drinking wine in the cellar. "Sofia? An agent? Holy shit! Though that does explain a few things. So, what has all this got to do with me? W-what did it ever have to do with me?"

"What has it to do with you is that . . . is that I love you. And I need your help." She wiped at her tearing eyes with her fingers, and Bartley's heart wrenched.

"What is it, Vio—I mean—the other name—Sofia. Boy, *that's* strange." She smiled through her tears, and Bartley produced a handkerchief from his suit jacket pocket and handed it to her. "It's a lot to take in at once. DEA— Jesus. How can I help you?"

"I don't know how to say—there are two people I love in the world. Only two, really. My father and you, Bartley. But now the agency, they threaten my father to take his farm if I don't do something I can't do! *I can't!* So I quit the job."

"You quit what job? As an agent or at the club?"

"The two. And you see it's a problem because Catania, that's the owner of the club—"

"Okay. Look, you can explain it all later. What do you want *me* to do?"

She paused briefly, took a deep breath, and said, "I want you to marry me, and then bring my father here to live."

"All right."

"I know you need time to think about it."

"I don't need to think about it. Yes, I'll marry you and we'll bring your father here—we need a real farmer here—and we'll all live together. We'll reopen the farm stand and even try our hand at a vineyard if you want."

"You are sure?"

"Of course. I mean, if you know what kind of grapes would do well in this soil."

She threw her arms around him, but he pushed her back. "Hang on, let me do this right." He drew her a few feet off the gravel driveway and knelt on the leaf-strewn grass. "Sofia—what's your name again?"

"Sofia Garcia Reyes."

"Sofia Garcia Reyes, will you marry me?"

She pulled him up to her and embraced him in her arms, and love encompassed him and girded his heart in a power more potent than any goddess, and he felt the wet tears on his neck and heard her dear voice whispering, "Yes, I will."

Two days later, a bald man wearing suspenders over a wrinkled white shirt, his jacket draped over one arm, entered the back room of the Big Moon an hour before the club opened. He placed a finger over his lips. Joseph Catania, the Teacher, nodded and began innocently to hum the Sicilian folk song, "Zumba Bimba."

The bald man set a briefcase on a chair and opened it. It was full of wires, headphones, and what looked to the Teacher like a random tangle of electronic components. From among these he drew a small hand-held device and, after making a few adjustments, began to carry it about the room.

Catania's old mentor, Francesco Galante, had always told him to have his office swept regularly, and he had gotten a little careless. But there was something about the way Violeta had disappeared on him in the middle of the big deal, the way she reacted when he tried to help her. He smelled a rat. Still, the deal had gone down pretty smoothly.

Catania watched the man from Northeast Bug Sweep as he moved about the room. From time to time the man would stop, shrug, shake his head, and change the setting on the device. "Oh well," he thought, "who can understand young women anyway?"

Then, at a frequency of 3 GHz, a red light began to flash. The device vibrated in the sweeper's palm. Catania's heart sank as the man looked him in the eyes and nodded. He turned off the device and pointed at the power cord behind his desk. Catania showed his teeth and growled. "*La puttana!*"

Just then his cell phone pinged; it was a text from Cold Fingers McGee: **Feds raid dodge square all go down I got out.** "*La porcaputtana!*" he spat.

A pounding commenced out at the front door, which was still locked. They were here! He stepped backward like a cornered animal as an outcry erupted in the lounge. He heard Coco and Sissy screaming and crying, "Police!" while simultaneously the back door to his office began to shudder under heavy blows.

The sweeper grabbed his jacket and scurried out toward the bar. Catania pulled a hammer from his desk drawer and ran into the bathroom, locking the door behind him. He tapped a text furiously: **violeta snitch**.

He pressed 'send' then brought the hammer down four times, hard, on the phone; he scooped the shattered parts and flushed them down the toilet as he heard the back door crash inward, slamming against the wall.

Catania emerged from the bathroom with hands raised and saw men in Kevlar vests and riot helmets storming his office. They threw him to the floor and cuffed him. A tired-looking DEA agent looked on, content, but not overjoyed, while another agent read Catania his rights.

Eighteen

Bartley found out, in a call from Manus's friend Brendan, even before he saw it in the paper, that there had been a drug bust at the Big Moon. Having heard Sofia's story, he was not surprised. In any case, the bachelor party was cancelled.

"Just as well," he told Brendan. "Not much good happens at bachelor parties." Brendan reluctantly acknowledged the truth of this observation.

The wedding party, however, was not cancelled. There was a no-frill marriage ceremony performed by the Honorable Michael Geary, City Clerk, who, by the power invested in him by the Governor of the Commonwealth, pronounced Manus and Jill husband and wife. A photographer friend shot photos of them—the groom in a gray suit and the bride in a simple blue body contour dress. Then they and their guests congregated at the Mt. Pleasant Golf Club to celebrate the nuptials.

Bartley, glowing, arrived with Sofia on his arm. In his head, a haughty little announcer described everyone's entrance in Downton Abbey accents. *Casually elegant for the occasion, Sofia is wearing a black satin knee-length dress with a flowered lace back and beaded strappy sandals with a matching clutch. Adele has chosen a more formal look, in a yellow, low-cut, sleeveless sequin dress. She appears as smug as ever, of course, on the arm of a balding but vigorous-looking man sporting a three-piece gray plaid suit that is clearly of better quality and sans doute more costly than Bartley Hannigan's, though Bartley may have a tad more swagger owing to the neat buttonhole flower, a twin to the one the groom is sporting. The mother of the groom is not wearing a corsage, since there isn't a lot of material in that dress to pin it to anyway! Hoh hoh hoh.*

The ex-spouses and their escorts exchanged polite handshakes and innocuous comments and took their seats at opposite ends of a long table reserved for the wedding party, Bartley and Sofia on Manus's side, and

Adele and Donald on the bride's side. The bride's parents looked like a pair of refugees from the Age of Aquarius; her father was a Jerry Garcia *doppelganger*, while her mother had so much turquoise and silver around her neck that Bartley thought she could have purchased Manhattan from the Indians.

Their meeting and introductions had been polite. Everyone was acting the adult, which was fine, though there was a certain amount of whispering and a few titters among those guests who had known Bartley and Adele as a couple for so long.

"You know why I love this whole idea, the city clerk and a party at the club?" Bartley asked Sofia.

"Why do you love it?" Her silver earrings flashed and quivered as she leaned toward him.

"*Minimum* of bullshit. None of the bridesmaids in matching gowns, and flower girls and tuxedos with ruffled shirts—no horrid band playing 'The bride feeds the groom,' and all that crap. Just a modest gathering of friends, a few drinks, sandwich and salad bar, assorted chicken wings and finger food, and they're off to Quebec City."

Manus's friend Brendan did have a turntable, a microphone, and speakers set up in one corner of the room, and soon the new couple danced to 'their song,' "Someone to Watch Over Me," after which Brendan raised a glass and the crowd stood for the toast.

"Manus and Jill," he said. He gazed toward the ceiling and after a thoughtful pause during which some serious cogitation seemed to work his brow. He shook his curly head and said simply, "Wow." A further pause ensued, after which Brendan continued haltingly, "My—my two best friends are now *married*, and . . . wow." His eyes opened wide and he blew what a poet had once called a "windy suspiration of forced breath," as if the full import of this new reality had just dawned on him. This realization evoked an even more earnest "Wow!" He scratched his noggin and concluded with a final wholehearted, "Wow!"

"Wow!" the crowd responded and raised their glasses.

"That was so sweet," Sofia whispered as the guests resumed their seats.

"I suppose—oh my God!" Bartley sat bolt upright, eyes fixed on something at the other end of the room.

"What is it?" Sofia asked.

"The psycho poet has crashed the party!"

"Bartley Hannigan!" she shouted as she advanced.

"Who the hell is that?" Manus asked.

Louise Andino, Daughter of the Mutant Muse, was bearing down on them. "You bring your Big Moon *stripper* girlfriend Vio-LETA to your son's wedding celebration? What class!"

Bartley stood. "Her name is Sofia. And she's not my girlfriend! She's my fiancée!"

Adele's voice, loudly: "*She is?*"

Bartley ignored Adele and glared at Louise. "And *you* were not invited!"

"No! You had to invite a *stripper* instead!"

"Get out!"

Violeta-Sofia was already on her feet, striding toward the psycho poet. "It is you who do not have class. Get out or I will make you regret to show your face here!"

"Oh, Violeta! You are *so cute* when you *butcher* the English language!"

"You're the one who butchers the language with your shit poetry!" Bartley cried, tripping over Sofia's chair as he extricated himself from his position at the head table.

"Dad?" Manus ventured, rising nervously, "Dad, can we—"

Bartley, still clutching his napkin, was on his way to join the fray, when he paused at the end of the table to explain to the stunned crowd who now sat with gaping mouths, "She's a stalker who writes poems about killing puppies!"

Brendan, at the microphone, gave vent to another "Wow," which reverberated through the room.

Things were degenerating fast. Bartley was charging toward Louise when Manus leaped over the table and tackled him. "Dad! You can't. . . !"

The sight of the struggling father of the groom pinned on the floor by his son elicited a collective groan of concern from the crowd.

Meanwhile, Sofia confronted Louise Andino in the middle of the dance floor. "Leave this place, *now*."

"Why don't you strip *here?*" The psycho poet let out her inhuman wild-cat howl and lunged at Sofia, fingers spread like claws, apparently intent on tearing down the top of her dress. In a series of rapid movements that left the struggling Bartley, and everyone else, shocked to stillness, Sofia Garcia Reyes, with steely calm, knocked the madwoman's hands away, slapped her face twice, forehand and backhand, struck her in the solar plexus, shot an arm under her attacker's arm and around her neck, spun her about, and wound up behind her, holding her criss-crossed arms by the wrists, forming the natural straightjacket in which, Bartley thought, she belonged. Louise Andino's upper body was immobilized as Sofia marched her toward the door.

"WOW!" Brendan announced.

Bartley and Manus rose. Jill ran to brush Manus's jacket, straighten his tie, flatten his hair, and re-pin his skewed and drooping buttonhole flower.

They then went along with the crowd which, almost silently, and of one accord, followed the victor and the vanquished out the door into the parking lot.

"Hers is the yellow Volkswagen!" Bartley called.

Sofia escorted the villainous versifier to her vehicle and whispered something to her before she released her. Louise fumbled with her keys for a moment, got in the car, and drove away without another word, poetic or otherwise.

Another scene was developing in the parking lot. Adele's date, who had been introduced to Bartley as a Donald Delaney, was in earnest conversation with a tearful woman while Adele looked on, imperious, indignant, and superior.

"I told you I just had to do this, Caroline," the man in the plaid suit entreated. "After today—" Donald was trying to speak softly, but he was getting louder as he attempted to make himself heard over her sobs.

"I don't understand! You don't *have to do* anything! If you want to be with me, like you *say* you do, why do you have to do anything with *that one?*" She snapped a wet Kleenex in the direction of Adele.

"I do want to be with you—it's just that—"

"Why are you *here*, Donald?" Caroline wanted to know.

He could think of no good answer, and Adele, in a demonstration of disdainful self-control, said, "Oh, for God's sake, go with her, Donnie! It's quite all right really."

She turned and some of the guests began to follow her back into the club. While her erstwhile gallant attendant stood there in a morass of indecision, Bartley couldn't resist repeating the question. "Why *are* you here, Donald?"

He turned on Bartley, fuming, "I'll take no questions from a man who believes in *leprechauns!*"

"Ah, don't disparage the wee folk, Donald, me lad!" As Sofia came up and took his arm, he added, "Or I may have to have my fiancée kick your ass!"

"Come on, Bartley," Sofia said, pulling his arm, "let's go back in."

"Unmitigated *quackery!*" Donald was shouting. "But that's the nice thing about being *crazy*, Hannigan. There's always a *leprechaun* to talk to!"

"Begosh and begorra, Donald, look! The colleen you *really* like is after leavin'! For God's sake boyo, go after her!"

Caroline's BMW was pulling away. Donald had to decide. After a quick exasperated glance in the direction of the retreating Adele, he ran to his Mercedes, tie flying over his shoulder, and followed the BMW. "Ah," said Bartley, looking after them, "Venus is a fickle goddess. She certainly turns the tables quickly, doesn't she?"

Inside, Brendan was back on the mike. "Is that entertainment, folks, or *what?*" Laughter, head-shaking, beer bottles clinking and jocular voices. "And how about Mr. Hannigan's fiancée?" Cheers and applause. "In fact, Jill just asked me to dedicate this song to Sofia!"

The bride led Manus onto the parquet, and soon the floor was filled with couples rocking to the Commodores: "She's a Brick House."

But when the song was over, Sofia pulled Bartley aside. "Do you think it is ruined, their wedding party?"

"Hell no! As long as the bride is happy, everyone is happy!"

Sofia looked in the bride's direction and smiled. "She is not a *prima dona*. Some women would be in the bathroom crying."

"Nah, Jill's what we call 'a hot shit.' They're gonna be fine. By the way, what did you say to Louise—the crazy woman?"

"I translated the Mexican proverb: *El que mucho abarca, poco aprieta.* 'The person who wants to hold everything, holds nothing.' I told her to let it go."

"Very sound advice. Though I could never figure out what she was hanging on to."

Bartley had told her that the young couple would be fine, but he wondered if Adele would be fine. The truth was he was starting to feel sorry for her. He knew that Jerry Garcia and his Birkenstock-wearing, granola-crunching mate were not her cup of tea, and he loved Sofia for not minding when he suggested they go and join the new in-laws and the ex-wife. Sofia was no *prima dona* either, thank God.

Adele would never change, though; she wanted none of their companionship. She was happy that Manus was happy, and was polite to them, but she excused herself to join some other friends, business associates whom Bartley did not know.

Eventually, the party began to wind down and Manus and Jill made their way to the exit and to the road that led to a new life, acknowledging with broad smiles and waving arms the chorus of well-wishers and their half-drunken cheers. Adele gave the other members of the wedding party a curt nod and a quick handshake and hurried off, saying she had a Uber waiting.

Bartley watched her go and squeezed Sofia to him. His son was a married man, the wife who had borne that son was in a cab going to back to her own mysterious and separate life, and he was with another woman, who was his fiancée. *How strange is this series of scenes that we call life!*

It was Saturday morning, and Cold Fingers McGee was having his breakfast of a bagel and a coffee at a table beside the plate window at the Coffee Mill. With his thin dark hair shining with a slick pomade, his crisp white shirt and neatly pressed autumn jacket, and his round tortoise-shell glasses resting on the ski slope of a connoisseur's nose, he appeared a Catholic priest, or a mathematics professor, or maybe Richard Nixon on holiday.

Appearances can be deceiving, however; he knew no Latin, nor could he have solved the most elementary algebraic equation, though he did always know the number of bullets that were left in the chamber of his Smith and Wesson. And who he was supposed to kill. All right, occasionally, he shot the wrong guy, but what the hell, those guys probably did something along the line that merited a bullet. This simple rationalization made the hit man chuckle over his bagel.

Cold Fingers was no Rhodes scholar, but even he could see that there was not much upside in dedicating a lot of time to hunting down this Violeta Martinez. Teacher had called him once from jail. Cold Fingers asked him if he was sure about that thing that he had told him. He said, *Almost positive.* Hmm. *Almost.* And who would pay him for the job?

There was enough evidence on the Teacher and the other members of Dodge Street to put them away for a considerable stretch. All their money would be going to lawyers to try to keep them in one of the better jails and maybe hide some of their ill-gotten assets. Coco and Sissy and the other girls at the club didn't seem to know much about this Violeta other than her name, which was probably phony. He had already spent a few days searching and had located two other women named Violeta Martinez in the area, but neither one of those could *ever* have worked as a dancer at the Big Moon. Cold Fingers had pondered the situation for a while after that jailhouse call before he threw his phone in the river.

He still wondered whether he should forget about the almost positive snitch. He'd heard they caught a couple of the cartel soldiers, but that was just the cost of doing business, wouldn't faze the top dogs south of the border. The guys the Feds picked up would be as silent as the grave as long as they had a family back in old Mexico.

Coco had texted him a photo she took of Violeta. It was better than the marquee photo, in which she wore a headdress and war paint. Whoever she was, she might be back by now. Of course, he would *like* to kill her, just as a last favor to the gang, and maybe for his own reputation. He wouldn't mind fucking her, either, though Coco said she was a tough broad—broke a guy's nose one night. Rape would be a lot of work—killing her would be easy. But he needed paying work and couldn't waste too much time trying to find her.

"Someone's lost who can't be found—please, Saint Anthony, look around." He mumbled the quick prayer. Short of that miracle, it didn't seem likely that he'd ever find her. In a couple of weeks, he would head out to Vegas, where there were always people who needed protection or whatever from a guy who could be relied upon to keep things confidential.

He finished his bagel and tipped the last of his coffee down his gullet. Then, just as he was getting ready to leave, he gazed out the window and saw a couple getting out of a shitbox of a spray-painted car. A slim guy in jeans and a V-neck sweater over a T-shirt, short hair, graying at the sides, and a woman, a good-lookin' woman, also in jeans and a light brown—he couldn't remember if they called it camel hair or cashmere jacket with a red scarf. She was Hispanic-looking, long dark hair in a braid. Cold Fingers watched them, how as the man came around the car and took her outstretched hand. They looked so comfortable together; he envied them because he had never felt really comfortable with any woman. He had never felt comfortable with anyone, unless it was business. While they put coins in the kiosk, directly across the street from him, he studied the woman's face, which looked vaguely familiar. *Wait a minute!* He picked his phone up off the table and opened Coco's text, staring intently at the photo of Violeta Martinez. *Holy shit.*

He zipped up his jacket and headed toward his car. From a box in his trunk, he extracted a 2" x 4" Dart Covert GPS Tracking Device with magnetic mount, an indispensable tool of his trade. So much easier than trying to follow a car through traffic; besides, if the girl was an undercover agent, she'd be trained to spot a tail.

When he was beside the rear of the shitbox, he bent to tie his wingtips. Before he rose, one hand reached up into the wheel well, and the magnet stuck. As he walked away, he promised himself to light a candle to that reliable old monk, Saint Anthony of Padua.

Sofia Garcia Reyes and Bartley K. Hannigan were drinking a tea and a coffee respectively, seated on a couch at Brew'd Awakening. They had been making the last few trips between her apartment and the farm, as she was moving in with Bartley.

"So," he said, "events are converging. Samhain, October thirty-first, is six days from today. The road is going in, but the tractors, we hope, won't quite be up to the stone circle. Your father is selling his farm to his neighbor and should be here by—well, whenever the paperwork is straightened out. And we are getting married—when?"

"November twenty-third. It's a Tuesday, just before Thanksgiving."

"Good. Anyway, they said we'd have the marriage license in three days. You want a party?"

Her nose crinkled. "I don't care about a party. Let's go to that town near the sea, Poor Smith?"

"Portsmouth, right. Good idea. I'll see how many days I can get off from the Institute."

"Bartley, what do you think is going to happen on that night?"

"Samhain? I really don't know. All I can say is that if you'd seen her—"

"I heard her. That was enough."

"Don't worry, Vio—I mean, Sofia. You'll no doubt be armed with a hazel wand and a Brigid's cross or whatever Cornelius comes up with. What's more dangerous is this: will you have to testify in open court against those gangsters?"

"They have got so much recording and photos, and of course the one hundred fifty pounds of cocaine. All that they need from me is—*una declaración jurada*—an affidavit. The judge says I don't need to appear. I mean the bail was five million dollars each, so they're gonna be away for a long time."

"And the Mexicans?"

"Once they check out the situation, meet the guys here and set up the deal, they get a couple low level guys to drive the boat. They will not come back."

"Then why are you always looking over your shoulder? Looking in the rearview mirror?"

"I just am being careful. It's how they train you to be." Sofia leaned forward and clasped his knee. "Maybe I put you in danger? Maybe I should go away until the case is over?"

He put on his lousy Humphrey Bogart impersonation, "We're in this together, sugar."

"You're sweet," she said. "Perez had me hand in my badge and gun, just like in the movies. But he has calmed down now. They know the choice they offered me was no good, an' now they think I'm going to be American, and I don't need them, they say *maybe* they can get me job at Logan Airport with the Homeland Security."

"Really? I thought you wanted to work with your father to make us the greatest farm in the Merrimack Valley."

"We have to decide about that, but until we are ready we need to keep some money coming in."

"Very practical." They put their empty cups in the collection bin. "Let's get the last of the stuff and give the landlord the key. Cornelius is bringing the U-Haul back to Middlesex Street."

"*Sí, el comandante.*"

A few days later, Cold Fingers downloaded the information from the tracking device onto his laptop. The base of operations seemed to be in Tyngsborough. He put the address into Google Earth and got an aerial view of the property. "Jesus, out in the boonies," he said to himself. "Look at all the woods up there behind the property. Must be the State Forest—lakes, swamps, and a lot of trees." He zoomed in on the house and barn and saw two cars parked in the driveway. Behind the house, and covering the hills, the trees appeared to be in rows, like the gravestones in Arlington. Strange.

He looked for neighbors—none for a mile along the road in either direction, or anywhere behind them. Perfect. There was a trailer and what looked like some tractors, a construction site about three quarters of a mile northeast of the farmhouse. No one would be around there after dark.

A brilliant idea was dawning on him. Halloween night had always been a favorite of his. On that night, you could wear a disguise, and no one would think it the least bit odd, not even the cops. And one might even wander onto the wrong property in disguise, looking for a Halloween party. He would pay Violeta a visit, and her boyfriend or whatever he was (bad luck for him), dressed as the Grim Reaper. Which, of course, he was.

A few hours before sunrise on Sunday, the 29th of October, Farmer Lambeau, in his army surplus cot in a Spartan room in his farmhouse upriver, was having a strange and vivid dream.

He saw himself in a winter landscape, snowshoeing an untrodden way beneath oak and ash, the spreading branches filigreed in white. He could taste the pure cold air; the only sound was the compacting of the snow beneath his feet and the exhalation of his breath, which curled about him in a milky vapor until the wind shifted and on it he smelled burning wood. A minute later he heard singing, a woman's voice as clear as the winter air, and he saw the glint of a fire through the trees and a thin column of gray smoke.

The winter traveler slowed as he approached, because he saw a stranger near the fire. But as he drew near, the stranger became a friend. It was old Happy Hannigan standing beside the only evergreen in the forest. Another figure was there, quite suddenly, with him—it was her voice that rang in the forest, and still she sang. She was an extraordinary creature—a tall woman in a gown of white, belted in green, and wearing a long, hooded cloak of green. Happy smiled amiably while the woman stood by the fire, singing in a language which Farmer had never heard.

"Can you understand her, Happy?"

"I can, now," he said.

The woman finished her song and pulled the hood from her head. Farmer saw a woman of astonishing beauty: dark-haired, queenly, eyes like the gold of autumn's leaves, with the black feathers of a raven in her hair.

"Quite something, isn't she?" Happy asked, winking.

She spoke to Farmer, sadly, in the strange tongue. Happy drew near him and translated. "She says the oak among the saplings has been felled, the gallant one, and his sons are across the sea. I'm afraid it's up to you, now, old friend."

"Oak among the saplings? Up to me? What?"

Happy took Farmer's hand earnestly in one of his and placed the other on his shoulder. "My boy is in great danger."

Farmer would hear those words over and over in his head as he drank his morning coffee, as he patched the air intake pipe on the John Deere tractor, and later, as he performed some maintenance on his shotgun with brake cleaner and a toothbrush.

The same day, Ricardo Perez and another agent were interviewing Joe Catania in Room 3473 of MCI Cedar Junction Prison. At Catania's left was his lawyer, Myles Prower, who occasionally interrupted the interview to report that his client did not wish to respond to a particular question. Perez would nod politely and continue to scan the copious notes in front of him.

"Are you familiar with a person named Thomas McGee?"

"Hmm. I think I've heard of him."

"You may know him as 'Cold Fingers'?"

"Cold Fingers. No, I don't think I know that name."

"Are you sure?"

"My client has answered the question," Prower said. He spoke in what struck Perez as a tone of permanent disdain, since, after all, he lived in Wellesley and his eponymous ancestor had arrived in Plymouth, Massachusetts, aboard the *Mayflower*.

"It's just that seconds before he was arrested, your client sent a text message to Thomas McGee claiming that someone named Violeta, we think he was referring to a stripper named Violeta Martinez, was a 'snitch.' The Thomas McGee to whom he sent the text is suspected of being the hit man in a number of murders in this state, and in New Hampshire and Rhode Island. Your client appears to be surprised, counselor." Perez leaned across the table toward Catania and said, "We had already cloned your phone, *dumbass*."

Catania closed his eyes and shook his head and Prower gave him a dirty look. "Don't care for surprises, Mr. Catania, *as I told you*."

"So," Perez continued, "I'm just sayin' that if anything, what is that word, *untoward*, were to happen to the person that you told the hit man was a snitch, you might be charged with something far worse than running drugs. A federal serial murder case. Your client might want to get that message out to his friend, though the phone number he used to text him is no longer operative and the man appears to be lying very low."

"I didn't say for him to hit anyone," the accused said in his own defense.

"Interesting defense. But if someone you suspected of being a snitch, someone *you told* an assassin was a snitch ends up in a shallow grave, hey, maybe the jury will believe that you were just making conversation when you sent him that urgent message as you were being taken down. Yeah, that's good. Try it."

Perez clicked his pen closed and stuck it in his shirt pocket. "We're done for now."

Catania was escorted back to his cell. Normally, he would have made conversation with his attorney, asked him how he thought it went, but he knew how it had gone, and Prower was too much of a prig to converse with anyway. He nodded and walked out ahead of him, down the long corridor to his cell.

On the way back to the car, Perez thought he'd better call Sofia. He hadn't been happy about the way she'd concluded her part in the case, but the truth was, he didn't blame her one bit. She paid her dues, and what he'd asked of her, or tried to force her to do, was far beyond the call of duty. The job had gotten the best of him. He felt like a bastard.

Nineteen

The following day, Monday, the 30th, Bartley took a walk up to the stone circle just after dawn. The new connecting road from Sherwood was approaching perilously close to what Cornelius called "the magic enclosure." Already, the light here seemed to have changed with the clearing of the trees for that road. He trotted back to the house.

Cornelius was up reading one of his ancient annotated texts from the Royal Irish Academy, while Sofia stood by the stove, from which arose a wonderful aroma that mingled with the percolating coffee.

"What are you making, beautiful?"

"Huevos rancheros."

"I love the smell of cilantro." He sat at the table beside Cornelius. "Hey, Seventh Son, we got a problem."

"I know. I was up there before first light."

"I have to go to work. You keep an eye on the site. If they get too near the circle, let me know. I'll call Carnadine and try to stall him. Can you think of anything else we can do?"

"My friend Eva, the librarian, knows the state archaeologist. She's asked him to come up—maybe he can slow things down. Later on, we've got to prepare a bonfire on the hill for tonight."

"And in Ireland? You said there would be a ritual there?"

"Two poets, an archaeologist, some farmers, a shop girl, an American with issues, some literature students from U.C.C. and the parish priest will be at the *Mur na Mórrígan*, performing a ritual there, to light the way, as it were."

"I hope the little man was right about that."

"My own study of the *Dinnshenchas,* the ancient "place lore," would confirm that hypothesis. It's not obvious, but 'tis there."

Sofia set a plate down in front of each of them. "*¡Dios mio!*" cried Bartley, "Look at this breakfast! Avocado, tomatoes, sausage, cucumber, and eggs on a tortilla! What a marvel you are!"

"A marvel indeed," affirmed the Irishman.

Sofia came back with a plate of her own and joined them. "*Gracias, mis hombres,*" she said. They ate in silence for a short time, enjoying the food and the Bach cantata playing on WCRB.

"One thing I don't understand, Cornelius, well, beside the 'American with issues.' You said that a priest will be at this ceremony? You mean a Catholic priest?"

"Father Dunleavy, yes."

"But it's a pagan ceremony! Isn't that against—"

"Yes, you see Father Dunleavy is a Catholic priest, but he's also a *henotheist.*"

"What the hell is that?"

"He believes in the Holy Gospel, but he believes in other things, too. He just doesn't apply them both *at the same time,* you see. The way Dunleavy put it to me was that to really do justice to reality, you have to understand it in different ways. He's been reading a physicist named Frank Wilczek, a Nobel Prize winner over at MIT, who posits, 'tis a fascinating paradox, that when you have a deep truth, you see, it's opposite is also true. He calls these contrary truths *complementaries.*"

Bartley shook his head as if he'd just taken a shot of particularly raw bourbon. "Look, I'm just saying, as a priest, doesn't he have to believe that the Catholic Church is the true church?"

"And so he does. He just doesn't deny that there are other truths as well."

"But I mean the Apostles' Creed says, 'I believe in *the one* true Holy Catholic Church.'"

"Well, there isn't any *other* Holy Catholic Church!"

"What?"

"Listen Bartley, I wouldn't puzzle over it too much. You probably have to be Irish to understand."

"I think," Sofia said, "that the world would be a much happier place if all the people were the henotheists."

The men agreed that she had a point.

"What are you up to today, Sofia?" Bartley asked as he rose and got his bag ready.

"I have to meet with Perez. . . ."

"Thought you quit!"

"Yes, but I don't want to be a total *pendeja,* even if he is. He asked to see me about some detail of the case."

"Don't let him bully you!" After he had slung the strap of his bookbag over his shoulder he paused and said, "Never mind that last remark. I forgot whom I was talking to."

As Bartley drove past the entrance to the Stonehenge Condominiums, he saw men in hard hats milling around a trailer. One had a set of plans rolled up in his fist and walked with a sense of purpose. Depressing.

At school, he had to get coverage for his class while he attended a Special Ed meeting for Byron Leeman, who sat slouched and sullen at the conference table, looking like a sack of dirty laundry. His teachers were there, as was his mother, and his Special Ed liaison, Donna Archer. Donna was wont to see herself as "an advocate" for every student on her caseload, a noble calling which in her mind worked out to a simple equation: the onus for the student's academic success lay squarely and entirely on his teachers. To suggest that *the student* bore some of the responsibility for his or her own success would have amounted to hate speech.

Ms. Archer opened the meeting. "Let me begin by reading over Byron's Individualized Education Plan and the accommodations and modifications to which he's entitled under the plan."

She then launched into three pages of accommodations and modifications. "Byron may need extra time to complete assignments and classwork. He may retake tests and quizzes in his Assisted Studies class. Please do not call on Byron. If he wants to contribute he will raise his hand.

Byron is an auditory learner; he should be provided with recordings of the lesson that he can listen to at home. He gets stressed out easily and may need to take breaks during the class. He should be allowed to go out in the corridor and take a walk for up to five minutes to refocus. Byron should be given a reader to work with him on academic tests." On and on she droned, while the teachers sat there glancing at the clock and grimacing.

"So! Ms. Toner, would you like to begin? And please start by describing the accommodations you're making for Byron in your class so that he can succeed."

And so, the Annual Review began with discussions of Accessible Instructional Materials and Positive Behavioral Supports and Continuous Improvement and Focusing Monitoring Systems, but there was no continuous improvement. There had never been any improvement. And the meeting would conclude with further modifications to the Corrective Action Plan, and more paperwork, none of which would have any measurable effect on Byron's academic profile, which could be summed up in one word— the word that Harris used for his ilk: *slug.*

Finally, there was a pause in the discussion and Donna Archer looked earnestly at Byron, who was, understandably, nearly asleep, and asked, "What can *we* do, Byron, to help you succeed?" And Byron roused himself enough to shrug.

"Mr. Hannigan, you're next. Could you begin with a discussion of the modifications and accommodations you're making for Byron in accordance with his IEP?"

"I'd be happy to do that, only I should preface my remarks with the observation that it doesn't much matter what accommodations I'm making because he has been absent eighteen days and it's not even Halloween."

"Yes," Ms. Archer, admitted, "his attendance is *an issue.*"

"It's the major issue," Bartley said.

"When he *is* in class, what accommodations are you making for him?"

"I give him alternate assessments. I allow him extra time. I let him take quizzes open book; sometimes I write on his tests the page numbers where he can find the answers. I let him use a dictionary. I seat him right in front of the Smartboard. I've told him to come after school for help, which he has never done. I've tried pairing him with more motivated students—"

"Excuse me, Mr. Hannigan," his *advocate* interrupted, "but we encourage teachers not to use judgmental words like 'motivated' and 'unmotivated.' It's not helpful, and it can be hurtful. Byron *has been* diagnosed with ADD/ADHD and ODD."

"I'm sorry. That's a new one on me. What is ODD?"

Ms. Archer didn't seem to know, either. She paused and squinted; her lower jaw slid sideways as she pulled up the official educational diagnosis. "Oppositional Defiant Disorder," she said finally, nodding gravely.

The teachers stole straight-faced looks at each other, each daring the next to crack a smile.

"So," Archer wanted to know, "after making all of these *necessary* accommodations, why does he still have a 19 in your class, Mr. Hannigan?"

"Aside from the absences? He has a 19 because I can't make him care. He *doesn't care.*" He addressed the student's mother. "Mrs. Leeman, have you ever seen him do *any* homework?"

"He says he doesn't have any."

"He does. And he doesn't do it in his Assisted Studies class, either, where Ms. Stackpole will tell you she spends a lot of her time trying to keep him awake."

Ms. Archer squirmed as if her seat was getting uncomfortable. "Let's not start to blame the victim, here."

"Who *should* we blame? His teachers, right?"

"As was just explained, Byron suffers from ADD/ADHD and ODD."

"He also suffers from L-A-Z-Y!" Bartley said.

Ms. Archer's jaw fell, which fortunately seemed to render her speechless for a moment. Bartley addressed himself to the young man, who was finally stirring and sitting up a bit. "Byron, let's be honest. Do you give a shit about school *at all?*"

Archer's hands were waving in front of her, as if she'd like to cover his mouth. "No," he said, before she could stop him.

"Have you ever tried to study *anything* for *any course* in this school, *at all?*"

"No."

"Have you ever tried to read—"

"I *hate* reading."

Archer had regained her voice. "All right. We're getting way off track here. Far afield from the purpose and scope of the IEP meeting . . . and frankly, rather inappropriate and unprofessional—"

But at that point, without warning, Byron's mother reached over and gave him three rousing slaps in the head.

"Ow!" Byron said.

"Yes!" Bartley said.

"Please!" Archer implored.

"Your English teacher is right! You're a lazy bastard! You're gonna start doin' some homework and stayin' after school or I'll take your car away! And you're gonna get your lazy ass to school! You're not gonna sit here and tell me you don't give a shit when I'm working my ass off to pay for your phone and your car insurance and keeping a roof over your head!"

The angry mother wanted his teachers to write in his notebook every day what his homework was so that she could see it. Bartley didn't know if this method would work, but it was certain that no other method had. Sometimes kids did begin to care if something was on the line—a car, video games, or being able to play on the baseball team.

Bartley didn't usually carry his phone at school, but he had tucked it into the inside vest pocket in case Cornelius had news on the circle. On the way back to his class he felt it vibrate next to his heart. The text read: "Grand news. Dozers stop. Arch find."

Archaeological find!

The clock moved slowly toward the closing bell, and even then, Bartley had to stay to help Wilfredo with *Romeo and Juliet*. "So, after he kills Tybalt, Romeo goes to hide in Friar Laurence's cell, while—"

"He hides in Lawrence?"

"No. Wait, let's go over the names of the characters again—"

"Mister, do you believe in that love at first sight?"

"Yes, I'm certain that it happens all the time."

Back to the graphic organizer with the names of the characters, and the modern English version of the text, but in one part of Bartley's brain two words loomed larger than all of Shakespeare's: *archaeological find!*

On Bartley's way out, Bede lumbered out of his office and said he needed to see him. "Your PLC team meeting notes—you forgot to align curriculum with 'Can-Do Descriptors!'"

"Family emergency!" he called over his shoulder and set off running.

The farmhouse was empty. A few minutes later, Bartley reached the stone circle, where a crowd milled about. Cornelius, who had been busy taking notes and making drawings, introduced him to Eva Angelina, his particular friend from the Special Collections room of the Dunstable Library. A petite blonde in the stereotypical librarian's glasses, she in turn introduced him to Dr. Steinberg, a state archaeologist whom she had convinced to come up from Boston on very short notice.

A short distance away from the circle, the steel shovel of a backhoe rested its crenellated teeth against the earth. The construction workers had left the immediate area and were walking about with cell phones and talking in groups of two or three down near the trailer.

"The backhoe uncovered it," Eva said, "and Cornelius spotted it right away."

"What is it?"

The archaeologist waved him toward a hastily set up field table on which sat a stone slab about a square foot in size. On it was engraved a sort of triangle made up of three spiraling concentric circles.

"Can you carbon date it?" Bartley asked.

Dr. Steinberg smiled indulgently as he adjusted his horn-rimmed glasses with a thumb and forefinger. "You can't carbon date stone. Only organic matter."

"Right, of course."

"But I think we will be able to make certain assumptions based on the layer of earth in which it was found. It's certainly very old. I think somewhere in this vicinity a thorough excavation, not that little summer intern study the people from Cambridge conducted, would reveal ancient fires, maybe other things that can be dated. My belief is that it's certainly pre-Columbian, and possibly the biggest find this side of the Atlantic since L'Anse aux Meadows."

Bartley's index finger turned in a circular motion as he pointed toward the graven slab. "The design looks familiar, somehow."

"It should. They're classic Newgrange spirals."

"*Sí an Bhrú*," Cornelius explained. "Newgrange, the prehistoric site on 'the plains of royal Meath,' and very close to the *Mur na Mórrígan*."

"Yes, of course, I've seen photos of those stones." Bartley whistled softly. "Newgrange! Isn't that five thousand years old!"

"Quite right," Steinberg said. "Now I don't think it's likely that visitors arrived from across the sea in the Stone Age, but stone circles were constructed in the Stone Age, the Bronze Age, and the Iron Age. We do know that Europeans—Vikings—reached North America a thousand years ago—"

This conversation was cut short. Without ever having met him, Bartley was sure that the man approaching in nervous haste was Jack Carnadine, a robust fellow whose dark suit jacket set off a thick crop of white hair. Bartley thought of the old metaphor: *There's snow on the roof, but there's fire in the hearth.* Carnadine introduced himself and asked, "What's up?"

The others all looked to Dr. Steinberg, who began to explain how he had come to arrive there and then showed the developer the stone that had been uncovered. He also referred Carnadine to Massachusetts General Laws, Chapter Nine, Section 26A, under which he and a team of experts would halt all work on the site while they "conducted surveys and field investigations relative to the recovery and preservation of scientific, historical or archaeological information, and analyzed and published said information."

"You don't mean the entire thirty-six acres?"

"No, I don't think so. In particular, this hill. And of course, if you come across anything down there. . . ." He waved at the construction encampment below.

"Absolutely! Newgrange-type spirals, you say? Could they have been made by Indians?"

"Indians didn't build stone circles or make stone carvings like this. There could also be Indian artifacts in the area, in which case we'd have to excavate in conjunction with the Commission on Indian Affairs. We'll know more after we dig test pits and begin to screen the earth. We'll also be studying satellite imagery of the area."

"And to think I was going to move the circle. Jesus, Hannigan, it looks like you may have been right."

"I told him that we, well, that Cornelius here, thought the circle might be an ancient monument of some kind."

The businessman nodded and looked about in what appeared to be honest wonder. "You did. You did, indeed. You know what? To hell with the Stonehenge Condominiums! We'll rechristen it Newgrange Condominiums! But I intend to leave this hill alone. The backhoes will be out of here this afternoon, and we'll figure out what to do about the site after you conduct your investigations. Maybe a modest museum for the artifacts, lectures, a gift shop, a parking lot and restaurant over that way, tours of the hill. . . ."

"At fifteen dollars a head?" Bartley asked, grimacing.

"Depends what you find, I suppose. But nothing excessive. Senior citizen and veteran discount."

"I should tell you, Mr. Carnadine," Dr. Steinberg interjected, "that depending on what we find, or already have found, the Natural Heritage Trust Program will probably authorize the DEP to take the land by eminent domain, since—"

"*What did you say?*" The look of wonder was gone, and now his expression resembled that of a prize fighter just before the bell for round one.

"—since I think they would feel it is 'threatened with conversion to incompatible uses or contains sacred sites or archaeological sites of state or national importance.'"

"But—it's my property!"

"You'll get just compensation. First the town would have to vote to take the site, but I can't imagine they would not vote to preserve it in public ownership."

Bartley wondered how he might describe the developer's visage as he heard those words. Carnadine's face was . . . *encarnadine.*

After a few seconds of mental tumult accompanied by labial contortions, his mouth exploded with the words: "My attorney is going to have something to say about this!"

"Oh, I think your attorney will tell you very quickly that a site of this kind, which may be the *only one* of its kind in the United States, is bigger than you, or him, as is the legal team that DEP has at its disposal. If he's as smart as you seem to think he is, he'll tell you to take the compensation. Really."

"This is bullshit!" Carnadine shouted. He glared at them for a few seconds before turning and storming off. And Bartley thought, "This is the opposite of bullshit. This is the state actually doing something that matters." So, it was possible.

After Dr. Steinberg had gone, with the slab wrapped in blankets in the back of his Land Rover, and Carnadine and the workers had gone, and Sofia had returned, and the afternoon was growing as gray and somber and still as a Breughal landscape, Cornelius, Bartley, and Sofia constructed a tall sort of teepee of wood near the stone circle, for the Irishman had said that it would be necessary to light a Samhain bonfire.

"This is it, then?" Bartley asked when they had finished.

"I've skyped with the folks in Meath, and we're pretty well synchronized."

Bartley looked through the bare branches to the dull pewter sky and shivered. "I'm no seventh son, but even I feel something impending."

"Yes," Cornelius said, gazing about like a man who has just entered a strange cave, "the door between this world and the other world is opening. The veil is thinning."

There was a stirring in the dark branches and a column of withered leaves rode upward in the sudden gust, while papery rinds of peeling bark shivered on the birch trees, reminding them all that Samhain foreshadowed the incoming winter.

"Well," Bartley said, "If we're all set here, let's go back to the house, have a sandwich and open a bottle of that Château Sainte Marguerite. We need something born under a southern sun to take the chill out."

"Right, so. But we must be back before long."

They were quiet as they trekked through the woods, but when they sallied out of the path and reached the broad hillside, Bartley put his arm around Sofia. Cornelius, to lift their spirits, twirled his blackthorn about and began to sing.

As I came down through Dublin City at the hour of twelve at night
Whom should I see but a Spanish lady washing her feet by the candlelight
First she washed them, then she dried them, o'er a fire of amber coal
In all my life I never did see a maid so sweet about the soul.

Wack for the too-ra-lo-loo-ra laddy
Wack for the too-ra-loo-ra lay

"What would our lives be like without the music?" Cornelius wondered aloud when he had finished his song. He swung his blackthorn like a sword at an imaginary opponent and said, "No better friend on a road than a blackthorn, Bartley, against mad dogs, blaggards, and evil intent. I'll be leaving this one with you."

At the house, Bartley uncorked the vino without preamble and grilled some turkey and cheese sandwiches while Sofia poured the glasses and set the table. Cornelius was pacing about, rechecking the mysterious contents of his backpack, and *What's Apping* the henotheistic Father Dunleavy in Ireland.

While Bartley stood at the stove, pressing the spatula down on the sandwiches and sipping the wine, Sofia told him about her meeting with Perez, who seemed to have softened, and who was trying to help her get a job with Homeland Security. She updated him on her father, whose application was complete, and who was still planning to come and live with them after they were married.

"This is going to be the best farm," she said, rubbing his back. He nodded and forced a smile. The wine may have warmed him, but it had not taken the edge off his apprehensions about the night ahead of them.

Sofia was hiding her apprehensions, too. She hadn't mentioned that Perez had told her to keep her wits about her until they located the assassin, Thomas McGee. Nor had she mentioned that since Perez was unable, at present, to issue, or get someone to reissue, a gun permit, she had borrowed Bartley's father's pistol from the night table drawer. It was in the inside pocket of the coat she would wear.

When they had eaten, and the sun was setting, they set off once again for Druid Hill. Behind them, at a cautious distance, something that looked like a human skeleton flitted among the deepening shadows at the edge of the lower fields.

Twenty

"Cold Fingers" seemed an apt moniker for its owner as he stared at the bones of a hand outlined in chalky white over the black glove that clutched the pistol. He wondered what the three were doing, heading into the woods as darkness fell. A Halloween outing?

He followed the path they had taken, which led up a hill into a thicker wood. A waning gibbous moon was rising into drifts of ragged clouds. It was his only light. He cursed as he came to a fork in the path and finally set off along the one that led right at a steeper incline. He stuck the pistol into his waistband as he picked his way among the boulders.

Beside the farmhouse, by the field below, where all was as silent as a landscape portrait, a black Cadillac pulled onto the gravel driveway, bearing its own Totenkopf, a skull and crossbones beside the motto: DEATH TO TAXES. Farmer Lambeau noticed that there was a car parked off the shoulder of the road, pulled in close the hedges, and he wondered why a guest would do that when there was a spacious dirt parking lot to accommodate all the folks who came to buy Christmas trees. He found it—odd.

He found it odder that there were cars in the driveway—he recognized Bartley's and another, and that there was a light in the kitchen, but there was no one about. *My son is in great danger.* Crazy dream. But still.

He had told Bartley that there could be bears in these woods. Could that be the danger? Why go to the woods at night? But they were certainly not here. *What the hell—I'll check it out for Happy, and for my own peace of mind.* He opened his trunk and took out a flashlight and the newly-cleaned shotgun.

Farmer turned his flashlight off as he approached the fork. First, he knew the path well, and the moon was rising. But he also heard something or someone descending the path from the Top Pond. He moved off the track and slipped behind a tree, leaning his cheek against the rough oak bark as he

244

peered into the darkness. He had come upon bears in the woods, pumas, and even gray wolves, but his old heart beat faster when he saw what seemed to be a skeleton taking shape in the darkness. At the fork, just a few feet from him, the skeleton pivoted and headed up the left-hand path.

Farmer saw that it was no walking dead, but a man in some kind of Halloween suit. And for a second, he saw in the moonlight the glint of blue metal at the figure's waist. The older man moved quietly, but faster than he had since the days when his own skeleton had its original hips and knees.

Then, before him, and several feet above him, standing so that he was silhouetted against the sky as the path rose to the crest of the hill, Farmer saw the figure of the skeleton man clearly. For beyond that strange silhouette, up where the old stones jutted from the earth, blazed a fire that lit the woodland grove. And from that direction now, carried on a gathering wind that sent sparks rushing and crackling into the night, Farmer heard an incantation of sorts. The sound reminded him of something he had heard—somewhere.

He looked upward again and saw that the figure had disappeared. He began to run up the hill, forgetting that he really *could not* run until he felt a twinge of acute pain and heard a popping sound. He collapsed to the ground and his shotgun clattered beside him.

He tried to rise but the burning pain that stretched from his heel to the back of his knee weakened his leg so that it buckled under his weight. He grimaced and swore and began to crawl forward, the smell of burning wood growing stronger in his nostrils.

Cold Fingers felt the wind picking up, and near the crest he saw flames wavering like a fiery banner. Stranger than that was the sight of a man at the center of a sort of circle of stones. He was flourishing a stick in the air and declaiming loudly in Russian or some crazy language.

It may have sounded like Russian to the hit man, but Cornelius O'Tuama was incanting in the ancient tongue of the Gael. In his right hand, he held a branch of the hazel, in his left a branch of the quicken or rowan-tree. He had drawn a Newgrange spiral with chalk dust in the earth before him. He raised his arms and called: *Oscail an doras, cairtheand, ar an éalaitheoir iarmharán!*

Cold Fingers drew out his gun. He strode forward, because he enjoyed a dramatic entrance to a scene he could direct, and end. "Hello my friends! It's me! Death! Don't reach into that jacket, Violeta Martinez! *Manos arribas,* as Butch Cassidy once said. Hands up!" He was pleased with his wit.

Bartley drew closer to Sofia, thinking, "So this is how it ends. *Shit!*"

Farther down the hill, Farmer Lambeau had heard Cold Fingers' threats, and pressed on with all his might.

"Thomas McGee!" Sofia shouted, "They know you!"

Hearing his name rattled Cold Fingers a bit, but it also angered him because he now felt foolish in the ridiculous costume that wasn't fooling anyone. He made some rapid mental forensic calculations of a criminal nature which led him to the conclusion that he expressed aloud, "They'll have to find me, and they'll have to prove it."

Then Cold Fingers went cold all over as he felt a wind or something with the force of a body hurtle past him, nearly knocking him over. He saw nothing, but seemed to hear a murmuring, barely audible—or was it audible only in his head? It filled the night with a soft humming buzz like a thousand whispers.

The target was standing there beside a man—the one she'd been with downtown. Kill them! Kill the girl, kill the boyfriend and kill the Russian! He tried to ignore the voices in the wind, which he thought must be the result of an atypical case of Halloween nerves. *Pull yourself together, McGee! Do the job!* But he hesitated, the gun trembling slightly in his right hand as it never had before.

Cornelius had turned at the sound of the stranger's voice and saw Death's double holding a gun instead of a sickle. "*Fri demnaib, fri armaib, fri áraib!*" he cried.

The wind rose, and the flames rose with it, brightening the three living faces and the skull mask, and Cornelius sensed at this moment that he did not belong inside the circle of stone. He edged out of what he felt was the center of a gathering power, in the way that those who had escaped the stricken Titanic rowed far from the foundering ship.

The space before them all appeared wavy in the heat, as if the air itself, or reality, were melting. The voices that Cold Fingers heard in the wind grew louder. And then he saw, *right there*, before him in the firelight outside the circle, an old woman taking on substance, condensing or thickening from the ethereal to the corporeal.

He tried to blink the vision away, but every time he reopened his eyes the woman was more visible, more real, with her long white hair, her haggard face, the rags of an ancient crone, a crooked staff, and her eyes *on him*. And there were other eyes in the darkness beyond the firelight, watching him.

Farmer Lambeau, meanwhile, had managed to crawl to the hilltop, and as Cold Fingers, now gripped with the cold fingers of a terror he had never known, turned to flee, he found a man kneeling on the path before him holding a double-barreled shotgun that was aimed at his chest.

The hit man was raising the pistol when Farmer blew him five feet backward. Strangely, though, Cold Fingers did not land on his back. He staggered, falling ever backward, or *being drawn*, toward the stone circle.

A few words escaped from Bartley—no more than, "What the—?" He was about to run toward Farmer, but other things were happening. The old woman's transformation from vision to being of substance was complete, and she was moving toward the stone circle. At the center of the magical enclosure, and above the Newgrange spiral, the air grew darker, a deep blot on the night that began to form a hole in the air itself, like the entrance to a cave.

A crow descended with a sharp cry from somewhere—a tree, the sky— and disappeared into the hole. Cold Fingers, who was still careening backward, as if caught in an inescapable vortex, was now swept up in a rapidly tightening circle, and, with a cry no louder than that of the crow that preceded him, disappeared into that dark portal in the air.

Meanwhile, the old woman, with each step she took toward the center of the circle, grew younger and more beautiful. Her back straightened, her white, wispy hair turned gray. It thickened and darkened until it was raven black and full, and she grew into the goddess they had once seen with her wild crown of dark feathers. Her rags were transformed into a mantle of thick fur; her crooked staff was gone, and her hand now rested on the stag head pommel of the sword that hung at her side.

When she reached the portal, she turned and raised her arms toward them, her hands open in what Bartley thought must have been a kind of blessing. The darkness bent over her, and the heartbeat of the universe seemed to pause, to miss a beat before it resumed. Bartley understood that the cry of the Mórrígan would rend the night air around Druid Hill no more.

She was gone, and the only sound was the crackling fire and the wind in the pines.

As reality, or normal reality, resettled over the scene, Bartley, Sofia, and Cornelius ran to Farmer, who had pulled himself into a sitting position on a rock, leaning on the stock of his shotgun. "You get some pretty wacky shit going on up here, kid," he said.

"Well, yes. And how did *you* end up here?"

"I'll try to explain that, but where the hell did the guy with the gun go? I blasted him full-on, and it wasn't no birdshot."

"Yeah, Cornelius, where the hell *did* the guy with the gun go? Ireland? The Otherworld?"

Cornelius, for the first time since Bartley had known him, was speechless. His cheeks puffed, and he blew a baffled breath and said, "I'm gobsmacked." None of the others were familiar with the term, but they all felt they understood. The wind was ebbing and the fire settling when Cornelius received a text from County Meath.

"Unusual atmospheric upheavals at the *Mur na Mórrígan,*" he reported. "A strange glow of silver-blue light bathed for a while the larger mound. Three ravens or hooded crows soaring above it. Then a sort of funnel swirled down into mound and they say, *something* flew out into the night. Dark again." He looked up. "No mention of a fellah with a gun. Jesus, I dunno where he went—'tis a puzzler."

"I suppose there is no need to call the police," Sofia said, "since there is no body."

"Just an abandoned car by the side of the road," Farmer said.

For a moment, they stared at the ground where the body *should have* been. Then Cornelius pulled a bottle of whiskey out of his backpack and they passed it around and talked until the fire died.

At the end of it all, Cornelius and Bartley carried Farmer back to the house while Sofia lit the way with a flashlight. The Irishman expressed his gratitude to the old New England farmer with an old Irish proverb: "It's true what they say, then. You can die without a priest, but you can't live without a neighbor."

A Relevant Digression

The LIGO Hanford Gravitational Wave Observatory, (46°27′18.52°N 119°24′27.56°W / 46.4551444°N 119.4076556°W / 46.4551444; −119.4076556) and the LIGO Livingston Gravitational Wave Observatory, (30°33′46.42° N 90°46′27.27° W 30.5628944°N 90.7742417°W / 30.5628944; −90.7742417) operate in unison. Each observatory houses as many as five interferometers within a four-kilometer high vacuum system. Together, they can detect discrepancies in gravitational waves of as little as ten milliseconds. These tiny differences have come to be known as "tremors in space-time."

On November 1st, theoretical physicist Stanislaus Stanowicz reported to work at LIGO Hanford, coffee in hand, bade security a good morning, and slid his ID through a scanning device mounted on the wall. Glass doors glided back with a sibilant hiss and he passed into the dust-free, climate-controlled expanse of well-lit, white-tiled corridors.

He had hoped to have a chance to look at Simone Napolitano's new research project entitled, "Non-Destructive Qualitative Analysis of Crystallinity Via X-rays Diffraction Measurements" while he drank his java, but he found fellow physicist Harold Greene waiting in his office with a printout of the trilateration report from the previous evening.

Stanowicz was a heavy man, and his swivel seat creaked and groaned as he settled his weight on it. "Whatcha got there?"

"LIGO detected a quite fascinating, or maybe I should say inexplicable, tremor in space-time last night."

Stanowicz's head tilted inquisitively as he uncapped his coffee. "From which quadrant? A charted galaxy?"

"That's the thing. It was from Earth."

"From Earth? That's impossible, or at least, it's unheard of—unimagined? What on this planet could produce the mass and velocity?"

"Certainly is strange, but I've got the data here. Look for yourself." He passed the flowing spreadsheet across the table and Stanowicz donned his glasses and perused it.

"Hmm. 42.67665° N, –71.4256° E. What's that? Massachusetts? New Hampshire?"

"Tyngsborough, Massachusetts. A nearly simultaneous event at. . . ." He pointed to some figures.

Stanowicz read, *N53.694567 W6.4463*. "Where's that, exactly?"

"It's in Ireland. County Meath."

He frowned, and after a moment, said, "Crazy shit."

"Weird shit," Greene concurred.

"I think we'd better recalibrate the system. Run a test on the hydraulic actuators, take a peek at the active vibration isolation system. Maybe look for anthropogenic sources from the 0.1–5 Hz band that might have created microseismic interference or nanometric surface aberrations."

Greene looked skeptical. "O-kay?"

"What's our alternative? Look for black holes in—what's it, Tyngsborough, and, eh, Meath?" Stanowicz seized his phone and punched in an extension. "Judy? Stan here. We're going to run some tests. Meet me in five minutes at the main interferometer. Bring the photon calibrator. Can you examine the new flex joint in the feedback loop? And while we're at it, we might as well check the photon actuation on the mode-cleaner cavity. Good. Oh, and bring a can of oil." He paused, and looking at Greene, rolled his eyes, "I think I realize that, Judy. I *do* have this Ph.D. from Princeton in Quantum Chronodynamics. The oil is for my chair!"

Clouds, gray and violet, purple-edged, stormed across the sky, casting deep rolling shadows over the verdant plain. Cold Fingers was flat on his back. He was shivering because he found himself inexplicably naked and inexplicably alive. The guy sitting on the ground had fired a shotgun at him at ten-yards range, and he had felt the slugs tear into him with terrible force, driving him backward—and then?

It was day now, and he was alive and somehow unscathed, but where the hell was he? He looked around—nothing but a few raised mounds of earth and low walls of stone.

And then he saw them: two horsemen cresting a hill. Instinctively, he cast about for a place to hide, but as he scrambled for a patch of tall grass, he heard the horses' hooves quickening into a gallop. They were soon upon him.

While the animals snorted steamy breath and whinnied and nodded their great maned heads, he gazed upward at the riders. They were mud-stained warriors, wearing ornate breast plates, braided beards, and long hair. Leather bracers were laced up their forearms, but their uncovered upper arms bore strange tattoos of twisting circles. Mantles of bearskin, flung back from their shoulders, were fastened with circular broaches. Their horses had no reins, but the warriors' fists were entwined in their horses' manes.

In addition to the swords that hung at their sides, Cold Fingers saw that one of the men had a large crescent-headed axe secured at his back; its curved head, with blood-spattered silver edge, was visible over his shoulder. But what troubled Cold Fingers more than any of this, and caused him to piss himself, and the two warriors to burst into a fit of laughter, was that hanging from leather cords before their grimy knees were the severed heads of men.

The warriors understood nothing of his babbling speech, but Crimthann told Meic Ruaid that if they could housebreak the fool, he might make a serviceable slave to tend the fire and drag water from the well. Meic Ruaid agreed they should take him back to Rathra.

"*Mrogaid!*" With this sharp command, and a hand signal, Meic Ruaid ordered the naked and gunless gunman to walk along beside them.

"I'm afraid there's been some kind of mix-up." Cold Fingers' protestation was apologetic, deferential: "You see, I'm from Boston! Massachusetts!" He pointed to his breastbone, "Me *American!* Yes! *O-oh say, can you see?* You know, *Superbowl?*" He pantomimed taking a hike from center and dropping back to pass but caught sight of the baffled expressions on the faces of the horsemen who were circling him slowly.

"*America!*" he pleaded. "*Superman!*" He stretched his arms out, leaning forward, and made a *shshshsh-ing* with his pursed lips that was supposed to sound like air rushing over an invulnerable body. "*Truth! Justice! And the Ameri—*"

The flat of Crimthann's sword swung down hard across his bare ass and the imposing, bear-skin clad warrior, with a twisting motion of his arms, directed the horse's head around in front of Cold Fingers so that the animal slobbered over his bony chest.

Crimthann, son of Cruithnechán, then leaned down from his saddle, and touching the arced blade over his shoulder, growled a string of words which the time-lost hit man did not comprehend in literal terms, but was able to deduce might very probably be understood as: "Shut the fuck up and walk before I get my fucking axe out!"

He walked in the indicated direction toward his new life.

Twenty-One

When shall we three meet again?

—Shakespeare

Bartley had thought that all of the brouhaha with the stone circle and the Mórrígan and the developer and the psycho poet and his divorce and the guy who was trying to kill them all constituted *stress*. But he found that when it was over, and he was stuck with nothing to think about but his job, he was not relieved, but desolate.

Yes, he had Violeta—he corrected himself—*Sofia*, who had become his wife in a quiet ceremony attended by Cornelius, Harris, Manus and Jill, and sanctified with several bottles of Dom Pérignon. Thank God for Sofia. But the prospect of another twenty years of reporting to an aging and increasingly cantankerous Bede, and of enduring the endlessly renewable stream of bullshit handed down by the Department of Elementary and Secondary Education, was depressing in the extreme. And Cornelius was preparing to leave, and Bartley had grown accustomed to having him about.

Nevertheless, the day arrived, and Bartley and Sofia sat with Cornelius in the Gold Circle Lounge near the departure gate on the third floor of Terminal E at Logan International Airport. The Irishman was wearing his tweed cap, a clean shirt and jacket, and of course, his UCC tie with the Celtic knot tie tack. They were drinking the parting glass, and the mood was somewhat somber.

"Well now, I'd say we've been through a fair bit together," Cornelius said. "And I'll be hoping that the two of you buy a farm in Ballyvourney one day."

"Well," Bartley said, "the one thing the three of us should know better than anyone is that anything is possible."

"Could you not get an extension on your visa to stay?" Sofia asked, wiping a tear with a Kleenex.

"You've got six older brothers to run the farm, don't you?" asked Bartley.

"Ah sure, there's none of them wanted to stay around that old place," he replied. "It's my two sisters are runnin' it without me. And then, my sister Bríd forwarded this letter to me from a Colm Lorcán in the County of Mayo."

He pulled a folded envelope from inside his jacket pocket, and handed it to Bartley, who put down his Guinness and withdrew the letter it contained. He read,

Dear Mr. O'Tuama,

It is given out that you are the man to see with regard to questions of faeries and other troublesome visitors from the Otherworld. I was disturbed one evening last June in my home where I live as a bachelor, having retired from the Electric Supply Board in April at my 65th birthday. Well there I was by the fire with the dog, Barney, when comes a knockin' at the door, and Barney, who is in general a mighty watch dog, goes off wimperin' and tryin' to get himself under the bunk. I answered the door. 'Twas a woman who looked awful distraught asked me for a drink of water. She was pale and rather frightening, but I give it to her out of pity for the thirst that was on her, Mr. O'Tuama, an' now she won't leave me alone. She seems to come out of nowhere at odd hours of the night, an' I can't get rid of her any way, always askin' for water. Can you help me, Sir? I enclose my address.

"Jesus, Cornelius, what'll you do about that?"

"I've heard of similar cases. I think that if can get Mr. Lorcán, the next time, to give her a cup of water taken from a place I know where three streams meet, he will be troubled no more."

"Then who is she? Or what is she?"

"I shouldn't like to say, lest ye have bad dreams. But I'll sort it out."

"I have no doubt."

"And what about yourself, Bartley?"

"Oh, you know," he said, "I guess I've got to keep working at the high school, gathering 'Professional Development Points,' and making up 'Smart Goals,' and gathering 'artifacts.'"

A metallic voice interrupted him. "*Aer Lingus Flight 136, to Shannon International Airport, now boarding at Gate 7.*"

The three of them rose. "*Slán go fóill*," Cornelius said, and the men gulped their Guinness.

"I don't like goodbyes!" Sofia declared. She hugged Cornelius and kissed his cheek.

"Reminds me of the old tune," the departing Corkonian said, "'Happy to Meet and Sorry to Part.' *Vaya con Dios, Señorita.*"

Sofia pressed the Kleenex to her eyes and said, "You go with God, too, Cornelius."

Bartley shook hands with his former house mate, but Sofia said, "Give him a hug!" and he did. The flight was called once more, but Cornelius paused and said to Bartley, "Ye really hate that school, don't you?"

"I used to like teaching. But the bureaucrats have turned it into just a dreadful profession. But I mean I'm a teacher. That's all I've really done. I'm not a farmer! You know, I looked up my name, I mean Hannigan, once. It said, 'the grandson of little Annadh, meaning 'delay,' the descendant of the little slow man.' That's me—I never take any action—I seem incapable. I just react. Inaction is my name and superscription, sadly."

Cornelius shook his head. "You're mistaken, boy. I looked it up, too. Ó h-Éanacháin your family was in the beginning, the son of the bird, and you'll see three birds on your crest. Maybe they're crows. All I can do, in parting, Bartley, is to quote the late Seamus Heaney. I forget the line exactly, but it's something like, 'What you do every day—*that's your life.*'" He nodded significantly and recited a few lines of one of his storehouse of enigmatic Irish poems, "Till a splash from the Lake of the Son of the Bird, and your soul would have stirred and waked anew."

"You think I should quit."

"Sure, you know yourself," he said, and for the first time since he'd heard that puzzling expression, Bartley thought, 'I do know myself.' Cornelius winked at the two of them and ambled off, singing,

In the merry month of June from my home I started
Left the girls of Tuam so nearly broken-hearted,
Saluted father dear, kissed me darlin' mother,
Drank a pint of beer, me grief and tears to smother

A few of the other passengers milling toward the gate looked at him, and with his free hand he tipped his cap to them, but he never looked back.

Then off to reap the corn, leave where I was born
Cut a stout blackthorn to banish ghosts and gobbalins.
Brand new pair of brogues, rattling o'er the bogs
Frightened all the dogs on the rocky road to Dublin. . . .

They heard his song fade into the general hubbub and the robotic announcements.

What you do every day—that's your life. The simple words struck Bartley with such force that, on the way out, Sofia asked if he was all right. With an effort of will, he smiled and nodded and redirected some part of his attention to their conversation.

Those words were still resounding in his mind several days later, on Saturday, when Phil, the Marine letter carrier (no such thing as an 'ex-Marine' he had told Bartley) informed him that he had to sign for a registered letter. He added that he had to take a photograph as Bartley signed!

Obviously, nothing was being left to chance, and Bartley saw, to his horror, that the missive was from the Department of Elementary and Secondary Education. He knew what it must be, and the notice inside confirmed his apprehensions. He had been selected for a "random audit" of "professional development points" toward his teaching license. "Random my ass!" he muttered. "*Bede!*"

DESE informed him through the unwelcome directive that he was to provide proof within thirty days that he had gathered sufficient "PDP's" for renewal of his teaching license in English. The points should be 'bundled," under the headings of "Content" and "Pedagogy," and a new 15 PDP requirement for Special Ed.

Naturally, there were forms to fill out—multi-colored and redundant, and professional development plans that had to be completed and signed. And so, instead of relaxing and taking a walk in the woods with Sofia, he had to update his Educator Licensure and Recruitment (ELAR) account and confirm his Massachusetts Educator Professional Identification (MEPID) number on the DESE website and begin to pull together evidence from worn folders stuck in a dented file cabinet where he had shoved certificates of attendance at forgotten seminars, report cards of horrid evening courses taken for recertification, classes with titles like "A Mindfulness Guide to Teaching," and "Twitter: A Teacher's Guide." All of the detritus of a modern teaching career.

He dumped the pile on the kitchen table beside the multi-colored forms and development plans, and as he sat there staring glumly at it, Sofia, good wife that she was, brought him a glass of golden liquid from the bottle of West Cork Whiskey that Cornelius had left behind, and went to paint the room that her father would take upon his arrival in two weeks.

Bartley wanted to help her, but she told him it was easy and that she liked to paint. "It will be good to have a *real farmer* back on the farm," he said.

"*Te amo,*" she said, and headed into the back bedroom with her roller and tray.

At least there was this corner of his life, he thought, where he was lucky. He looked blankly at the hateful mess of papers before him, and then sat back and sipped the whiskey. He saw Cornelius's blackthorn leaning beside the fireplace and smiled ruefully.

At the departmental meeting, Bede, with the air of a man whose work was vital, had the secretary hand each English teacher a stack of yellow placards measuring approximately 14 by 12 inches. He informed the staff that DESE had decided that it would be necessary, from now on, in addition to writing goals and mastery objectives and power standards on the board every day, to hang up in the room the placard bearing the number of the standard or standards being taught that day.

This announcement was greeted by profound silence, until Harris was overheard to mutter, "The only thing that's gonna be hanging in my room is *me*."

Bede shot an admonitory look in his direction and said, "After all, this is *standards-based* education, and so both the teacher and the students should be aware what standards are being taught each day."

He flattened his tie over his paunch, as Bartley wondered, once again, "What maniac would put this guy in charge?"

"Another thing that the state has decided. . . ." He paused until a collective audible groan subsided. "And remember, they are only following the orders of the Justice Department. They are *rolling out a new initiative*." (Bartley winced involuntarily at that phrase). "This new initiative, is called RETELL, or Rethinking Equity in the Teaching of English Language Learners. It will require each of you who has even one ELE student in your class, which is *all of you*, to get an 'SEI endorsement.' This will involve taking a class which will be offered on Saturday mornings for three hours, for ten consecutive Saturdays, and without which you will not be able to renew your teaching license."

Bartley felt as if he'd been hit with a hammer. "*What?*"

"You will learn about language acquisition theories, and do a 'capstone project' involving—"

Bartley heard nothing more. He could only imagine the useless bullshit that DESE governmental eggheads would come up with to fill in that many hours. An ounce of patience and a bit of compassion would be worth more than all the language acquisition theories. *What you do every day—that's your life. What you do every day—that's your life.*

The meeting was to end at 3:05, so when Bede asked at 3:03 if there were any questions, the older teachers glared at the younger teachers, a look that said: *Don't even think about it.*

When the meeting had concluded, Harris sidled up to Bartley near the exit and said, "Our workplace has become a volcano of idiot lava. For now, we're scalded and burned by it, but *eventually* we may be assimilated into some other reality where it's totally inoffensive, like the guy in *1984* who learned to love Big Brother."

Bartley groaned and then stopped short. "I don't want to win this victory over myself." Then he shocked himself and his friend by saying, "I've got to go talk to Bede."

"Have you completely lost your mind?"

"I'll catch up with you later."

Bartley turned the corner in time to see the boss twisting the key in his door and lumbering into his office. He was about to follow him when Amy Proctor came out of the superintendent's office farther down the corridor.

She waved an index finger and picked up her step. "Congratulations are in order, I understand, Bartley. You were married recently."

"That's right. Thank you."

She nodded, her lips compressed, looking at him as if she was trying to bear up under some grievous insult. "Out with it, Amy. What's the problem?"

"You married—a woman."

"As many have done before me."

"So, this whole thing of pretending to be gay. . . ."

He considered his options for a moment. He could tell her that Sofia was a transgender male. Or he could tell her that he was 'gender fluid,' as he'd heard one man describe himself at the city council hearing on who could or should use what bathroom and change in which locker room. But the bottom line was, he didn't want to lie any more, and he didn't want to make her feel bad, or insult anyone. He was worn out with it all. "Amy," he said, "it's just a movie."

"What? What's just a movie?"

"All this. Things you think are bullshit, well, sometimes they turn out to be real, and then the things you think are real, your marriage, your job—turn out to be—bullshit. OK. You got me. I just said I was gay because that consultant was accusing me of being anti-gay, which I'm really not. I'm sorry. I like you. I didn't mean to make your life difficult."

She had that sort of look on her face that a dog has—not that she was ugly. In fact, she was good-looking—but that look a dog has when you are trying to give him a biscuit, but he doesn't know you, and doesn't quite trust you, yet. A wary look. "Bartley . . . maybe you *should* see a counselor."

"No. I know what's wrong with me."

"What is it?"

"It's that what you do every day is your life—and you only get one."

At that point, Bede came out of his office with his briefcase in hand. He gave the two of them a look that combined puzzlement and annoyance. Amy Proctor nodded at Bede, and at Bartley, with perhaps a hint of sympathetic understanding, and then she walked away, her heels clicking across the tiled floor.

Bede looked at Bartley as if he smelled something noxious, grunted, and was heading away with briefcase swinging at his side when Bartley called out, "I need to see you for a few minutes."

He whirled about. "I don't do drive-bys."

"I need to see you."

"There's nothing you need to tell me that can't be better said in an email."

"Fine. I'll see if the superintendent is available."

Bede shook his head and muttered down in his throat with his mouth nearly closed, but he returned. A civilized person would have unlocked the office door, Bartley thought, so they could have their conversation in private, but Bede was not civilized. Also, he was a close talker. He was a large man, and he liked to hover over people from a distance of four inches. He now loomed over Bartley, the customary petulance souring his features.

"Back up, will you?" Bartley said. "I'm not one of your little minions you can terrify."

He didn't move, and Bartley took a step back.

"What's so urgent?" Bede wanted to know.

"The mass of men lead lives of quiet desperation. You know who said that?"

Bede put down his briefcase and crossed his arms. "What is this, a quiz show?"

"If it were, you would be eliminated quickly. That's part of the problem. They made you head of the English Department, but you've never read Thoreau. I don't think you've read much of anything. So why *are you* the boss? Because they could see that you like to push people around, that's why."

"They made me department chair because I get things done and I have high expectations of my staff."

They heard a rumble as a custodian turned the corner, pushing a wheeled bucket, using the protruding handle of a mop as a tiller to guide it. Bartley wondered fleetingly if anyone had imposed a lot of bullshit ideas on him about how he should clean the floors.

He turned back to Bede. "You're a cheerleader for a bunch of pointless, impractical nonsense. I mean, do you really think it's a good use of our time to hang up these *stupid* placards with numbers of standards all over the wall every day? Or to spend hours at meetings on 'text-dependent questions?' If I'm going to ask a kid a question on a reading, *what else* will it depend on but the text? Flipped classrooms and backward design and U.D.I. and P.I.M.S. and D.D.M.'s and rediscovering the wheel every five minutes— why did I go to school? Why did they train me just to robotize me and standardize me?"

Bede held up the palm of his hand as if he were a traffic cop. "It's been determined that kids learn best when they understand that learning is standards-based, and they know what standard they're working on each day."

"Kids learn best when the teacher is enthusiastic and patient and rested. And this never-ending *bullshit* saps our enthusiasm and tries our patience and keeps us up at night wondering why we got into this—*volcano of idiot lava!*"

"I think you need to be more open to the coaching that Esme Gath offered. I'm also going to recommend in your professional development plan that you take the Skillful Teacher class, and a class on Formative Assessment."

Bartley laughed sadly and shook his head. "You know, you are the champ—the undisputed master, of *bullshit*."

"You're deficient, Hannigan. I'm recommending corrective action. It is in the students' *and your* best interest."

"Maybe if I get an A in your classes, I'll be able to win the victory over myself and love the Big Brother Department of Ed, eh?" He could see that Bede did not get the reference.

"Frankly, having a teacher in my department with your attitude is bad for morale."

Bartley considered this for a moment, and then he said, "What's bad for morale is a boss who's unqualified and who seems to enjoy being a *dick*."

Bede now got as close as his belly would permit. "You don't even *know* what a dick I can be. By the way, the state informs us that you're being *audited* for your license. How's *that* going?"

Bartley had to restrain an impulse to punch him in the grinning gob, because he knew that it was not a "random audit." That was bullshit, too. Bede had requested the audit from one of his pals in the Department of Ed. Their noses were six inches apart, and Bartley could smell the Polo cologne.

"You know, Bede, there's only two reasons we're here on this spinning rock that make any sense to me. The first is to help each other, and in this building, especially, to help the kids, and the second is to have fun. You don't help anyone. And you kill the fun. I have Christmas trees to sell. I quit." Bartley brushed him with a hard shoulder as he departed.

"Wait a minute, Hannigan. Under the contract, you'll need to give notice. What about the students? I can't replace a teacher overnight in November."

Of course. Now that he *wanted* to leave, Bede would try to keep him. "Fine—you have a month's notice. But with this stipulation. I won't be hanging any damned placards around my classroom! I won't be filling in any indicators any backward design templates. I will delete all emails that refer to 'backward accountability,' 'PIMS,' or 'DDM's.' I won't be 'debriefing' with Esme Gath! I will be reading with the kiddos, and discussing ideas, and learning new words and exposing them to culture. My room will be a bullshit-free, DESE-free zone for the next month. And I will not be going to any of your *stupid* departmental meetings. *I'm done with all that!*"

Bede grimaced, and as Bartley made his exit he heard him say, "You're very full of yourself, Hannigan."

Bartley whirled and cast his final dart. "You're very full of shit, Bede!"

"You need counseling!"

"You need an enema!"

On the way home, he stopped at the post office. He took the green form and the blue form and the yellow form and tore them into tiny bits and stuffed them into the DESE return envelope and dropped the shredded remnants of his career in the mailbox, before which he paused, flicking his fingers backhand under his chin like the Godfather.

Then he got into his car and slipped Jimi Hendrix into the CD player. "Voodoo Child!" Hendrix was a master of the guitar and a master of the wah-wah pedal, which was a far greater achievement than being a master of bullshit. He headed to The Old Court for a Guinness.

Eva Angelina set down her tea cup gingerly and settled herself at her desk in the library beneath the Dunstable town seal, which featured a puzzled-looking man at a plough beneath the motto, "The profit of the field is for all." She let her tea steep while she opened the letter and read.

December 2016
Balleyvourney, Co.
Cork

Dearest Eva,

It is a queer thing, but I find, especially after receiving your last letter, that I hear your voice in my head, like, at odd times of the day, and I see your face when I close my eyes, and I long for your company and don't sleep very well with missing you. All of these are signs, as I understand, and do believe, that I am very much in love with you, Eva. And this is a sort of spell no charm can break. If you agree, I think we should be married. Of course, I would prefer to live in Ireland and that means one day that you would be buried with my people. And, of course, with me. But that will be many years from now, please God.

If you will accept my proposal but cannot abide a life away from home, I will go to you.

If you come here, you need have no fear that you will be confined to a pig farm in West Cork, my dear. That would be hard for a woman not bred to the farm, but you see anyway my sisters and I are selling the farm to Des Doyle and sons. I never realized what dirty work it was until I got so bloody clean.

I am being awarded an honorary degree from UCC in Irish Folklore, and have been asked by RTE, (Irish television) to work with a Professor Harmon from that college on a series called "Sacred and Pagan Ireland." So, I can now wear my UCC tie boldly and honestly, which is a burden off my mind. All that to explain that if we wed, and you agree to come here, the two of us would live in Cork City or in Dublin. I am hoping to receive word that you will have me, and that I will soon hear your dear voice in a home of our own.

By the way, speaking about RTE, I saw a film on it lately about a factory in Sweden where nearly all the cars are built by robot-machines. They work 24 hours a day and they never go on strike. But sometimes they break down. Can you blame them, Eva?

I hope you will answer in the affirmative and I can promise you I will never make you regret it, but will work for you and try my best to make you happy. Please give my regards to my old friends Bartley and Sofia. They must be very busy with the trees.

Yours Devotedly,
Cornelius O'Tuama

After she had read and reread the letter, Eva Angelina put it down on the desk. She picked up her teacup in two hands and held it before her lips without drinking until her glasses fogged in the rising vapor. She took off the glasses and stared over the top of the cup for a moment, out the window toward the two great pine trees whose indistinct branches rose and fell in an unseasonably mild breeze. She watched the laden boughs nodding like a horse's head, or like a dory in the rolling wake of a schooner.

It seemed to her that the natural world was breathing softly while her own breath was nearly suspended. She smiled as she recalled his words. *Can you blame them, Eva?* Who but Cornelius would interject robots and burial plots into the middle of a proposal letter? She loved him, and a new life beckoned. Paralysis was not an option. She closed her eyes and sipped her tea, then whispered, "Yes, Cornelius. Yes, I will. Yes." She got up to call her mother, and to tell her that she would be returning to the land of her mother's mother.

Epilogue

(Four years later)

Bartley Hannigan situated himself in the tub chair as the audio technician clipped the tiny wireless microphone onto his tie. Dick Diggins, host of the *Diggin the Scene* TV show, sipped from his *Diggin the Scene* coffee cup and said, "I think it's better to have you here after the commercial break, Bartley. We'll be back on air in about two minutes. You seem relaxed—have you done this before?"

"When I was a teacher, I was always in front of students. And since the book has come out I've done quite a bit of radio, TV. I don't stress out about too much, you know."

"Well, I guess that's the point, right? A lot of it is bullshit, anyway?"

"Most of it, and these days most people are full of shit. Like, I just decided, after this interview, I'll never wear a tie again. Why do I need this thing hanging from my neck?"

"You don't."

"So, why should I? It's uncomfortable."

"You shouldn't. Except that your microphone is attached to it."

The cameraman gave the high sign and Diggins patted his hair, sat up a bit, took on a look of focused attention and began abruptly: "And we're joined tonight by Bartley K. Hannigan, the author of the runaway best-seller, *The Age of Bullshit*." He held the book up, and turning to his guest, one Digginsian eyebrow arched over the rim of his Woodrow Wilson glasses, asked, "Do we live in an age of bullshit, Bartley?"

"Absolutely, Dick. We are inundated with bullshit, plagued with it, cursed by it, and most of us have surrendered to it. It's useless, time-consuming and expensive, and it wears us down."

"Take us back, Bartley. You quit your job because of the bullshit. How did you decide to write the book?"

"OK. So, I tell my boss I quit, I sent my teaching license audit forms back to the Department of Ed in little pieces, and I went down to this great Irish pub in Lowell called The Old Court. I need a drink, right? So, I order a Guinness—it's late afternoon, and there are some other people in there, and we get talking, and I tell them how I quit my job because I couldn't take—"

"—the bullshit."

"Exactly. And you know what, this sad lookin' guy pipes up and he says, 'At my company, we are required to appraise our employees, but we are told what level of achievement they can hit, because only so many people in the company can be 'exceeds' or 'far exceeds.' Therefore, we have to go through the motions of evaluating everyone, but they expect us in the end to grade everyone as 'meets.' '*Total bullshit!*' And then one of two women at a table says, 'Today I was in Burlington for a sales conference where all of us needed to play act a sales call. Total bullshit. In the meantime, my customers are screaming for support and I'm in a room pretending. Tonight, after I pretend all day, I must do a sales forecast. Total bullshit because the forecast is already available via the corporate accounting system.'"

"So, you began to see that it was all around us."

"Ubiquitous! By the time I had finished my second Guinness, I knew I had to write the book. It just kept coming. And I realized that many people have two jobs, their real job, and then all the other stuff that I call the 'meta-work,' the work about work. One guy came in, a railroad conductor, an old-timer. You could just feel the frustration and resentment as he was telling us about the bullshit on his job. 'Every day' he says, 'my box is full of papers that have nothing to do with my job! OSU's and ASU's, general orders, bulletins, crew date memos, service standards, 'must carry,' regulations—the company response to every eventuality. But when a kid gets on the train with a plastic sword, you don't have time to look up in the employee handbook how you're supposed to handle it—you use your common sense and then you look in the rule book later to see if you're fucked.' Oops, sorry, Dick."

"I think we caught it but be careful or the FCC will do that to us!"

"That old timer told me about a young woman who worked as a conductor. They have all these 'must carry' rule books and handbooks on that job. She had it all stuffed in this big knapsack, which was caught by a passing train and she was dragged to her death. She became a metaphor in my mind for all the bullshit that is killing us, and I began to think about how much better life—the quality of life would be for all of us—in so many professions, if we could eliminate this nonsense—this Everest of drivel produced by bureaucrats and lawyers and foisted on the rest of us to make us miserable."

"You did quite a bit of research?"

"I interviewed cops—oh, cops or military—forget about it—I won't even begin. Anyone who works for government—that's obviously the worst, particularly state or federal. The state is just *killing* teachers with bullshit—that's how I got caught up in the machine. But, doctors, all kinds of people in the medical field, business people, real estate agents, dentists, engineers, prison guards . . . a prison guard told me, 'Christ, if some guy hangs himself in his cell, you'll spend a week on paperwork that no one will ever read, and the poor guy is still dead!' The response to everything, including death, is more paperwork! And so, more and more people started to reach out to me to tell me their stories. Some amount of paperwork is inevitable, but I found that we are *buried* in paper, in buzzwords, in pointless checklists, in reports no one reads, in committees that decide on formats that no one wants to use. In short—in bullshit."

"The book has certainly resonated with the public. It has been on the *New York Times* best-seller list for ten straight weeks."

"Time is such a valuable resource—time is *the most* valuable resource—and people are frustrated because everywhere they see themselves and their co-workers spending this limited resource on things that don't help them, don't help their clients or the people they serve, that don't help anybody! Maybe they could use that time to do something that would improve a situation for themselves and those they serve. But they see the product of their valuable time put in some file never to see the light of day again, just so their boss can tell his or her boss that they are conforming to guidelines in some useless, redundant memo—it kills the spirit! We have to fix it. We have to take our lives back! We cannot—working people cannot permit theoreticians to justify their jobs by continuing to 'roll out' bullshit programs! We have to stop promoting bullshitters who have no better qualification than that they have perfected the art of bullshitting!"

Diggins held up the book once more. "Workers of the world unite! Bartley Hannigan, ladies and gentlemen, *The Age of Bullshit.*"

Epilogue II

The new Vice President of Cloud Solutions, Adele Smollet, formerly known as Adele Hannigan, had concluded her initial meeting with department heads, but she had held one 'team member' back in her office for a private conversation.

"Donald," she said. "I noticed that your F.P.T. report is missing several components, including key analytical data."

"Come on, Adele. You know those reports are on the way out, so I'm just waiting to see what's going to replace them. I understand it will be soon, and I'll work on those."

"We have not switched over yet. Have the F.P.T.'s on my desk tomorrow. I need all of my staff to be in compliance and up to date with company policies as I assume my new duties. I run a tight ship, you know. Which reminds me, I'll be needing a log of daily phone calls with a brief description of the nature of the call and how it contributed to either supporting present clients, gaining new clients or to your professional growth goals."

Donald's entire figure seemed to slump, and his face to melt. "But I cover seven states! Do you know how many calls I make in a day?"

"No, but I will! *Thank* you!" she said in a chirrupy voice, looking past him to the door by way of polite suggestion.

Donald stood his ground for the moment. "But none of this matters—*to anyone!* And the analytics are already available from our accounting department. And logging phone calls? I just don't see the point!"

"Yours is not to reason why, Donald. You'll just have to trust me that there is a point. F.P.T.'s! On my desk. Tomorrow."

Head hanging, he stumbled out of the office like a child who has just been told he cannot go to out to play until he cleans his room—and paints it.

When he had closed the door, Adele sat back in her reclining seat and smiled, saying, "Oh, believe me, there's a point, Donnie. A *very sharp* point." She spun in the chair and laughed.

At his desk, Donald packed his belongings. He could see this would never work. She had won. H.M.S. *Adele* had left him listing and demasted, and now he must strike his colors and crawl away under the tattered remnants of his sails to the nearest port.

His secretary passed by with an armful of folders but decided not to ask what was going on because she noticed that he was slamming things into a box and uttering imprecations. The last thing he pulled from his drawer was a copy of *The Age of Bullshit.* "I'll never understand it," he muttered, gripping the text in both hands as though he would strangle it, "a guy who believes that *leprechauns* visit his farmhouse, and he makes *a fortune* telling *everyone else* they're full of shit!"

He shook his head and choked back tears as he carried the box to the exit.

Coda

Bartley made it home the following afternoon. *Home.* He was filled with pride to see, from the road, the old red barn, which had been entirely remodeled and repurposed. The farm equipment, tractor, and horse stalls had been replaced with a grape crusher-destemmer, a hydraulic wine press, stainless steel tanks, a bottling line and corker, all gleaming in a well-lit space above a concrete floor retrofitted with modular slot drains. He pulled up beside the boxy truck that delivered 7,000 cases of wine a year to various outlets in New England. On its side were painted the words:

Stone Circle Vineyards
Vintners: Ramon and Sofia Reyes
Tyngsborough, MA.

He found them all sitting on the porch: Sofia, her father, Don Ramon, and Don Nippery Septo, who had given up European ostentation in favor of New World comfort. The bicorn hat that had been wont to sit athwart his head, a gift from an admiral, had been replaced with a Panama hat, a gift from Sofia. It was made from the plaited leaves of the toquilla palm, sturdy and light. She had also presented him with a Jacques Cartier watch; he said he didn't mind a bit that it was supposed to be a woman's watch—'twas a lovely article, and he checked it often, though he didn't *really* care much about minutes and hours. As shy as he normally was about human company, he had made an exception "for the lovely Sofia," and had promised to stay about the place "until 'twas time to leave." Only he knew what that meant, but Bartley suspected it would not be long, now that he had shared his expertise and the winery was running well and ready to hire more help.

They were all sharing a bottle of wine and conversing in Spanish as Bartley came up the steps. He had been studying the language for a couple of years, but when the three of them really got going, it was still too fast for him. His wife picked up the bottle, and Septo, with a characteristic clurichaunian flourish, produced a glass from inside his jacket, which Sofia filled with the deep red Syrah, saying, "We saw you on TV. You're famous!"

"Fame is bullshit."

Sofia laughed and winked at Bartley as she handed him the glass, and it struck him once more what a beautiful woman she was, with her beloved crooked smile, and their cherished child on her lap. Septo pointed at his glass and told him, "Now put that under your shirt, boyo. It may not be a Chateau Haut Brion, but it's a very special oul' plonk, and no nonsense about it!"

Don Ramon's eyes shone in his bronzed, weathered face. "*Órale, que loco el enano que tenemos en la casa.*" Which Bartley understood. "What a crazy dwarf we have in this house."

Bartley and Sofia's two-year-old daughter, Constance, or Constancia, depending on who was addressing her, slid off her mother's lap and went to her father, one hand in front of her face (since it was attached to the thumb in her mouth), the other raised toward him. Bartley set the wine glass on the table, picked her up and hugged her until she giggled, and said, "Papi!"

Don Ramon requested '*una cancion*' from the 'crazy dwarf,' who was only too happy to oblige. Bartley felt a perfect calm in his heart as Constance rested her head just over it and the little man sang:

Good luck to you all now barring the cat
That sits in the corner a smelling the rat
Ah whisht you philandering girls and behave
And saving your presence I'll chant you a stave
I come from a land where the praties grow big
And the girls neat and handy can dance a fine jig
And the boys they would charm your heart for to see
They're wonderful fellas round Tandragee!

Bartley felt his cell phone vibrate. He pulled it from his pocket while Septo sang and peered sideways at a text message. It was from Harris. *Hope you and the family are well. I miss your creative noncompliance here at Disfunction Junction. My motto for the year is Hunker in the Bunker. I have developed through some unconscious reflexive animal process of self-preservation a sort of Teflon life-skin that comes in handy at the concrete shoebox institute of learning dementia.*

"Learning dementia," "idiot lava," "analysis paralysis." Harris was the poet laureate of the Resistance in the war on educational bullshit. Bartley smiled at the thought of his "life Teflon skin." He sipped his wine, breathing quietly a Neil Young sort of blessing on his old friend, "Long may you run." He slipped the phone into his pocket and kissed his daughter's forehead as Septo concluded:

Here's to the boys that are happy and gay
Singing and dancing and tearing away
Rollicksome frolicsome frisky and free
We're the rollicking boys around Tandragee!

Bartley, his wife, and his father-in-law cheered, while the little girl laughed, and the little man danced a quick jig before taking a full bow, sweeping the Panama hat before him with courtly grandeur. Quite suddenly, Bartley recalled a line that he had read in Thoreau's *Walden*, long ago, and apparently forgotten for many years, "If one advances confidently in the direction of his dreams, and endeavors to live the life which he has imagined, he will meet with a success unexpected in common hours."

Note: The poem recited by Cornelius O'Tuama at the stone circle is the prophecy of An Morrígan from Part 167 of *Cath Maige Tuired: The Second Battle of Mag Tuired, London, British Library, Harleian MS 5280, 63a–70b (Catalogue of Irish Manuscripts in the British Museum, by Robin Flower (London, 1926) vol. 2, 318–319)*. The poem in Old Irish is in the public domain, but translations are not. There are several available for those who are interested. For example, see "Prayer in Gaelic Polytheism" copyright ©2012 Kathryn Price NicDhàna.

In general, the best free database for "Irish literary and historic culture," including a wide range of ancient Irish texts, is available at *Celt: Corpus of Electronic Texts, The Free Digital Humanities Resource for Irish history, literature and politics*. Website: https://celt.ucc.ie

I'd like to thank Dr. Maria Tymoczko, a world-renowned authority on translation studies and early Celtic Literature, under whom I studied Irish folklore and translated Old Irish texts back in the late '70s at UMass, Amherst. Those were good days, and interest she awoke has never faded.